TERMINATION ORDERS

LEO J. MALONEY

PINNACLE BOOKS
Kensington Publishing Corp.
www.kensingtonbooks.com

PINNACLE BOOKS are published by

Kensington Publishing Corp.
119 West 40th Street
New York, NY 10018

All Kensington titles, imprints, and distributed lines are available at special quantity discounts for bulk purchases for sales promotions, premiums, fund-raising, educational, or institutional use.

Special book excerpts or customized printings can also be created to fit specific needs. For details, write or phone the office of the Kensington special sales manager: Kensington Publishing Corp., 119 West 40th Street, New York, NY 10018, attn: Special Sales Department; phone 1-800-221-2647.

ISBN-13: 978-0-7860-2989-1
ISBN-10: 0-7860-2989-7

First printing: September 2012

10 9 8 7 6 5 4 3 2 1

Printed in the United States of America

This book is dedicated to John Peterson (Code Name Cougar), who was both my colleague and best friend for many decades. John and I met on our first day of black ops training and developed a special bond that made us closer than brothers. We had each other's back one hundred percent of the time and were so in tune that we knew exactly what the other was thinking. We had talked about writing a book about our many missions together, but he was not able to complete our last mission together as he lost his battle to cancer in 1997.

I think about John every day and know how lucky I was to have him in my life. I miss you, my friend.

CHAPTER 1

Three sharp raps at the door yanked young Zalmay Siddiqi from uneasy dreams, and the adrenaline hit him like a kick in the face. He froze with the primitive instinct of a rabbit cornered by a fox, hoping against hope that whatever predator had come knocking would go away of its own volition. He listened. The knocks came in a familiar pattern of three shorts and three longs: Cougar's signal. As his blazing panic subsided, he realized that he had been holding his breath. He exhaled, but the smoldering dread remained. Even friendly knocks were unwelcome in the middle of the night.

He rolled nimbly out of bed and pulled the lanyard on the light fixture above him, spilling the bulb's dim yellow glow onto the sparsely furnished room: a lone mattress on the floor, a plastic chair draped with his clothes, his few possessions huddled in a corner where cracked plaster walls exposed the concrete underneath.

Tugging on a plain Afghan *khameez* tunic and *salwar* trousers made of rough cloth, he hurried out of the bedroom to the hallway door. The knocks were still coming intermittently in their steady pattern. Zalmay gingerly turned the lock, and no sooner was the dead bolt released than the door was flung open, nearly knocking Zalmay back into the wall. A tall, wiry American, a man he knew as Cougar, rushed into the apartment, also wearing Afghan garb and carrying a black duffel bag. His movements were jerky, his voice breathless.

"Grab your things. You've got thirty seconds."

Zalmay's thoughts were forming a protest at Cougar's abruptness, but the urgency in the American's speech stayed his tongue. With a sudden clarity, he asked only, "Am I coming back?"

"No," Cougar responded, and he looked over his shoulder. "Pack only what you can't live without."

Cougar stood at the door, his head cocked like that of a prey animal listening for stalking predators. Zalmay threw his single other outfit and his prayer mat into a canvas knapsack. From under his mattress, he took out a slim roll of cash tied with a rubber band. He reached in again, pulled out a creased old photograph, and hid it, along with the money, in the folds of his shirt. Then he turned to face Cougar, doing his best to look brave.

"I have been expecting this," he said. "I am ready."

Fear and anxiety had marked Zalmay's life since he'd met the American and agreed to help him. Zalmay was well aware of the consequences of being caught. The thought usually kept him awake and tossing on his mattress at night. And on this particular night, his nightmare had finally come calling. He could only feel glad that it was his friend and not an enemy assassin at his door.

"Good," said Cougar, "Now let's . . ." Cougar trailed

off and turned his head as if listening for something. Then Zalmay heard it, too, and it stopped him cold. It was the rumbling motor of an approaching car, which came to a halt down below the open window. Zalmay walked to the window to see who it was. Looking down, he saw a black sedan with two men climbing out of it, Americans in Western suits, each with a submachine gun in his hand.

"No, get away from there!" said Cougar.

Too late—one of the men below looked up, called to the other, and pointed right at Zalmay. Both black-suited men dashed for the door of the building. Zalmay's apartment was on the corner, all the way down the hall; the men would have no trouble at all finding them.

"Come on!" said Cougar, motioning for him to go out the door. Zalmay dashed out and was halfway down the hall, past a row of silent, closed doors on his right, when he noticed that Cougar had stayed behind to shut the door to the apartment. He waited, nervously, as Cougar caught up, and they hurried to the stairs. From there, he could already hear the footsteps of the two men scrambling up, closing the distance with each footfall. Zalmay's apartment was only three floors up, so it wouldn't take them long to get there. And there was no other way out.

Cougar drew his weapon from its shoulder holster. "Upstairs," he whispered. "Quietly." He took the lead, and they tiptoed up a flight of stairs, keeping their footsteps as light as possible. Cougar crouched behind the bend of the fourth-floor corridor, and Zalmay ducked behind him, breathing heavily, his mind blank with panic, the way a rabbit must feel when confronting a tiger. The American kept his Glock pointed toward the stairwell as the sound of the men's shoes on the steps grew louder and louder, and then they heard the footsteps receding down the hallway toward Zalmay's apartment.

"Zalmay," whispered Cougar, pulling a set of keys from his pocket, holding them tightly in his palm so they would not jangle. "Take these. I'm going to hold them off. While they're searching your apartment, you run down as fast as you can and start the car. If I'm not the first one down, you take off without me, understand?"

"But . . ."

"Don't argue, just go. Now, after me!"

Cougar walked back down the flight of stairs, quickly and silently, leading with his shoulder, arm extended and gun pointing down, at the ready. They heard a crack as the men kicked in Zalmay's door. Before reaching the landing on the third floor, Cougar motioned for Zalmay to jump over the rusting railing onto the next flight down, so he wouldn't be seen from the hallway. Zalmay clambered over and vaulted down, but his foot slipped on the metal, and his arm smacked painfully on the railing below. A hollow, metallic sound echoed up the stairwell. They heard voices and then the sound of the two men running out of the apartment.

"Go!" said Cougar. "I'll hold them off!"

Zalmay nodded and started down. He leapt down the stairs two steps at a time, one hand clutching the keys and the other the strap of his knapsack, which was slung over his shoulder and slammed against him with every step.

Gunshots, three sets of them, blasted through the hallway upstairs; the single reports from Cougar's Glock were answered by volleys of fire from the two men's semiautomatics. He slowed down and for a split second considered going back to help his friend. Honor demanded it. But no; Cougar had told him to go on ahead, so that is what he would do. He had learned that the honorable thing to do was not always the right thing. He pressed on, and an inchoate, wordless prayer for his friend's survival formed in his mind.

Zalmay raced into the dusty night air, easily spotting Cougar's beat-up jeep, parked at a hasty angle to the building, the headlights left on like the still-open eyes of a dead ox. He pulled the door open and swung into the driver's seat, tossing the knapsack onto the seat beside him. He fumbled to slide the key into the ignition and then turned it; the engine rumbled to life. Gunshots reverberated from inside, but now they came from much closer. Cougar had made his way down the stairs. Zalmay leaned over to unlatch the passenger door and then kicked it wide.

Cougar burst out of the building. He stopped just long enough to shoot out one of the front tires of the men's sedan. Then he ran over and hurtled into the jeep's passenger seat, pulling the door shut as he did in one fluid motion, yelling, "Go, go, go!" Zalmay saw the two men appear at the door as he hit the gas. They sped off under a barrage of bullets. Several slammed into the back of the jeep, making dull, metallic *thunks*, and one shattered the rear window. Zalmay mashed the pedal to the floor. The sound of gunfire slowly faded in the distance and then stopped altogether.

"Are you okay?" Zalmay asked, his eyes on the dark dirt road. "Were you hit?"

"Still in one piece," Cougar said, with ragged breath and looking back. "You?"

"I am fine. Are they behind us?"

"They won't be getting far. Not in that car."

Zalmay exhaled. "Where are we going?"

"Turn here." Zalmay turned the jeep into a narrow side street. "We'll take the inner roads, just to be safe," Cougar added. "It's best to make sure we're not easy to follow."

Zalmay breathed deeply, trying to calm his frantically beating heart. "Where are we going?" he asked again.

"Highway One, toward Kabul," said Cougar, shuffling through his duffel bag.

"We are going to Kabul?"

"You're going to Kabul," Cougar replied pointedly. "And then out of the country."

"You are not coming, then?" Zalmay said, trying his best to hide his anxiety and disappointment. Cougar did not respond, and Zalmay didn't press it. He knew the answer already.

"I need you to bring something with you when you go," said Cougar.

He reached into a pocket and produced a small black plastic chip, no bigger than his fingernail: a camera's memory card. "You know what's in there?" Cougar said.

"Is that what those men were after? The photographs?"

Cougar nodded. "This, and you."

"How did they know?"

"I tried to transfer them electronically, and the files were intercepted. That's how they knew to look for us. Now I can't get them through from here—they're watching every single connection. It needs to be carried out of here. And you're going to be responsible for getting it to the US and into the right hands."

"America . . ." he said in a whisper barely audible over the engine's growl. Through everything that had happened, the dream of going to that Promised Land had never left his mind. But he had never allowed himself to fully believe it was possible. To hear Cougar say it now suddenly made it a reality.

"We'll travel together as far as possible, but it's better if you don't take the jeep. If nothing else, these fresh bullet holes are going to be a tad suspicious. We'll stop where you can find alternate transportation—something less conspicuous."

"But, Cougar . . ."

"We don't have much time, so let me finish. While you're on the road, tell no one your real name. Call as little attention to yourself as possible. If you have any identification, get rid of it now. Burn it, or toss it into a storm drain or down a well. Do what you can to change your appearance. You have some money; here's more." Cougar handed him a wad of bills—American currency. "If anyone asks, you're visiting family in Kabul. Come up with a story, and practice it. And always keep an eye out for tails, just like I taught you. I can't promise you'll make it there safely, between the Taliban and our American friends. But I've done all I can to give you a fighting chance."

Zalmay sat in silence as the morning twilight rose upon the city, making it appear ghostly and unreal.

Even now, while they drove alongside light traffic on an arterial road, the scene already felt like a distant memory.

"Why will you not come with me to Kabul?" he asked.

Cougar hesitated, as if gathering his thoughts. "This is the safest way for both of us. I can't get us a flight out of here, not anymore, and I would attract too much attention on the highway, from soldiers and the Taliban."

"The Taliban!" Zalmay bristled. "They would have no love for me, either, if they knew I have been helping you."

"Plus," Cougar added, ignoring Zalmay's interruption, "I have some unfinished business here." He gave a wry smile.

"I will stay and help you," Zalmay declared. "I am not afraid."

"No way."

"I want to stay," he protested, and anger welled up in him. "I want to stay and fight!"

Cougar sighed and took on a stern but fatherly tone. "I need this memory card delivered. I can't do it myself, and there's no one else I can count on to do it. This is your mission, Zalmay."

Zalmay looked away. "It is a coward's mission. "

Cougar frowned, and his tone became distinctly one of rebuke. "This isn't about you proving yourself, Zalmay. Delivering those photos is our top priority. People's lives might depend on those pictures getting into the right hands. If you want to do something meaningful, this is it."

Zalmay assented wordlessly. Then he scowled and

looked out the window as Cougar proceeded to give him specific instructions for what to do in Kabul. Being sent away like this filled him with shame, because he would be unable to help his friend right there in Kandahar. At the same time, his heart ached with thoughts of America, which had always seemed so impossibly far but was now so tantalizingly close—and that filled him with even more guilt, the guilt of choosing a comfortable life while others like him would remain no better off. Ultimately, he knew that Cougar was right. For now, however, he needed to brood.

With daylight approaching, the city was beginning to show signs of life. They were on the outskirts now, where the streets gave way to Highway 1. This highway was one of the Coalition's most ambitious projects in Afghanistan, cooperatively built by troops from among twenty-six NATO partner countries. Once called the Ring Road, the highway stretched to the capital and beyond, going around the entire country before coming full circle back to Kandahar from the west.

Cougar had Zalmay pull over to the side of the road a short distance from a small bazaar where many drivers stopped for food and tea and to trade information about the conditions of the road before the haul to Kabul.

As Zalmay and Cougar popped open the doors and climbed out of the jeep, the muezzins' voices began to drone over the minaret loudspeakers, calling all Muslims to their morning prayer. Zalmay's hand instinctively went for his prayer mat.

"I'm sorry, my friend, I can't wait for prayers," said Cougar. "But I'm confident Allah will forgive a short delay while you say good-bye to a dear friend."

Zalmay smiled, and they embraced tenderly.

"Thank you, Cougar."

The older man laughed hollowly. "I'm the one who should be thanking you, Zalmay. You did far, far more than anyone could ask for."

"And yet I am eternally grateful to you."

Cougar nodded, and Zalmay knew that he understood.

"I'm sorry you have to go alone, Zalmay. But I promise you, what you're doing is important. I'm counting on you."

Zalmay nodded in assent. "Will we meet again?"

"In the States, if everything goes right. And let's pray that it will. Good-bye, Zalmay."

"Good-bye, Cougar. Peace be upon you."

Zalmay gave the American the keys to the jeep and watched him as he climbed into the driver's seat and started the engine. Zalmay watched him as he drove off, feeling more the loss of his friend than of leaving his home. When Cougar disappeared into the city, Zalmay turned his thoughts to the road ahead: a harsh, dry land punctuated with towns and villages and a thousand enemies between him and his destination.

CHAPTER 2

Dan Morgan turned onto the small suburban cul-de-sac, the familiar tightness gripping his knee as he forced himself with gritted teeth to pound the pavement harder. *Embrace the pain; love the pain.* He pressed on for the last few dozen yards to his house, feeling the cutting chill of the early-March air in his throat as he inhaled.

Neika, who absolutely would not be tired out, had been straining at her leash to chase a squirrel but now set her sights on home. She let out a frustrated half bark, half whimper, muffled and choked off by her collar. Somehow, she still retained the exuberant energy of a puppy, but he knew she could really do some damage when she was threatened.

"Easy, girl," Morgan chuckled. He broke into a slow trot and then slowed to a smooth stroll as he walked into his front yard. He took a minute outside to catch his breath, letting Neika off her leash. She trotted into the garage to sit at the kitchen door, panting, tongue lolling, and eyeing him impatiently.

Morgan stretched his calves and, feeling another jolt

of pain, rubbed his aching knee. "Well, Dan," he muttered to himself as he opened the door and Neika plowed inside, "I guess you're officially not a young man anymore."

As with everything else, Morgan took aging stoically in stride, even now, with forty-one just around the corner. However, those little signs that his body was no longer what it once was always had their own particular sting, especially in the way that they carried a stark reminder of the life he no longer led.

As he walked into the house, he was met by the smell of coffee and frying bacon. His daughter, Alex, was at the stove, cracking eggs on the edge of a skillet. She was as tall as he, and her brown hair had been recently cut shorter, to chin-length. She combined Morgan's athleticism with Jenny's slender frame, and even her casual movements were full of grace.

"Well, this is a nice surprise," he said.

She turned around nonchalantly, looking at him with sharp, intelligent eyes, and gave him a good-natured smile. "Mom's out running errands, so I thought I'd be a good kid and make breakfast." Alex turned back to the counter and scooped crispy strips of bacon from the skillet onto a paper towel.

"Are you sure you should be handling bacon?" Morgan asked, gently ribbing. "Isn't that against the rules?" She had not eaten meat for nearly three months.

Alex laughed. "Whatever rules there are, Dad, I'm the one who makes them."

"So it wouldn't actually be cheating if you had some, just this once?" He grinned with feigned hopefulness.

"And look, eggs over easy, just the way you like

'em," she said, ignoring his comment. She poked the spatula at one of the three sizzling in the pan and then, a bit too abruptly, flipped it over. The yolk began to ooze out from under it. "Ah, crap."

Morgan walked over to her and reached for the spatula. "Here, let me show you."

"I think I can handle frying an egg, Dad." That was his daughter: independent to the bone.

Neika, who had gotten her fill at her water bowl, sauntered over to beg for scraps.

"Nothing for you here, puppy," Alex said. The coffeemaker sputtered, then beeped as the last of the brew dripped into the pot. She poured out two mugs and scooped two spoonfuls of sugar into one. "Still take yours black, Dad?"

"You got it."

She handed him a mug and took a sip from hers. "Ooh, sweet, sweet caffeine."

"So," he said, "big plans for the weekend?"

"Oh, I might meet up with Tom and Robbie later today, if they're around. Nothing definite yet."

While she fussed with the eggs in the skillet, he took a moment to regard her, with her new and yet-unfamiliar chin-length hair. She really was becoming a lovely young woman, charming and vivacious. It was more than that, though: there was something about her that seemed much more composed and self-assured than the moody adolescent she had been even six months ago, when she had turned sixteen. He had always been unconditionally proud of her, but, now more than ever, she seemed to really command it.

"So, your mother mentioned there's a boy you've been seeing," he said, as casually and good-naturedly as possible. He expected her to roll her eyes and clam up, but he was surprised to find not a hint of annoyance in her voice.

"His name is Dylan, Dad. He's a good guy, and I like him a lot."

"That's great, sweetie. I'm happy for you."

"And if you promise to behave," she said, "I might even bring him home to meet you."

He grinned and sipped his coffee. It was steaming hot, and it made him realize how cold he was. "How did you two meet?"

"An APS event."

"APS?"

"You know," she said. "Americans for a Peaceful Society. Remember I told you I joined up?"

"Oh, the peaceniks . . ." said Morgan, chuckling, He sipped more coffee.

"I think the preferred term is *pacifist*, Dad," she said, with an edge of irritation to her voice.

"In the sixties they called them *hippies*." He had meant the comment to be good-natured, but he knew immediately it was the wrong thing to say at the wrong time.

Alex scowled. "I guess it would be too much to ask for you to take me seriously."

Morgan frowned. Things seemed to have taken a turn rather quickly. "I didn't mean . . ."

"I know what you meant," she said dryly. "I know how much respect you have for people like—well, people like me, I guess."

"Of course I respect you, Alex," he said. "But you have to admit, this whole pacifist thing tends to be a bit . . . *unrealistic*, don't you think?" He was trying hard not to anger her, to humor her, this new passion of hers, but he could tell he wasn't doing a very good job of it. *So much for being a master of deception*, he thought.

"Dad, do you know what's happening out there? Do you know how many soldiers are dying in our wars? How many civilians? Just innocent bystanders, at home, going to work or to school? Do you know, Dad, what our government does to terror suspects, many of whom turn out to be innocent?"

He nodded. He wanted to tell her he knew more than she could imagine. He wanted to tell her things he had not only heard about but *seen*. Instead, he bit his lip and let her continue.

"So maybe APS is a small ripple in a big pond. So maybe I can't change the world. At least I'm doing *something*."

Dan bit down harder, doing his best to keep from saying something he might regret. "Maybe, Alex. But the truth is, there are evil people in this world. People who would much rather you and I and everyone we know be dead. It's not like we go to war just for the fun of it. The people who make those decisions always weigh everything carefully, to make sure it's really, absolutely necessary."

She scoffed. "Right. And even then, it still never seems to solve anything, does it?"

"Isn't it ironic," Morgan said, grinning in an attempt to change the tone of the conversation, "that we're fighting over this?"

One of the eggs in the skillet let out a loud pop. Alex sighed. "How about you go sit down, I'll bring breakfast in a minute, and we'll forget I ever mentioned anything?"

It may not have been much, but it was a peace offering of sorts. Morgan took it as an opening. "Truce, then?"

"Truce."

"Hey, listen," he said. "I was saving this until after breakfast, but, you know, the Bruins are playing at the Garden this Friday. I thought you might like to go, too."

"Yeah, Dad," she said, with a measure of genuine excitement in her voice, though still tempered with her irritation. "I'd love to." Sports had always been their bond; whatever the arguments between them, this common ground brought them together. He wondered if it would be enough as she grew older and drifted further and further away. He wanted to tell her that he loved her, that he would do anything for her happiness.

"Okay, then," he said instead, and he turned to walk into the dining room. The table was set for breakfast for two, the silverware slightly askew but with pretensions of luxury, like linen napkins clumsily folded into fans, and a copy of the *Boston Globe* sitting neatly next to his plate. What a sweet kid, he thought, even if she was a little misguided by her own naivety. He sat heavily into the chair, relieving his knees with a sigh, and shivered at the chill of his damp shirt against his skin as he leaned back.

He picked up the paper and flipped through to the National section, which had a long piece on Lana McKay, an up-and-coming senator from Ohio who was making waves in Washington. A fresh face in politics, she had been catapulted into the national spotlight in the past year by her powerful appeals to ethics and political reform. She was bold, had a reputation for getting things done, and had emerged as a presidential hopeful in the next election. Morgan knew well how political fads came and went, and he knew even better that politicians sang a radically different tune inside their cabinets than they did to the press. But even he thought there might be something to this one.

He scanned the article but he couldn't concentrate on the words; his heart just wasn't in national affairs at the moment. Then he looked below the fold to find the smarmy mug of Senator Edgar Nickerson smiling at him. He and McKay were shaking hands at some political event. It made sense, of course, for McKay to be seen with the man widely considered to be the most trusted politician in America. But Morgan's image of her suffered from the association. Nickerson was one of the top players in DC—an old-money aristocrat who had a way of making people trust him implicitly. But Morgan knew better than to believe his public image: the man knew how to play the political game, with a reputation among insiders for masterful behind-the-scenes manipulations that no one ever dared speak of aloud for fear of reprisal.

Morgan decided he wouldn't let politics spoil what was already not the most pleasant of days, so he turned to the sports page for a March Madness update and was immersed in reading when the doorbell rang.

"I'll get it!" he called out to Alex. He walked to the foyer and opened the front door to find a narrow-shouldered man with thinning blond hair and nervous eyes. It was a familiar face, and one he thought he'd never see again. It fell somewhat short of being a pleasant surprise.

"What the hell are you doing here, Plante?"

"Hello, Cobra. How are you?" said the man softly, with an edge of anxiety to his voice. "It's been a long time."

"There's no Cobra here," said Morgan. "Not anymore."

"Would you rather I called you by your civilian name?" Plante asked. "I can do that, if you prefer."

"I would *rather* you tell me what the hell you're doing at my front door," said Morgan. "Or are you here just to catch up on old times?"

"I need to talk to you," said Plante, the apprehension obvious in his tone. "Please."

"Dad, who is it?" called Alex from the kitchen.

"Just a couple of Jehovah's Witnesses, sweetie, " he yelled to her. Then he turned back to Plante. "You know what? I changed my mind. I don't care why you're here. Get the hell off my property before I exercise my right to shoot you as a trespasser."

"Won't you—"

"Listen here," Morgan interrupted, lowering his voice to a growl. "I don't work for you anymore. Whatever it is, I don't care. It's not my problem. It belongs to you and the rest of the clowns at the Agency."

"What if I told you it's a matter of life and death? What if I told you no one else could help us?"

"Jesus, it's always life and death with you people, isn't it?"

"You know that better than anyone else, don't you, Cobra?"

Morgan gritted his teeth. "Listen, Plante, my daughter's here, and she just cooked my breakfast. So I'm going in, and I'm going to sit down with her and eat, and you're going to get the hell away from me and my family."

"You won't even listen to what I have to say?"

"There's nothing you can say, Plante. Now, go away." Morgan began to swing the door shut.

"Cobra, it's Cougar," said Plante. The name stopped Morgan dead in his tracks. "Your old partner, Peter Conley. He's been killed. I'm sorry to tell you like this. But now you're the only one who can help us."

Morgan looked at Plante in shock, then took a deep breath.

"Fine. You can come in. But if I find out you're bull-shitting me . . ."

Morgan stepped aside to let Plante into his home. And just like that, his past had flooded back to wash away his life of suburban tranquility.

CHAPTER 3

Morgan walked into the kitchen hunched in the posture of apology and found Alex with a plate of eggs and bacon in each hand, ready to walk them into the dining room.

"Who was that, Dad?" she asked.

"I'm sorry, honey," Morgan said. "It's a business associate of mine. He has an urgent issue, and he needs to talk to me about it right away. I'm going to have to take a rain check on breakfast."

"Oh," she said, obviously disappointed. Then she asked, scrunching up her brow, "What exactly is an emergency for a classic car broker?"

He chuckled. "There's a surprise entry at an auction that my client is interested in. Sometimes these things can be extremely time-sensitive."

"I see," she said blankly.

"I'm going to try to get rid of him as soon as I can, and then we can spend some time together."

"Okay, Dad," she said, with a pride and stoicism that he knew masked some hurt feelings. "You should take your breakfast in with you, at least. You need to eat, and I wouldn't want it to go to waste."

Morgan figured that accepting the food would be the least bad choice, so he took the plate and walked to the foyer, where Plante was standing. He ushered the surprise visitor into his office, shutting the door behind them and setting the plate of eggs and bacon down on the desk.

Morgan sat down in his chair, behind his desk. Plante pulled up a green leather upholstered chair. He was a thin, balding man with a weak nose and chin. He looked aged, too, his hair getting prematurely white and perpetual worry carved into his face even more deeply than before. But some things hadn't changed: he still wore a rumpled button-down with a loosened tie and sleeves pushed up to his elbows, just like he did eight years before and for as long as Morgan had known him before that. And he still had the same steady anxiety, which, if anything, as Morgan remembered, made him a more rather than less effective handler.

"I gotta tell you, Plante, you were the last person I expected to see show up at my front door."

It was true. He hadn't heard from Plante in years, not since Morgan's bitter departure from the Agency. The moment Morgan saw his old associate, a million possibilities had flooded his mind, and he instinctively began to think of how he might take Alex and his wife, Jenny, and leave the country. A lot of these plans involved killing Plante right then and there.

Morgan checked himself. If he were in that kind of danger, he wouldn't be sitting down with Plante for a chat. He'd be a corpse already. They needed him. And he would have slammed the door in Plante's face if he hadn't mentioned the one person who prevented him from doing that, the one person Morgan held dearest from his past life.

"It's been a long time," said Plante.

"Yeah. Plante, how did it happen?" Morgan wasn't in the mood for small talk.

Plante didn't need to ask what he was referring to. "We're not sure, Cobra. Cougar was working undercover in Afghanistan. Someone shot him and set fire to his apartment with his body inside."

Morgan shut his eyes in grief. Conley and he had been partners ever since they left The Farm, up until Morgan's retirement. Being in life-and-death situations had been routine for them, and they had developed a deep and abiding trust and admiration for each other. He couldn't count how many times they had saved each other's asses. Morgan would have readily given his life for his friend. He could hardly hold back the shame and guilt at the thought that if only he had been there with him . . .

"Who?"

"Who what?"

Morgan's eyes were set with grim determination. "Who did it, Plante? Who pulled the trigger?"

"We don't know exactly."

"You're the goddamn Central Intelligence Agency. Where the hell is your *intelligence*?" His grief was turning into anger, and all the past bitterness he had felt for the organization welled up inside him.

"It caught us by surprise. And he had enough enemies—you know how it is. What do you want me to tell you?"

Morgan got up, slamming his hand down on the desk. "I want you to tell me who did this so they can get the slow, painful death that they deserve."

Plante regarded Morgan as if he understood, with a look of pain that might have been guilt. Morgan bit his lip and sat down.

"That's what we all hope for, Cobra. That's why I'm here, asking for your help."

"That's not why you're here," said Morgan. "What's going to happen to his body?"

Plante looked at him contritely. "We couldn't bring him back and risk exposing what he was. I don't think I have to explain to you why that is. Given that he had no immediate family and that his body was badly burned . . ."

"*Plante*," Morgan insisted.

Plante sighed. "We let the locals handle it. He was buried in an unmarked grave in Kandahar. I'm sorry, Cobra. He deserved better, but he knew the risks. Just like you did, every time you went out on assignment. That's just the nature of the mission."

Morgan took a deep breath, trying to calm his rage at imagining his friend buried in some lost little mound of dirt, a mangled corpse mourned by no one. He tried to keep his mind on practical matters.

"What was he doing there?"

"You know I can't tell you that," said Plante.

"Fine," said Morgan. "Then don't. But I know you're not here just to give me the bad news. What is it, then? Let's hear what made the Agency suddenly remember that I exist." Morgan scowled at him.

Plante returned a look that blended apology and commiseration. "We need your help."

"I figured as much," said Morgan acerbically. "I didn't suppose this was a social call. I was looking for something a bit more specific."

"It's a sensitive matter that I'd rather not discuss here," said Plante. Morgan shot him a look of incredulity, but he continued. "I'd like you to come with me down to Langley. There's a helicopter about ten minutes away that can take us there, and if everything goes smoothly, I promise I'll have you home in time for dinner."

"I don't have time for your bullshit, Plante. *You're* here for *my* help, so as I see it, you're not in any position to bargain." Morgan leaned forward for emphasis. "Tell me what you need, or get out of my house."

Plante was apologetic. "Come on, Cobra, be reasonable here. My hands are tied, and I need your help. I wish I could be straight with you, but the order came from above."

"Then forget it." Morgan got up and started for the door.

"Cobra . . ." said Plante, getting up as well.

Morgan stood face-to-face with the man and spoke in a low voice. "I mean it, Plante. I'm done with that life, done lying"—he looked around to make sure Alex wasn't within earshot, and his voice sank to a rumbling whisper—"to my family. Done putting my life on the line for a bunch of spineless politicos and backstabbers."

"If you won't do it for me, do it for Cougar," said Plante.

Morgan feinted a lunge at Plante, who flinched in response. "*Don't you dare!* You have no right to use his memory to get me to do what you want."

Plante seemed to make an effort to gloss over being intimidated and to assert himself, but his speech still had a slight tremble. "What about what *he* wanted, Cobra?" he asked. "Have you considered that?"

Morgan stepped back. "What are you talking about?"

Plante hesitated, looking down.

"Don't pull this crap on me, Plante," said Morgan. "You're not getting anywhere with this cryptic bull-shit."

Plante considered that for a moment. "He sent us a last message before he died. I can tell you that much."

"What did it say?"

Plante just stared back at him.

"That's it, we're done."

"Stop!" Plante's voice took on a new urgency. "Look, Cobra, truth is, we don't know. It's in some kind of code, a code that we've had little luck breaking. And we suspect we're running out of time."

"Why are you asking me about this? What makes you think I'll do any better than the pros over at the Agency?"

"Because there is only one thing that's perfectly clear."

"Oh, yeah? What's that?"

"It's addressed to you."

Morgan faltered. "Come again?"

"'For Cobra's Eyes Only.' That's how it starts. In plain English. The rest of it seems to be in a kind of code, but the words don't match up with any of ours. We can only conclude that it's actually meant for you and that you're the only one who can tell us what it means."

Morgan frowned, deep in thought. He didn't know

what it could be about. There was a time in his life when coded messages from Cougar would have been business as usual. Just another day on the job. But that time was gone, long gone. Their interactions these days were limited to exchanging cards on Christmas and the occasional afternoon spent over beers, reminiscing about all the times they'd cheated death together. It was so implausible, all he could manage to say to Plante was an incredulous, "Why?"

"Your guess is as good as ours."

He thought for a moment. Knowing Cougar, it had to be important. And in this line of work, *important* could mean *urgent* and *life threatening*. Suddenly, Morgan felt as if he had a mission again. He didn't waste any time. "Do you have it?"

"Have what?"

"What do you think? The *message*. Do you have it?"

Plante seemed taken aback by Morgan's sudden intensity. "Sorry, Cobra. I'm not authorized to take it out of headquarters."

"You're kidding me," said Morgan. "What if it's too late by the time we get there?"

"I'm sorry, I just don't have the authority," said Plante, shrugging.

"Then talk to someone who *does* have the damn authority!" Morgan exclaimed, exasperated.

"I already did. Kline said specifically—"

"Kline?" asked Morgan, his eyes narrowing. "You mean *Harold* Kline? What's he got to do with it?"

Plante hesitated. "He's Deputy Director of the Clandestine Service."

"Boyle made *that* worthless, spineless little pencil pusher *Deputy Director of the NCS*?"

Plante stiffened and adopted an affected, professional tone. "Regardless of what you think of him, Cobra, that's what he is. And that means he has final say, unless you want to personally take it up with the Director himself."

Morgan leaned forward in his chair as if he was about to lunge at Plante. "Well, you can tell that asshole . . ." He was too beside himself to finish the sentence.

"Look, I know you've had your disagreements in the past. But he's running the show now. This kind of thing has to go through him."

"I get it. I know him. I know what all this bullshit is about. He wants me to come down there so I can kiss his ring, doesn't he?" Morgan fell back angrily in his chair. "Wants to gloat and lord his new position and his fancy new office over me, and Cougar be damned— isn't that it?"

Plante softened. "Look, Cobra, I wish I could help you. I really do. But I've been working under Kline for a while now. I frankly don't believe that he's purposely stonewalling this. My impression is that he just happens to believe fervently in protocol."

"Well, screw him," Morgan said, with incredulous impatience. "You need to do what's right by Cougar."

"Nothing I *can* do."

"Then screw you, too. Let's see what Boyle has to say about this shit."

Plante sighed. "NCS Director Boyle is aware of the situation, and he gave Kline the authority in this matter. Calling him is only going to delay this even more. Cobra, this is the only way it's going to happen. If you want to see the letter, you need to come down with me to headquarters."

Morgan exhaled, barely containing his anger. He could easily be as stubborn as Plante. He could play this game. He did brinksmanship as well as—hell, probably better than—any of those clowns. But how long would it be until Kline caved in? These missions tended to be time-critical, and he knew that Kline would always privilege his own authority over everything else, good intentions or no.

"There was a time when you wouldn't have put up with this bureaucratic bullshit," he told Plante, knowing that, by saying that, he had, in effect, caved.

"Maybe I've come to realize that there's a reason why we follow the chain of command," said Plante.

"To hell with the chain of command." Morgan exhaled, closing his eyes, letting his anger subside. "I'll come. But not for them. For Cougar."

"You're doing the right thing, Cobra."

"Yeah. That's always been my weak spot."

Morgan escorted Plante out of the office and to the front door.

"Look, Cobra . . ." Plante seemed newly contrite, his face full of heartfelt pain. "This—Cougar . . . It was a blow. He was my friend, too. I can only imagine what it must be like for you. Why don't you take a few minutes? I'll be right outside when you're ready to go."

Morgan assented tacitly, then closed the door and walked back to his office. He took down a picture of Peter and himself that hung on the wall next to his gun cabinet. Sinking into his chair, he looked at the framed photo, in which he still had a full mustache on an unlined face. Peter Conley towered next to him, wiry, with a high forehead and a prominent chin. Both were smiling widely. The picture had been taken just a few years after they graduated from their year of CIA training and began work in Black Ops. They were showing off new arm tattoos, corresponding to their code names: Conley's a cougar, and Morgan's a coiling cobra, ready to strike—deadly animals for deadly men.

He glanced at the eggs and bacon, still untouched on the plate, undoubtedly cold by now. He thought of Alex and couldn't help remembering the night he had told Jenny he didn't really make his money—or most of it, anyway—dealing in antique cars.

He told her all he could say without breaking his oath of secrecy. All those business trips to car auctions, celebrity auto shows, private collector negotiations, and fleet deals—most were covers for dangerous forays into foreign countries, and often into enemy territory, to protect American interests. They were full of excitement, yes, as well as deception and violence—he had cheated death again and again. He did it by being stronger, faster, smarter, and better prepared than the enemy—but he knew that others had been, too, and had not survived. He was good and he knew it, but he also knew he owed Lady Fortune his survival on more than one occasion.

Jenny had been a mess of emotions when he told her. She had been proud, yes, of his bravery and service to his country, but she was also livid that he had deceived her into living, unwittingly, under the constant threat of being widowed by a foreign bullet, a car bomb, or a cyanide capsule. Even worse was that little Alex, almost nine years old at the time, could lose her father. They had made a decision together that night:

Alex would not grow up fatherless. Morgan had called Plante in the morning and told him he was out for good. That was almost eight years ago.

Morgan looked down at the picture in his hand and wondered whether Conley would be alive at that moment if they had still been partners. As he brooded on their friendship and what could have been, Morgan heard the sound of Jenny's car pulling into the driveway.

CHAPTER 4

"**W**hat do you mean, you have to go to DC?" demanded Jenny. After helping unload the groceries from the car and put them away, Morgan had pulled her into the bedroom, away from Alex, and told her that he had to go. The soft gentleness of her face became uneasy, and she pushed her short brown hair nervously behind her ears. She knew, of course, what was in DC.

"Plante is outside, waiting," he said, not knowing where to begin.

"Plante? You mean your old supervisor?" she asked, bewildered. She walked over to the window and looked out.

"My old handler, yes." He tried to project reassurance in his voice. Its effect was limited, at best.

"Dan, what's going on? What does he want?"

"It's Peter. Peter Conley was killed on a mission."

"Oh, Dan, I'm so sorry," she said, as her natural kindness asserted itself, and she took his hand in hers and held it tightly. "How are you?"

He looked at her stoically, but he knew he couldn't hide his grief.

"Oh, Dan . . ." she said, embracing him. She pulled away and then asked, "Is there going to be a funeral?"

"No," he said bitterly. "Apparently it was more *convenient* to have him buried over there."

"Wait, I'm confused," she said suspiciously. "I assumed . . . Why do you have to go to DC, then?"

"Something to do with his last mission. They say they need my help."

She pulled away from him, opened her mouth as if to speak, then closed it on a second thought. Then she finally said, "*Help* how?" Her sympathetic dark brown eyes took on a familiar steely glint that was the only thing that still had the power to intimidate him.

"It's strictly paperwork, I promise. They want me to take a look at something. Some kind of coded message."

"They're the CIA," she said sharply. "Don't they have people who can take care of that there?"

Morgan wondered how he had ever managed to keep his life hidden away from her for so long. "It's a special case, Jen. It's got to be me."

"Dan . . ." she said, half pleading, half admonishing.

"I have to do this, Jenny."

"Do you remember what you told me back when Alex was a child?" she asked. "Do you remember what you promised?"

"Yeah," he replied, with a pinch of contrition. "I said that I was done. Out. And I meant it." He moved in closer and put his arms around her. "I'm coming in only as a special consultant. This could be important, and I might be the only one who can help them. Believe me, I would not be going if that weren't the case."

She backed up slightly and raised an eyebrow. "No running around in a war zone?"

"No," he said firmly.

"No gunfights? No flying halfway around the world to put your life at risk?"

"No and no. They show me a printout, I tell them what it means, and I'm out of there. That's all."

She sighed and looked away. "I know you're upset about Peter. I am, too. But that won't make me forget your promise."

"I know," he said. "I didn't expect it to."

"Did you ask Alex to the game already?" she asked. He nodded.

"Have you told her?" she asked.

"Not yet," he said.

"She'll play it cool, but she really craves your company, you know. She will be disappointed."

"I know," he said, and he kissed his wife tenderly. "Look, Jenny, I wouldn't be doing this if it weren't perfectly safe. And if everything goes smoothly, I'm out of there in less than twenty-four hours." Even if Plante were done with him by evening, Morgan had his own questions. "I'll be back in time for the game with Alex. No harm, no foul."

"And if it doesn't?"

He didn't have a chance to answer before they heard light footsteps approaching from the hall. The door, which had been ajar, opened, and Alex walked in breezily.

"Oh, hey, Mom," she said, pointedly avoiding eye contact with Morgan. "I just wanted to tell you that I'm off to meet my friends in a few minutes." And then, reading their body language, she asked, "What's going on?"

"Your Dad has to go out of town."

"Oh. Is this about that auction?"

"It's just for a day or so," said Morgan. "It's happening in Virginia. I wasn't planning on going, but an important client, the man who was just here—he wants me to be there to bid on a Duesenberg, and, well, long story short, I need to fly down today."

"Are you going to be back for the game?" she asked, with affected nonchalance.

"Are you kidding? I'll be back before you know it. I wouldn't miss it for anything."

"Yeah. I mean, no pressure, Dad," she said, and he thought he saw the trace of a smile playing at the corners of her lips.

CHAPTER 5

"I hope that there is no one waiting for you tonight," said Faqeer to Zalmay as he maneuvered the truck around another crater in the highway. The right front tire rolled off the edge of the road, and the entire truck groaned and teetered dangerously as the back wheel followed suit. Faqeer was obviously not new at this, so Zalmay did his best not to imagine the truck tipping over onto its side.

Zalmay had hitched a ride with Faqeer at the bazaar not far from where he last saw Cougar and the bullet-pocked jeep. Faqeer's rig was what the Americans called a jingle truck, with beads and baubles hanging off the sides and with every surface painted with ornate designs. Faqeer, a Pashtun man in his late thirties with a trim black beard and a beret-style *pakol*, had been mostly silent at first, but he became more relaxed, even gregarious, after Zalmay answered his probing questions regarding his attitude toward the Americans.

Faqeer was as pro-American as they came—uncommon among the Pashtun, the largest ethnic group in Afghanistan to which the great majority of the Taliban belonged—but Faqeer had little to thank the Taliban for and much reason to be grateful to the Coalition forces. He had started his fruit business almost entirely thanks to their nation-building efforts and strategies to wean local farmers off growing poppies, from enlisting the support of fruit producers in the Kandahar province to the renovation of Highway 1, through which he brought all his produce to the capital.

He had a particularly soft spot for the military, even though their presence at checkpoints all along the road caused significant delays. Highway 1 was plagued by attacks, and the craters in the asphalt provided an all-too-clear reminder: Taliban militia prowled that span of the highway, ambushing all kinds of passing vehicles. The sight of troops was always a relief: a guarantee, if only partial, of safe passage.

Zalmay had heard about the dangers of this highway, yet even though he hadn't been on it in years, the peril was obvious at a mere glance. It wasn't only the blackened asphalt and mortar holes; looking out the window, he saw the bullet-ridden carcasses of cars and trucks on the edge of the road, now monuments to travelers who were not as fortunate as they had been—so far, at least.

If he had taken Cougar's jeep, Zalmay could have made it to the capital by noon. The fact that they were in a truck capable of carrying a few tons of weapons and explosives meant that they were stopped at every checkpoint and had to wait behind a line of similar trucks for inspection, even though Faqeer's truck was, at the moment, mostly empty—it being much too early for harvest season. What should have been a six-hour journey was taking all day, and it was now getting dangerously close to sundown.

Zalmay had days before he was to meet Cougar's contact—he was not worried about that. But at any moment on the road he could be found by the enemy. Every time a soldier motioned for them to pull over, Zalmay wondered if they had his picture, if he had been flagged as a person of interest, to be detained and delivered to the enemy's doorstep.

Even if he weren't suspected, what would happen if a soldier were to find the small black memory card, which he had nervously pushed through a hole in the upholstery of his seat so that it wouldn't be found when he was searched? He had some comfort in the knowledge that the soldiers weren't looking for small things. They were more interested in finding Kalashnikovs, from the AK-47 to the AK-100 rifle, or a pallet of hand grenades, stacked like eggs, thirty to forty per carton; but what if one of them had a sudden hunch while searching the cab of the truck, and he casually probed the plushy orange foam for hidden objects?

"This is why they will lose, you know," said Faqeer, as they passed the blackened shell of a bus, a memorial on the roadside.

"What?" said Zalmay, distracted by his anxious musings.

"The Taliban. This is why they will lose, in the end. They are destroyers, and this is all they know how to do anymore. Just to kill and to make our lives miserable. They are now the enemies of the people of Afghanistan. For this reason, their unjust regime will not return, and their insurgency will be defeated by the will of the people. Even if the Americans leave, we will be free of these vermin."

"*Insha'Allah*"—if God wills it—Zalmay muttered. At that moment, he noticed that Faqeer was looking intently into the rearview mirror. The truck slowed and veered to the side of the road, as two American army vehicles—what they called Humvees—sped past them, leaving a trail of dust. It didn't take him long to notice where they were headed; they were following a pillar of smoke rising in the distance, where the terrain rose into jagged hills.

As they drew closer, they came upon a long row of stopped vehicles, most pulled over to the shoulder of the road randomly and askew, as if they didn't expect to go anywhere anytime soon. The smoke seemed to be coming from the bridge over a shallow ravine a couple of hundred feet ahead, where the two American vehicles had carelessly parked.

Faqeer pulled the hand brake and opened the door. "Stay here; I will see what's going on." The driver climbed down from the truck and walked toward the gathering of vehicles. Zalmay watched uneasily as his companion talked to other drivers who were hiding from the punishing sun under the shade of a short cliff. Faqeer came back about fifteen minutes later.

"The bridge is out," he said, sitting back in the driver's seat, against the colorful seat cover. "Taliban sabotage. An entire segment crumbled, and there is no way to get across. It will be many weeks before it is fixed. But do not worry. The Americans will not allow the road to be impassable for long. They will bring a temporary bridge, and we will be on our way soon. There are some who are waiting here, but I do not be-

lieve that it will be done tonight." He started up the engine, and the truck rumbled under Zalmay's seat.

"What happens to us in the meantime?"

"There is a small village, not far, where we can get
lodging and food," said Faqeer, as he maneuvered the
truck into a three-point turn. "I have stopped there before. It is a simple place, but it will allow us to resume
our journey tomorrow."

It was only some twenty minutes until they reached
their destination, a collection of a couple dozen houses
just off the main road. There were two trucks and three
cars there already, no doubt for the same reason they
were. Faqeer brought his truck to a stop near the other
vehicles, and two men in rustic dress came to meet
them.

"Are there beds for two more?" Faqeer asked as the
two clambered down from the truck.

"All are welcome," one of them said warmly, and he
waved them toward the village. Zalmay followed him,
his sandals dragging across dusty terrain to a collection of about a dozen single-story adobe huts arranged
haphazardly on a shrub-speckled hill. It was a peasant
village, though there was no sign of electricity, and village water came from a hand pump, attached, presumably, to a well. On drawing closer, Zalmay noticed that
the sides of some of the houses had rows of bullet
holes—not befitting a war zone, but the place had obviously not been untouched by violence.

As they arrived within the limits of the village, Zalmay and Faqeer were introduced to their hosts, two
brothers named Gorbat and Mirzal. They were both
short, with sun-browned, prematurely wrinkled skin
but also with broad smiles that lit up their faces. The

brothers showed them the house and room where they would sleep, with two straw mattresses laid out on the floor. Two small children, a boy and a girl, looked on curiously. Zalmay noticed that there were no other mattresses in the house; their hosts had given up the only beds they had.

Gorbat and Mirzal made no mention of charging for their hospitality; the Pashtunwali, the code of honor that the rural Pashtun people of Afghanistan still lived by, forbade it. These customs were all but forgotten in the city, and Zalmay was amazed that, even this close to the great highway, people still kept to it.

They left their things in the room and went outside. The village seemed to be abuzz with activity as pots, sacks of grain, logs and slabs of meat were carried to and fro. The coming of visitors seemed to be shaping up to be a celebration—more of a pretext than a real reason, Zalmay thought.

As Zalmay's spirits began to rise from the festive mood, he saw an old man with a wild, bushy beard walk out into the square. Mirzal said to Zalmay and Faqeer jovially, "That's Malang, our muezzin. He does the daily calls to prayer." He said the word *muezzin* mockingly, as if Malang had as much claim to the title as he had to call himself President of the United States. In a harsh, croaky voice, Malang began to chant the evening *adhan*, the Islamic prayer called out five times a day for all within earshot: "*There is no deity but Allah, and Muhammad is the Messenger of God.*" The inhabitants stopped what they were doing and shuffled slowly to get their prayer mats.

Once the villagers and their guests were done with their prayers, preparations for the celebration continued. "Tonight, we feast!" Mirzal explained with relish and anticipation. "We have many guests this evening, so Patasa is butchering a lamb. We will roast it here and have a banquet."

Faqeer smiled contentedly.

Zalmay made a show of appreciation, but his own apprehension would not allow him to enjoy the festivities.

Time passed. By the time it was dark, the fire was blazing high. The villagers and guests had gathered around for light and warmth, when he heard a *rubab*, the stringed national instrument of Afghanistan, which had become somewhat rare after confiscations during the post-Soviet and Taliban government music ban of the 1990s. Its three-string twang of hypnotic rhythms was joined by the percussive beat of a *tabla* and *dohol*. Dozens of voices joined in, enchanting the night with epic narrative songs about heroes and heroines, brave death, and struggles between men over land, women, and status.

All that was missing were the belly dancers for an evening of *klasik*, history sung as folk music. The villagers sang of love, of war, of cruelty, and the national identity of a people who had never once been defeated, not by the Mongols, not by the Soviets, not by anyone, ever.

Meanwhile, the lamb was cooking over a pit, and they were served plain, slightly undercooked white rice in a clay bowl. It wasn't much, but to Zalmay, who hadn't eaten all day, it was a feast.

Despite the merry mood, Malang, the muezzin, was skulking around and scowling at them. "Malang does not approve of our mirth," said Mirzal, when Zalmay asked him about it. "He fancies himself a mullah. Thinks he is the keeper of propriety. But we in the village don't have patience for his preaching."

The lamb was carved and the meat distributed to the guests first, as Pashtun hospitality demanded. Zalmay, for the first time since leaving his apartment, felt relaxed, and he allowed the joy of the moment to enter his heart.

And then he saw the headlights. They were coming fast toward them. Others saw them, too, and the music trailed off. The vehicles stopped at the edge of the village. By the light of the fire, Zalmay could make out two pickup trucks, with men in the truck beds. A group of them jumped to the ground, and as they came into the light, Zalmay saw that they wore turbans and had dark, scraggly beards. Each cradled an AK-47. He didn't have to see Malang's manic glee to know that the village had just been overrun with Taliban insurgents.

CHAPTER 6

One of the insurgents raised his Kalashnikov into the air and fired. The villagers recoiled in fear.

"We are fighters for God, and we demand hospitality in your fine village," he said. "We will need beds and food for all my men."

Zalmay tried to remain calm. He had nothing incriminating on him, and the memory card was safely tucked away back in the truck. He had a well-rehearsed story about why he was on the road, and he did not look like a Tajik farmer, whom the Taliban, who were almost exclusively of the rival Pashtun ethnicity, would undoubtedly target first. As long as he stayed quiet, he told himself, he would live through this.

"You will stop your sinful music now, and the women will cover up appropriately," said the leader.

Malang, looking positively triumphant, came forward to greet the man.

"Welcome, *talib*," he said. The word was the proper singular of Taliban, and meant *student*. Malang continued, "We honor your presence in our simple village."

Everyone else was too terrified to move, but a few

were suppressing looks of indignation. Zalmay looked at Faqeer, who was standing across the square and whose fury was barely checked. He was fuming, and his eyes were wide with mad hatred.

"We claim all the vehicles in this village, along with anything else that might aid us in our fight against the invader."

Don't do anything stupid, Zalmay urged Faqeer in his mind. *Please*. The leader, who had been ambling as he spoke, now stood in front of Faqeer and apparently saw the expression on his face.

"Do you have something to say?" the *talib* demanded.

Faqeer did not answer but managed to restrain his emotion; his face became blank and accepting. The *talib* seemed satisfied that he had cowed Faqeer into submission, and he turned away. But it was a mistake: as soon as his back was turned, Faqeer pulled out a short revolver and shot the man twice in the torso.

Everyone watched in complete silence as the dead man fell to the ground. Faqeer panted, with wide-open, crazy eyes. And then, almost immediately, there was a burst from the AK-47 of a nearby insurgent. Faqeer crumpled to the ground, his final expression of wild anger frozen on his face. One of the villagers, a wizened old woman who had been in the line of fire, fell down as well. She began to wail pitifully. All the villagers and their guests gasped and recoiled, except for Gorbat, who ran to succor her. The assailants raised their weapons to make very clear what would happen if anyone decided to pull a similar stunt.

"Throw him into the fire," said one of the Taliban with practiced authority, pointing at Faqeer's body.

Zalmay was shocked. Cremating a body was forbidden, a grievous sin. His heart burned with rage against these thugs. He knew that this was equally intolerable to the villagers—even more so, since their honor would compel them to protect their guests. But they did not move; instead, he saw, their heads hung in shame. Zalmay remembered the bullet holes on the sides of the houses. This village had seen their share of misfortune, and war, apparently, had broken their will.

As his underlings moved to carry out the order, this new leader pulled Malang aside and conferred with him. Malang spoke and then pointed directly at Zalmay. *So much for not attracting too much attention to myself,* he thought. The man walked toward him, and Zalmay spoke a quick prayer under his breath.

The man stood in front of him, commanding, "On your knees!"

Zalmay complied, trying to hold steady while clinging to whatever desperate hope he could find.

"You were with the pig that shot our brother?"

Zalmay tried to speak but was frozen, the barrel of the man's Kalashnikov inches from his face.

"Speak!"

Zalmay couldn't. Another man said, "Shoot him!"

The man raised his rifle and prepared to fire. Zalmay shut his eyes and braced for the bullet, the end of everything. But it never came. Instead, Zalmay heard shouting.

He opened his eyes and saw that Mirzal had stepped forward defiantly, preventing anyone from moving Faqeer's body. Despite his shortness, Mirzal's silhouette against the bonfire seemed tall and proud. One of the thugs yelled for him to step back, but that just prompted Gorbat to step up to stand beside him.

Emboldened, the villagers came forward to stand with them, one by one. The insurgents shouted, "Back! Back!" But the villagers moved forward instead, edging the armed men back toward their trucks.

The man who had his rifle on Zalmay turned to deal with this new situation. The armed men were shouting and motioning for the villagers to step back, but they would not. They continued to advance.

Zalmay realized that all the thugs were distracted. If he took off at a sprint, he could probably make it far enough into the darkness to get away from the armed men and then run back to the highway. All he had to do was dash out of there.

Instead, he stood up and walked to stand by his hosts, facing the men with guns. Zalmay saw that most of the men seemed uncomfortable, unwilling to actually open fire. All but the man who had almost killed him, the one who seemed to be in charge. His cruel face seemed murderous in the flickering firelight.

"Swine!" he said. "Step back, or you die!"

Zalmay knew this was not an empty threat, and so did everyone else. But nobody faltered, nobody stopped. Whatever they were grasping on to, whether it was their honor and hospitality or just being tired of the thuggery of the Taliban, the people of this village were willing to die that night. And Zalmay was prepared to die with them.

At least he would die on his feet. He braced himself, ready for it this time. The cruel man raised his rifle, and the others followed suit. All he had to do was give the order, and then—

There was a *pop!* of a gun from the darkness beyond, and the insurgent's head erupted, splattering red onto Zalmay's face. The man fell to the dust. Almost immediately, there were three more reports, and three more Taliban collapsed. The rest, realizing what was happening, turned around and started shooting wildly into the darkness. The villagers dropped to the ground to avoid incoming gunfire. The thugs, shooting ineffectually into the darkness, continued to drop. They tried to run, but bullets caught up to every one; soon, they all had dropped like flies.

That's when Zalmay noticed that the square was surrounded by men in desert camouflage, wielding M-16s and shouting at everyone in broken Pashto, *"Stay down! Stay down!"*

Americans.

They had been saved by the Americans.

CHAPTER 7

Less than three hours after they left the Morgan home, Plante was ushering Dan Morgan into the CIA's New Headquarters Building. Called the George Bush Center for Intelligence, it had been added to the original building in the nineties. It was a complex of steel and glass that always made Morgan think of a shopping mall, with its flower gardens, arched entrance, and blue glass. It brought to mind the last time he had seen Plante, when he had come down to tender his resignation as an operative (even if, officially, of course, he had never worked for the CIA).

Plante had been Morgan's handler and usually his only contact in the CIA, summoning him whenever he was needed. Plante had accepted his resignation without much protest. He gave Morgan no grief, other than reminding him that the confidentiality agreements he had signed at the beginning of his service still held. Then Plante wished him well in his new life, and that was, Morgan thought, the end of it.

But then, in the coming weeks, Morgan began to notice things. Things like an unfamiliar car parked near

his house. Or odd phone calls in the middle of the
night, when there was nothing but a ominous silence
on the other end. Or, even, strangers in public places
who bumped into him deliberately and whispered menacingly, "We're watching you."

Morgan tried to call Plante, to get them to stop, but
all he got was the bureaucratic runaround. His calls
were never transferred to Plante, and he was reduced to
yelling at powerless underlings. The harassment eventually stopped, but it had left a lot of bad blood between himself and the Agency. Since then, he had all
but completely cut ties with Plante and everyone else
in the CIA's hierarchy.

There was one exception to that silence. Morgan had
left certain items in a personal locker at headquarters
during his days as a wet contractor in Black Ops, items
he wanted to get back. He didn't return for them right
after his resignation, partly out of pride but mostly out
of fear of calling attention to the locker's contents: incriminating records and documents that he should have
destroyed long ago, and some that never should have
existed at all. Among them was a diary of everything
he had ever done in the service of the CIA, with dates
and detailed accounts of his every Black Ops mission:
a little black book filled with the Agency's dirty little
secrets. He had thought of it as his insurance policy, in
case things ever got really bad. The situation soured
before he could collect them, and so there they had remained.

Years had passed by the time he decided to retrieve
the stash in his locker. He had called the National
Clandestine Service—formerly known as the Direc-
torate of Operations—to find that Plante was still there.

He scheduled an appointment, but they never met. When he arrived, Morgan had been told that Plante was in a meeting. He was left waiting until some desk flunky told him there was no record of any Code Name Cobra ever working at the CIA. He had lost his temper, made a scene, and burned his bridges with the Agency. As far as he was concerned, at the time, he was done, for good.

And yet here he was again, being escorted through security by Plante himself. He first walked through a bulky metal arch much thicker than any metal detector. He hadn't been asked to remove anything from his pockets. They then took digital prints of all his fingers, a head shot, and scanned his retinas.

"What, you're not going to ask me to take off my clothes?" he said sarcastically.

"No need," said Plante, pointing at the scanner he had just passed. "That machine has already revealed everything and more. If you were trying to sneak in here with a bomb up your ass, we'd know. Hell, if you were trying to sneak in here with a straight pin up there, we'd know."

Morgan signed a pile of nondisclosure agreements and was issued a visitor ID and admitted into the building. Plante escorted him down a long, sparse, antiseptic hallway, where he passed busy, professional-looking people who had that familiar intensity of CIA employees. Plante stopped in front of a door and swiped his employee ID through the key-card reader. The door unlocked with a buzz and a click, and Plante led him into a small conference room.

"I'm going to have to leave you here for a few minutes, Cobra. I'll trust you to behave." Plante walked

out, and the door clicked shut behind him. Morgan figured he might as well sit down. He took the chair opposite the door and looked around the room. At the far
end was a chalkboard-size computer screen. The table
was sleek and functional, the chairs comfortable enough.
Behind him, the metallic-blue windows offered a view
of the woods that separated the Agency headquarters
from the Potomac.

It was an unremarkable room, especially after he'd
seen what they had deeper in this building. Behind layers and layers of security, people rushed past one another in hallways abuzz with activity, briefing rooms
that had the latest technology, bunkers and safe rooms
that could hide the entire staff in case of emergency, a
thousand operations going on at any given moment.
And then there was the Ops Center, the nerve center of
the whole facility, with more monitors than NASA's
Mission Control, with live feeds from every surveillance satellite available. There was far more here than
met the eye, beyond this sleepy office environment.

Morgan had been in the room for a few minutes
when the door clicked and swung open again. But instead of Plante, the person who came in was a stocky,
baby-faced, freckled man with light red hair who didn't
look a day over eighteen, even though Morgan knew he
must be at least thirty by now. His name was Grant
Lowry, a computer prodigy who worked as an analyst
for the Clandestine Service.

"Hiya, Cobra."

As a rule, CIA employees kept to themselves. Apart
from getting a beer now and then with members of
their work group, they did not fraternize, and the
Agency liked it that way. There was nothing like a

company holiday party to leak sensitive information. As a Black Operative, Morgan had even less contact with the people who worked at headquarters. In fact, Plante was practically the only one with whom he'd ever had any sustained contact. People who do what he did don't exactly like to advertise their identities to anyone, even within the Agency. But Lowry had consistently run support and intel for Morgan on missions. The two men had formed an unlikely bond, and Morgan was pleased to see his grinning mug again.

He exchanged a warm handshake with Lowry and then sat across from him at the table. "Hi, Grant. I didn't know you were working on this op."

"Hey, Cobra, you know that kind of talk is off-limits. But I'm not here on official business. I heard you were in the building, and I thought I'd drop in and say hello."

"I thought the CIA was good at keeping secrets," Morgan said with a smirk. He sat back in his chair, resting his arms on the table.

"Nothing's a secret if it's on a computer," said Lowry, with a devilish look on his face. "You just have to know how to ask."

"I swear, people put far too much trust in machines."

"Machines just do what you tell them, Cobra. It's people you have to watch out for." Grant gave a light-hearted chuckle. "So how've you been, old man?"

"Old man? I'm three years older than you." Morgan looked at him with mock anger.

"And retired," said Lowry.

"I *was* enjoying my 'retirement.' You?"

"Ah, you know, same old," said Lowry, half reclining in his chair. "Thinking of leaving the life behind me—maybe start my own consulting agency."

"No shit?"

"It's what all the cool kids are doing. Plus, it's hardly any fun anymore. This whole gig has been a little too stressful since 9/11." He sighed. "It was always difficult to tell friends from enemies, but lately, things have been ridiculous. And then there's this McKay character."

"The senator? I thought her whole business was corporate regulation."

"Oh, she's a busy little bee. She's heading up the Senate Committee on Intelligence." Lowry looked around, leaned forward, and lowered his voice, as if he was worried people might be listening. In this place, he was probably right. "She's taking a real hands-on approach, and apparently she's taken a special interest in the CIA. She's been around to tour the facilities a few times. Seems like she's planning a major review of operations—some transparency and accountability business. Gonna rattle some cages and all-around raise hell around here, from what I heard."

Morgan raised an eyebrow. "Can she do that?"

"If she gathers enough support. Not," he said, lowering his voice again, "that I'm exactly happy with the management here. Or, should I say, the micromanagement."

Morgan could sympathize. Nobody really got promoted in the CIA because they were competent, at least not those above a certain rank. The higher-ups, the career bureaucrats, were there because they were masters at the game of politics. That, or because someone even higher up the ladder had decided they could be controlled. That made the bosses almost invariably grade-A assholes, even though, by all accounts, the current head of the NCS, Jeffrey Boyle, was an exception. Morgan had worked with him in the field in the old days, and fieldwork formed a bond of trust that wasn't easily broken.

"So what about Kline getting to be number two at the NCS?" Morgan asked, grimacing.

"Oh, plenty of us called foul, but Boyle swears by him. If you ask me, Kline plays the game well and knows how to keep the bigwigs happy. He's even got a lot of us underlings legitimately on his side."

"Yeah. From what I understand, Plante is one of them."

"Hey, who knows? Maybe the guy has qualities that the rest of us are missing. At least I can vouch that he's not a total incompetent." Morgan looked at him doubtfully, and Grant shrugged. "So what exactly is it that brought you here?"

"Cougar," he said simply.

"Ah, so you heard. My condolences, Cobra. He was one of the best." Lowry smiled wanly, looking down. "You know, maybe you should've stuck around. We could use more men like you around here. Don't you ever miss it?"

Morgan grinned. "Do you even have to ask? Of course I miss it. I loved it. And it *mattered*, too, Grant. There's not much I can do now that's as important as what I did here. And all I can think of ever since I heard about Cougar is that, if I had been around, he might not be dead now."

"Or you might be dead, yourself."

Morgan looked at him ruefully.

"Well, why not come back?" Lowry said, changing the subject.

"Because it wouldn't be long until I remembered what made me leave in the first place. And in any case, I made a commitment to my family, and I intend to keep it."

Someone outside swiped an ID card and opened the door. Harold Kline walked in, wearing a stiff black suit. He was a slight man with a thin hooked nose and thin lips that hid tiny sharp teeth. In tow was Plante, carrying a slim folder marked CLASSIFIED.

"Lowry," said Kline, curtly.

"Just leaving, boss," he said, getting up and slipping past the two men and out the door.

"Code Name Cobra," Kline said perfunctorily, with affected formality. "I hope you had a pleasant flight down." He held out his hand, but Morgan just glowered at him. "Very well," he said. "Let's get right to it, shall we?" He sat down opposite Morgan, and Plante took the adjacent chair. "Let him have it, Eric, would you?"

Plante took a single sheet of paper from the folder and handed it to Morgan. "This is a copy of the last communication we received from Cougar. The original is still in Afghanistan. We had experts on the ground analyze the paper, and there was no secret message on the paper itself, apart from what's plainly written. Can you make any sense of it?"

Morgan took the sheet and looked at it. It read:

> *For Cobra's eyes only.*
> *A fruit vendor in Kabul once said to me,*
> *"Afghanistan is always the same; it is only the*
> *invaders who change." "Well, you know what*

*they say," I replied, "variety is the spice of life." I
am pleased to report blue skies over Kandahar
and hope that things are the same stateside. It
reminds me of the days I would tear down the
highway in that GTO to make it in time for the
daily ritual—remember, in Stoney? The.re is no
such happiness to be f.ound here. Still, people
persist. Let it never be said that the Afghans are
not a resilient people.*

*Yours truly,
Cougar*

It had obviously been hastily written, with no pre-
tension of having a surface meaning. Conley must have
been pressed for time.

"Well?" asked Kline impatiently.

"Looks to me like he's having fun at summer camp."

"Very funny," said Kline dryly. "I think that's very
funny. Don't you, Plante? Listen, Cobra, did you come
down here to waste our time?"

"No, you brought me here to waste mine," said Morgan, with a touch of anger, sitting up in his chair. "You
can't give me this without any context and expect me
to tell you what it means."

"So you're telling me what?" said Kline.

"I need to know the facts on the ground," said Morgan. "If you keep me in the dark, you can't expect me
to be able to read, can you?"

"So you want to hear sensitive details about a classified operation because you need *context*?" said Kline.

He was trying to sound incredulous because he wanted
to weaken his opponent's position, Morgan knew. And
so he parried.

"It looks like the idea is getting through your thick skull."

"What it looks like," said Kline, on the offense again, "is that you don't know a goddamn thing, and you're bullshitting me for some reason. What it looks like is that you want to pretend you're still a spook. You get a nice little tour of headquarters, and you think you're working for us again?"

"I think you want something from me, and you want it bad enough that you sent Plante right to my doorstep to fetch me." Plante looked at him, increasingly uncomfortable with the verbal sparring that was unfolding in the room. Morgan kept a firm stare on Kline. "So are you going to fill me in, or aren't you?"

"You have my answer," said Kline curtly.

"Then we're done here." Morgan got up.

"I suppose we are," said Kline, getting up as well. "Mr. Plante, please escort Cobra out of the secure area."

Kline walked out, and Plante held the door open for Morgan. When they were walking side by side, Plante spoke.

"I know he can be a prick. But decoding this message could be far more important than your spat with Kline." Morgan continued to walk, half ignoring Plante. "I know I have no right to. But I'm asking you to be the bigger man here."

"So you're playing good cop to Kline's anal-retentive, shit-for-brains cop?" said Morgan.

"I'm playing the handler who doesn't want to see Cougar's work fall to pieces," said Plante, frustrated. He exhaled, and his voice became unusually earnest. "There's no strategy here, Cobra. I'm not trying to manipulate you. He was your friend, and my friend, too. He died for this assignment. And you know he didn't take assignments unless he knew they were good and worthwhile." Plante looked at him. "He was like you that way."

"Well," said Morgan, feeling a twinge of guilt, "there's nothing I can say. I can't tell you what it means unless I know what I'm looking for. And if Kline wants to deny me that in order to prove his own superiority, then there's nothing I can do."

They walked into the elevator in silence. Plante's phone rang, and he flipped it open. Morgan heard the voice on the other end but too faintly for him to understand the words. Plante responded, "Still in the building, sir. Yes, sir. Right now? Understood." He flipped his phone shut and said to Morgan, "Looks like Kline had a change of heart."

"Is he going to give me what I want?"

"No. Not himself, at least. He wants me to send you up to see Boyle."

CHAPTER 8

The office of the Director of the National Clandestine Service was decorated with the austerity of a military man. It was not large, and it was sparsely furnished. There was a desk, sturdy and plain, which had Boyle sit with his back to a wall rather than the windows—an arrangement born, Morgan knew, of the die-hard instinct never to turn your back on anything. The wood-paneled walls were unadorned except for one dominating artifact: an American flag, frayed and singed, whose thirty-four stars, set in a circle, revealed that it had been flown in the Civil War.

Jeffrey Boyle himself had started his career as a Marine, and Morgan liked to joke that he had never really gotten over it. Boyle's discipline was legendary. He was known to be up every day at 4:00 A.M. for a five-mile run. He worked tirelessly, pausing only for a single, sparse daily meal. On the days that he left the office at all, it was usually after midnight.

His character showed through in his figure, and age, Morgan noticed as the man rose to greet him, had done little to diminish him in any way. Even though he was nearing sixty, he was still a remarkably powerful man. He wore a crisp black suit, matching his stern, focused expression, that did nothing to hide his broad shoulders and the muscles underneath.

"Dan Morgan," he said, with practiced levity. "Or should I say, Cobra? I had to see it to believe it." He was a serious man, and even though he had none of Kline's stiff fussiness, joking still seemed unnatural on him.

"I could say the same about you, sitting behind that desk," Morgan said, as he shook Boyle's hand. "Who did you have to sleep with to get this job?"

Boyle laughed heartily. "I like to think that it's a different set of talents that brought me here."

They sat.

"And you've definitely come a long way, haven't you?" said Morgan. "I'm surprised you ever got out of the field. They used to say that you'd still be nailing bad guys even if you had to do it from a wheelchair, hooked to a respirator."

Boyle smiled. "I did love the work. But I've discovered that there's a lot of good to be done from behind a desk. If you stick with this work long enough, you start to realize that leading and managing isn't a privilege. It's a duty. Because if you don't, somebody else will. And what I also realized is that you can't trust anyone else to do the right thing."

Morgan had to agree. At the same time, he saw a grim ruthlessness in the man that put him off. But it was gone as suddenly as it had come.

"Can I offer you a drink?" Boyle said. "I have some whiskey in the cabinet."

"I don't drink," he replied.

"Of course, how could I forget? I don't, either, of course. Sound body, sound mind, and all that. But the politicians who frequent this office don't usually share my philosophy about alcohol."

"Not much else, either, I would think," said Morgan.

Boyle thought for a moment, then said, "Yes, that's true, much of the time."

"It makes me wonder how you manage to put up with it, Boyle. Politicians. That whole world of back-stabbing and double-crossing, all done with a perfect smile plastered across their faces. At least spies are up front about being liars."

"You have to play the game," said Boyle, matter-of-factly. "That's the price you pay for influence, Morgan."

"You mean *power*."

"Someone needs to have it. Who would you rather it be?"

Morgan didn't respond. The two men stared at each other for a few interminable seconds.

"In any case," said Boyle, breaking the silence, "we should discuss the reason you're here in the first place. Kline tells me you've been making trouble for him."

"If you'd asked me, I would have said it's the other way around."

"You would, of course, say that," said Boyle. "Well, he wants me to lock you up until you cooperate."

Morgan laughed. "I'd like to see him try to do it himself."

"I'm sure you understand," said Boyle, ignoring Morgan's interjection, "we're not in the habit of sharing the kind of information you want with just anyone. And I'll be honest. I don't like the idea of bringing you in on this. It's unusual and exposes things that are strictly confidential. But I'm going to do something that's not often done in this business." He pulled out a pen and laid out a printed form on his desk, which he began filling in. "I am going to trust you. You're an honorable man, and I know that you have the best interest of this country in mind." He signed the form and held it out for Morgan. "Are you going to make me regret this, Morgan?"

"My country has always come first," said Morgan, with heartfelt conviction. "That's as true today as it was when I first joined up."

"I'm going out on a limb for you here," said Boyle.

"And I'm grateful for that," Morgan said. "You're doing the right thing."

Back in the conference room where they had met earlier, Kline sat down across from Morgan for the second time that day, but this time he looked like he was ruminating on something mildly bitter. "Evidently, Director Boyle disagrees with my assessment of this situation. Eric, please brief Cobra on Operation Pashtun Sickle."

"Did you come up with that one all by yourself?" said Morgan.

Plante began, ignoring him and turning on the screen at the far end of the conference room. "The purpose of this operation was to take out this man." On the wall-size screen he brought up a picture of a fat, middle-aged, bearded man in fancy-looking traditional Afghan garb, sporting a smug, vicious smile. "Afghan warlord Bacha Marwat. He controls a sizeable portion of the drug trade in the Kandahar region. He produces count-

less tons of poppy seeds. He has ties to the local government and commands a good deal of corruption. A
significant amount of his revenue goes toward maintaining local militia, many of whom are in league with
the Taliban and who are giving our soldiers hell over
there."

"Cougar was embedded as an aid worker," Plante
continued. "His primary mission was to get close
enough to terminate Marwat. But there were difficul-
ties. Marwat is a well-guarded man. Cougar had an
asset, someone in Marwat's organization who might
have been able to get him inside the operation."

"Who's this asset?" asked Morgan.

"All we know is his name," said Plante. "Zalmay
Siddiqi."

"Spell it for me." Plante did. "And how were you
communicating with him?"

"Dead drop," said Plante. "The mail slot in a house
in Kandahar City. We had a communications officer
check it twice every day."

Morgan nodded. It might be inefficient, but when
working deep undercover, paper communication was
harder for someone to detect or stumble upon. Paper
could be destroyed. Electronics always left traces.
"Were these messages in your own code?"

Plante nodded. "Except, of course, for the one you
have in front of you."

"Pen," Morgan said. Plante handed him one from
his shirt pocket. Morgan pored over the paper, making
illegible annotations.

"Well?" said Kline impatiently.

"The asset's dead," said Morgan, leaning back in his
chair.

"Dead? Are you certain?" asked Plante nervously. Kline looked at Morgan with suspicious eyes.

"That's what it says here."

"That's an awful lot of text for that to be the whole message," said Kline dubiously.

"It's not all," said Morgan. "The rest says he's been found out and requests immediate extraction. Although that's moot at this point, isn't it?" he said witheringly.

"What else?" insisted Kline. "There has to be more."

"That's all there is."

Kline leaned forward and looked Morgan in the eye. He looked like he was trying his best to appear intimidating. "It had better be. Because if I find out you're lying to us . . ."

"Are you accusing me of something, Kline? Because I think you'd better come out and say it."

"I just think it's strange," said Kline, with mock perplexity, "that Cougar would encode this in a way that only you could read it. Don't you think that's strange, Eric?"

Plante held his uncomfortable silence.

"I can think of a few reasons why," said Morgan. "But it all boils down to the fact that, for some reason, he didn't trust you."

"Now you're the one who apparently has something to say," said Kline.

"Cougar was compromised, and he must have wondered whether the issue might be here at home."

"Are you suggesting," said Kline, in disbelief, "that Marwat has a mole in the CIA?"

"I'm suggesting maybe Cougar thought this ship wasn't run as tightly as he liked. Maybe he only wanted someone he could trust to be able to understand his message."

"I see," said Kline, through his small teeth. "Well, as you said, the point is moot. Mr. Plante, kindly escort Cobra out of the building."

"We've arranged for a car to take you to the airport," Plante told Morgan as they walked out of the building. He handed Morgan a piece of paper, folded in thirds. "Here's a copy of your itinerary. Your flight to Boston leaves at five. I'm sorry we wasted your time."

"You know I'd do anything for Cougar. There was a time, Plante, that I would've done anything for you, too."

"There are things I wish I could tell you, Cobra. Things that would convince that you I was always on Cougar's side. And that I'm your side now, too."

"But you can't," Morgan said, with deadpan sarcasm. "Because it's classified."

"I really wish I could. There's a lot that you don't know."

"And that you can't tell me. How convenient."

"Maybe one day we can put our differences behind us," said Plante sincerely. "Maybe one day, when you have the full picture of what went on."

"Yeah. Maybe."

Morgan turned and walked toward the town car that was waiting for him, leaving Plante standing on the curb next to the Headquarters building.

Morgan had an uneventful ride to the airport. Once there, out of the driver's sight, he picked up a pay phone and dialed Information. His call connected, and after a few minutes, he hung up and called Jenny, telling her that he would have to stay in DC overnight. Then he hopped into a cab and took off, away from the airport, to see an old friend.

CHAPTER 9

"Let me see if I understand you correctly. You wish to go into the heart of an occupied country, and you want no one to know about it?"

The man with the serenely quizzical look on his face was Kadir Fastia. His hallmark beard, neatly trimmed, was now a near-white that stood out against his olive skin. Fastia was a deliberate man, and every movement he made, down to each small gesture, seemed measured, considered. He was the image, Morgan thought, of a man at peace with himself. A cigar smoldered between his fingers. Smoke permeated the air in his study, trapped by closed doors and windows with the blinds down, keeping out the evening sun except for thin slivers that spilled onto Fastia's desk. Through the window, Morgan could hear the laughter of Fastia's grandchildren, who were playing outside.

"For starters, yeah."

"Am I correct in assuming that you do not wish to use your real name?"

"You are."

Fastia took a scrap of paper and scribbled a name

and a number on it. "This man can help you. Passport, driver's license—local, European, Chinese—anything you need, he can get it to you. Tell him that I sent you, and he will get for you what you ask."

"Much appreciated, Kadir," he said, pocketing the paper. "This will be helpful. But what I really need"— Morgan sighed—"is wings."

Fastia looked at him pointedly. "You wish for help getting into the country? For my help?"

"Getting in isn't the problem. It's getting out afterward. So I guess the question is, can you do it?"

"The question, my friend, is what do you intend to do while you are there?" Fastia puffed on his cigar, and the smoke filtered out of his mouth in dense curlicues.

Morgan looked out the window pensively, then said, "What's your relationship with the CIA like these days?"

"Mutual toleration," said Fastia. "I don't ask too many questions about the work that I do for them, and they don't ask too many about the work I do on my own."

"What do you know about Cougar?"

"I have worked with Cougar since you departed, but not for some time now," said Fastia.

"Did you know he's dead?"

Fastia's eyes widened slightly, and grief lined his face. "No. This is the first I have heard of this. How did it happen?"

"He was running a mission, solo, in Kandahar. I guess someone sniffed him out."

"In Kandahar, you say. So I assume this is the reason that you are going?"

Morgan nodded. "He sent me a letter through the

Agency. Coded in a way only I could decipher. He was working an asset in Kandahar, and he wanted that asset extracted. I'm guessing it was insurance, in case something happened to him. I'm supposed to meet this guy in Kabul in three days." *The.re is no such happiness to be f.ound here*, the letter had said. The number of characters before each of the two strangely placed periods had told him the date: 3/24.

"I take it that the Agency does not know about this."

"They're in the dark, and I'm going to keep it that way."

"Are you sure that this is the wisest course of action?" Kadir said, with typical understatement.

Morgan answered the question by ignoring it. "I'm also going to need some support on the ground, a local who knows his way around, who can drive me and can set me up with certain supplies. Now, Kadir, pay attention: if there's any part of this that you can't deliver, you need to tell me now."

Fastia leaned back in his chair and rested his chin on his hand. He took a puff from his cigar and closed his eyes.

Morgan had first met Fastia on the dunes of the Libyan Sahara when they crossed over on their way to Tripoli for their most important mission yet: to kill Colonel Muammar Gaddafi.

It was one of his and Cougar's first Ops together. They were young men, fresh off The Farm and full of piss and vinegar, their corresponding tattoos still smarting from the needles that had made them. He and Conley had flown into Alexandria and were driven westward in a rickety jeep by a man named Azibo. Conley, who had a way with strangers and an endless curiosity about foreign cultures, sat up front, prattling away with the driver in Arabic. Morgan sat in the back, restless in the suffocating heat. He tried to focus on the mission ahead, but it was nearly impossible to concentrate on anything. Their initial enthusiasm was flagging from the dull strain of transportation. It would be different once they arrived at their destination, but for now, Morgan closed his eyes. He tried fruitlessly to sleep as he bobbed along with the vehicle until he noticed that the engine had cut off, and the jeep was coming to a halt.

"What's going on?" he asked Conley, who in turn said something in Arabic to Azibo.

"He said the engine died on him," Conley told Morgan.

Azibo turned the key, but the engine didn't respond. Conley had another brief exchange with him.

"He doesn't know what's wrong. It looks like I'm going to have to go out and take a look."

Morgan got out, too, and stood a few feet from the jeep, keeping his eye on Azibo as Conley opened the hood.

"We'd better hope we haven't been leaking oil since Alexandria," said Conley, "or this jeep might have just become a three-ton paperweight."

Morgan looked up and down the desert road. There wasn't a car in sight. He took a drink from his canteen. "I'll keep my fingers crossed," he said sarcastically.

Conley rooted around in the engine. "This thing is a nightmare," he said. "It's basically held together by string and duct tape. I'm shocked we even made it out of the city."

"That's just great," said Morgan, shielding his eyes from the scorching sun. "How the hell are we going to make our rendezvous?"

"I said it was a nightmare. I didn't say I couldn't fix it."

Morgan went to sit on the jeep's backseat with his legs out the rear door as Conley struggled with the engine, a shirt wrapped around his head like a turban to protect him from the punishing rays of the sun. Azibo reclined in the driver's seat with the door open, looking on with heavy-lidded eyes.

Squinting at the bright sands and with sweat dripping into his eyes, Morgan thought about what would happen if Conley wasn't able to get the motor running again, about failing this mission. This was about more than just removing one piece of human scum from the face of the earth. Without Gaddafi, the Libyans had a chance for freedom. This could alter the course of history for millions of people. And who knew what sort of repercussions there could be after that? Who knew what other people, living under the yoke of oppression, would be emboldened if freedom happened in a place like Libya? It seemed ridiculous that everything should hinge on this rickety old hunk of junk. But if there was one thing he had learned so far, it was that everything depended on the smallest details. A penny on the tracks could derail an entire freight train.

Those thoughts had been running in Morgan's mind for nearly two hours when Conley announced, "That ought to do it."

"So it works?" asked Morgan. Conley exchanged a few words with Azibo, who turned the key again. The engine rumbled to life, and the three men cheered.

"Now I just need to . . ." said Conley, trailing off, and he began forcing something in the engine with a screwdriver, putting his weight into it. The screwdriver slipped, and he jerked away suddenly, clutching his right hand. "Damn it!"

"What is it?"

"God*damn* it. Nothing, it's nothing, just a cut." Conley tried to wave it off, but Morgan saw that his hand was bleeding, small drops falling and congealing on the dusty ground. Morgan reached into the car for the first-aid kit. "Goddamn stupid thing to do," said Conley.

"I guess now we know who the shooter is going to be," said Morgan. It had been a point of contention; both were crack shots, and each wanted to be the one to pull the trigger. Morgan was glad it had been decided for them.

Conley held out his hand and winced when Morgan cleaned out the cut with rubbing alcohol. It was deep but not enough to do any permanent damage. Azibo watched curiously as Morgan sutured it over a sterilized plastic sheet and wrapped bandages around Conley's hand.

They crossed the border into Libya sometime after nightfall. Shortly beforehand, Azibo had left the road entirely, making the crossing in the open desert. It was bumpy, slow going. All Morgan could see was the dusty ground directly in front of the headlights, and the stars above, brighter than he had ever seen them. A fresh breeze began to blow, a blessing after the scorching heat of the day.

When they came to a rise in the terrain, Conley told Azibo to stop. The driver cut the engine, plunging them into darkness. The absence of the motor also brought on an eerie quiet, with no sound except for the drifting sand hitting the side of the jeep.

Morgan took the night-vision binoculars from his pack and leaned out the window. He swept the horizon, a barren, godforsaken wasteland, no more alien for being entirely green in the night-vision goggles. He didn't spot what he was looking for, so he pulled out his flashlight and clicked it on and off in a sequence of longs and shorts, alternately pointing in several different directions.

"There!" said Conley, pointing north. It took Morgan a moment to make out a faint flashing dot.

"That's got to be him." Morgan clicked the flashlight on and off in its direction several times to acknowledge the signal, then sat back down. "Let's go."

Five minutes later their headlights shone on a battered, oversize jeep not too different from their own, and a lone man standing next to it, wearing a traditional robe and a desert scarf, the kaffiyeh, on his head. Azibo stopped thirty feet away in a cloud of dust. Morgan opened the door and got out of the jeep, his MAC-10 machine pistol firmly in his hand, safety off. He approached the man with tense caution. Conley, flanking him, did the same.

The man held out both of his hands, palms upward, in a gesture of friendship that also served to demonstrate that he was unarmed. He stared at the two men intently and said, after a moment: "One of you is Cobra. The other is Cougar." The statement had a slight, hopeful inflection to it. His accent was minor, but the precision of his pronunciation revealed that English was not his first language.

Morgan brought the aim of his MAC-10 to the stranger's chest. "And you are?"

"Code Name Wings. I am Lieutenant Colonel Kadir Fastia."

Morgan lowered his weapon but remained tense, like a snake coiled and ready to strike. The man in the turban smiled, bowed, and said, "Salaam."

"Salaam," they each responded in turn.

Salaam. The word echoed in Morgan's head. *Peace.* Not in this world.

Morgan rode shotgun as Fastia drove them down an old dirt road, not a sign of humanity in the encroaching darkness. "The main highway is not safe for the three of us traveling together," Fastia told them. "This way will take us longer, but we will not be stopped. I am afraid we have a long way to go. I have arranged safe lodging near Tripoli. But you may sleep now if you wish." Morgan looked back at Conley, who was sitting behind Fastia, alert and with his gun resting loosely in his hand, ready to shoot Fastia through the seat if necessary. Trust only went so far.

"Cobra . . ." said Fastia idly. "Tell me, did you choose that name yourself?"

"Yeah, I did," said Morgan curtly.

"May I ask why?"

"The cobra is a killer," Morgan responded. "Agile,

cold, ruthless, and efficient. You don't want to mess with a cobra. And I wanted everyone I encountered to know," he said, looking pointedly at Fastia, "that you don't want to mess with me."

"Not all men are able to choose their own names," said Fastia. After a few minutes' silence, Fastia began to speak again, still staring dead ahead at the road before them. "A man under my command was bitten by a cobra once. We were running exercise drills in the desert, and he stepped in the wrong mound of sand. The snake bit his ankle, right through his boot. It was an unfortunate circumstance. The man responsible for bringing the first-aid kit, which had the antivenin necessary to save this man's life, had forgotten it. We were too far into the desert to get him back to safety in time. He convulsed violently for interminable minutes as we tried in vain to suck the poison out of the bite. His ankle grew swollen and black. He screamed and screamed, in pain. For us to save him. Yelled out for his mother. A grown man, yelling for his mother. It was not long before he died. Do you know how people who are bitten by the cobra die?"

Morgan did not respond.

"Of asphyxiation. The cobra venom attacks the brain and causes paralysis. The victim soon loses the ability to breathe. Within half an hour, this man's heart was not beating anymore."

There was a long silence between them, during which all they could hear was the rumble of the engine. Morgan later remembered wondering about what Fatia's purpose was in telling this story, whether it was some kind of test. He glanced back at Conley, who looked at him but made no sign in response. Finally, Morgan spoke. "You're an intelligence officer in the Libyan Armed Forces, is that right?" he asked.

"Yes, that is right," said Fastia, looking ahead, his expression cool and blank.

Morgan continued. "That has to be some kind of big achievement, yeah? Years of strict training, following orders, giving your complete loyalty to your superiors. Isn't that right? Or is there something special about how we do things in the US?"

"No, it is the same."

"Do you know what they call it in the US when someone does what you're doing right now to your country?"

"I believe you call it treason," said Fastia bitterly.

"That's what they call it. They'd give you the chair for it there. Fry your brains and put you in the ground. Tell me, is it the same here?" Morgan glanced at Conley, who gave him a look that said, *You'd better know what the hell you're doing.*

"No," Fastia said, his grip on the steering wheel making his knuckles white. "Here, it is done by firing squad."

"And it's not only the dying, either, is it?" continued Morgan, as if he had not asked Fastia a question before. "Dying a traitor—that's a shameful death. Maybe the worst death for a military man."

Fastia was trying his best to offer no reaction, Morgan could tell. But his line of questioning was getting to the guy, as he had hoped. He wanted to make sure of this man. And, one way or the other, he would get a response.

"So my question here, I guess, is—why do it, Kadir? Why are you willing to be a traitor to your country?"

"It is Gaddafi who is the traitor," Fastia spat back, rage finally breaking through his stoicism. Then, composing himself, but still in anger, he added, "He has betrayed this country. It is for love of Libya and its people that I help you."

Morgan shot him a glance. "As I understand, it's about more than just love of your country, isn't it?"

Fastia's faced tensed, and his back straightened. "They have told you more, then, than I wished," he said, with renewed but strained courtesy. "Yes, Cobra, I do this for vengeance, as well. Gaddafi is a murderer. He killed my family—my mother and father and my sister—in one of his purges." Bitter tears streamed down his face despite himself. "The love I had for them has turned to hatred for the butcher who killed them. I want nothing more than to see him dead."

Morgan saw a passion and resolve in Fastia that couldn't be faked. "You're a more patient man than I am, Kadir. If it had happened to me, I would have taken matters into my own hands a long, long time ago."

Fastia regained his composure and was once more stiff and impassive. "It is as they say, Cobra, that revenge is a dish best served cold."

"Do you believe that?"

"No, I do not. But it will do."

They hardly spoke for the next several hours as they made their way along twisting country roads toward Tripoli. Finally, they arrived at an isolated, two-story, adobe house.

"The people who live here," said Fastia, "will give you lodging for the night. Here, you may rest and eat without worry." He then introduced the two of them to a wizened little man and woman who welcomed them inside by candlelight, to a room with two ratty mattresses on the floor. Fastia stood at the door. "I must go, but I will be back in the morning for you," he said. "Rest well. You will be safe here. Get some sleep, if you are able. Tomorrow will be a historic day."

Fastia arrived early the next morning dressed in his Air Force uniform, with two more uniforms for Morgan and Conley. "I believe that these will fit you both. I don't think I need to remind you that if you are caught, you will be tortured and executed as spies."

"If they take us, they won't take us alive," said Morgan, running his tongue over a molar crown that concealed the standard-issue cyanide capsule. On a mission, the possibility of death was always an immediate reality.

"Good," said Fastia, and he waited for them to get dressed. Once they were in uniform, Fastia stepped forward and made minor adjustments to their clothes, starting with Morgan. "With your mustache and dark complexion, you will have no trouble passing for Libyan," Fastia told him. He then moved on to Conley. "Cougar, you look more Western. Many will not question your appearance if you are in uniform, but it would be best if you would hide your face whenever possible." He stepped back to examine both of them. "This should be enough to fool any guards along the way, as long as you keep your mouths shut. Now come. It is time. I will give you the details of the mission en route."

Fastia had arranged for an official-looking town car, black and polished. Conley took the wheel, with Morgan and Fastia in the backseat, and they arrived in the city in about an hour. Tripoli was abuzz with its annual International Fair, which attracted thousands of people. The heavy traffic was exacerbated by military checkpoints, and security forces patrolled along every major street. They would have been stuck for hours if they hadn't been in a military car. Instead, they passed the barricades unchallenged as the checkpoint guards snapped to attention and saluted. Still, Morgan held his breath every time, and Conley tried to hide his face as much as possible.

"This, all this security, is for him. *Colonel Gaddafi*." The name sounded like a swearword coming from Fastia's mouth. "It will not save his life today."

The traffic grew heavier and the barricades more frequent as they approached the square where Gaddafi was going to address the throng of businessmen and tourists who were in town for the fair. When they were within view of their destination, Fastia had Conley turn into a side street and park the car.

"This is it," he told them. They were parked in front of a tan five-story office building. The glass front door, built into an arch, led to a modest lobby. There was a guard posted on the sidewalk, a mere ten feet from it. "The building has a clear view of the plaza, and it has been emptied out for the event. There will be another guard inside."

Conley got out and opened the door for Morgan and Fastia. The guard approached them, motioning for them to leave, but when he caught sight of Fastia's uniform, he snapped to attention and saluted them. Fastia spoke to him authoritatively in Arabic, and, with a final salute, the guard returned to his post. Conley took the duffel bag from the trunk. He sagged slightly from the weight.

Fastia led Morgan and Conley to the entrance and tapped on the glass door with his ring to get the attention of the guard inside. The guard looked up, surprised, and Fastia motioned for him to open the door. He walked over, fumbled with the keys at the lock, and then swung the door open to admit them.

Once inside, Fastia exchanged a few words with the guard, walking slowly farther into the building's lobby until they were no longer visible from the street. Morgan, meanwhile, walked a little ahead of them, pretending to head toward the elevator door. Fastia pointed to something in a corner, and at his signal, Morgan pulled out a knife concealed in his boot and, in a flash, pulled the guard's head back and slit his throat. The guard dropped to his knees and fell to the floor gurgling, blood pooling around his head in a macabre halo. Fastia walked to the door and, knocking against the glass again, motioned for the other guard to come in. This time, Morgan was waiting by the door, and he pounced just as the guard walked through, dispatching him in the same way. They dragged the bodies into the elevator with them. There would be no witnesses to their presence.

They got off on the third floor, and Morgan checked his watch: 11:09. According to Fastia's intel, Gaddafi's motorcade would arrive in twenty-one minutes. There were three windows on the floor that faced the stage where Gaddafi would make his appearance. Morgan chose the best vantage point, took the duffel from Conley, and dropped it next to the window. He took the leather shooter's gloves from the bag and slipped them on. Then he removed the dismantled weapon and assembled it, slowly and deliberately.

The Dragunov semiautomatic sniper rifle, also known as an SVD, was ideal for the job. Named for the Soviet weapons designer who'd created it, the SVD was built for extreme accuracy and power, with an effective range of over 2,500 feet. The magazine held ten 7N1 special precision loads. The rifle was fitted with a muzzle flash suppressor and a custom silencer, so that no one could figure out where the shot had come from until they made a sweep of the buildings. When they did locate the source, all they would find would be two dead guards and an abandoned Soviet weapon, with nothing to tie the operation back to two American assassins.

Morgan attached the telescopic sight to the barrel of the rifle and secured it onto the tripod, then placed the gun at the window ledge. Conley took his position next to him, scanning the area through high-powered binoculars, while Morgan looked through the scope, sweeping the crowd for guards who might spot them. Conley checked the billowing flags for wind speed and direction.

"Looks like you have a steady wind, about five miles per, coming across your path on the right."

Morgan acknowledged this and cracked open the window just enough so that he had an unobstructed view of the podium where Gaddafi would be standing. The noise of the crowd filtered into the room, a cacophony competing with a rousing military march that was being played by a brass band.

"Five minutes," Conley said.

Fastia, who had been sitting in an office chair behind them, watching eagerly, got up and stood by the window, nervously. Meanwhile, Conley removed a radio transceiver from the pack and said into the mouthpiece, "This is Cougar. Come in, Eagle's Nest."

"This is Eagle's Nest," crackled a voice from the radio.

"We are in position; repeat, we are in position."

Onstage, the band stopped, and a local dignitary began delivering an introduction that went mostly ignored. Morgan put an invisible bead on him, rehearsing the countdown in his mind.

"Two minutes," said Conley. "Careful. Wind's picking up." Morgan shifted the crosshairs just to the right of the speaker's heart. Sweat began to run down his face.

"One minute . . ."

The band struck up a patriotic march. After a few measures, the music was overtaken by sirens, and they saw the flashing lights of the motorcade approaching between the long lines of parallel barricades. A wild cheer erupted as Gaddafi's black Mercedes and five security vehicles pulled up to the stand. The dictator's private guard, officially called the Revolutionary Nuns, comprised exclusively of highly trained and beautiful young women, spread out and stood at attention.

Conley focused his binoculars on the darkened windows of Gaddafi's Mercedes. "I wonder if he's really in there. Might be a decoy or a look-alike."

Morgan didn't respond. It couldn't be. Not today. At last, one of the security guards opened the car's rear door. Two men wearing military uniforms, each with a chestful of medals, emerged from the vehicle.

"Come on. Come on." Morgan placed his gloved finger on the trigger with just the lightest touch.

Finally, he emerged: Colonel Muammar Gaddafi, wearing a red and black patterned ceremonial Bedouin robe that reached the ground. His long, greasy dark hair spilled out from under a matching cap.

"That's him," said Conley, looking through his binoculars. "Positive ID. That's the target."

Gaddafi beamed and waved to the crowd, who cheered on cue as he made his way to the podium.

"Target acquired," Cobra spoke into the radio. "Cobra requesting go-ahead."

"Mission is go, Cobra."

"Everything looks good," Conley said to Morgan. "It's up to you now."

"Do not fail," said Fastia, in a whisper.

Morgan released the safety as Gaddafi adjusted the microphone to his height. The bastard was right in his crosshairs. There was no escape for him now. Even at this range, Morgan would not miss. He never missed. Taking a deep breath, Morgan touched his finger to the trigger and began his countdown, out loud. "Five. Four." He added pressure to his trigger finger. "Three. Two."

"Abort mission!" came the voice on the radio. "Abort, Cobra! Abort! Do you copy?"

Morgan stopped the countdown but kept his finger on the trigger, the target in his scope.

"Do it," demanded Fastia. "It is our only chance."

All he had to do was squeeze the trigger.

"Confirm abort order, Cobra!"

Why should he abort? *What reason could there be to let this mass murderer live?* Morgan wondered. He could allege radio failure. A tragic miscommunication. They would throw the book at him, but what could they do? The bastard would be dead. He looked through his sight at Gaddafi, still talking at the podium.

"Cobra!" said Conley sharply. "They gave the order to abort. *Let it go.*"

Fastia crouched and snarled, "Shoot! Take the shot, Cobra! Do it now, before it is too late!"

Morgan tensed his trigger finger. The crosshairs remained on Gaddafi, who was talking boisterously to the crowd.

"Confirm abort order, Cobra!"

Conley put a heavy hand on his shoulder, and Morgan, exhaling, let go of the trigger.

"Abort order confirmed," he said.

"No!" said Fastia, falling to his knees, his voice breaking. Morgan jumped to his feet.

"Let's go, Kadir," said Morgan. "It's over."

"No! It's not over yet! Pick up your gun and shoot!"

"Let's say I do that. What then? Do you think they're just going to give you and your wife and daughter safe passage to the US if you disobey orders? Trust me, Kadir, we're your only friends right now, and we're telling you, it's over."

"Why would they stop us? Why?"

"We might never know," said Morgan. "The suits always have their reasons. All we can do is hope that they made the right call."

Conley was at the door. "Cobra, we gotta go."

Fastia gave a last bitter look through the window, where the crowd cheered wildly for Gaddafi. Resigned, he said, "He lives, then."

"And so do we, Kadir," said Morgan. "Come on. The clock is ticking."

Slipping out of the building and back into their sedan, Morgan, Conley, and Fastia drove to an air base where Fastia had arranged for a military aircraft with a flight plan to Egypt; once in the air, they would divert their course to London. Fastia's family had already boarded and sat waiting for them. They would eventually fly to America, to start a new life. With two guards killed and the Russian weapon left behind, Gaddafi would discover there had been an assassination attempt on his life. There would be repercussions. Lives would be lost. But nothing would ever be tied back to the CIA. The dictator himself would rule for years more before being toppled by a Western-backed popular uprising.

"Well, Kadir?" asked Morgan.

Fastia took a puff from his cigar and let the smoke flow slowly out of his mouth. A child's exuberant laughter came from outside his office.

"Tell me something," he asked Morgan. "You have a family, like me. A home, a child. You are a different man now, with a different life. Does the past call you so strongly that you would leave it all behind on the spur of the moment?"

"I thought you, of all people, would understand," said Morgan.

"It has been a long time since I left Libya," said Fastia. "I have changed much since then. And history, as it seems, does catch up eventually."

"Did they ever tell you why they aborted the Libya mission? Why they chose to let Gaddafi remain in power when we could have eliminated him back then?"

A sudden intensity came into Fastia's eyes, and then he sighed deeply, as if trying to soothe a profound pain. "The geopolitical circumstances changed abruptly. That, or OPEC interceded on the butcher's behalf. What does it matter?" Changing the subject, he asked, "Do you still call yourself Cobra?"

"If I have to," Morgan said simply.

Fastia put out his cigarette in an ashtray on his desk. "I will need money," said Fastia. "I will not charge you my normal fees, but the airplane and the asset in Afghanistan will not come cheap."

"I have the money, Kadir. I need to know if you can deliver."

Fastia took a deep breath. "Yes, Cobra. I will help you. For Cougar's sake, and for yours."

CHAPTER 10

Leo Guzman's fingers flew across the keyboard. It was daytime, but his little nook was a dark burrow. The daylight, he found, would set his biological clock to a day-and-night cycle, which interfered with the alternative sleep cycle he was training himself to follow. At the moment, he was interspersing bouts of furious typing with sips of an energy drink. He was hitting the sweet spot, his wired mind racing, and feeling in a very real sense, as he often did at this job, that he had the world at his fingertips. He was concentrating so deeply and intensely that he didn't even notice the knock on the door; he only saw the light streaming in from the hallway outside when someone opened it.

"Guzman?" he heard coming from behind him.

He swiveled around in his chair, mildly irritated at the interruption. "Oh, hey, Plante, can I help you?"

"I need you to run a trace on a phone."

"Got the number?"

Plante told him. "Think I can get a real-time feed of the trace at my desk?"

"What, did you think I'd make you look over my shoulder?" said Guzman, grinning.

"Oh, and one more thing. Think you can keep this one quiet, too?"

"Be careful, Plante. Someone might think we're running some kind of covert intelligence-gathering operation or something."

Plante grinned at the joke.

"Anyway, it'll be ready by the time you're back at your workstation."

"Appreciated, Guzman."

"You got it."

Plante closed the door, and the room was plunged back into its previous denlike darkness. With a few strokes of the keyboard, Guzman began to run the trace. The program connected surprisingly fast, immediately placing the cell phone in a residential neighborhood in Bethesda. He noted the speed only long enough to deduce that someone else must be tracing that same number. But having done what Plante asked, he only cursed the disruption and began to work himself back into sublime hyperconcentration.

CHAPTER 11

"I hope you understand, Barry, that this is a career ender." Nickerson watched with well-concealed pleasure as the young senator squirmed in his seat. It had been over a full minute since he had set the pictures down in front of the man, and Lamb still hadn't taken his eyes away from them. "If the media got ahold of this . . . I mean, we can already see the story play out, can't we? Senator Lamb caught with a pretty young thing named Erika Dillon. Speculations abound on whether she's a call girl. Political base disgusted. Your own party dumps you like a barrel of toxic waste."

"What—" said Lamb, trying to keep his voice steady. "What do you want?"

They were in Nickerson's office. Nickerson had pulled the drapes shut for a claustrophobic effect and left his standing lamp as the only light source. It cast enormous dark shadows on the walls. It looked, he observed with pleasure, like an interrogation room.

"Barry . . ." said Nickerson. "Barry, Barry, Barry. What kind of man do you suppose I am? I hope you see this for what it is. I hope you realize that this is me helping you."

"*Helping* me?" said Lamb. He was sweating. And Nickerson loved to watch them sweat. He loved that special blend of shame and fear they got when they sat in that chair. He wondered if Lamb would cry.

"Why, Barry, this is your second chance. Your new lease on life."

"What are you talking about? Oh, Jesus . . ." Lamb rubbed his temples.

"Think about it. If these pictures were in someone else's possession . . . How many people do you know who would not immediately turn them over to the press? No, Barry, this is good news. This is your wake-up call. This is when you are confronted by your folly, Senator Lamb, and given the chance to turn things around."

"Do you mean—"

"That I'm not going public with this? Of course not! Give me more credit than that, Lamb. I do not destroy a man's life lightly."

Lamb let out a sigh of relief, but his anxiety did not leave his face, and he still glanced nervously at the photographs every few seconds.

"Of course," said Nickerson, "courtesy does go both ways, does it not?"

"What d-do you m-mean?" Lamb stammered. He was beyond the deer-in-the-headlights stage now. He fidgeted nervously with his hands.

"I mean, I need a stalwart ally on the Intelligence Committee. I believe we are going astray in the push for greater oversight."

"Ah," said Lamb, as it dawned on him. "So this is the price of your friendship?"

"It's crass to talk about price. What we face here is a gentlemen's agreement. A mutually beneficial relationship."

"It's blackmail. That's what this is." Lamb's fists were balled up white.

Nickerson's expression grew cold and flat, but he said nothing.

"I see what you are now, Nickerson. Jesus Christ, and to think you've actually got a reputation as a— Listen. I won't be bullied, Nickerson. Do what you will. I'm not folding."

Nickerson nodded. "I suppose I have to respect your integrity. Say, what do you think will make a bigger splash, Lamb—sending these to a reputable newspaper or going tabloid?"

Lamb stood up to face him. "You wouldn't!"

"I suppose we could always split the difference and do both. What do you think?"

"Nickerson . . ." he said, pleading.

"Or maybe we trickle them out online," Nickerson continued, ignoring him. "Make a game of how long we can keep this in the news cycle."

"Please don't do this," said Lamb.

"*Or*," said Nickerson, "you have a change of heart in the next three days and come out officially against Intelligence oversight."

"I can't just—"

"You can, Senator Lamb, and if you have any love for your career or your marriage, you will."

Lamb just stood there, speechless and forlorn. The phone rang.

"You can go now," said Nickerson. "I'll be expecting news of your change of heart."

CHAPTER 12

Dan Morgan walked out onto the tarmac, the sun shining on his face, as the plane Fastia had arranged awaited him, door open and engines running. They had made all the arrangements with a man in Afghanistan, and Morgan had called Jenny and told her the CIA wanted to keep him around for a few more days. He told her he wouldn't have his cell phone for security reasons but that he would call her when he could. He didn't like lying to her, and the thought of breaking his promise made him sick. But he had to do this, and he had to keep it a secret, even from her. He couldn't let the CIA find out about it, and they had their ways. For all he knew, they were tapping his home phone.

"Cobra!" someone shouted from behind him. Alarmed, he turned around and saw Eric Plante jogging to catch up with him. *That didn't take long,* he thought.

"What are you doing here, Plante?" Morgan asked. "You could have just called if you needed me for anything else."

"Come off it, Cobra. I know you're going to Afghanistan."

"Afghanistan?" said Morgan, laughing incredulously. "I'm going home."

"In a private jet piloted by Kadir Fastia?" Plante asked, with a knowing smile.

"I thought I'd catch up with an old friend on the way," Morgan said.

"Right. Of course you did."

Morgan sighed. "How'd you find me?"

"Cell phone."

Morgan took his phone out of his pocket and stared at it. He'd turned it off but had left the battery in. He cursed himself. Rookie mistake.

"These things make it almost too easy, don't they?" said Plante. "Listen, Cobra. I can't say much, but since you're determined to go through with it, I'll tell you this much. You might not have gotten the whole story back at headquarters."

"What are you saying? Did Kline make you hold back?" asked Morgan.

"Kline doesn't know everything, either."

"What are you telling me?"

"Just be careful out there," said Plante. "Marwat isn't the only enemy you should watch out for."

"Plante, if you know something, I need you to tell me now," he said impatiently.

"All I know is this: Marwat isn't getting the opium out of Afghanistan by himself."

"Then who is involved?" pressed Morgan.

"That's something Conley was hoping to find out. Maybe he did, and maybe that's what got him killed.

Just watch your ass, Cobra. Things might not be what they seem."

"Thanks for the warning," said Morgan. He threw his phone to the ground and stomped on it. "I'll be sure to send you a postcard when I get there." He turned around and headed for the plane.

The beeping of the satellite phone woke her at 4:30 A.M. She stretched, catlike, out of her cot and switched on the display. The message, coming from halfway around the world, glowed on the screen: *Cobra going to Kabul to extract target. Intercept them there. More information to come.*

Cobra. What the hell was his part in all this, she asked herself. Did he know? And if so, how much?

But ultimately, it didn't matter. The thought of her Ops team's failure to capture the boy stung her, like failure always did. But this time, it would be different. This time, they were coming to her. And this time, she would personally pull the trigger on both the kid and Cobra.

Cobra. What a lovely new development. She couldn't suppress the smile that played on her lips. It would be a reunion that had been a long time coming.

CHAPTER 13

Morgan had not been to Kabul since shortly after the rise of the Taliban. It had been a dreary city then, worn down by constant war and terrified of recent repression. The city now seemed to be bursting with new life; people and cars moved chaotically through streets of market stalls, which seemed to have popped up like mushrooms after a rain. There were construction sites rising all around the city, and the mood among the citizens was one of guarded optimism. But many of the buildings were at least as old as the Taliban and still bore bullet holes to prove it.

"How do you like our beautiful city?" asked the man driving the taxi.

"Always thought there'd be more sand," Morgan said, looking out the window through his sunglasses. The man smiled, showing a mouthful of white teeth. His name was Baz. He was clean-shaven and wore a white, Western-style, button-down shirt and mirrored Ray-Bans. He chain-smoked Marlboro knockoffs and drove one of those boxy Russian-made cars, colored powder blue.

They had just left Baz's safe house, which was really

just a room in the back of a tea shop. Morgan had changed into traditional local clothes and applied a fake beard. He had never felt at home in foreign dress, and while the loose, pajama-like pants and tunic shirt Baz gave him might have been a comfortable cut, this set was made from a rough and scratchy material. At least the flowing *khameez* shirt was perfect for concealing his shoulder holster.

"You got everything else that I asked for?" Morgan had asked back at the safe house, as he applied the gray and scraggly beard in front of a wall-mounted, stained mirror shard.

"With Baz, there are no problems. You remember to tell your friend that. Never problems."

"The gun?"

"I could not find the Walther, but I got you one just as good." Baz handed him the pistol.

Morgan examined it: a Glock 17. He pulled back the slide, feeling its weight in his hand. It had the characteristic sleek, square muzzle, not quite as short as the PPK, and, of course, the most obvious feature: the plastic casing, which Morgan knew had been met with skepticism when the gun was first introduced. But the Glock had long since proved its worth. It was tough, reliable, and packed a nice punch with little recoil. He deftly took it apart on the table and checked each piece before putting it back together.

"Yeah," he said. "This'll do." He strapped on the holster under his *khameez* and tucked the gun away.

Baz also produced a tactical knife, used but well-honed, which Morgan strapped to his ankle; a disposable cell phone, from which Morgan extracted Baz's number before removing the battery; a first-aid kit; a roll of Afghan money in mostly small bills; and a blank EU passport to get this Zalmay person out of the country. This mission was of the quick-and-dirty variety, with little time for planning and, of course, with no real-time support.

"So where are we going, baby?" Baz asked, after they drove away in the cab. Morgan gave him a sidelong glance.

"Kabul Zoo. Can you get us there by noon?"

"You got it, boss."

This was the location of the rendezvous, according to Conley's letter. The clue had been in the phrase *the daily ritual*. The reference was from their early days as partners, when they often went to the Stone Zoo in Massachusetts—the mention of *Stoney* confirmed it, and also put the time of the rendezvous at noon: because at noon, without fail, a couple of orangutans put on an elaborate mating ceremony and went at it on the cage floor, to the consternation of parents and the delight of teenage boys. It had become a running gag between them over the years.

Baz steered them along a busy thoroughfare, where pedestrians and jingle trucks vied for space with cabs— the city's cab fleet, for some reason, seemed to be made up almost entirely of old-model Toyota Corollas. Baz negotiated this anarchy with the effortless ease that only a professional could pull off.

"The Kabul Zoo," Baz said, pensively, his eyes on the road. "You know, it is too bad you did not come some years ago, when Marjan the lion was still alive. Do you know of Marjan, the world-famous lion of the Kabul zoo?"

Morgan grunted noncommittally. He had to focus on the mission now, to mull over every possible scenario. He struggled to keep his mind in the game and ignore his latent uneasiness about the whole affair—the sketchiness of the information on his end, the lack of preparation and support, and, of course, more than anything, the possibility of a traitor working in the CIA—the only reason he could think of why Conley would want to keep that information from the Agency

He looked askance at Baz, who was still prattling away. Morgan had remained on his guard around him. Running missions halfway around the world forced him to rely on local assets as guides, but Morgan made a habit of distrusting them—a practice that had saved his life on more than one occasion.

Instead of dwelling on his apprehension, he continued to ignore Baz's story about the lion and tried to focus on practical issues, mentally rehearsing the call-and-response that was indicated in Conley's letter. His own line, which he would say when he met Zalmay, was the opening of the letter: "A fruit vendor in Kabul once said to me, Afghanistan is always the same; it is only the invaders who change." The next line of the letter read, *Well, you know what they say: variety is the spice of life.* This was a decoy, a plausible response that was meant to throw off anyone who might have intercepted the communication. The correct response was, according to their code, the final line in the letter: "Let it never be said that the Afghans are not a resilient people." He repeated his and Zalmay's lines under his breath until he was satisfied that he knew them through and through.

". . . and then his brother comes back the next day with a hand grenade! Do you believe it?" The cab was lazily weaving through traffic down an arterial road, which seemed to be leading out of the city. Morgan checked his watch: a sliver past 11:45.

"Yeah, that's nice. How are we doing, Baz?"

"Not far. Here, you see? Mountains on both sides. We are passing into Deh Mazang. We are close. The zoo will be on this road, on the left."

They drove for another few minutes, and Baz said, "Here," pointing to a gated area on the far side of the road. "That is it right there." He circled back around a rotary a few blocks down and pulled over to an unofficial drop-off area. There, a collection of taxis and cars sat parked, their owners in the driver's seat or leaning against the driver's door.

"I will wait here," said Baz.

Morgan nodded. "Keep the motor running." He got out of the car, feeling the reassuring weight of the gun against his chest, and walked purposefully to the entrance of the zoo. There, a concrete lion stood perpetual watch, and a sign announced that the admission price was ten Afghanis for locals—about twenty cents—and ten times that for foreigners.

Here was the first test of his disguise. It would hold up to a cursory glance, but anyone who examined him too closely might notice that his skin tone, his facial features, and his mannerisms were a bit off. Although he was hardly inconspicuous, with his wide shoulders and relative height, he knew the secret to passing unnoticed was in his bearing: avoiding eye contact, not speaking, and adopting a timid gait. All of which were entirely unnatural for him, but after years of practice, he was able to switch into the mode effortlessly. He joined the short line at the entrance and, when he reached the booth, laid two coins on the counter. The attendant waved him in without a second look.

The zoo—a dingy collection of bored, lanky animals—turned out to be a bad location for a rendezvous. It was busy but not enough so that he could disappear into a crowd if he had to. Also, the people were there in groups and families—boisterous young fathers, barefoot children, even women in pale blue burqas, hard to tell apart in a flurry of the indistinguishable. As a lone man, he not only stuck out but was likely to draw stares.

Despite himself and all his apprehension at the poorly planned mission, Morgan couldn't suppress his excitement. The danger awoke in him an animal alertness that he had not felt since his days in the Clandestine Service. It was a feeling that, in his suburban life, he could only approximate, shooting at the firing range or speeding down the highway in his classic GTO. But even these were pale parodies of what he felt at that moment.

Morgan looked around for a visitors' map and didn't find one that he could understand, so he walked around, looking at the cages and forming a mental layout of the place. He spotted the orangutan enclosure close to the far end of the zoo. It was a tall cage that bordered two others on either side, with the service access in the back wall. It held two unhappy-looking apes that several teenage boys were trying to taunt into activity.

He walked over to the cage and leaned against the railing, scanning the crowd discreetly every few seconds. He soon spotted a young man, twentysomething, walking in his direction with a little too much nervous resolution. He was not tall, but Morgan could tell that he was very strong even through his baggy *khameez* shirt. They made eye contact and broke it almost im-

mediately. With affected nonchalance, he pretended to
be interested in the apes and planted his feet next to
Morgan.

Anxiously, expectantly, Morgan said, "A fruit vendor in Kabul once said to me, 'Afghanistan is always
the same; it is only the invaders who change.'"

The youth gave Morgan a knowing look and responded in stilted, accented English,

"Well, you know what they say. Variety is the spice
of life."

*The wrong response. It was the wrong goddamn re-
sponse.* Morgan stiffened slightly and hoped the other
man hadn't noticed. His mind raced. Had he made a
mistake in deciphering the code? It had been so long,
maybe he had misread it. Maybe Conley had gotten it
wrong. Maybe—no, he stopped himself. He hadn't remained alive so long by doubting himself. This man
had just failed the only possible test of his identity. He
was an impostor. The question that remained now was
what to do about him.

"Cougar sent you?" the man asked, still pretending
to look at the two orangutans, who sat picking at each
other's nits. "You are Cobra?"

Morgan nodded. "I assume that he sent you, too?"

"That is right. I am Zalmay."

"Nice to meet you, Zalmay. Is there any chance you
can tell me what was so important that Cougar sent me
here to get you?"

"I would prefer to do it once we leave this place, if
that is acceptable to you."

"Yeah, that's fine," Morgan assured him. "We can
go. I just need to show you something first."

"It cannot wait?" The young man began to look nervous.

"It needs to be now. Somewhere private."

Morgan led the way along the zoo path. He had to act fast. For all he knew, the real Zalmay was still coming, and he needed to get back to the orangutan cage before someone else beat him to it.

As Morgan led the impostor toward an out-of-the-way bathroom, each man was careful not to turn his back on the other. Did the man know that he knew? Were both of them walking with feigned cordiality, only prevented from turning on each other by the public location, knowing full well that they would attack each other as soon as they were out of sight? Morgan had no way to know for sure—but neither did the other man. This made the timing extremely tricky. Making a move too early might be a mistake, but making it too late could be fatal. The situation was a boulder teetering on a precipice, where even the slightest nudge would send it hurtling over the edge.

In their tentative walk, they reached the bathroom. It was more of a hut with two small external niches, each formed by an L-shaped wall that hid its respective door from the sight of anyone walking along the path. Morgan walked to the men's side, kicked the door to the lavatory lightly to make sure no one was inside, and motioned for the impostor to follow him.

"Cougar told me to give you this," Morgan said as soon as they were out of sight, reaching into his shirt for his gun. But the impostor caught on too quickly, rushing him and slamming him against the wall before he could take aim. The gun flew from his hand, falling out of close reach. Morgan caught a glint of steel in the man's right hand—a small switchblade. He deflected the man's thrust but felt a sharp pain as it made a glancing slash in his torso. Morgan struck back with an open-handed blow that smashed the man's nose, then grabbed the impostor's right hand, knocking it twice against the wall so that the knife fell to the ground. Morgan kicked it away and then threw a lateral hook that was thwarted by the close quarters: his elbow hit the wall, and the punch landed ineffectively on the man's arm. The response came quickly: the impostor punched Morgan in the gut, causing him to double over. The man maneuvered himself behind Morgan, who felt a thick, beefy arm wrap around his neck.

Morgan elbowed him as hard as he could, but the impostor just tightened his hold. The lack of circulation to his brain began to take its toll, and Morgan knew he was as good as dead if he didn't somehow get free. He had one last idea. Pushing against the man, he swung both his feet upward and rested them against the wall only long enough so that he could reach his hand into his right boot and grasp the hilt of his knife. He then pushed off the wall as hard as he could. The man staggered backward into the tiny bathroom, and his hold loosened just enough for Morgan to free himself, spin around, and plunge the knife, now in his hand, deep into the man's gut. The man gurgled, slumped against the wall, and crumpled to the floor.

It had been many years since he had killed a man, and it filled Morgan with a sudden mental clarity. He searched the man's pockets for something that might identify him and found a slim wallet in a shirt pocket, sticky with blood. He opened it and ruffled through it, taking the money to make it look like a robbery. He then checked the cards. "What the . . ." It was an employee ID, with the dead man's name and along the bottom, the words, ACEVEDO INTERNATIONAL. Why was a man who worked for a government contractor posing as a CIA informant? Morgan got up and closed the bathroom door. He didn't have time to think about that, not at the moment; with luck, the body would remain hidden long enough for Morgan to escape from the zoo.

He picked up his Glock and ran, making his way out of the grove and around a number of cages back to the orangutan habitat. People stared at him and backed away, and soon he noticed why: his shirt and arms were spattered with blood. He reached the orangutan cage to find two men standing there, playing out the same scene that he'd had with the impostor minutes earlier. *Screw it*, he thought, and he pulled out his gun. This was no time for finesse.

"I was sent by Cougar," he said, holding up the Glock. "Which of you is the man I'm looking for? Which of you is Zalmay?"

The slighter of the two, a bewildered young man, sheepishly raised his hand. The other immediately reached for a gun, and Morgan quickly fired two rounds into the man's chest, prompting screeches from animals and bystanders alike. The young man stood frozen, wide-eyed and open-mouthed.

"You need to come with me," Morgan said, but Zalmay backed away, terrified.

"We need to get out of here now! There'll be others!" Morgan insisted, and then he caught something out of the corner of his eye. While most of the zoo's visitors were now running as fast as they could away from them, one figure in a burqa had just drawn a submachine gun from under her garment. This seemed to convince Zalmay. He and Morgan bolted just as she opened fire on them.

They dashed as fast as they could, bullets whizzing past them, hitting the ground and walls around them. Morgan was taking the most direct route to the exit when he spotted a man up ahead, running toward them, with a black submachine gun of his own.

"Turn here!" Morgan yelled to his companion, and they took a right on a path that led them along the perimeter of the zoo. There was a tall fence to their right, and to their left, a low wall separating them from the sunken animal habitats ten feet below.

Then Morgan saw him—the same man who had cut them off before had doubled back to intercept them on their current route, and he was now only about fifty yards away in front of them. Behind him and Zalmay, the woman in the burqa was still approaching. To go forward or backward and try to face either of them with only his handgun would be suicide. There was only one possible way out.

"Jump!" he yelled.

"What?"

But Morgan had already climbed over the wall to the animal habitat. Looking only at the dusty ground below, he pushed off. He tried to land on his good leg but still felt fire in his bad knee when he hit. Moments later, his companion landed beside him, tumbling over.

Morgan got up, and as he looked around, he saw piercing green eyes staring at him from no more than six feet away. She had been reclining lazily, at least three hundred pounds of sleek tendon and muscle. Now she seemed to be taking an inordinate interest in these intruders who had just landed in her home.

They had jumped, literally, into the lion's den.

CHAPTER 14

Morgan looked into the lioness's eyes, and out of the corner of his he could see her muscles tense. Half-remembered words from the story Baz was telling him in the car flashed in his mind: some jackass who'd wanted to show off for his friends had jumped into the lions' enclosure, presumably the very one he was standing in right now, and had been mauled to death. One wrong move, and Morgan would meet the same fate. He stared into the lion's eyes, at the tips of her long yellowed teeth, at a jaw that could crush steel. The first rule of surviving an encounter with a predator, passed on by an asset during a mission in sub-Saharan Africa, echoed loud and clear in his mind: don't act like prey.

Zalmay stumbled to his feet, and a gasp told Morgan that he had finally become aware of where they were.

"*Don't move*," Morgan said to Zalmay. His eyes did not stray from the lion. "If you run, you're dead." She was reclining on a waist-high wooden platform. On the other side of it was the service access gate. It was padlocked. There was, he noticed, no place to hide in the habitat apart from tall grass, and no other way out. But there was a shallow recess in the wall at the gate that could provide them with cover from enemy fire.

They couldn't have more than a few seconds before their pursuers caught up with them. He wasn't about to be caught like a sitting duck. "We're going to walk, slowly, to that door," he said to Zalmay, and he began to take measured, deliberate, sideways strides, keeping his eyes on the lion. Zalmay followed with timorous steps. The animal's gaze was locked on them as they moved, her muscles rippling as if she was aching to pounce. He remembered his handgun, tucked inside his *khameez*. How fast would he be able to draw? And how many bullets would it take to kill a lion? He decided against it. *The slightest misstep*, Morgan thought, *and we're dinner*.

They inched their way around the wooden platform, and Morgan wondered whether a lifetime of living in a cage had made the lioness tame or even more hungry for prey. But with every step they took toward the gate, she seemed to relax and grow more accustomed to their presence. No sudden moves, and they would be fine.

They had almost made their way to the other side of the platform, only a few feet from the gate, when Morgan's eye was drawn to the far end of the long habitat, where bars kept out visitors on another of the zoo's paths. People had been watching them through the iron barrier and yelling, but now they weren't pointing at him or the lioness anymore. They were looking directly above them.

Morgan had scarcely a split second to react. He lunged, pulling Zalmay with him into the recess in the wall as a round of bullets hailed down on the spot where they had just been standing. There was another burst, close to them, from what Morgan recognized as a submachine gun. But they were well protected; the bullets wouldn't hit them, not from above.

The gunfire was not entirely without effect, however, as the sound seemed to have angered the lioness. She had leapt from the platform and now paced the ground right in front of them, looking up at the pursuers.

Morgan took a moment to examine the gate behind them. It had a rusty old padlock, holding a dead bolt in place. He knew better than to try to shoot it open; all that would accomplish would be to seal it shut permanently. He shoved his shoulder against the gate with all the momentum he could muster in the limited space he had, hoping the dead bolt, or a piece of the wall around it, might give. It didn't budge. Time was running out.

Zalmay began shouting through the gate, into the tunnel egress; his cries for help were in an Afghan dialect—Morgan couldn't tell which.

There was another burst of gunfire, but this time it wasn't directed at them. Several bullets pierced the lioness's flank; several red spots on her tawny skin erupted in blood. Her legs buckled, she collapsed to her side, and with a few last, wheezing breaths, she died.

There was only one reason, Morgan realized, that they would shoot her. He drew his Glock and listened for it. Sure enough, a few seconds later, he heard the soft thud of someone's feet hitting the dust in the cage. The other pursuer would probably have stayed above, ready to rain bullets on them if they poked out of their little nook. They were completely cornered. But he wasn't going to be taken down, not without a fight. He held up his Glock and motioned for Zalmay to stand back.

He heard a man's voice, in the accent of a native English speaker, shout from just out of sight, "Drop your gun! We only want the kid. Come out peacefully, and we'll let you go."

Morgan looked at Zalmay, who was wild-eyed and breathing heavily. "We're going to get out of this," Morgan told him, but it didn't seem to help.

The man fired a burst of bullets against the edge of the wall, spraying dust into their faces.

"You really think you can take us on?" the man continued. "Even if you survive today, what are you going to do? We found you *here*. If you run, we'll find you again. Just give us the kid, and you're free to go."

"Go to hell!" said Morgan.

"All right, you—."

"Ramos!" someone yelled. It was a female voice, coming from above. Accented but not Middle Eastern. Something European. It seemed strangely familiar to Morgan, and it stirred up old, long-forgotten memories. But before he could place it, he was interrupted by a scream. The man in the cage had tumbled backward into their line of sight; on top of him was an enormous male lion with a wild, orange mane, teeth bared, its claws sunk into the man's chest, crimson with blood.

Morgan was so startled, he didn't notice that a panicky zoo employee had arrived on the other side of the gate and was yelling at them as he fumbled and cycled through keys on a ring as big as Morgan's fist. Having picked one out, he pushed it into the padlock, and, with a turn, the lock fell open. He undid the bolt and swung open the gate, urgently motioning them outside. They got out of the cage and into the service access tunnel. The zoo employee closed the gate behind them, securing the dead bolt and clicking the lock shut. He obviously wasn't about to risk his life for the other man. Morgan looked back into the cage and saw the lion dragging his prey, screaming, out of sight.

Morgan surveyed the tunnel. It was long, curving out of sight in both directions. He noted which way was the exit. Then he noticed his companion, whose eyes showed a state of mind past fear and horror.

"Look alive!" Morgan exclaimed. "We're not out of the woods yet." He took Zalmay by the shoulders and shook him; the youth seemed to snap out of it. They started down the tunnel in the direction of the exit. Pain gripped Morgan's bad knee as they ran; with every impact of his right foot on the concrete, he fought through agony. But he kept on moving as fast as he could.

Eventually, they reached a flight of stairs that led them up to a custodial building. The door to the outside was locked, but it was made of flimsy, decaying wood. Resting on his bad leg, he raised his left foot high and kicked the door. The weak jamb splintered around the lock. Sunlight flooded in, and Morgan saw that they were at the entrance of the zoo, where patrons were swarming, funneling through the narrow door to the outside. *No better plan than to get lost in the crowd*, thought Morgan. "Let's go," he told Zalmay, holding his arm so they wouldn't get separated.

They pushed and jostled, but everyone was as eager as they were to get through. Rather than let go of Zalmay, Morgan let the pushier patrons pass; they finally made it outside with the last of the stragglers. Morgan heard police sirens approaching in the distance.

They found Baz looking apprehensively at the crowd that was streaming out of the zoo. He frowned at Morgan as they approached and said, "Did you cause this?"

"I thought I told you to keep the engine running. Where are the keys?" he demanded. Baz took them from his pocket and held them up. Morgan grabbed them.

"Hey!" Baz protested.

"Get in the backseat. You!" he said, pointing at Zalmay. "Up front."

They complied, Baz reluctant and Zalmay bewildered. Morgan got into the driver's seat, turned the ignition, and maneuvered around the frenzy of pedestrians. As they rolled onto the road, the police cars were pulling up to the zoo's entrance.

Morgan drove as fast as he could without attracting undue attention, keeping his eyes on the rearview mirror to spot any possible tails. As the zoo receded into the distance and they approached the city, Morgan took a deep breath. When he inhaled, he felt a sharp pain on his right side where the knife had sliced his skin, pain that up until that point had been dulled by the adrenaline. He lifted his shirt to look at the wound. It was bleeding freely, a long cut but not very deep. *I've had worse*, he thought, and he pressed his hand to the wound to stanch the blood. He would have to get somewhere quickly to attend to it. But first there was a pressing issue he was eager to get out of the way.

He turned to the young man in the passenger seat. "You're Zalmay, then?"

"That is r-right," he said, with a slight stammer. "Zalmay Siddiqi."

"All right, Zalmay. You can call me Cobra." He reached for the radio dial, turning it on and cranking it up until cheesy Middle Eastern pop music blared from the speakers. "I need you to tell me who's after us," he said just loudly enough so Zalmay could hear him but Baz could not. "And while you're at it, tell me what they have to do with Acevedo International."

Zalmay looked back at him anxiously, a bit surprised. "So you know they are from Acevedo, then? They are enforcers. Mercenaries."

"Yeah, I figured," he replied. "And why do they want you dead?"

"Because of what I know—what Cougar and I uncovered. Because I'm carrying this." He took something out of his knapsack and handed it to Morgan: a tiny memory card. "Pictures that show Acevedo is involved in the Kandahar drug trade."

Morgan frowned, turning the memory chip in his fingers. If what the kid was saying was true, this whole thing was much bigger than he had imagined. Acevedo was a major contractor, a multibillion-dollar corporation. And it had major ties with politicians. Whatever separation there was between government and business was especially porous when it came to Acevedo. The object in his hands would put him in the sights of some major players.

"I think I'd better hold on to this," he said, slipping the chip into his pocket. "I'm going to need you to tell me everything you know later. Right now, I just need to know this: is there any possibility that you were followed on your way to meet me?"

"No, I do not think so," said Zalmay. "I have been hiding in Kabul for days. If they knew where I was, I believe they would have come for me already."

"That's what I thought." Morgan took his left hand off his wound, which promptly began to bleed freely. Taking the wheel with his bloodied hand, he used his right to remove his Glock from its shoulder holster. Zalmay recoiled. But Morgan held it out by the muzzle for the boy, keeping his eyes on the road. "I want you to take this and keep it pointed at our friend here." He motioned to Baz. Zalmay took the gun gingerly and trained it on the driver.

"What is the meaning of this, Cobra?" said Baz with shocked indignation. He apparently had been straining to hear their conversation.

"Don't play dumb," Morgan answered, looking at him through the rearview mirror. "You sold us out."

"What are you talking about?" he said, looking astonished.

"There were exactly three of us who knew the location of the meeting today, and two of us were nearly killed in there."

"That is crazy, Cobra, my friend. I did not—"

"Save it," Morgan interrupted. "Just sit tight, and do as I say." He looked at Zalmay and spoke again so only he could hear. "We need a place to lay low for a while."

"There is the place where I have been h-hiding out," he stammered. "An abandoned house in the north city. I will tell you how to get there."

"Good. When we get there, you and I are going to have a nice, long chat. And I'm going to get some answers."

As he drove, Morgan's thoughts were haunted by the mysterious figure in the burqa and that strangely familiar voice that stirred up something obscure in his unconscious mind.

CHAPTER 15

Zalmay's hideout was a cramped adobe house with a half-collapsed wall and rubble on the floor. Among the few amenities were a couple of chairs, a blanket, and a small battery-operated radio, left there, he gathered, by Zalmay, himself. Morgan tore the blanket into strips and used them to tie Baz securely to some pipes under a cracked porcelain sink.

"This is crazy, Cobra!" he protested. "I have not betrayed you!"

"That's not a chance I'm willing to take," Morgan said, tightening the knot around Baz's wrists.

"What are you going to do to me?"

"Just sit tight and be quiet, and you'll be fine," he said, gagging Baz's mouth with another of the strips. Morgan knew he could be jeopardizing the mission by sparing the driver's life. In the old days, he would have killed a man for less. Maybe he was going soft, but he was willing to give Baz the benefit of the doubt—or at least enough to keep him alive for now.

Morgan walked into the next room, bringing a chair and motioning for Zalmay to follow him. He took the small radio and turned it up as loud as it would go—the broadcast was scratchy, and the speakers weren't exactly potent—to drown out their conversation. Then he sat, removed his fake beard, and cracked open his first-aid kit. He lifted his shirt to examine the slash. The bleeding had all but stopped, dried blood crusting on his skin. Although not too deep, it would need stitches. He poured ethyl alcohol onto a piece of gauze and began to dab at it, which allowed the blood to flow more freely. It stung like hell, but he had long ago learned to suppress the pain. He scrubbed it harder, to clean as deeply as possible. The alternative was risking a deadly infection.

"Zalmay," he said to the young man, who was pale at the sight of the seeping blood. Morgan began to suture his wound as he spoke. "Sit down. I think it's time you answered some of my questions. I want you to tell me what you and Cougar were doing in Kandahar before he died."

Zalmay pulled up another chair and sat facing Morgan. Having finished the sutures, Morgan took a good look at the boy for the first time. Zalmay was a skinny kid, no older than twenty-five and probably younger. He had dark olive skin, with large eyes and a wholesome-looking face marred by deep grooves of worry and anxiety.

"I will tell you what I can," Zalmay began. "What Cougar and I learned, it is damaging to many people. He believed it was the work of many to keep it quiet, a . . . what is the word?"

"A conspiracy?" Morgan suggested, as he secured a wad of gauze over his wound with surgical tape.

"Yes, a conspiracy. To hide Acevedo's connections

with a local drug lord, a powerful man in Kandahar named Bacha Marwat."

"Yeah, I've heard of him. What's his relationship with Acevedo?"

"He is one of the great opium traders in the region," said Zalmay. His tone made it clear he had no love for the man. "He has many, many farmers under his command, who altogether harvest tons and tons of poppies. But transporting opium is not easy. Acevedo has many big planes that take off and land every week in their own airfields, with no oversight but their own. Cougar and I found out that this is how Marwat's opium is getting out of Afghanistan."

Morgan wiped his hands of blood, put his shirt back on, and took the memory card from his pocket. He took out the cheap digital camera and batteries he had instructed Zalmay to buy on their way over as he watched over Baz in the car. He put the batteries in the camera, then inserted the little black plastic memory card in the appropriate slot. He turned on the camera, and switched to the replay function. It showed that there were ninety-seven images in all, which he began to click through. In the first several frames, he could see a plane clearly marked with Acevedo International's logo, a curled eagle's claw. After that, there were crates, each filled with bags. Another series of pictures showed the contents of one of the bags spilled open: opium.

He paused to take this in. If Acevedo International was running opium for a local warlord, the charge against them was more serious than just drug trafficking, or even war profiteering. Much of Afghanistan's drug money ended up funding the Taliban or other insurgents—usually as protection money, or a way to

keep the Americans busy. This was out-and-out treason. If it were true, this kid had evidence that could
bring down one of the most powerful corporations in
the world. A lot of very rich and influential people
would want to silence him. And now it was Morgan's
duty to get him safely back to the United States.

Morgan looked up at Zalmay and couldn't help feeling sorry for this jumpy and confused kid, who was not
that much older than Alex. "How did you get involved
with Marwat?" Morgan asked.

"Because of my English. I was a translator for Marwat's men."

"Why did you turn on him? Did Cougar promise
you money?"

"No," said Zalmay, with an offended scowl. "No, he
did not promise me money. I did it because it was correct. Because I see it as the will of Allah. The man I
worked for, he has connections with the Taliban. He
forces all the farmers to grow poppies and pays them
less for the crops than the price of wheat. They are starving, but they cannot stop working, or Marwat's men will
kill them. The longer I worked for him, the more I discovered what he did, and the more I hated myself for it. I
stayed in his service because I needed the money, and
because I was scared and alone and they provided me
with some protection and security. But every time I accepted payment, I felt that I was unworthy to live."

A wave of anguish passed over his face. He turned
away, and spoke with a trembling intensity. "My parents were killed in the beginning of the war. The invasion made the Taliban even more cruel and fanatical,
perhaps because it made them feel their power slipping
away. My mother and my father were wealthy city

Tajiks who opposed the Pashtun Taliban. They had Western sensibilities, and my mother did not like to wear the *chadri*—what you may know as the burqa. One day, an angry mob of Taliban loyalists caught them on the street. They called my father a dog and my mother a whore and stoned them to death. This was when I was only a boy. I have been on my own since, and I have made many compromises to survive." He looked right into Morgan's eyes. "I am helping Cougar because I wish to do something worthy. This is my redemption."

Morgan had known many foreign collaborators in his life, and each had his own reason to help. A great many wanted money or asylum, and many did defect as a matter of principle. But rarely had he seen anyone so certain in his purpose as this kid.

"Well, Zalmay," Morgan said, "I hope you find what you're looking for. And if you're telling the truth, it means we're on the same side, and I'm going to do everything I can to help you. Just one more thing." Morgan knew that this would be a shock to the young man, and so he had waited to tell him. Morgan turned down the radio. The gaudy pop music played in stark context to the solemnity of the moment. "Did you know that Cougar was found dead in Kandahar?"

Zalmay looked at him with wide, pitiful eyes. "No," he whispered. "It cannot be."

"I'm sorry, Zalmay. His death came as a shock to me, too. He was a great friend of mine."

"And mine," Zalmay said weakly.

Morgan could tell that it was more than mere friendship for Zalmay, however. If the young man had found some sort of paternal protection among men like Marwat's, then a man like Conley would have been much closer to a father figure to this orphan. *Shit. This must be hell on the kid.*

"Listen. We can't bring him back. But what we can do is finish what you two started together and stick it to the people who did this to him. Everything's prepared to get you into the United States. What do you say to that?"

"I say, we shall do it," said Zalmay, with angry resolve.

Morgan nodded at him. "Now we have to figure out how to—" He was interrupted by muffled yells coming from the next room. Before he could even get up to see what was happening, Baz was hushed by two whispers from a silenced weapon. And then *she* appeared in the doorway.

The figure in the burqa stood in stony silence, a faceless ghost, the sky blue of her garment contrasting with the black of the pistol she held in her left hand. She was looking right at Morgan through the mesh covering her face. She had the drop on him, and he had no way to defend himself. She took careful aim.

Zalmay sprang up with a bloodcurdling howl and charged at her. She turned the gun toward him and fired wildly, too fast to aim. Two shots missed their mark; two pierced his chest. He staggered but maintained his momentum. She fired again, aiming straight for his heart this time. He crashed to the ground at her feet.

Without wasting a millisecond, she turned the gun toward Morgan and pulled the trigger.

Click.

There was a flicker of recognition between them. Judging his own gun to be too far out of his reach, Morgan lunged straight at her instead. But with a lightning-quick about-face, she evaded him and dashed out the door as quickly as she had come in. Morgan ran after her, passing Baz, the poor bastard, still tied to the pipe, dead, in a pool of his own blood.

Morgan rushed into the street and saw her sprinting to his left, only a few yards ahead. He set off after her. His knee still ached and kept him from running at full sprint, but it was obvious her restrictive garments were cramping her speed. Within a block, he was hot on her heels.

With a final push, he grabbed at her, clutching cloth. She stumbled and fell; her head covering remained in his hand. She rolled on the dusty street, ending up on her back, so that he could see her face. It was striking, if a bit lined with age, haughty and high-cheeked, framed by short blond hair: a face he knew all too well.

"Natasha? *T*?"

She looked at him contemptuously and then at something behind him. He lifted his eyes from her. His single-minded chase had made him oblivious to everything around him, but now he saw that a number of men were running toward them. They had obviously spotted him as a foreigner. And even if she was obviously not one of their own, this was a culture of honor; he could easily get killed by a mob. They held back, but they were clearly ready to rush him and do some violence. He would be able to manage this, but not if he had to take Natasha prisoner at the same time. Plus, he knew very well that if he so much as touched her, he would be lynched. Begrudgingly, he cast her a look that said, *you win this time*. He turned around and dashed back to the safe house. A dozen indignant Afghans were left in his wake, screaming their resentments at him, but fortunately none followed him.

When Morgan got to the house, he saw that Zalmay still lay where he had fallen, his blood pooling on the ground. Morgan checked for a pulse. Nothing.

Morgan gritted his teeth. If it weren't for this kid, T would have killed them both. He wished he had time to take care of the body, but he wasn't safe staying in this place. T would find her way back at any moment. Morgan picked up the camera containing the memory card, his gun, and the car keys and ran out to Baz's taxi.

As he drove away, he opened the glove compartment, ran his hands under the seats, searching until he found what he was looking for, what he knew had to be there—a tiny electronic bug, stuck to the bottom of the mat on the passenger's side. So this was how Natasha had known where his rendezvous with Zalmay would be, and this was how she had found them afterward. *Sorry I doubted you, Baz*, he thought, as he tossed the bug out the window.

He popped the battery into the back of the cell phone that Baz had given him. He had to make two phone calls. The first was to Jenny. She didn't pick up, so he left her a message on her voice mail. The second call was to Fastia.

"Two hours according to plan. But," he added bitterly, "only one passenger." Fastia acknowledged, and they hung up. Morgan removed the phone's battery again.

T. Shit. He didn't know what it meant, but he did know one thing—he could no longer trust the CIA. If she was involved, there had to be a traitor on the inside. To go back to the Agency without knowing who it was would be as good as suicide. He was, and would remain, completely on his own.

CHAPTER 16

Morgan sat in the stretch limo, dressed to kill in a tailored tux. Even though he was still a fresh-faced youth—this was barely two years after Libya—he had the broad-shouldered frame of a man, with a look of grizzled determination to match. But their destination that night was rather more pleasant than the Libyan Sahara. They were headed to a charity ball at the DC Mandarin Oriental Hotel. It was a swanky event, full of diplomats, politicos, businessmen, and other assorted Washington bigwigs. Champagne, caviar, and expensive women—a playground of the rich and powerful. But Morgan would be going in on business.

The suit sitting across from him, an unnamed Agency case officer with droopy, dead eyes and a deep, rasping voice who was balancing a glass of expensive Scotch on the rocks on his knee, proffered a folder taken out of his briefcase.

"Natasha Vasiliyevna. She's here as a member of the Ambassador's security detail, but the word is she's intelligence. We've had reports that she's looking to defect."

Morgan opened the folder, in which there was a letter-sized photograph of a woman. Blonde, with high cheekbones and intense, piercing blue eyes looking at something off to the side. A deadly beauty.

"She's a looker," Morgan said.

"Say what you want about the Russkies," said the suit. "One thing the commie bastards have is taste."

"She doesn't look Russian," said Morgan. "Looks more Swedish to me."

"On her mother's side," said the Agency man. "An Olympic gymnast."

"Good genes. How'd she end up in Russia?"

"Her mother was one of those few people who defected *into* the USSR," he said, with a sneer.

"And now her daughter wants out," said Morgan blankly, his eyes transfixed by the photograph. "Ironic. Why doesn't she just walk out the door?"

"She's concerned that the Foreign Intelligence Service won't take too kindly to it. She wants assurances of safety and protection."

"Can't say I blame her." In spite of himself, Morgan was stirred by the thought of meeting her in person, to see her beauty and intensity up close. He could immediately see himself being lured in by her, however, and that frightened him. "How do we know this isn't a ploy?" If there was one thing he had learned from his work, it was that there could be multiple levels of deception going on with any given interaction.

"That's how she'll play it, of course. Her bosses will believe it is *she* who wants to turn *you*. They will expect her to extract information from you—which we will provide, just enough for them to get a taste."

"And what if it turns out we are the ones she's playing?"

"We have, of course, foreseen the possibility. It is part of your task to determine her true intentions."

"And how do you want me to accomplish that?" asked Morgan, raising an eyebrow.

"It's my understanding that you have a particular . . . *talent* in dealing with women. Exploit it."

Morgan looked at him wordlessly as the limousine pulled in to the red carpet at the Mandarin Oriental.

"We're counting on you, Cobra. Break a leg," said the Agency man.

"Anyone gets in my way, and I'll break two," Morgan said, and he walked out onto the red carpet.

Morgan quietly scoped the schmoozing crowd of sharply dressed and well-coiffed jet-setters. This Natasha was gorgeous, if her picture was any indication, but he felt that even she wouldn't stand out too much in this milieu. Everything was perfect, as one would expect. The waiters made the rounds in a precise dance, and the stiff-necked private bodyguards were so numerous that men in black suits practically lined the walls. And the people spoke with a canned wit so smooth, it seemed thoroughly rehearsed.

Then he saw her, and he realized how wrong he had been. She did stand out, even among the surgically enhanced escorts and trophy wives who populated the ballroom. She was wearing a plain black dress, with her light-blond hair done up. Seeing her like that, Morgan noticed that Natasha Vasiliyevna was not only a beauty among beauties; there was something that seemed far more alive in her, something almost animal-like, which was so different from the glossy sheen of all the polished personas in attendance.

Natasha had been cornered by some young heir type, and though they were out of earshot, she was visibly ignoring him and surveying the room instead. Still, the boy nattered on with the obliviousness that overconfident, underexperienced, privileged youths always seemed to display when talking to a member of the opposite sex who was not completely fascinated by them.

His lips were still moving when Morgan approached. "—it's just this full-body sensation, and I'm telling you, you've never experienced anything like it. It's just wave after wave of—excuse me, can I help you?"

"Yeah. You can get the hell out of here."

Natasha looked at him, intrigued.

The young man said in a huff, "Hey, buddy, do you know who I am?"

"What you are is leaving," he said. "Now."

The kid frowned. This lack of deference was obviously a new experience for him. He turned to face Morgan, chest puffed out, hands made into fists, in his best imitation of a tough guy. "What if I don't?"

Morgan turned to face him. The other man was taller, but Morgan was a fighter, and it showed. "Don't tell me you're actually threatening me," he said dismissively. He noticed that the kid had looked toward his bodyguard. "I wouldn't," said Morgan.

"Oh, yeah? Why not?"

"I'm not afraid of a fight. But you, on the other hand . . ."

"I know karate and capoeira."

"And I've killed a man with my bare hands. Now listen. You get out of here now, or I start breaking fingers. How many do you think I can get to before your bodyguard pulls me off of you?"

The kid recoiled, then turned to walk away. "Savage plebeian," he said under his breath as he went.

Morgan was left alone next to Natasha, who had been ostentatiously ignoring the interaction. "Lovely crowd, aren't they?" said Morgan nonchalantly.

"Give a trained monkey a decent suit and a professional haircut, and he would fit right in," she replied, without missing a beat. She had only the slightest accent.

"I don't know about that," he said. "Dressing a monkey in a suit would constitute *fun*, and I don't think they allow that here."

"I think they do," she said without looking at him, "but only if it comes here to die."

Morgan chuckled. "Sounds like you're not crazy about being here."

"I am counting the minutes to when I can leave this excruciating event."

"Funny," Morgan retorted. "I've been told that you're actually fairly eager to stay."

Her cunning eyes flashed on him with immediate understanding. "Perhaps," she said. "Now that you're here."

Natasha opened the door to her suite at the Mandarin and pulled him in by his tie for an aggressive kiss. Her breath was fragrant, like wine, and her kisses were fervent, almost desperate. She held his head in her hands, leaning her forehead into his, noses scrunched up against each other. She breathed heavily with desire and smiled.

She was a subtle seductress. A lesser manipulator would have just used her body, leering stares, pure sex. But this, this was passion—real passion, calculating as it might have been. This was, without a doubt, a cat-and-mouse game, but it was unclear who was which. Both their masks were layers deep, and there was no way of telling how far down sincerity was, if it was there at all.

Morgan walked into the room warily. As assassinations went, this was the oldest trick in the book, and he would not fall for it, not even for a woman like Natasha. But there wasn't anyone else in the suite. All that caught his eye was—

"Is that a checkerboard?" he asked, with a hint of authentic enthusiasm. It was the first chink in the armor, a tiny wrench in the works of their mutual manipulation. It was a touch of sincerity, of something genuine in what would have been, for both of them, a completely fabricated interaction.

"My favorite pastime," she said. "It helps to while away the long hours of boredom. Do you?"

"Do I play? I've only been wiping the floor with any opponent since I was eight."

"Then we play," she said, decisively. "We shall find out if you can wipe the floor with me."

She set up the board, and she chose black. They sat across from each other.

"Care to make it interesting?" he said.

"And how do you propose that?"

"An item of clothing for each captured piece," he said.

"That's hardly fair, is it? Capture six of my pieces, and I'll be . . ." She smiled and blushed—a blush that Morgan suspected was not born of modesty. "I suppose that would be acceptable."

She made her opening gambit, and he made his. As they made their plays, Morgan began to get a feel for her style. It seemed naïve, unsophisticated. He captured one of her pieces. With an alluring smile, she slowly removed a shoe, black and high-heeled, letting him get a look at her stockinged leg. She placed the shoe on the table next to the board.

This is going to be easy, he thought. And then he lost three pieces in one move. There went a jacket, a tie, and a shoe. Only then did he realize she'd been toying with him, leading him to underestimate her, get overconfident. She was a far more subtle player than he'd realized. He thought, *this is going to be fun*.

"I hope you have as many moves in bed as you have on the checkerboard," he said.

And then the game really began. She, like he, seemed to be able to see many turns ahead. Every move became a sally or parry in complex strategies as each player tried to find an opening.

The game progressed, and Natasha was down to her dress and nothing more. He advanced, but it had been a trap—and there went his shirt. But the move had left her vulnerable. He took another one of hers.

She smiled slyly and pulled him in, by the hair, for a kiss. Then she turned her back to him, slowly unzipped her little black dress, and let it fall to her ankles. They never finished the game.

CHAPTER 17

Boyle shut the door to his office and almost bumped into the Deputy Director for HUMINT, or Human Intelligence, Julia Carr.

"Boyle," she said, "I was just coming in to see you."

Carr was an ex-Marine and had been a HUMINT handler herself, in her earlier days. She had a face that was both ordinary and attractive, which, with the right makeup and hair, could even be called beautiful. But she downplayed her beauty as much as possible. Her hair was cropped short, she wore no cosmetics, and she donned clothes that, while not exactly ugly, made it plain that she refused to rely on her looks to establish her authority or to gain the respect of others.

"I'm on my way somewhere," Boyle told her. "Can it wait?"

"I'd really rather talk to you right away," she said.

"Then walk with me," he said. "You have about a minute and a half."

They started down the hallway together. He could tell that she was straining to keep up with his vigorous pace.

"Sir, I'd like to know what's going on in Kandahar."

"Just what do you mean?" he asked. "Kandahar's a big place. There's plenty going on there at any given time."

"I think you know what I'm talking about, sir," she said.

"What you're meant to know will come to you through the appropriate channels."

"Jeff, come on," she said, lowering her voice. "Don't bullshit me here. Something's going on. I've got people in the field. I gotta know if they're going to be in some kind of danger."

"My answer's still the same, Julia."

She held out her arm for him to stop. He did and turned to face her.

"Throw me a bone here, Boyle," she pleaded. "I can't be left out of the loop like this."

He sighed. "Rogue agent. Purpose unclear, whereabouts unknown. And that's all I'm giving you."

"Isn't much," she said.

"It's as much as you need to know. Now if you'll excuse me . . ."

He gestured down the hall and walked on to his meeting. When he burst into the conference room, Kline and Plante were already waiting for him.

"One of you care to tell me what the hell is going on with the Cobra situation?" said Boyle.

"We have reports of gunfire and several dead at the Kabul Zoo," Kline began. "Witnesses describe the shooter as a man who closely matches Cobra's description. Witnesses also say—get this—that the man shot a lion during his escape."

"Any idea where to?" asked Boyle.

"He flew out of Kabul under the identity of an Italian citizen named Antonio Bevelaqua," said Kline. "He took off in a private jet at the Kabul airport eight hours ago, headed for Amsterdam."

"So we—"

"The plane," Plante cut in, "was forced to make an emergency landing in Istanbul. Where he went from there is anyone's guess."

"Then we need to focus on finding him, right away. Kline. Put together a task force. I want them concentrating exclusively on finding Cobra. Do what you have to, and make provisions to bring him in."

"Sir," interjected Plante, "do we need to treat him like a fugitive?"

Kline cut in. "As far as I'm concerned, this is what he chose, and we should treat him accordingly."

"I know Cobra," said Plante. "Probably better than anyone else here. He's a good man. An honorable man. Whatever he's doing, there's got to be a reason. I think the best thing we can do is to bring him in quietly and just *ask* him what's going on."

Boyle seemed to think about it, even swayed. "In any case," he said, "I want someone at the ready, in case this really is some kind of vendetta. I'm not going to have a highly trained ex-operative on the loose without a contingency measure. I want Wagner on standby."

"*Wagner?*" said Plante, taken aback. "Sir, isn't that a little drastic? I mean, Morgan used to be one of us, after all."

"That's exactly what concerns me," said Boyle. "Kline, you have a problem with any of this?"

"No, sir."

"Then get to it. I want this taken care of. And everything goes through me, understand? You make a move on him when I say so." His voice became low and grave. "I don't even have to tell you how dangerous it would be to have a rogue operative out there. Find him, gentlemen. Do whatever you have to, and find him."

CHAPTER 18

Nickerson set the receiver down and sat motionless in his office, a deep frown on his face. Things were not going according to plan, and he did not like that at all. It was unworthy of his intelligence and cunning. He would, of course, be the first to admit that he was a vain, proud man. But he did not consider this a fault or a weakness. He knew his own worth, his own power. That was all. Except, when it slipped through his fingers, it was almost enough to make him dizzy, thinking of himself as fallible. All he could do was remind himself of his many superior talents and attributes—

He was brought back to the here and now by the ring of his intercom.

"Sir? Senator McKay is here to see you. Shall I send her in?"

"Please do."

He'd almost forgotten about this appointment. It should serve as a pick-me-up, at any rate. He looked over himself in a small mirror mounted on his wall when he heard the knock on the door. He ran his fingers through his hair, flashed himself a winning smile, and, satisfied, said, "Come in!"

Senator Lana McKay walked in with quiet assurance. She had short, carefully coiffed brown hair, a strong and harmonious face, and fierce, determined green eyes. Her presence was enough to fill a room. Admirable, almost worthy of jealousy to Nickerson. She was quite a bit older than the women he usually pursued, but he toyed with the idea of making an exception, just this once.

"Hello, Senator Nickerson," she said, extending her hand.

"Oh, hello, Lana. It's good to see you," he said warmly. "Thank you so much for coming. Please, call me Ed."

"Well, thank *you*, Ed," she said, settling down where Lamb had previously sat. "It's always a pleasure to speak with you. Now, what can I do for you?"

"Right to business, then," he said, with a broad smile. "The way I like it."

"No point in wasting each other's time when there's work to be done, right?"

"Of course. So here is why I asked you to come. I'd like to discuss this new bill you're pushing for."

"I was actually hoping I could count on your support, Senator," she said, picking up the thread of the conversation. "Tightening up the rules and oversight of government contractors in Iraq and Afghanistan is not only extremely urgent—it's a no-brainer."

"Yes," he said, dragging the word out so that it sounded like it had three distinct syllables. "Undoubtedly, it's an issue of some importance. I understand what has you fired up about it. But I favor a more cautious approach. Frankly, I believe it's premature."

"What do you mean, 'premature'?" She drew herself back slightly, defensively.

"This is a sensitive point in the reconstruction effort." The practiced words rolled smoothly from his tongue, designed, in tone and content, to elicit confidence and understanding. "Our contractors are out there helping to ensure the safety of our troops and to aid us in our efforts to reshape Iraq and Afghanistan. They are under a lot of pressure, and their success is our success. I'm afraid no good can come of our meddling with these companies. I believe that it would be in the best interest of the American people to table your bill for the time being."

She was clearly taken aback. "Ed, contractor oversight is a vital issue. Some of these companies aren't only working outside of the law, they're doing evil things in our name, and with our money! They're undermining the reconstruction and putting our troops in greater danger!"

"I've read all the media hysteria—"

"'Hysteria'!" she exclaimed in disbelief. "We have incontrovertible evidence of serious criminal malfeasance!"

"—but the truth is more complicated than that," he continued calmly. "It always is. Reform like this isn't always possible without serious compromises. And politics, as you know, is the art of the possible. The timing just isn't right for something like this, Lana. Perhaps in two more years, we can talk about it again."

"This is an intolerable situation! Something needs

to be done, and I'm going to do this with or without your support."

"Are you certain about that, Lana? I have significant influence in the Senate. How far do you really think this can go without me by your side? You can't do it without me. Right now, your choice is to have it die in committee or on the floor."

"I will not abandon this issue," she said.

He smiled gently. "I understand that you've committed yourself to this already and that there is a political cost to abandoning it altogether. But I believe we can come to a compromise on a . . . more *moderate* bill, one that will satisfy your constituency without causing potentially disastrous interference in the war effort."

She jumped out of her chair. "I will not defang this bill for the sake of political expediency!"

"Lana, please calm down and listen to me. I know you are passionate and idealistic, and I know you feel strongly about this. But our legislative body is built on compromise." He cleared his throat. "As you know, we're going to pass an energy bill later this year. I know how important the coal industry is in your state. This is going to be a major issue with your constituents. Work with me on this, and I can guarantee that whatever bill gets passed will protect your interests."

She laughed wryly. "I guess it's true what they say about laws and sausages."

"Why don't you take a couple of days to think it over . . ."

"I don't need to," she said curtly. "The answer is *no*."

"Lana . . ."

"I am not interested in compromising my principles for the sake of votes, Senator." She got up to leave.

"I admire your moral courage," he said, standing up as well. "Just remember, that can be a dangerous thing in this town."

"I know what I signed up for. Good-bye, Senator."

You have no idea, he thought to himself, smiling as she stormed out of his office.

CHAPTER 19

As she drove home, Jenny Morgan reached into her purse and cursed herself for forgetting her cell phone again. She had just spent hours going over swatches and fabrics with a client who had rejected option after option Jenny showed her with a slight, snobbish flick of the hand. To keep herself from saying something outright rude, Jenny had promised to come back with more samples the next day. And still, she would likely lose the client, anyway. But worst of all, another day had passed and she still had not heard from Dan.

Her instinct was to trust him, but his story about having to stay in DC was more than a little fishy and alarming even on the face of it. Jenny was not stupid. There was obviously more going on than her husband had told her. But as she neared home, she tried to push it out of her mind. She knew there was nothing she could do once Dan had decided something.

As she turned into their street, her eyes were drawn to a white van parked across from their house, marked BALD EAGLE PLUMBING. *Strange*, she thought. She seemed to remember seeing that van there that morning. Jenny looked at it suspiciously, then, in a moment of self-consciousness, laughed and shook her head. Living with Dan over the years had really made her paranoid. They were there for a big plumbing job, and that's all; perfectly normal, nothing to be concerned about.

She parked in the driveway and went inside. Neika ran to greet her, panting and licking her hand. Jenny said hello to Alex, who was sitting cross-legged on the living-room couch, sullenly staring down at a book, her short hair concealing her eyes. Jenny wished she could tell her daughter that Dan hadn't just gone away on business, that he was doing things of serious consequence. But it wasn't her place. Dan would have to be the one to tell her. What's more, Jenny knew about Alex's new political inclinations and that, if anything, her daughter would probably be appalled if she found out. Dan at least deserved a chance to be there to explain his own side of things.

"Did your father call?" she asked Alex, who shrugged in response. Jenny walked to the kitchen counter and found her cell phone there, still attached to the power cord. Seven missed calls; three new messages. She flipped it open and clicked through to voice mail. One message was from a client who wanted a consultation, and there was another from her sister, who had just called to say hello.

The third was from Dan: "Hi, Jen, it's me. I'm calling to tell you that everything's fine here. I've been held up at the auction, and I'm not sure when I'll be able to call again. I'll probably be home in a couple of days. I can't wait to see you and Alex again. I hope your friend Clara's surgery went well. I know how worried you were about her. Oh, and make sure you take the GTO out for a spin. You know how it needs a little air now and then. I love you."

Her friend Clara. She didn't have a friend named Clara, and no one she knew was in the hospital. *What was this*—and then she remembered. It was their code, something her husband had made her memorize, along with emergency plans, in case anything happened. The meaning of the message was vivid in her mind: *Danger! Get away!* She had always thought this business with secret codes was a bit ridiculous, but now that she had gotten the call, she didn't feel ridiculous. She felt afraid.

She walked into the living room, where her daughter was still on the couch. "Alex," she said, "do you trust me?"

Alex looked at her quizzically, appearing slightly worried. "I . . . guess?"

"I'm serious, Alex. If I ask you to do something without asking me why, would you do it?"

"Mom, what's wrong?" Alex asked, alarmed. "You're scaring me. Are you okay? Did something happen? Is Dad okay?"

"As far as I know, your father is fine, and so am I. But I don't have time to explain. I need you to pack a suitcase as quickly as you can. We need to leave home for a few days. Pack warm."

Alex laughed in disbelief. "What's going on? What is this about?"

"I don't know. But please, Alex, trust me, and do it now. We could be in danger."

The fear must have been obvious in Jenny's voice, because Alex's demeanor became completely serious, and she didn't raise any further objections. She just asked, "When do we leave?"

"Right away."

"Okay," she said. "Are we taking Neika?"

"I'll take care of Neika," said Jenny. "Just hurry."

Jenny rushed to the master bedroom and tossed together a bag as quickly as possible, filling it with comfortable clothes, a jacket, and some winter items in case the cold returned. She rummaged through her sock drawer and found the stun gun that Dan had given her years ago, which she hadn't felt comfortable carrying around with her. She picked it up, checked the charge, and dropped it into her purse.

Just then, the doorbell rang, and her heart sank with foreboding.

Jenny breathed deeply as she walked downstairs, trying her best to calm her nerves and appear normal. Whoever it was, it would be better to dispatch them quickly and coolly, without arousing suspicion. With one more deep breath, she turned the doorknob. Standing at the door were two men in black suits.

"Mrs. Morgan?" said one of them, stepping forward. "I'm Agent Baird, and this is my partner, Agent Pace. We're with the FBI." They held up their badges. "We'd like to ask you a few questions about your husband."

Their badges looked legitimate enough, and if she had any doubts, she would have asked to examine them closely and take down names and numbers. But she knew immediately and instinctively that it wouldn't have helped, because these men weren't really from the FBI. "Is he in trouble?" she asked, hoping that her feigned apprehension was convincing.

"Not as far as we're concerned, ma'am," said the one who called himself Pace, who was skinny, had a shaved head, and spoke in a Texas drawl. "We'd just like to talk to him. And you might be able to provide us with information about an ongoing case."

"Is this about the cars?" she said, doing her best impression of a worried, naïve housewife.

"No, ma'am," said Pace.

"He isn't in trouble, is he?" she asked again, wide-eyed.

"That's not what we're here for, Mrs. Morgan," said Baird, who was short and stocky and had eyes that seemed too close together for his face.

"I don't know what I could help you with, then. Dan's the one you really want. I'm afraid he's out of town, but I'll certainly let him know you came by next time I talk to him."

The two men exchanged a look. "Actually, Mrs. Morgan," said Baird, "you're the one we want to speak to. May we come inside?"

She hesitated before saying, with all the cordiality she could muster, "Yes, yes, of course. Come in." She stepped aside to admit the two men into the foyer. "Can I offer you gentlemen anything to drink?"

"No, thank you," said Pace.

"So how can I help you?" she asked, obligingly. "I don't know what *I* could possibly tell you that might be of any—"

"Mrs. Morgan," Baird cut in testily, "do you know the whereabouts of your husband?"

"Yes, of course!" she said. "He's in Seattle, advising a client at a car show."

"Is that a fact?"

"Why, yes, as far as I know. When you're married to a man, Mr. Baird, you do tend to know these things."

"I'm sure, Mrs. Morgan," said Pace. "Now, has your husband attempted to contact you in the past two days?"

"He called me, if that's what you're asking. He left me a message this morning telling me he might be away for a few more days. Do you want to hear it? It's right—"

"That won't be necessary, Mrs. Morgan," said Baird.

"Could you tell me what this is all about?"

"We can't reveal too much," said Pace. "This is an ongoing investigation. But your husband might have key information about a murder case. Our chief suspect is a client of his, you see."

"Oh, dear," she said. "I hope it's not anyone I know. I couldn't bear to think I knew a murderer."

"Do you know of any way we can contact him?" asked Baird.

"Not if you've already tried his cell phone. You can leave a card if you'd like, and I'll have him call you as soon as he's available."

The two men looked at each other and then back at her. "Actually, ma'am," said Pace, "we're going to need you to come with us."

"Excuse me?" she asked, feigning outrage, her increasing alarm showing through her façade.

"You heard us, ma'am. Just cooperate, and everything will be fine."

Jenny looked at the men, not knowing how to respond. At that moment, Alex walked into the foyer with her backpack, holding Neika on a leash.

"Were you going somewhere, miss?" said Baird.

"Who are these people, Mom?" she said. Neika was straining gently at her leash, growling under her breath at the two strangers in her territory.

"Ma'am. Come with us now, please," said Pace. "You, too, miss," he said to Alex.

"Me?" asked Alex. "What is this? Mom, what's going on?"

"She's not going," said Jenny. "If you need me to go, I'll go, but she stays."

"It's for her own safety, ma'am," said Pace.

"Mom?" insisted Alex.

"We're not asking, Mrs. Morgan," said Baird.

"Okay," said Jenny. "We'll come. Alex, darling, these gentlemen are from the FBI. We're going to go with them so they can ask us a few questions about your father."

"What about Dad?" asked Alex. "What about what you told me five minutes ago—"

"Alex, it's okay. We should cooperate with them." She turned to the two men. "Let me just grab my purse."

Pace nodded in assent, and Alex just stood there with a perplexed look on her face. Jenny picked up her purse and walked back toward them. As she drew within an arm's length of them, she slipped her hand into her purse and clutched the rubber handle of her stun gun.

She flicked the switch and jabbed Baird with the twin electrodes; he fell backward with a startled yelp. She turned to do the same to Pace, but before she could, he grabbed her arm and twisted it. The stun gun zapped ineffectually in the air and fell to the floor. Neika was now snarling and tugging at the leash. Alex let go.

Barking and growling savagely, Neika bounded toward Pace, knocking him onto his back. Jenny looked at Alex and shouted, "Garage!" Both of them dashed for the door, and Jenny grabbed the keys from the kitchen on the way. Alex followed her into the garage.

"Mom, your car isn't in here!"

"We're not taking my car."

Jenny pulled the tarp off a hulking shape on the opposite side of the garage to reveal her husband's classic 1967 Pontiac GTO. As Alex clicked the button to open the garage door, Jenny got into the driver's seat. She turned the ignition, and the muscle car rumbled to life.

"Neika!" Alex cried out, and a couple of seconds later the German shepherd came galloping from the kitchen. She jumped in through Alex's open door and onto the backseat.

As the outside door rattled open, Jenny looked toward the kitchen and saw Pace storm into the garage, his suit jacket ripped wide from Neika's attack. She looked back at the garage door, just open enough now for them to make it out. Jenny stepped on the gas pedal, and they lurched forward and stalled.

"Mom, can you even drive this thing?" Alex exclaimed.

Jenny turned the key. In the rearview mirror, she saw Pace draw a gun.

"We'll see." She stepped on the gas pedal, and the GTO roared down the driveway past her SUV and onto the street.

The wheel was a lot stiffer than she was used to, but,

man, the thing could go! They tore down the road, soon leaving their street and the unmarked white van behind, and headed for I-93. They didn't speak for several minutes, sitting quietly except for their heavy breathing, the atmosphere in the car laden with tension, fear, and exhilaration. Even Neika panted restlessly in the backseat. After a few minutes, Alex broke the silence.

"Mom," she said, still breathing heavily. "Who the *hell* were those guys?"

CHAPTER 20

Morgan arrived at the Philadelphia International Airport early the next morning. From Istanbul, he had hired a driver to take him to Thessaloniki through Bulgaria, and from there he took a commercial flight to the United States with a connection in Zurich under the third alias he'd used in the past two days. While at the airport, he bought two disposable prepaid cell phones—burner phones. The first he used to call home, Jenny's cell phone, and then Alex's. If he knew anything about how the CIA operated, they were by now tapping all of his family's lines, and he had just effectively announced his location to everyone who was looking for him. But if there was a chance that Jenny and Alex were still at home, that meant they were in danger. He was only partly relieved when no one picked up at his house and both Jenny's and Alex's cells went straight to voice mail. He hoped they had gotten his message and were by now safely hidden away in his father's tiny hunting cabin in Vermont, where Morgan had instructed Jenny to go, many years ago, in case something ever happened.

He dropped that phone into the open backpack of a teenaged traveler who was headed for the check-in counter. If they were going to track him, let them try. By the time they realized they had the wrong scent, he'd be long gone.

He looked up the address of a used car lot in the phone book and took the commuter rail into the city. Airport cabs were much too easy to trace. Once inside the city, Morgan switched to buses. He kept an eye out for tails and took the usual evasive precautions, getting on and off vehicles at the last minute and making frequent, unexpected turns.

About an hour and a half later, he arrived at the Mercado used car lot, where a man in a yellow jacket approached him and asked, "What can I do to get you to drive out of here in your new car today?"

Morgan grinned.

Half an hour later, he was driving away in a 1999 Sebring convertible. From there, he made a stop to pick up some supplies at a drugstore to replace his bandages. In the parked car, he laid out the fresh rolled-up bandages, surgical tape, and scissors on the passenger seat and carefully undid the older dressing. He examined the wound, which had been restitched by a doctor in Istanbul. Considering the circumstances, it was healing fine.

Once finished, he sat in the car and mulled over his next step. He had a visceral urge to go north to reunite with Jenny and Alex, who were alone, scared, and possibly in danger. All he wanted was to be there to protect them.

But things, of course, weren't that simple. He couldn't just forget what had happened in Kabul. He took out the little memory card he'd received from Zalmay and clutched it in his fist. He'd looked through the rest of the photos, and they just got more and more incriminating. Several featured T approaching the airplane and talking to a man that he recognized as Bacha Marwat. The last few showed T, still at the airfield, speaking to a man whom he did not recognize, with a face that reminded Morgan of a bulldog.

As far as Morgan was aware, he was now the last living person who knew about the Acevedo International conspiracy who wasn't also in on it. Even if he chose to ignore the fact that Acevedo was funding the enemy and reported nothing to no one, he would still be too dangerous to them at large. Morgan could take his family and disappear, but how long could he stay vanished? How long until he slipped up and T or someone else came knocking? No, he couldn't let this go. He needed to get answers, and the answers wouldn't be up north.

He picked up the second phone and dialed. It was a shot in the dark, and like any shot in the dark, it could go terribly awry.

"Is this line secure?"

"Is this who I think it is?" asked Plante.

"Is this line secure?" he insisted.

"Hold on," Plante said. Morgan heard a click, and a low hum came over the line. "It's safe now. Cobra, you need to come back in. Where are you?"

"Isn't that the million-dollar question?" he said bitterly.

"Why are you on the run? And why did you shoot up a zoo?"

"Will it help if I say I didn't start it?"

Morgan could imagine Plante's disapproving stare. "I hope for your sake there's a good reason for this. And if there is, you need to get back here and explain before they send an operative to kill you."

"It wouldn't be the first in the past few days."

"What are you talking about?"

"Someone was waiting for me in Kabul," he said. "Someone knew I was coming. I met Conley's asset, and they killed him. He left me with a memory card that would make a lot of very powerful men very uncomfortable."

"Oh, God. What are you going to do?"

"Who knew, Plante? Who knew I was in Afghanistan?"

"I thought I was the only one."

"Well, you weren't. Someone sold me out. I bet it's the same person who sold Cougar out. And I bet it's someone inside the CIA."

Plante went silent.

"Do you know something I don't, Plante?" asked Morgan.

"I have . . . suspicions. Compromised agents and missions, signs of leaks . . . But getting ahold of any evidence has been like grasping at smoke. Nothing concrete, only suggestions and vague wisps of clues."

"Does it have anything to do with Acevedo International?"

There was another long pause that said that the answer was yes. Plante said, "I have something to show you. When can you meet me?"

"How do I know you're not setting me up?" said Morgan.

"You don't know," said Plante. "Honestly, there's

nothing I can say to prove it. You're just going to have to trust me."

"Trust is something I'm not exactly brimming with right now," said Morgan. "But as I see it, I don't have much of a choice. I can make it to DC by tonight."

"Good. Then do it," said Plante. "My house, nine o'clock. I have lots to show you. Maybe together we can get to the bottom of this."

"And find the son-of-a-bitch who sold out Conley and me," added Morgan. "There's just one thing that I need to know right now, and God help you if you lie to me. Do you know where my wife and daughter are?"

"Kline sent two agents to bring them in, but they gave our men the slip. It looks like you taught them well, Cobra."

Morgan couldn't help smiling with pride as he hung up and removed the battery from the phone. He tossed it out the window and turned the key in the ignition. As he drove out of the city, he tried to focus on Plante and the possible connection between Acevedo and the CIA, but his heart was elsewhere, with his wife and daughter, wanting to protect them from all those who would harm them to get at him.

CHAPTER 21

It was early afternoon, and Nickerson was sitting in his office, with his feet up on the desk, annotating a draft bill, when in stepped Roland Vinson, a burly, greasy man with bulbous, heavy-lidded eyes and back hair that crept down the back of his neck. Nickerson swung his feet to the ground and leaned forward in his chair.

"Sit down, Roland," he said. "We need to discuss what to do about this Lamb situation."

"What situation is that, sir?"

"Don't tell me you don't follow C-SPAN, Roland," said Nickerson, pausing for a beat. Vinson looked at him blankly. Nickerson continued. "It seems that he decided to grow something that vaguely resembles a backbone and come out in favor of greater Intelligence oversight. This makes him rather, well, ungracious in light of our kindness toward him, does it not?"

"Must be losing your touch, boss."

"Let's call this a rare slip," said Nickerson, with a hint of irritation.

"So now what? Do we nuke him?" asked Vinson.

"No. Send a copy of the photos just to his wife. Tell

him next time it's the *Washington Post*. Hopefully he'll get the message."

Vinson nodded. "Sir, there's also the matter of this McKay woman. What are we going to do about her?"

"It will be taken care of," said Nickerson tersely.

"Sir, she didn't back down. We need to do something to—"

"I said it will be taken care of," interrupted Nickerson. "*I* have taken care of it. I am well aware of the threat she represents. She is popular and inflexible. She can inspire other senators to do things against their best interests. Against *my* best interests. But I'm not concerned. She won't be a problem for long."

Vinson shifted in his chair. "And what, exactly, is your solution?"

"That's for me to know, Roland, and you to find out—if and when it's necessary. Are we done here?"

A scowl played for an instant on Vinson's face, and then he said, getting up, "Yes. I'll deal with this Lamb situation."

"Good, good," said Nickerson from his seat. "Be sure to keep me updated. And shut the door on your way out, will you?"

Nickerson barely had time to make himself comfortable when his intercom chirped. He picked up.

"Senator?" came a voice over the intercom.

"Yes, Greta?"

"Your three o'clock is here. A Vera Blackburn, an aide to Senator Weidman."

He frowned. "Did she have an appointment?"

"It's on the planner, sir."

"All right, then." He shrugged. "Send her in." He placed the receiver back in the cradle, picked the draft bill up again, and put his feet on his desk, pretending to be engrossed in the document. He looked up nonchalantly as the door opened, and he nearly upset his chair when he saw who it was.

He knew her only from photographs, and they did not tell the whole story. She was tall and in her late thirties with slight wrinkles around her eyes but still a knockout in her sleek business outfit that was perhaps slightly too flattering for the part. Her walk was naturally seductive, a rhythmic gait that accentuated her sensuous curves. Hers was a striking, murderous beauty, with high cheekbones and sleek, light blond hair. But most of all, it was her eyes that were frightening, deep blue eyes that betrayed nothing but casual pitilessness, like that of a tiger regarding a baby antelope that had stumbled into its lair.

Natasha. "Wh-what are you doing in my office?" he demanded, trying to be intimidating but not convincing even himself.

"Come now, Senator," she responded, with honeyed undertones in her barely accented speech. "Surely you wouldn't turn away the person who has been doing your dirty work."

"How did you get in here?"

She shrugged. "The door. You *saw* me come in." She ambled slowly around the office as if she owned it, touching this and that, running her hands along various surfaces. "You seem to think you're a lot safer than you really are. Like a handful of fat, middle-aged security men will keep someone like me out of here. I barely even had to try." She had made her way around the office and now stood in front of him. "Good thing I work for you, no?"

"You can't be here," he said through his clenched teeth. "What if you're seen?"

"What of it?" she said, casually. "Do you think I care? *I* don't exist. *I'm* not the most trusted politician in America. Isn't that right, *Senator Nickerson*?" Her voice dripped with sarcasm. She looked up at a crucifix he had nailed to the wall. "Are you a religious man, Senator?" She was mocking him, with just a hint of a threat. "Or is that only a show for the voters? *Or*"— she grinned maliciously—"do you truly believe you will go to a better place when you die?"

"What are you, a reporter? How about we cut the small talk and you tell me why you're here?"

"My, you are all business, aren't you?" She gave him a cool smile. "Okay, then. I am here for two reasons," she said. "First, I wanted to see your face when you saw me. Men like you, they do not face the truth of their actions. They sit in their fancy cars and big offices and let people like me do their dirty work. Well, here I am. The face of all your sins. And I must say, it gives me pleasure to see you squirm."

"I'm glad you're having fun," he said, losing his patience. "But I'm not the one who failed to kill Cobra in Afghanistan. I'm not the one who let him escape with the goddamn photographs and I'm not the one who let the Agency spook take the goddamn pictures in the first place. So instead of coming in for this very pleasant meet-and-greet, maybe you should be out there trying to fix your own screwups."

She eyed him menacingly; her tone became ice-cold. "Cobra was more slippery than I expected. I underestimated him. But that is a mistake that I will rectify soon."

"You'd sure as hell better, or—"

"The second reason I am here," she said, interrupting him, "is that I want you to know that our relationship is going to change. As of now, my fees are doubled, and you are no longer entitled to secrecy. You will tell me what I want to know when I want to know it. Do you understand?"

"You think you can come in here and tell me what to do?"

"The alternative is to come in here and slit your throat." She pouted seductively. "Do we have an understanding, Senator Nickerson?"

"Yes," he said, gritting his teeth. "We do."

She chuckled. "Of course you say 'yes.' But you are a coward at heart, and like any coward, you will turn back on your word as soon as I walk out the door. But it is of no matter, because I will be enforcing our little agreement."

He glowered at her.

"I want to know what your plan is. The master plan. What are you in for, Nickerson? What are you trying to accomplish here? And don't give me that bullshit about doing important things away from government oversight. You don't give a shit about improving humanity."

"I guess you're right about that," he said, with a wry smile.

"What's the endgame, Nickerson? What's your angle? Money? Is that it?"

Nickerson laughed. "Money? My family already has *money*. Money buys you yachts and fancy cars. It buys you a house on Nantucket and the French Riviera. Hoarding money is the ambition of small people. Me, what I want is power." He smiled. For a man who wore a mask nearly every minute of every day, it was liberating to speak freely. "What I want is power," he repeated. "Real power. The power to do anything I want. The *capo di tutti capi.* Politicians, those Wall Street assholes, the President himself—they are all going to line up to kiss my hand."

Natasha laughed.

"What?"

"Your delusions of grandeur," she said, smirking. "Very amusing."

"Trust me. You are small-time. You know nothing of real power. How to get it or how to wield it."

"Perhaps." She slinked closer to him. "And yet I could kill you right now. It wouldn't even be difficult. And for all the power you say you have, there's nothing at all you could do about it."

He instinctively backed away from her, regarding her with the impotent fury of defeated pride. She stood there, her gorgeous face inches from him, her faint perfume smelling like death. She snapped her teeth at him, as if she was going to bite him. He flinched. She grinned.

"By the way," she said, turning and stepping away from him, tracing her finger on his desk, "our mutual friend has already alerted me to my next assignment. I must say, you are a bold man, for a senator."

He looked at her with wounded pride, but he knew how to take things in stride. "So you accept it?"

"Yes, I will do it."

"And the Cobra situation?"

"He will be dead by morning." As she turned to leave, she looked back at him over her shoulder. "You will be hearing from me, Senator."

CHAPTER 22

Morgan parked the Sebring around the bend from Plante's suburban home. It was in an out-of-the-way neighborhood, sparsely populated and cut with twisted streets that wound around in a lightly forested area. The thick old trees, which during the day would provide pleasant shade, now seemed to fill his line of sight with ominous dark corners. He got out of the car and started making his way to the house. He kept to the shadows as much as possible, all the way up Plante's inclined front lawn and the house's front steps, lit only by the flickering lamppost on the street below.

Plante's home was a two-story, two-car-garage brick house. Morgan was hoping that Plante would be waiting for him, but no one came to the door as he approached. He knocked lightly—the doorbell would too easily announce his presence to anyone who might be nearby. Getting no answer, he tried the handle and found that the door was unlocked. He pushed it ajar, and it creaked slowly open, the streetlight behind him casting his shadow far into the entrance corridor.

The house was mostly dark, but there was one visible source of light, spilling from a room all the way down the hall. The stillness gave Morgan a bad feeling. As he crept toward it, he wished he had the comforting weight of a gun in his hand. That feeling hit him harder when he reached the door, looked inside, and saw Eric Plante.

Plante was slumped over on his desk, his face turned away so that the back of his head was turned towards Morgan—or what was left of it, anyway. Most of it had splattered on the wall behind him. Blood, sticky and deep crimson, had pooled around him and was trickling down to the floor, where it formed a dark stain on the carpet. Without thinking, Morgan stepped into the room to examine the body. From the blood spatters on the wall, he unconsciously worked out the trajectory of the bullet, following it backward with his eyes to a broken pane on double French doors to the outside.

Sniper.

Instinctively, he dodged out of the way, just as he heard another pane crack and a bullet whiz past his ear, hitting the opposite wall. He stood flat against the far wall—with the floor-to-ceiling window in between him and the only way out of the room. Exiting would now move him into the shooter's line of sight. Any sniper with decent reflexes would be able to hit him before he made it halfway to the door. If it was T holding the gun, which was all too likely, he would not even get that far. He was trapped.

Morgan told himself that panicking would not help. He let himself breathe and assessed his situation. Outside, by the light of the room, he could only see a few feet of the backyard lawn. The rest was engulfed by the darkness, and he had no hope of catching a glimpse of the sniper. The French doors had curtains, which were currently open, but they were too wispy to provide any decent cover. Plus, any move to shut them would get him killed. Behind him was a built-in bookcase with below-waist-level cabinets that held, along with books, a couple of Plante's nicer pipes and tobacco. He knocked on the interior wood backing, hoping for a hollow sound, but it was solid, with no way to break through to the other side. There was no way out of that room that wouldn't get him a bullet in the head.

Morgan's gaze was drawn to his dead friend. The damage was mostly from the exit wound, and his face was marked only by a single round hole in his forehead. He stared blandly out of his still-open eyes, a blank look on his face, showing no surprise. He had never even known what had happened to him. Under his head was a file folder, half-covered in a puddle of blood.

Plante had known something. Could he have been looking over the relevant files before he died? Things he wanted to show Morgan? And how could Morgan make a grab for it, right in full view of the sniper?

His mind raced. The only light in the room came from a metal lamp on Plante's desk. It was an architect-style lamp, heavy-based, articulated, and intensely bright with a metal reflector. He followed the cord to where it was plugged into the wall, just a few feet away on his side of the room. He had seen no other light on in the house; unplugging it would plunge the room into total darkness. It would leave the sniper blind—unless, of course, they—*she*, he was almost certain—had night vision.

Well, he thought, *only one way to find out*. He reached

out to grab the plug, knowing that if his hand was within the sniper's line of sight, he would lose it. In one quick movement, he pulled it, and the room went dark. He stood in silence for a few seconds. No gunshots. If the roles were reversed, and he was suddenly blind, he would be shooting up the room right now. Not a good sign. But he had to make sure.

He grabbed a large hardcover book from the bookshelf, about the size of his head. *Let's see how good your reflexes are*, he thought, and he flung the book past the window. The shot came immediately, hitting the book and sending it flying toward the opposite corner of the room.

Damn. The cover of darkness wouldn't help him.

But . . . He had a thought. The sniper might be able to see in the dark, but too much light too quickly would temporarily overwhelm the night vision. The lamp on Plante's desk was powerful and would again suit his purpose fine.

He grabbed the cord and edged the lamp off the table, careful not to pull too quickly. It teetered off the table and landed on the thick carpet with a thud, base down, as he had hoped. He pulled it quickly out of the sniper's sight. Then he clicked it off at the base and plugged it in once more. Picturing the spatter patterns on the wall and the broken windowpane, he worked out the shooter's approximate position. This would have to be quick.

He positioned the lamp just out of sight, adjusting the blistering hot reflector with his hand, burning himself slightly even through his tugged-down sleeve. Then he took a deep breath. *Here goes nothing*, he thought, and in one motion, he clicked the lamp on and pushed it out into the sniper's line of sight.

Immediately, he heard the cracking of a glass pane, the shattering of much thinner glass, and the metallic *clang* of the bullet hitting the reflector. Sparks flew. The bulb, which had barely had time to flash on, was instantly extinguished.

The shot had come fast, too fast for a sniper who should've been shooting blind. How had the shooter known his move before he made it? He felt the pain of the burn in his hand, and it became obvious: the heat signature. The sniper was using a thermal scope. Even with the lamp off, that scope would have been lit up like a Christmas tree.

It was hopeless. His only choice was to risk running out in front of the window and hope that the bullet wouldn't find its target, knowing that, if it were he at the other end of that scope, he couldn't miss. *Here goes*, he thought, his calves tensing in preparation for the sprint.

And then his eye caught a single point of light in the room: a spark from the lightbulb still smoldering on the sheer curtains. And he had one last, mad idea.

He opened the cabinet and groped around through a series of small objects. *Please, Plante*, he thought, *tell me you kept it here*. His hand found a cool tin container, and his heart skipped. He picked it up and shook it slightly. It was about half-full of liquid. He brought it up to his face, and the unmistakable odor of lighter fluid wafted to his nose.

He sprinkled the fluid at the curtains and the floor in front of the door, shaking the tin hard enough that its contents would reach the other side. He did this until he exhausted the container, and then he went back into the cabinet. He found what he was looking for: a matchbook, the kind that restaurants and hotels give out. He ripped out one of the thin paper matches and lit it. He then touched it to the rest of the match tips, and they ignited. The flash of phosphorus burned brightly in the darkness.

He smiled as he dropped the matchbook onto the fluid-soaked carpet. It lit up in a blue blaze that climbed the curtains and raged toward the ceiling. He heard numerous tinkles of cracking panes and realized that the sniper was shooting blindly. The smoke alarm started beeping maniacally, and in the din, Morgan laughed out loud and yelled, "Can you see me now, bitch?"

Now he had to make his move. The sniper wouldn't be able to target him, but he could easily get hit by one of the bullets sailing past. And he had another problem now, too—the fire was spreading fast. It wouldn't take long for the whole room to turn into a blazing inferno.

Then he happened to look at the desk and saw, by the orange light of the flames, the file on Plante's desk. He couldn't leave it behind.

He listened for the shots. Soon the sniper would take a brief respite. It would be only moments, to take a second look and reassess, but it would be enough. And then . . .

The bullets stopped coming, and he sprang from his corner. He found the bloody file with his hand as he passed and yanked it from under Plante's dead head. The bullets came but too late—he was already outside the line of fire. He dashed through the door to the hallway and out the door. It was a short run to the car from there. He was out of the woods, for now.

So long, old friend, he thought as he glanced back at the house. The only response was the rising smoke and the faint flicker of the consuming flames inside. It was a funeral, of sorts, a final blaze of glory that would consume his former handler's slim body.

Morgan ran as fast as he could back to the Sebring. He got in, tossed the bloody folder onto the passenger seat, and sped off toward I-495, his eyes darting constantly to the rearview mirror to make sure that T hadn't managed to follow him. His next destination was to see his wife and daughter, and he would not sleep until he reached them in Vermont. He glanced at the folder on the passenger's seat. What kind of answers would it contain? Would it tell him who the mole in the CIA was?

But what if it did? He was running out of allies. The only one in the Agency whose loyalty he could be certain of was Plante, and that was because he was now dead. But he was on his way to see his family. That was more important than any investigation.

While he was still wired from the adrenaline, his first two hours of driving flew by. But the stress of the past few days finally caught up to him. He had barely slept in four days, during which time he had flown halfway around the world and back, while continually being chased and shot at. He forced himself to keep going, saying Alex and Jenny's names like a mantra as exhaustion threatened to make him delirious. He had to get to them, had to stay ahead of his pursuers. He gripped the steering wheel, hunching over, holding on by a thread. He tried to slap himself awake, but still sleep encroached on him. Several times, he awoke with a start to find the car drifting onto the shoulder of the road.

He couldn't help his family if he was in the hospital, he thought, or dead from a traffic accident. He pulled onto the shoulder and backed onto a dark, rutted access road so that the car faced the highway for a fast getaway yet was just far enough in to be hidden from view. At least he could avoid being spotted at a rest stop. *Twenty minutes. That's all I need.* He reclined his seat and closed his eyes. *Twenty minutes, and I'll be back on the road.*

CHAPTER 23

Harold Kline yawned into his hand, and as the elevator doors opened, he was startled to see CIA Director Boyle standing in front of him.

"Sir," said Kline, flustered, shifting the heavy folder in his arm.

"Good morning, Kline," said Boyle, stepping aside for Kline to walk out into the hallway. "What's the latest on this Cobra situation?"

"The forensics team at Plante's house found evidence of an accelerant," said Kline, walking along with Boyle.

"Not surprising." Boyle opened the door to his office. "Please, come in."

"That's not all, sir," continued Kline, sitting down at Boyle's desk. "They found a couple dozen bullets in the walls and floor of the room. It seems likely it was one of those bullets that killed Plante."

Boyle sat down at his desk stiffly. "What's the official story?"

"He will have died in bed, in a tragic house fire started by faulty wiring. He will be buried in a closed casket, with a large wreath from the CIA acknowledging his service. There'll be no indication of violence."

"Good," said Boyle. "Any word on the identity of the shooter?"

"We found a shell casing under a tree a few hundred feet from the house and signs of a hasty cleanup. Definitely a sniper. But nothing that would lead to a positive ID," said Kline. "That's why I had Plante's communications pulled." He placed a small digital audio player on the table. "This is a recording made yesterday on Plante's line." He pushed play.

"Is this line secure?"

"Is this who I think it is?"

"Is this line secure?"

"Hold on . . ."

There was a click, and the recording went silent.

"What am I hearing here, Kline?"

"To my understanding, sir, that is Plante circumventing our surveillance to speak to Cobra."

"Is there any way we can find out what he said?" asked Boyle.

"No, sir."

"You think this is related to his death?"

"I don't know how you can escape the implication, sir," said Kline. "And that's not all. I also pulled Cobra's file. He apparently had some personal effects in storage in our facilities. Took the storage clerk over an hour to find it, buried with other stuff that hadn't even been touched in years." He put a thick folder on the table. It was old and bent, with deteriorated elastic holding it together, barely containing the documents inside.

"Is this what I think it is?" asked Boyle, undoing the elastic and opening the folder.

"Records from his old missions. Termination orders, transcripts . . . And that"—Kline pointed to a small black bound notebook—"is a detailed diary of every mission he undertook for the CIA."

Boyle leafed through the documents with furrowed brow. "Why do you suppose he kept these?"

"Impossible to say, sir," said Kline. "But it is a serious breach of protocol."

"That it is. But I can guarantee he's not the first one to do it," said Boyle.

"The facts of the situation are damning."

"Give me your assessment, then," said Boyle.

"Based on the evidence," said Kline, "I would say Cobra snapped. Whether it happened in Afghanistan days ago or years ago, I don't know. But it's clear that he did. It's also clear that he isn't just a garden-variety traitor. He's going after people he worked with. This is personal to him. For whatever reason, for whatever imagined crime against him, he wants revenge."

Boyle sighed. "It doesn't seem like the Cobra I knew."

"I know that you think highly of him, sir," said Kline. "Should I alert the FBI, in your opinion?"

"No," said Boyle. "The damn Feds won't know what to do with a man like Cobra. We clean up our own messes. Are Rivers and Buckner still active?"

"Sir, Rivers and Buckner failed to capture a high school girl and a middle-aged woman. I can think of few things more dangerous than Cobra going rogue. We need to fight fire with fire."

Boyle's look became solemn. "You're talking about activating an operative."

"I believe the circumstances warrant it, sir."

"The President will not okay this," said Boyle.

"The President doesn't have to know. Sir, we have a dangerous man at large that nobody but us is equipped to deal with. He is smart, deadly, and obviously has an agenda. There's no telling what he'll do if we don't stop him."

Boyle ground his teeth and banged his hand on the table as if he was arguing, not with Kline but with his conscience. "Get Ramirez to contact the Bat. Keep him on standby. And expand the search on Cobra. I want him found."

"Understood," said Kline, getting up. "And, sir," he said, before he walked out the door. "You made the right call."

CHAPTER 24

Morgan woke up, chilled to the bone, to the sounds of birds chirping and the sun peeking through the branches of the trees. *Damn it*, he thought, checking his watch: 6:50 A.M. He had slept for more than five hours. *Shit*.

He drove the rest of the way as fast as he could, tires squealing at every curve. If Alex and Jenny had been found while he was asleep, he would never forgive himself. The wooded highways of the Northeast were a blur as he pressed on with a single-minded purpose, weaving through sparse traffic and stopping only for gas on the way.

Just after 1:30 P.M., he turned onto the short stretch of dirt road in the woods that led to his father's hunting cabin. The undergrowth had already crept onto the path, and there were even a few saplings that had taken root. From the flattened plants and broken branches, it was obvious that another car had passed through recently. *At least they made it here*, he thought hopefully. But thoughts of Alex and Jenny dead or captured still invaded his head and refused to leave.

He pulled up to the cabin a few minutes later and found the GTO parked near the door. The cabin itself was a small hunting lodge in the forest a mile or two from the highway, where the noises of civilization didn't reach, except for the occasional plane passing overhead. Morgan parked and got out of the car. As he approached the entrance, he could hear Neika scratching at the door from inside. He raised a hand, shaking in anticipation, and knocked.

The door opened, and there stood Jenny, tired and disheveled, holding a stun gun in a defensive crouch. To Morgan, she had never looked more beautiful. Her kind brown eyes, exhausted from the past few days, widened in surprise. Dropping the weapon to the ground, she fell into his arms and a deep, passionate kiss.

Neika, puppylike, had already bounded outside and was jumping for joy, not knowing what to do with herself. Alex emerged from inside, holding a knife in her trembling hands, her athletic frame showing the weariness of nervous, sleepless nights. She approached slowly, repeating, "Dad? Dad?" with tears in her eyes. Morgan put an arm around her, as well. Relief poured over him. For a moment, as he held his wife and daughter tightly in his arms, everything was right in the world.

"Are we safe?" asked Jenny, finally. "Dan, tell me we're safe."

"I can't know for sure," he admitted, as they walked inside. "But this is the safest place I know of right now."

The cabin was old but sturdy, and structurally, it had held up well over the years of disuse—his father, who suffered from a bad back, had not been hunting in over a decade. It was furnished with two rustic beds in the bedroom, a few wooden chairs, and a table. Jenny had clearly been working to make the place livable. No amount of her interior design skills could transform it into a dream home, but it was as comfortable as Morgan had ever seen it. The floor and other surfaces were mostly free of the dust that had no doubt accumulated, and there were some groceries on the table, mainly snack foods that required no preparation or refrigeration. He was surprised to find the room cozy with warmth, and he noticed that a fire crackled in the iron woodstove in a corner.

"There was an old pile of chopped wood out in the back," said Jenny. "A couple of logs were still good enough to burn. I figured we'd have what comfort we could manage."

Dan smiled. Jenny Morgan certainly wasn't a helpless woman in need of being saved.

"Speaking of which," added Jenny, "Alex, could you go get a couple more logs for us?"

"Sure, Mom."

Jenny waited until Alex walked out the door, and then she turned to Morgan. "Dan, I know there are things you don't want Alex to hear, but I sure as hell deserve to know. Why are we here?"

"It's a long story," he said, sighing. "Did you tell her? You know, about me?" he asked.

"No," she answered calmly. "It's important for you to explain it to her yourself. But you have to, Dan. She needs some explanation for what's going on. There were armed men in her home. You need to tell her. Today."

"Yeah . . . ," he said. "You're right. I do." He wasn't looking forward to that conversation.

"And I need some answers, too. Like, who were the men who came to our house?" asked Jenny.

He frowned. "What did they look like? What did they say?"

"They were two men in suits claiming to be with the FBI. They wanted Alex and me to go with them. Dan, who are they?"

"Boys from the Agency, if we're lucky," he said.

"If we're *lucky*?"

Alex kicked the door open, carrying two large, partially rotted logs in her arms. "These were the best I could find," she said.

"You seem to be getting the hang of this roughing it stuff," Morgan observed.

"Well, it *has* been three days," said Alex, with a hint of coolness to her tone.

"I'm sorry you had to go through all this."

"It's all right," she said, sighing stoically, tossing the logs into the smoldering embers. Then she turned and looked him straight in the eye. "Dad, what's going on here?"

Morgan took a deep breath. "Some people, some very bad people, are out to get me right now. I had your mother bring you here because they might have come after you to get to me. And from what she tells me, it sounds like they did."

"Who, Dad? Who's coming after us? Why would anyone want to do that?"

"They're bad people with a lot of power. It's all very complicated, sweetheart."

"*Stop* talking to me like I'm a child."

"Alex—"

"I'm not a kid anymore," she said, her voice crack-ing. "You need to be honest with me. For once."

"Sweetie, it's complicated."

"Don't give me that!" she exclaimed, tears forming in her eyes. "Don't even! I mean, you miss the game and leave for days to go God knows where. Then Mom tells me *we* have to leave home. Then two men with guns show up at our front door. And now we're in a cabin in the woods I didn't even know existed, and I still don't know *why*." She stopped, out of breath, look-ing at Morgan, her eyes pleading for an answer.

He sighed. He'd always known this day would come. He had put it off, again and again, and now he was forced to come clean at the worst possible moment. "You're right," he said, pulling a chair out for her. "I think it's time we had a conversation. One that we should have had a long time ago."

She sat down, her weary expression now mixed with confusion and apprehension. He pulled up a chair in front of her, and Jenny sat a few feet away. He began.

"For over ten years, Alex, I was a spy for the CIA."

She gaped at him, speechless, looking bewildered and unsure. She opened her mouth to speak, closed it again, then said, "What? Dad, that's ridiculous. I *know* you deal in antique cars. I've met people you work with. I even came with you to Los Angeles once, re-member?"

"That wasn't a lie. For many years, it's been my real, honest-to-God job. But before that, it was only a side job. My cover."

"For your career as—as a *spy*?" she asked incredu-lously.

"Yes."

"What does that even mean?" she asked. "Being a spy. I mean, like in the movies? I'm trying hard not to assume anything. I'd rather hear it from you."

"I was in Black Ops," he explained. "I ran missions that officially never happened. Dangerous missions."

"You mean like . . . assassinations?" She spoke carefully, looking down.

"Yes," he said solemnly. "Among other things."

"I see," she said.

"Look, Alex . . ."

"Sorry, Dad, this is just a bit much, all right? I mean, suddenly you're telling me that you've been lying to me my entire life? I mean, this is about who you are! You're what's wrong with the world . . . You, personally, represent what's wrong with the way we deal with the rest of the world! I mean, I knew what your politics were, Dad, but I didn't know you were at the heart of everything I'm against! Just how am I supposed to react to that?"

"I'm your father," he said. "I love you, and I have always wanted the best for you. That has never been a lie. That's stronger than politics. It's stronger than anything."

"But you've *killed* people! How am I supposed to live with that?"

Morgan took a deep breath. "I don't know what I can tell you to make you accept it. All I can do is try to make you understand. I did this work because it was the right thing to do. There are evil, dangerous people out there, Alex. People who look for ways to harm Americans. People who would destroy our government and kill our citizens. I know this sounds vague and distant, but I saw it up close. It's real. They're real, and this country needs people like me to keep them at bay.

"I know you believe that everything is going to be fine if we all just try to get along," he continued, "but this isn't *Sesame Street*. I've been there; I've seen things; and, trust me, sweetie, things just don't work that way. And even if you don't believe me, if you can't see why, I still don't regret anything I've done, because I know it made the world a safer place for you to grow up in."

Alex sobbed quietly and said, through her tears, "I don't even know you, Daddy."

"Alex . . ." he said, reaching a hand out to her. "It's still me. I'm still your father."

"No," she said, recoiling, and she stood up. "I can't just accept that. It's not that simple." She grabbed her coat.

"Where are you going?" Morgan asked.

"I just . . . I need to be away from here right now." She turned and walked out of the cabin, slamming the door.

"You could have said something," Morgan said to Jenny, sadly, without bitterness.

"You did well," Jenny reassured him. She laid her hands on his shoulders and stroked him tenderly. "It's just a lot to lay on her. Let her go be angry, blow off some steam. This can't be easy for her. I know it wasn't easy for me, either. She needs this time. Let her have it."

"What makes you so sure she'll come around?"

"Because you're her father. You're more important to her than any political cause."

"I hope you're right." He sighed.

Jenny sat down in Alex's chair, across from Morgan. "Dan, I know Alex wasn't ready for this, but I need to know what happened. Why are people after us?"

"It's a long story."

"I'm not going anywhere."

Morgan told her everything that had happened since Plante knocked on their door. She winced at every turn where he might have died had it not been for a stroke of luck or a split-second decision. She demanded that he show her the wound in his side and gasped when she saw it. As he told her about Plante, with her gentle touch she removed the bandages, cleaned away the dried-up blood, carefully placed fresh gauze from their first-aid kit over his sutures, and wrapped the bandages around his torso.

"And those two men who came to our house, they were from the CIA?" she asked him, as she pulled the end of the bandage taut and taped it.

"I think so," he said. "But they're not the ones I'm worried about. They wouldn't have had clearance to kill. They would have just brought you in. The one I'm really worried about is the one who attacked me in Afghanistan."

"You said it was a woman you recognized?" asked Jenny.

"Yes. She's a Russian spy who turned double agent for the CIA many years ago. I originally helped to turn her to our side." He didn't feel compelled to tell her their shared history in any further detail. "Now she's hunting me because I have information that could hurt her and whoever she's working for." He looked into his wife's eyes. "Jenny, this . . . I never wanted this for us.

CHAPTER 25

Alex walked down the dirt road, crushing the incipient undergrowth beneath her boots. She wept, and it made the afternoon light and everything around her misty, the whole world quivering through her tears. But she pressed forward without destination, doggedly refusing to look back.

Even though she was sixteen and entitled to some rebellion, she had never spoken to her dad like that before. It hurt her, like she had willfully broken something precious. And at the same time, her rage at his deception, at the details of his secret life, burned inside her.

It was like he was two different people, and she couldn't join both conceptions of him in her mind. She loved her father. But a killer? Could that really be him? It seemed impossible to square this with the loving, doting, if often absent father she had always known. She couldn't conceive of him being both.

And even if she did manage to, what was she supposed to do, anyway? On the one hand, he was her *father*. And he was a good father, a good man. She knew that. What right did she have to doubt him like this? How could she do anything but love him and trust him? But, on the other hand, what good were her political convictions if she didn't stick by them now, when they mattered most?

She buried her face in her hands. It was too much. She was confused, hurt, angry, and *so tired*. She wished she was at home but at the same time felt that she wouldn't be comfortable there, that it wouldn't *feel* like home right now. Not after her father's confession. Not now that she knew about the big lie.

She was so confused. She was so alone. She needed to talk to someone, someone who wasn't her father or mother.

Her hand slipped into her pocket, and she fingered her cell phone. It had been off since they left the house. Could it really do that much harm if she used it? What if she just—

No. Her mother had warned her. Cell phones could be tracked, and she should only use hers in a dire emergency. It would stay right there, in her pocket. But what if she . . . Maybe that would be okay. Yes, it would do fine.

She trudged on, still not looking back. She was, however, no longer aimless.

CHAPTER 26

The iron connected with the ball satisfyingly at the nadir of the swing. Edgar Nickerson raised a hand to shield his eyes from the setting sun as he watched the white dot follow its lazy parabola until it hit the grass in a narrow stretch between a sand trap and a grove of trees, a cool 250 feet away.

"What did you think of that swing, Vinson?" he said jovially, squinting against the sun at the pin on the green.

"Just peachy, Mr. Nickerson," said Vinson, standing near the cart and looking at him with his piggy little eyes glazed over with blank impatience. Nickerson had a habit of making people wait on his whim. He put away his club and motioned for Vinson to put the bag on the white golf cart, which he did, grudgingly. Nickerson had done without a caddy so he could talk to Vinson, but he was damned if he was going to carry his own bag when there was help around.

"Come on," he said, motioning for Vinson to get on the cart. The vehicle moved silently.

"I take it the affair with Miss Dillon is taken care of?" Nickerson asked, hands on the wheel.

"As usual," said Vinson. "I'm here because I need to know what's going on with the Cobra situation."

"I'll tell you what you need to know," he said.

"Well, Hodges is on my ass. If you want to tell him yourself, I'm sure he'd appreciate it."

"Tell him it's being dealt with," said Nickerson.

"That's not going to be enough to shut him up," said Vinson.

"Then you can tell him that we have the full extent of the resources of the Central Intelligence Agency backing him. I thought the reason you were here was so I wouldn't have to—"

"Mr. Nickerson," Vinson interrupted, urgently, and motioned toward where his ball had landed. There stood a woman, dressed in tight black pants, with short, light blond hair and a deadly beauty that was obvious even from far away. She had picked up his ball and was tossing it lazily upward and catching it as it fell. "Do I take care of this?" Vinson asked.

Nickerson looked around to make sure there was no one else in sight. One paparazzo looking for a senatorial scandal was all it would take for pictures of him standing with a CIA assassin to be plastered on the front page of every major newspaper.

"No," said Nickerson, agreeably. "I'm the one who asked her to meet me here."

"I don't think I like this bitch too much."

"Then it's a good thing that's not what I pay you for," said Nickerson. He brought the cart to a stop a few yards from Natasha "My, they do let anyone into this place these days," he said, loudly enough for her to hear.

She had caught him off guard last time, and he had acted like a schoolboy afraid for his lunch money. She wouldn't get that pleasure this time.

"I am here," she said curtly. "What do you want?"

"Would you believe me if I said I enjoy our little talks?" he said jovially, motioning for Vinson to pull his clubs from the cart. She remained impassive. Vinson sighed and picked up the bag, setting it on the ground. "Would you mind?" said Nickerson, and he took the golf ball from her. "I don't think anyone will mind if I *don't* take a penalty over your interference." He dropped the ball and positioned himself to swing . "Vinson," he said. "why don't you take a little walk?"

Vinson practically snarled at that. He shot Natasha a homicidal look, then walked away.

Natasha stood silently until he was out of earshot and said, "I hear Marwat is dead."

"Yes. Drowned in his own tub," said Nickerson flatly. "How tragic."

"Was that your doing?"

"Marwat was greedy and predictable. That made him a good associate. I had no reason to get rid of him." He practiced his stroke, brushing the grass with the sole of his club.

"What will happen now to our business in Afghanistan?" she asked him.

"I'm not too worried," said Nickerson, switching out his club for a five iron. "Another will take his place. Nature abhors a vacuum." He cleared his throat. "Meanwhile, you have again failed to kill Morgan, and those photographs are still at large. I thought you were a professional. What is it you said last time? 'Dead by morning'? Tell me," he taunted, interrupting his practice swings to look at her with a derisive smile, "are you *trying* to fail?"

He savored her seething silence and, after a calculated pause, said, "Well, it's no matter now. I'm not the only one who grew impatient with your ineptitude. I'm told that the CIA has sent an operative after Cobra. This time, he *will* be dead by morning."

"*What?*" she spat in venomous indignation.

"You are reassigned to focus on your primary task," he told her. "Which, by the way, you should have been doing to begin with."

"That is unacceptable." she fumed. "*I* kill Cobra!"

"Ah, yes," he said, as if he had forgotten. "Your little . . . *vendetta*." He packed the last word with contempt. "How very old-world of you."

"I do not expect a man like you to understand," she said. "Nor do I care. You will not deprive me of my revenge."

"Think of it as outsourcing, my dear." He swung, punctuating his statement with a *thwack,* sending the ball into a smooth arc. The ball bounced three times on the green and came to rest a few feet from the hole.

"You pathetic little man," she said in white-knuckled anger. "What stops me from killing you where you stand?"

"We both know why you haven't killed me already, and why I'm quite sure you won't," he said, sounding unperturbed. "But I'll humor you. What stops you is that, while at my side, you will become fabulously rich and powerful."

She looked at him with restrained contempt. She had enormous pride. It made her irrational, but Nickerson understood that it also made her formidable.

"You will do what I tell you. At the rally, in five days," he said, like a schoolteacher giving homework instructions.

"Cutting it a bit close," she grumbled.

"Are you suggesting that you can't do it?" he said airily. "I thought you were supposed to be the best." She scowled at him in response. "Excellent. That's the kind of spunk I expected from you. And I understand you found yourself a way to get close?"

"You understand correctly," she said acerbically.

"I have something for you," he said. "Look in the large pocket of my golf bag."

She unzipped it and found a cardboard tube. She popped the top and slid out the schematics from inside.

"You called me here just to deliver these? You could not have sent your trained monkey to do it?" She pointed at Vinson, watching them from the tree line and looking surly.

"Since you were kind enough to make your introduction before, I thought it best to conduct our affairs face-to-face when possible. Now tell me this is going to go off without a hitch," he said.

"There will be no problem," she said.

"Then that's that, isn't it?" he said, satisfied, and he motioned for Vinson to come over. "I knew I could count on you, *partner*. Now, if you'll excuse me, I have a ball to sink."

He hopped onto the golf cart, let Vinson get into the passenger's seat, and drove away, watching in the rearview mirror as Natasha receded from his sight and disappeared into the wood.

"She's trouble, sir," said Vinson. "You won't be able to keep her on her leash much longer."

"Not like you, eh, Vinson?" said Nickerson. "Faithful as a dog." The man scowled at the comparison, but kept quiet. "But you're right. She's becoming a liability. We will have to dispose of her in good time. But for now, she is still useful."

"Yes," hissed Vinson. "For now."

CHAPTER 27

Morgan sat at the rough wooden table in the hunting cabin, perusing Plante's documents by the light of a single, flickering, lightbulb that hung from a wire from the ceiling. Alex had been gone for several hours now, and the sun was close to setting.

He had been staring at the same piece of paper for the past half hour, unable to concentrate—not because of the bloodstains along the corner of the page but because his eyes were anxiously drawn to the door every few seconds. His ears caught every rustle he heard, over the low rumble of the generator, wondering if this time it might be the sound of his daughter returning. He had taken the old hunting rifle from its rack on the wall, loaded it, and shot at a few squirrels outside to see how it handled. It had one hell of a recoil and was so unpredictable, he couldn't count on hitting a stationary target twenty feet away. Still, he left it on the table within reach, just in case.

Neika, meanwhile, sat underfoot, relaxed and oblivious. Jenny was keeping busy adding the first woman's

touch the cabin had known, rearranging the sparse fur-
niture, throwing out a chair that had rotted through,
and confining a large deer-antler lamp with its long-
ago-burned-out bulb to a corner of the room. Morgan
knew this was Jenny's way of coping with her daughter's absence. He had half a mind himself to get into
the car, find Alex, and bring her back, but Jenny had
been right. Alex needed her space.

Meanwhile, the file that his old handler had compiled was plenty to keep him occupied. It was thick
with papers, printouts that, Morgan presumed, Plante
had prepared to give to him when they met. It seemed
that Plante had been conducting his own investigation
into Acevedo International. He must have had reams of
documents to compile this kind of data. Clearly, he had
been at this for months. There were copies of flight
manifests for supposedly empty Acevedo cargo planes
flying out of Kandahar, and yet there were fueling logs
showing they couldn't possibly have been empty. Another packet of papers was devoted to the connection
between Acevedo and the CIA, but the evidence Plante
had dug up linking the two was nebulous and uncer-
tain. It consisted mainly of suspiciously convenient oc-
currences, like investigations that had been called off,
inquiries that had led to dead ends, informants who
had wound up dead. But there was nothing definite to
tie Acevedo to any of it.

Morgan waded through stacks of financial documents. A calculation in the margin of one of the last
pages added up all the money unaccounted for and still
came up short of the billion-dollar profits Acevedo
should be making from the drug trade. Plante had

scribbled, in a hasty, frustrated hand, *Where is the money going?*

Morgan turned the page to find a profile of Lester Hodges, head of something called the Special Projects division at Acevedo. The attached head shot showed a tough-looking man with the square face of a bulldog. Morgan recognized him as the man who had been talking to T in Zalmay's photos. Behind the profile page was a single document, signed by Hodges, authorizing transportation of materials to Kandahar. In a corporation shrouded in secrecy, this seemed to be Plante's only solid lead.

Was anyone at the Agency aware of any of this? It seemed unlikely. If any of the higher-ups knew, the investigation wouldn't have fallen to Eric Plante alone. Maybe, like Morgan, Plante had suspected a mole. He again lamented his old friend's death, and especially now that he knew that, if Eric were still alive, he would have had a faithful ally in all this. As it was, he couldn't trust anyone.

He had to decide what his next move was going to be. Careful consideration wasn't usually his style. He would rather throw a wrench into the works and see what happened. But he wasn't going to gamble where Alex and Jenny were involved. He needed to be cautious.

He couldn't go to the CIA, of course. Any other government agency might help him, but they would be all too happy to screw the CIA, along with him, in the process. What about the media? He could expose the whole thing to the world—but he couldn't go to the press without exposing himself and, along with that, revealing a dozen state secrets. He felt that shining the light of public scrutiny on this would do far more harm than good.

No. He would have to find out who was behind this, and he had to do it alone. He would go after Lester Hodges and follow the evidence all the way to the top, wherever it led him.

He waited for Jenny to move into the bedroom, then gathered up Plante's documents and placed them, along with the memory card Zalmay had given him, in a white shopping bag, which he hid discreetly under a loose floorboard in a corner of the cabin.

He sat back down on the hard wooden chair and stared at the wall, and as the first outlines of a plan formed in his mind, he heard light footsteps outside, approaching the door. His hand automatically moved to rest on the rifle. The door opened. He breathed a sigh of relief when he saw Alex at the door, standing against the encroaching darkness outside. Jenny rushed past him to hug her.

"Where were you?" said Jenny. "We were worried sick!"

"Around. I needed to think, so I just walked along the road until I reached the highway."

"Well, I'm just glad you're back," said Jenny.

Morgan looked at his child with relief, but it was still painful to be reminded of the things she had said.

Hesitantly, she spoke. "Look, Dad . . . I took some time to think and . . . I'm not saying everything's okay, or that I forgive you. But I don't want to do this right now. I don't want to hate you. I don't want to be angry." She was picking up steam, speaking louder and faster. "Maybe we can fight later, have it out and everything.

But not right now. Right now I need things to be okay, at least until this is all over." He began to speak, but she interrupted. "I'm not done yet, so let me finish. So we don't fight for now, okay? And even when we do fight . . . Damn it, you're my dad, you know? Even if I'm compromising my ground just by saying this . . . I don't know. I love you, and nothing, not even this, is going to change that." She finished, nearly breathless, as if getting it all out had been an enormous effort.

Morgan's lips turned up in a smile of restrained relief. "I know I shouldn't presume too much here," he said, "but I'm really thankful for the benefit of the doubt."

Jenny hugged her daughter. "That's my girl. Twice as thoughtful and caring as any adult I know."

"I just had some time to think, is all," Alex said, holding her mother. "And I can't take all the credit. Dylan said some things that really got me to see things a different way."

Morgan's heart sank as he heard these words. It was as if a black cloud had suddenly obscured the silver lining. "'Dylan said'? You mean, you talked to him?"

Alex stepped back nervously. "I gave him a call, and we talked for a while," she said, faltering at the change in his expression. "It helped a lot. Don't worry," she added quickly, "I didn't tell him any of the specifics, about you or everything that's going on."

"I really wish you hadn't done that," he said, going through all the implications in his mind.

"Dan, come on," said Jenny. "She just wanted to hear a friendly voice. Maybe you could cut her some slack this once."

"Look, Dad, I knew you wouldn't like it," Alex said

apologetically. "But I didn't tell him what's going on or where we are. Not even a hint."

"When?" he said urgently. "When did you make the call?"

"I don't know. I-I . . . " she stammered. "It must have been hours ago. I was venting to him for a while, and then I walked some more. I had to think some things through." Her tone changed from defensive to self-assured. "I didn't use my cell phone. I'm not stupid, Dad. I'm not a spy, but I know *something* about this electronic-surveillance stuff. I called from a pay phone in the gas station down the road."

Morgan wasn't reassured. "There are pictures of you two together online, aren't there? Connections in social networking sites and whatnot? Meaning that anyone with an Internet connection could easily find out that he's your boyfriend?"

"I . . . I guess . . ."

"Dan, don't hound her," said Jenny.

"We need to go right now," Morgan said with adamant resolution. "Take only what you can't live without."

"Again?" exclaimed Alex.

"Could you just stop for a minute and explain?" demanded Jenny.

"There's no time! We need to get moving right now."

"No," said Jenny, firmly. "I need you to tell me what's going on before we pick up and leave again."

He looked at her, ready to argue; but he was incapable of speaking harshly to her, even in this situation. Instead, he took a deep breath. "I know how the Agency works," he said, hurriedly but methodically gathering up items that were strewn around the cabin.

"They won't be just tapping our phones. They'll be monitoring the people we're likely to call. Family. Friends. And, unfortunately, that includes boyfriends."

"But I called him from a pay phone, Dad! How will they know it was me? How are they going to find us here?"

"You mean even if they weren't listening in to the call?" he said, without looking up from packing. "They would still check out the number and send someone out here regardless. And this place is registered under a known alias of mine. If we hadn't called their attention to this area, they never would have found us. But now it won't take them long to put two and two together. We need to go. Now."

He walked toward the loose floorboard to retrieve the hidden items, when he noticed Neika scratching at the door. "Quiet!" he mouthed, holding up his hand and perking his ear to listen over the low rumble of the generator. "There's someone out there," he whispered. "Get under the table."

An ashen Jenny ushered Alex below and then huddled underneath it, as well. "Dan, what are you going to do?"

He picked up the rifle from the table and switched off the light, immersing the cabin in darkness. "Stay put. I'll be back as soon as I can." He patted Neika, who was still clawing frantically at the door. "Sorry, girl, but you're taking the lead on this one."

"Dad, no! What if she—"

"She could save our lives, honey. Sit tight."

He opened the door, and Neika shot out of the cabin, her syncopated gallop rustling the undergrowth. He followed her into the darkness, treading as lightly as possible, the sound of her footsteps and her intermittent grunts leading him through the dim, branch-filtered moonlight. She ran off ahead of him into the blackness. He continued to run after her until he heard her yelp and then tumble to the ground. Someone was out there. Someone had gotten her. He raised his rifle, but it was no use. There was nothing to see or target.

He stepped behind a tree and listened intently until he heard footsteps. Someone was running around him on his left. He stepped out from behind the tree and, aiming to the extent that he could, fired. The boom of the rifle echoed in the silent woods and left Morgan's ears ringing. He tried and failed to listen for the footsteps, until he heard, behind him, the click of a flashlight. The sudden light projected his own shadow, huge and ominous, onto the trees in front of him.

"Drop the rifle," said a harsh, accented male voice from behind him, "or I will make you drop it. And I promise that if I do, you will be dead before it hits the ground."

The man could have been lying for all Morgan knew, but this wasn't a time for taking chances. Not when he was the last line of defense for his wife and daughter. He tossed the rifle aside, and it made only the slightest noise when it fell on the soft forest ground.

"Cobra," the man said. "How nice to make your acquaintance." Morgan turned around. In the pale reflection of the flashlight, he could just make out that the man's face had a crooked ugliness, and its cause was a diagonal scar that ran from his cheek to his forehead. It was a face he knew from photographs, and he also knew the reputation that went with it.

"You're Wagner, aren't you?"

The man only offered him a lurid grin in response. "That is your family in there, is it not? Your wife and daughter?"

Morgan didn't respond. But of course, he didn't have to.

"Come on," the man said, motioning toward the cabin. "Let's have a chat together, all of us, shall we?"

Having no choice, Morgan started walking toward the door. It felt like marching to his own execution.

CHAPTER 28

Morgan trudged heavily into the cabin, with the killer named Wagner holding the gun on him from behind. The assassin was holding, Morgan now saw, not a firearm but a tranquilizer gun. But what really caught his eye was the man's face. The scar, though long healed, was deep and disfiguring. It started on his left cheek, swept up to take a chunk from his nose, seemed to pull up his right eyelid by an unseen string, and ended in a diagonal slash through his right eyebrow, giving him the appearance of a permanent scowl. His face was sunken, and he had tiny eyes and a thin nose, which made him look ratlike, despite his solid build.

Morgan knew the man, Ingolf Wagner, by reputation. He was an East German defector, ruthless and cruel by all accounts, who took pleasure in killing his marks. His brutality, it was said, was matched only by his skill with a bowie knife. And this man was going into a cabin where Morgan's wife and daughter waited. It was, for Morgan, the stuff his worst nightmares were made of.

As they entered, Morgan scanned the room for a way to turn the tables on the assailant, for any potential weapon; but there was nothing he could have reached fast enough. He wasn't going to risk the man opening fire with Jenny and Alex in here, even with just a tranquilizer gun. He had to bide his time and look for an opening.

"Stand up," said Wagner to Jenny and Alex, who were still huddled under the table. They emerged slowly, nervously. Alex was trembling, and tears were streaming down her face. Jenny put her arms around her daughter and held her tightly, staring at Wagner protectively, waxing with aggressive hostility. Alex, on the other hand, seemed far diminished. Despite her sinewy strength, the girl now appeared small and fragile. Morgan caught the assassin leering momentarily at Alex before averting his eyes.

Bastard.

"Sit down. You first, Cobra. Hands flat on the table. Move a finger, and I'll cut it off." He bent over, his eyes mere slits, and whispered, "Try anything funny, and your wife and daughter will not be so pretty anymore."

Keeping an eye on them, Wagner began examining the cabin. He picked up the suitcases one by one, opening them and spilling their contents onto the floor. Morgan's blood boiled at seeing the man paw through his wife's and daughter's underwear, his beady eyes lingering just a second too long on a lacy pair that must have belonged to Alex. Murderous thoughts welled up in Morgan's mind. *Stay cool*, he thought. *Make a move now, and we're all dead*.

"Can I help you find anything?" asked Morgan, with mock solicitousness.

"Shut your mouth," Wagner said gruffly, barely looking up from his search. He proceeded to pour out the contents of Morgan's duffel. He quickly rifled through the various items and then walked over to where Morgan was sitting.

"You know who I am, don't you?" His voice was a cool, menacing growl.

Morgan stared him in the face. "Yeah, I know who you are."

"And you know what I do to people who don't cooperate."

Morgan glowered at him.

"Good. I just wanted to make sure I set the right tone." He paced, circling the table. "See, Cobra, there is something I would like your cooperation with. And it's so much easier if I don't need to establish the consequences of your being uncooperative."

"Let my wife and daughter go. Once I hear them drive away, we can talk."

The man laughed, a hacking, barking laugh. "No, no, that's not how it works. You are going to die, Cobra. That is what I am getting paid for. But if you play ball, as they say, your family here might make it through tonight."

Morgan knew he was most likely lying. There was nothing in it for him to leave living witnesses after he got what he wanted, and from what he had heard about this creature, he was a ruthless, vicious hit man. As long as it was up to him, Morgan was convinced, Jenny and Alex would never get out of this alive. But the way he looked at Alex also told Morgan something: the man was undisciplined. Let his desires get in the way of the mission. This made him especially dangerous and unpredictable, but it could also make him sloppy. Morgan had to play along and stay alive as long as possible, while he waited—and hoped—for Wagner to make a mistake.

"What do you want from me?" asked Morgan.

"That's more like it," he said with inordinate satisfaction. "I was told you need to be eliminated because you've become—how did they put it?—*a grave liability*. But that is not the whole story. You've got something with you, something that some people are quite desperate to get back."

Morgan's mind was working. Wagner was playing mercenary, trying to make an extra buck by working both sides. "Who the hell told you that?" asked Morgan, feigning ignorance.

"Who is not important," he said. "You have a memory card hidden somewhere, and I want it. Where is it?"

"Do you know exactly what it is you're looking for?" Morgan asked.

"Why?" said Wagner. "Do you want to tell me?" His eagerness belied his intentions. He wanted to use the pictures himself, for blackmail or leverage.

"The pictures show that a CIA operative and a major war contractor are working together to smuggle opium from Afghanistan," Morgan said, slowly and deliberately. "Opium, I might add, that funds the militias that are killing our boys over there. It's the sort of thing that's going to make a lot of very powerful people very nervous, and you're going to be in possession of those pictures. They will know you saw them, examined them. Are you sure you want that? Someone's got the stones to be double-crossing the CIA here. What makes you so sure they're going to let *you* live after this? That they won't send someone after *you* like they sent you after me?"

Wagner scoffed. "I'm not an idiot like you, Cobra. I won't be found. Unlike you, I don't have anyone holding me back." He looked at Jenny and Alex. "And unlike you, I don't care. What I care about is that I get the money."

"And how much are they paying you?" Morgan asked.

"More than you can match," retorted Wagner, laughing his hideous, barking laugh. "No, Cobra, you cannot buy your way out of this."

"Who was it?" asked Morgan. "Who sold out the CIA? Who's paying you?"

"You know," said Wagner, "I'm getting tired of all this goddamn talk." He grabbed Alex by the hair, and she yelped as he pulled her to her feet. Unsheathing his knife, he brought it to rest against her throat. "Enough with the goddamn games, Cobra. I know you have the memory card with you, and you are going to get it for me." He tugged at Alex's hair, and she let out a small whimper. The knife, a long, wooden-handled bowie gleaming in the soft light, looked sharp enough to slice through bone. "Isn't that right, sweetheart? Tell Daddy I won't hurt you if he does as I say."

Morgan ground his teeth, his fists balled so tightly, his nails dug into his flesh. He wanted nothing more than to rip out the bastard's jugular.

"All right," Morgan said, defeated. "You win. I've hidden them right here in the cabin." He got up and walked backward, slowly, toward the corner, keeping his hands plainly visible. He crouched down and, with his right hand, lifted the loose floorboard.

"You had better not even be thinking about pulling out a gun on me, Cobra," Wagner said. "You try anything, and your little girl here goes first."

"Easy now," said Morgan. "I'm just doing what you said." Morgan removed the shopping bag from the hole, lifting up his hand to show that it wasn't a gun.

"Bring it over here."

Morgan walked over, hands outstretched, and held the bag out for Wagner. The assassin couldn't take it without first letting go of Alex, who nearly stumbled forward, trembling.

"All right, sweetheart, you can sit down," he said, keeping the knife at her throat. "Give it here," he said to Morgan.

Morgan handed over the thick folder. As he handed over the little plastic memory card, he fumbled, and it fell on the floor of the cabin, at his feet.

"Here, I'll get it," said Morgan, bending down. But instead of picking up the chip, he wrapped his fist around the deer-antler lamp that Jenny had placed on the floor. Before Wagner could react, he swung it hard, diagonally upward. The heavy base hit Wagner in the face, sending him reeling back. Before he could recover from the blow, Morgan swung again, connecting with the man's temple, and this time the assassin staggered and fell back hard on the wooden floor.

In a blind rage at the assassin's threat to his family, Morgan struck once more with the lamp, and this time the wooden base broke off, flying low to a corner of the room. Morgan bashed him with the now-free deer antler again and again, and the bones of the man's skull cracked sickeningly. The man convulsed and finally fell limp, his face beaten to a pulp, blood pooling around his head and seeping through the cracks in the wooden floor.

Morgan got up, panting, blood splattered on his face and shirt, feeling the relief of victory. Then he turned to Jenny and Alex, and only then, upon seeing the look of horror in his daughter's face, did he realize what she had just witnessed. Alex, who was too squeamish to watch even mildly graphic action films; Alex, who at age eight had insisted they have a funeral for a bird that had hit the living room window and died; sweet, sensitive Alex, who opposed aggression on principle, had just seen him lose control and kill a man in an act of naked violence.

"Alex . . ." he said, but he didn't know what to tell her. He wasn't sorry. He couldn't be sorry, after the bastard had threatened his wife and daughter. But he was afraid, at that moment, that he might lose his daughter, anyway.

"Why don't we go into the bedroom, sweetie?" said a breathless Jenny, putting a comforting if shaking hand on her daughter's shoulder. She nudged Alex, who then walked, wordlessly, through the doorway, looking blankly ahead. Jenny lingered with Morgan just enough to whisper to him, "I'm sorry, Dan. You just saved our lives—I know that. You did it to protect us. She'll understand it in time. She'll come around. Just . . . let me talk to her alone for a while."

She gave him a gentle touch on the shoulder before walking into the other room with Alex and shutting the door behind her.

Damn.

Morgan knew there was nothing he could do now about Alex without making things worse, so instead, he did something that always warded off apprehension—focusing on practical matters. He needed to dispose of the body, which was the least of his troubles, considering that they were in a national forest. Their greatest problem was the fact that they had been found out and needed to get the hell out of there quickly. Once *they* realized that this one was dead, they would send another. And then, as he pondered this, he heard the rumble of a car outside, approaching the cabin.

Morgan hurriedly searched the dead man's body and found what he was looking for—his concealed weapon, a five-round Ruger snub-nosed revolver, strapped to his ankle. He took it out, unlocked the safety, and rested his finger on the trigger. Whoever was coming, this time he would have more than a rusty rifle to fight them off with. He wouldn't get taken by surprise. This time, he'd be ready.

He barged into the bedroom. "Someone else is here," he told Alex and Jenny, who were huddled together on the bed. "It isn't safe. Follow me." He opened the window, which led to the outside, behind the cabin. He let his wife and distraught daughter climb out first and then hopped over himself. "Stand flat against the wall. If you hear gunshots, run into the forest, and don't look back."

The beam from the headlights went out, and then he heard the car door slam. Morgan skulked around to the side of the cabin, stepping carefully so as not to make a sound. In the dim light of the moon, Morgan could barely make out the parked car, which he identified as a Ford sedan. He heard footsteps approaching the door. They were light on the soft ground, but they still seemed too heavy to be T's.

Well, whoever it was, Morgan wasn't taking any chances. His grip tensed on the gun. This needed to be quick. Aim and shoot, no thinking. He heard the doorknob and the squeak of the front door. Morgan took a step beyond the corner and . . .

Crack.

Underneath his left foot, just a tiny twig, but it was enough. Morgan caught the fleeting glimpse of a man darting into the cabin, narrowly escaping twin bursts from Morgan's weapon. *Well, no point in subtlety now*, thought Morgan, and he fired twice into the cabin, shattering the glass in a front-facing window.

Morgan ceased fire and crouched behind his GTO, checking his ammo. One more bullet. He looked around and found that he could see the reflection of the light streaming out of the cabin on the window of the stranger's sedan. He raised his weapon, lying in wait. He could normally hit a fly at this range. But he only had one bullet. He'd have to make it count.

The silhouette of the man at the door appeared in the reflection. Morgan breathed deeply. He'd have one chance at this.

He shot up and swiveled in one quick motion, taking aim and ready to shoot.

And then he saw the man's face. He gasped in surprise and lowered the weapon. His hairline had receded, making his already high forehead, now wrinkled, look even higher. New lines marked the face, and his hair had been dyed dirty blond, but he was as familiar as ever.

Standing at the door of the cabin was Peter Conley.

CHAPTER 29

"**D**amn it, Peter, I need to know," said Morgan. "How the hell did you escape Afghanistan? And whose body did they find at your apartment?"

Morgan, Jenny, and Conley were sitting at a booth in an old and dingy roadside diner. They were sharing the cramped eatery with only Alex, at the counter, and two solitary truckers who wore blank stares of exhaustion and listlessly shoveled food from heaping plates into their mouths. A corpulent woman with a wrinkled face and a dirty apron filled their coffee mugs and tossed three peeling menus onto the table. Morgan picked one up and found that it was crusted with mustard.

"I tried to transfer the photographs electronically," said Conley. "They never went through. Acevedo controls key Internet infrastructure in the Kandahar region, and my guess is, they were watching Internet traffic very closely. That, I think, is how they found me out."

"The body," he continued, "belonged to a man who tried to ambush me in my apartment. But I was ready for him." He took a sip of his coffee. Jenny watched him intently as he spoke, hanging on every word, her soft, intelligent eyes slightly widened in interest. "When I went out that morning, I had left two hairs stuck between the door and the jamb. It's an old trick, but it works. When I came back, they were gone. In this line of business," he added, "it pays to be paranoid."

Morgan looked outside to the far corner of the parking lot, where the GTO and Conley's car were parked in the dark under a dead lamppost. They had driven separately, Morgan with his family and Conley on his own. When they were three hours into New York State, far enough to elude any possible search perimeter, they had stopped for the night. They had paid cash for two motel rooms—which would be easier to defend than the more comfortable three—and they had the management unlock the adjoining door, opening it wide. Morgan and Conley bunked together in a double room to avoid any awkward pairings.

Alex was still having trouble dealing with what she had witnessed at the cabin and had perched on a stool across the diner from them, her elbow on the bar, nursing a glass of Coke, looking distraught and making a point of keeping her back to them. She had wanted to stay behind in the motel room, but Morgan refused to let her out of his sight.

"So then, I had a choice to make," continued Conley. "I had no gun on me, only a knife, and I had the money and the papers to walk away and get out of the country. But I had left the memory card—*that* memory card"—he pointed to Morgan, who was absentmindedly fiddling with the little plastic chip as he listened—"hidden inside the apartment. So I decided to go in. I took off my shoes, walked right past my door, down the hall, and came back as quietly as I could. Then I crouched next to the door, and I listened hard until I heard the bastard inside cough. He was standing close, waiting for me right behind the door.

"It wasn't really much of a contest," Conley bragged. "I unlocked the door like I was coming home, and once it was open, I slammed it hard against him. He stumbled back just long enough for me to disarm him and slash his throat.

"He was smart enough not to have any ID on him, but I knew he was from Acevedo. I got the memory card from right where I'd left it behind a loose brick hidden behind the bed. I put my watch on him, I messed up his face, and then I torched the apartment. Then I raised the alarm and got the hell out of there. After that, I went straight to Zalmay's, and once I sent him on his way to Kabul with the memory card. I couldn't trust the CIA with it, not after seeing T there. I didn't know who else might be compromised. I couldn't contact you electronically, for fear that the message might never make it to you. So I left the letter at the dead drop, addressed to you, and trusted that, even if the chain of communications had been compromised, they would want to know what the letter said, hoping it might lead them to Zalmay."

The waitress came over to take their orders, which they gave her in turn.

"The young lady at the counter over there is with us, too," said Morgan. "Be sure to let her know you serve twenty-four-hour breakfast when you take her order. She'll be happy to hear that."

The waitress left, and Conley continued. "Once Zalmay was on his way, I had to finish what I started. That night, I snuck into Marwat's house and eliminated him. After that, I hid out for a couple of days before I skipped the country as a stowaway in one of Acevedo's own planes."

"Well done!" said Morgan, chuckling.

"I ended up in Frankfurt, where I finally called in that favor from George Koch. Remember him, Morgan? Well, he got me a fresh EU passport and a ticket back here.

"I tried to contact Plante. That's when I found out he was dead, that it appeared you were the one who killed him, and that now no one could find you. I didn't believe for a second that you were the killer. So I went to your father's old cabin, where I thought I'd be most likely to find you. I knew there was more to this than met the eye."

"There always is," said Morgan. He went on to relate everything that had happened to him since Plante showed up on his doorstep. At this point, Conley had already been told about Zalmay. It had been the first thing he'd asked about after making sure that Morgan and his family were all right. He listened to the story keenly, deep in thought and never interrupting, as if trying to make everything fit together in his mind. Morgan had just finished telling him about evading the sniper at Plante's house when he spotted the server walking toward them, balancing three plates of food.

She dropped a plate holding a soggy-looking burger onto the table in front of him, buns open steakhouse-style and topped with a wilted leaf of lettuce. But he hadn't eaten more than the odd snack picked up at a gas station convenience store for the last few days. To him, this was a feast. He could tell that Peter and Jenny were both also ravenous, and for a few minutes, they ate in silence. Then Morgan broke it, asking Conley, "Do you know about Plante's investigation of Acevedo?"

"Know about it? I was *helping* him. What, you think he did all that on his own? We had a couple of contacts in the company who sneaked out some of their financial files, whatever they could get their hands on. Apparently, some people still have consciences, even people who work for soulless traitors. Plante and I compiled that information, looking for the identity of the person responsible for running the drug trade and the traitor in the CIA who was helping them." He took a pregnant pause.

"But there's more to it, isn't there?" asked Morgan.

Conley frowned, thinking, and then said, "Jenny, would you excuse us for a moment? I think it's best that you don't hear any of what I'm about to say."

Jenny, who had been absorbed in the story, looked somewhat deflated by the request, but she acquiesced. "I'll go check on Alex," she said, getting up and bringing her coffee and food with her.

Conley lowered his voice. "Look, Dan, I'm telling you this in the strictest confidence. I'm telling you because I trust you, and there's no one else who can help me with this."

"You don't have to worry about me, Peter. I have your back come hell or high water."

Conley took a deep breath and bit his lip. "This investigation into Acevedo that Plante and I were running was entirely . . . extracurricular. The CIA knew nothing about it. And we had good reason to keep it that way. Our driving suspicion was that Acevedo had someone in the CIA who was leaking information and doing their best to disrupt any investigation or operation against Acevedo."

"Plante told me that much," said Morgan.

"Here's the part I'm certain he didn't tell you," said Conley, looking furtively around them and then leaning in closer, his voice scarcely louder than a whisper. "During the course of our investigation, I was approached by a man I didn't know. Called himself *Smith*. I had him pegged right away for an intelligence type, careful, measured, and deliberately vague. He accosted me in the street and asked me about the Acevedo investigation. I told him I didn't know what the hell he was talking about, but I could tell he knew that I did. He said he was a representative from some supersecret worldwide security organization of some kind. He said they were impressed with me and were interested in recruiting me to do some work for them."

"That's a likely story," scoffed Morgan.

"I didn't believe it myself, at first. Had 'trap' written all over it. Of course, we've all heard the rumors about such a thing existing, operating on a level that's even more secret than Clandestine Services, some kind of shadow organization. But I've always thought it was a sort of tinfoil-hat fantasy, the CIA bogeyman. Plus, even if I did think such a thing existed, no way in hell did I believe that this guy was associated with it."

"But you changed your mind?" said Morgan.

"I did. Not that I got a good feeling about this guy, but then again, I'm not one to go by my gut on this kind of thing. What changed my mind was that he was handing me intel. It was real, solid stuff. Checked out. And it pointed to the existence of a mole within the CIA. Someone high-level."

"Did you think it might be a smokescreen of some kind? To get you to give up what you had?" interjected Morgan.

"Yeah, I thought it might be, but it checked out, Morgan. Everything checked out. And meanwhile, they didn't ask for anything in return. And then they made their proposition—the mission in Afghanistan. Plante would help arrange for me to go undercover. The mission, as far as the CIA knew, would be to terminate a local drug lord. But I was also there to look into Acevedo. A deception within a deception. I got a tip about a plane that was going to be loaded with opium. I took the chance, recruited Zalmay to help me get in, and took those pictures in the memory card."

Morgan nodded. "Do you think this organization of yours will be able to help us?"

"I do, if I knew how to contact them!" said Conley. "But I have no idea who they are, much less where I might find them. They came to me. That's how it always worked."

Morgan nodded and said, after a pause, "But there's one thing I don't understand. Why did you reach out to me, of all people, to come and make the meet with Zalmay?"

"That was never part of the plan. I wasn't going to turn him over to CIA custody, where I was sure he'd turn up dead, a 'suicide' or the victim of an unfortunate accident. I didn't know how deep the rot in the Agency might be. So I was going to bring him over myself and defend him with my life if I had to." His tone was suffused with bitter sadness.

"What happened?"

"I guess I got spotted doing recon with Zalmay. I was ambushed. They knew where to find me—someone in the CIA had ratted me out. But it got worse. I was making contact with this shadow group by handing off written notes to a runner who was on Flower Street at 2:00 P.M. every day. Never talked, never made eye contact, just passed the note. The day after Zalmay and I managed to take those photographs, the runner never showed up. The next day, he didn't, either, and I was attacked.

"I would have trusted Plante to retrieve Zalmay, but we couldn't communicate privately between ourselves or in a way that others in the Agency wouldn't understand, too. There was just one person I trusted completely and to whom I could communicate a message without the possibility of anyone else understanding it."

Morgan nodded. "Any idea who the traitor is?"

"I don't have any evidence that points strongly to anyone in particular. I just know it's got to be someone with a pretty high security clearance. But . . ."

"But?"

"I have a hunch," said Conley, lowering his voice. "Kline. He's an outsider, the bureaucratic type, and a micromanager. He's into everything in the NCS, and he has top-level security access."

Morgan stirred his coffee. "I never liked that asshole," he said. "And I believe he's capable of it. But he hasn't got the brains or the guts to mastermind an operation like this. If he's in it, he's got a boss." He paused, then asked, "What about this Hodges guy, from Plante's file?"

"He's definitely in elbow deep," said Conley.

"Do you think he might be the guy behind it all?" Morgan asked.

"I think it goes farther up than that," said Conley. "No way he's doing all this without the higher-ups taking notice. But he's a solid lead."

"Good," said Morgan. "So we go after him. We get Jenny and Alex someplace safe, and we go after him hard. Then we find out who he's working for, and we go after *him*. We get to the bottom of this, no matter what it costs, Peter. Because we can't back out now. This is the only way we'll ever get out of this alive."

Morgan looked over his shoulder at his wife and daughter, who were talking quietly but intensely at the counter. Alex was sniffing and blowing her nose, her eyes red. "I need to do this, Peter. For them. Jenny and Alex. I couldn't stand the thought of them getting hurt because of this. We already came too close."

Morgan looked at his friend, who was gazing back at him sympathetically. But Morgan thought he saw something else there, a sad sort of relief. And he understood. Conley had never had a family of his own. He had never had a lack of lovers; Morgan used to joke that Conley had a woman in every city in the world. But he had not gotten married and settled down, and did not have any plans to. It made him a great spook. He had nothing holding him back and tying him down. Morgan imagined that it would be a lot easier, not having to worry about what might happen to his family. But at the same time, it was a sadder, emptier existence. As he looked at Jenny and Alex at the counter, he was filled with love. More than anything, they gave his life meaning, they gave his actions weight. He could not imagine giving that up for anything.

"There's one more thing," said Morgan. He took the memory card out of his pocket and laid it on the table in between himself and Conley. "I believe this is yours."

Conley picked it up and examined it as if it were a precious jewel. "This has traveled a hell of a long way to make it back into my hands."

"And now what are you going to do about it?" said Morgan.

"Nothing yet," said Conley, as he stowed the plastic chip in a jacket pocket. "It's not enough anymore. Especially now that we know for certain that we can't trust the Agency. We have to sit on this until we know the whole picture, along with the things you took from Plante."

Morgan nodded. "Then we know what the mission is."

"Cougar and Cobra, together again, huh?" Conley was smiling wearily, despite himself.

"Cougar and Cobra," said Morgan. He grinned, then looked over at Alex, sitting at the counter with her mother. "I need to go over there. I need to explain this to my daughter. About what happened. And about why we have to go."

"Good luck," said Conley sincerely.

Morgan walked slowly toward the counter, making sure that his daughter saw him approach. He stood with Jenny in between him and Alex. "Hi, I . . ." he said, trailing off, without knowing what to say.

Alex looked up, her moist, puffy, bloodshot eyes expressing both devastation and defiance.

Jenny tenderly kissed her daughter's head and got up. "I'll let you two talk," she said, excusing herself.

Morgan sat down on the stool beside Alex. She looked down at her plate, pushing a soggy fry around with a toothpick. He didn't know what to say. Morgan could go into a war zone and face off against the deadliest men on the planet without a second thought. He had undertaken missions that endangered his life again and again. By the odds, he should have died five times over by now. He had come out of all that alive, and on all those assignments, fear had never hampered him. And yet, here she was, a still-impressionable teenage girl, and he was terrified to speak to her.

She sure wasn't giving him an opening. *Well*, he thought, taking a deep breath, *I just have to go for it*. "Look, kiddo," he started, "there are lots of things I wish I had done differently. One is that I should have trusted you with my secret. I should have told you years ago, and I'm sorry I didn't." He paused for breath. Her eyes, still looking the other way, showed the slightest signs of softening.

"Back at the cabin . . . you saw a side of me that I hoped you would never know, and I'm sorry." He cleared his throat. "But I have never been sorry about anything I did to protect this country and my family. And in the end, it's really about you, because you're the most important person in the world to me. You and your mother. Did you know that?"

She didn't look up, but a tear rolled from her eye and dropped from her cheek to the counter, her aloofness melting. Her shoulders were hunched, and her hands were no longer playing with the plate but were in her lap. "That's supposed to make me feel better?" she said bitterly. "That you did all those horrible things for my sake?" She looked away, sniffling.

Morgan took a deep breath. "I've got to go away tomorrow, early in the morning. It will be hard for me, because all I want is to stay with you and watch over you. But I have to go to protect you, and I might not make it back. That's something I was always aware of, on every mission I went on. After I met your mother, I had to tell her, every time I left on a mission, everything I wanted to say to her, because I knew I might not get another chance. So I'll say this to you, Alex. If I never talk to you again, if you never forgive me or understand me, just know that I love you, more than anything, and that everything I did, I did it thinking about what was best for you."

She didn't respond, didn't look up, just sat there, choking on her sobs. He sighed, got up, and before he walked away, heard her say, quietly, "I love you, too, Dad. I just don't like you anymore."

He sighed. It would have to do.

CHAPTER 30

Lester Hodges checked his watch, but it was more a gesture of irritation than anything else. He had been sitting at his table for two at La Martine for over half an hour, and that was forty-five minutes longer than he was willing to wait for anyone, especially a punk junior senator from Pennsylvania. A waiter silently refilled his water glass. Hodges tapped the empty glass that had contained his gin and tonic. "Another one," he grunted. "And don't be stingy with the booze this time."

Soon another waiter placed his sixteen-ounce New York strip steak in front of him. *It better be rare*, he thought. "Make it so rare, it's illegal," Hodges always said when he ordered, chuckling. But he wasn't chuckling now. He took the steak knife and tore into the meat. It was a pale pink. He motioned to the waiter.

"You call this rare?" he growled, pointing to the steak as if the waiter had put a turd on the plate.

"My sincerest apologies, sir," he responded, obligingly. "I will send it back to the kitchen at once, sir. We'll have another one out for you right away."

"Goddamn better."

The waiter took the plate away, and Hodges hit his fist hard on the table. That idiot senator—some young Martha's-Vineyard-vacationing asshole playboy who had probably read a book on negotiation tactics once and thought that made him enough of a man to play with the big boys—establishing dominance or some shit like that. Hodges ate whelps like him for breakfast. He didn't need a book to tell him how to establish dominance. Hell, he'd *written* the book on intimidation. He could make that bastard shit his pants just by looking at him.

Hodges was so angry, he almost missed the man who had walked into the restaurant, cruised right past the hostess, and headed straight for his table. This was a man in his late thirties or early forties, wide-shouldered and solidly built, in serious shape, wearing a garish Hawaiian shirt, large sunglasses, and carrying a thin folder of some kind. Hodges had never seen the man before in his life, but like so many people he had just met, Hodges disliked him. The man pulled out the chair, straddled it, and sat down, encroaching on his space, facing him from across the table.

"Hello, Lester."

Hodges's eyes narrowed. "Who the hell are you?" Hodges saw another man approaching: Keller, his chief of security, who had been watching from a corner of the room. He stood by. If Hodges raised a finger, he would throw this guy out into the street like a dog and give him a couple kicks in the gut for good measure. All he had to do was give the signal.

"What the hell are you, a journalist? You with some newspaper or something?"

"No," the man said, laughing. "Not quite. I'm more of a freelancer. My name," he continued, "is . . . now listen well, because I want you to remember this, and it looks like you've had a few already, and you might forget. I'm known as Cobra."

Hodges looked speechlessly at the man, this man known up until this moment by code name only. The man who had been causing him so much trouble, whom no one seemed to be able to find, and who was now sitting so close to him at a table, it was as if they had a goddamn lunch date. All he could do was stare.

"So you've heard of me," said Cobra. "Good. That makes this even simpler. I want you to listen well. I know you answer to someone. You're not smart enough to pull this off on your own. I want you to tell him that I found you, and I want you to tell him that I'm coming for him. He can hide, but sooner or later, I'm going to get him."

Hodges laughed uproariously. "What the hell are you gonna do? As far as I'm concerned, you're a fly on the wall. You're an ant under my feet. In fact, I'm having a hard time figuring out why I shouldn't just have Keller here take care of you right now." He noticed that some people in the restaurant were staring.

"Oh, I don't think you want to do that, Lester."

Hodges gave the signal, and Keller reached out to put his hand on Cobra's shoulder. But Cobra was quicker. He blocked Keller's arm, grabbed two of his fingers, and snapped them back with a sickening crack. His leg swooped under Keller, causing him to fall hard, drawing gasps from other patrons and staff.

"What are you looking for here?" demanded Hodges

angrily. "A payoff or something? You looking for money, Cobra?"

"No, Lester, I'm not interested in your money," he said. "Here's what I want. I want to watch you squirm. I know what your division has been up to. Your dirty little secret: I know, and I want you to know that I know. And I want your boss to know, too. And I want you two to go on with your lives, knowing that I'm coming for you. When you least expect it, I'll strike, and I'll hit you both hard. You got that?"

Hodges could only glare at him, his right hand gripping the steak knife involuntarily. Through his fury, he said, "I don't know who you think you are or what you're hoping to accomplish here, but you should remember something, too. You've threatened the wrong man this time, and believe me, you're gonna pay."

Cobra got up, looking satisfied with himself, and turned to walk away.

You think you won, don't you? Hodges thought. He motioned for Keller to approach. Keller, who had quickly gotten to his feet despite his injured fingers, leaned down, and Hodges said quietly, "Follow that man. I want to know his real name, his address, and the name of his goddamn third-grade teacher by the end of the hour! And have the car brought around." Keller motioned to the other two bodyguards and gave them instructions while cradling his injured left hand. Then he rushed out the door to follow Cobra. Hodges got up and charged behind him. The maître d' made the slightest move to get in his way. "Put it on my tab," Hodges barked at him. "And don't you dare charge me for that overcooked steak!" He barged past, out of the restaurant, into the sunny DC street.

His town car pulled up. Once inside, he got out his phone, fumbled with the buttons, and made the call. The phone rang twice, and then he heard, "Les, what is it?"

"Ed," he said, "I gotta see you. I don't care where you are or what you're doing. I gotta see you *right now*."

Morgan hit the street at a brisk pace, and with a mere glance toward the gray sedan he knew was parked on the curb across the street, he turned and began walking west. The street was a wide, one-way thoroughfare, sidewalks packed with pedestrians who occasionally broke off randomly to cross the street. The use of the crosswalk here, if it ever happened, was purely incidental.

"You think he'll bite?" said Conley's voice in Morgan's ear.

"Yeah, he'll bite," said Morgan, after tacking a Bluetooth receiver to his ear for show. It would attract less attention if people thought he was on the phone, but the real transmitter was an undetectable earpiece that was lodged in his ear. It was state-of-the-art and practically invisible. Not the kind of equipment available at Radio Shack, but Conley still had the contacts in the city to hook them up. "I got a chance to size him up in there," Morgan continued, dodging a woman with a baby stroller. "He's got more balls than brains, that one. You got the tracker onto his car?"

"Without great complication," said Conley.

"That's why I always picked you as my partner, Peter. Now, what do you see?"

"You've got a tail," said Conley, unworried. It was all part of the plan. "About thirty paces back and closing. Tall man, black hair. He looks like he's holding something in his hands."

"Yeah, that'll be his fingers," Morgan chuckled. He went on without looking back or giving any sign that he was aware of the man following him. "Just like old times, eh?" Morgan said jovially.

"I'd love to reminisce, Cobra, but I think your attention would be put to better use by concentrating on the mission, huh?"

"Just be where you need to be at the right time, and leave the rest to me."

"Got it, partner. See you in"—a short pause—"three minutes, twenty-six seconds. Out."

Morgan squeezed his way past pedestrians, sustaining a pace that was quick enough to keep his tail on the verge of losing him but not hurried enough to actually lose him.

Two blocks down, Morgan turned a corner, and the busy road became a tiny back street, wholly residential, with parked cars half on the sidewalk, where an old woman carrying groceries was the only soul in sight. He walked another block and didn't have to look back to know that Keller was behind him and closing. *That's right, asshole, just keep coming.*

Morgan turned into the alley and made right for the trash can. He took off the lid, stuck his hand in, and his fingers closed around the grip of Wagner's tranquilizer gun, right where he'd left it, along with a tiny belt of spare darts. "Just in case," Conley had said.

Morgan and Conley had predicted that he would be

followed out of the restaurant and decided it wouldn't do to kill someone in a crowded city. A corpse attracted police and the media. On the other hand, when people see a guy passed out in the alley, they assume he's drunk and, for the most part, leave him alone.

Morgan hid behind a Dumpster and clicked the safety off. He had taken Keller by surprise in the restaurant. To be bodyguard to a guy like Hodges, Keller would have to have some serious combat training. Plus, he must be a good ten years younger than Morgan. This guy would be able to handle himself. *All the more reason to bring him down with the first shot*, he told himself.

He heard Keller's footsteps, hurrying down the alley. This was going to be even easier than he had thought. He raised the gun to take aim. Keller would be wearing body armor, but the needle would go right through the bulletproof mesh. Morgan aimed it about chest-high and inhaled. Keller passed the Dumpster, moving at a measured trot toward the end of the alley. The dart left the muzzle with a whisper and plunged into Keller's back. He yelped in surprise and spun around, a savage look on his face. *Fall. Fall, Damn it!* He didn't. He saw Morgan and charged. With no time to reload, Morgan tossed aside the gun and the darts and braced for impact.

He ducked as Keller swung at his face, but the bodyguard followed it up by sinking his fist into Morgan's gut. Morgan doubled down involuntarily, and Keller elbowed him hard in the back. Morgan fell forward on the paved ground.

He lay there for a second, dazed, until he felt Keller's

arm wrap around his neck, getting him in a choke hold. He groped for the dart gun, hoping to use it as a bludgeon. His hands hadn't found the gun, but they had closed around something—the tiny belt of darts.

Keller raised him to his feet, the meaty, muscular arm tightening its grip on Morgan's neck, cutting off his air and circulation. He could feel himself fading away as he thrashed, trying to break free, to no avail. He only had one chance. With fumbling fingers, he flipped the plastic covers off each needle in the belt. Holding the curled-up belt in his fist, he stabbed it, as hard as he could, into Keller's neck.

Keller released him and staggered back with a roar of pain. Morgan relaxed. But Keller didn't and retorted with a hell of a right hook to Morgan's temple, which caused him to trip on a discarded cardboard box and fall forward. His head fuzzy, phasing in and out of focus, Morgan was dimly aware of Keller bending down and picking up a two-by-four. Morgan rolled onto his back just in time to see this mountain of a man, looming for what seemed like miles over him, raise the piece of wood far above his head, ready to come down and crush Morgan's skull. Still dazed from the punch, Morgan could only raise his hands ineffectively, waiting for the blow.

It didn't come. He looked up at Keller and saw that he had an oddly blank look on his face. He blinked hard three times, frowning in dumb confusion. Then his fingers slackened, and the plank fell to the ground. He tumbled forward, onto his knees, and collapsed on top of Morgan.

It took more strength than Morgan expected to roll

him off and onto his back beside him. Morgan got up and wobbled to the far end of the alley, aching all over. The alley opened to a back street where Conley sat in the idling car.

"What the hell happened to your face?" asked Conley. Morgan touched his face and noticed that blood was trickling down his nose, which was tender and swollen.

"I thought you said the effect of the tranquilizer was instantaneous," said Morgan, his voice muffled because his nose was blocked by the blood and swelling.

"Well, you know," said Conley, "as with all your narcotics, your mileage may vary. There's a first-aid kit in the glove compartment."

Morgan took out the kit and applied some gauze to his nose. "Do you have a lock on Hodges?" he asked.

"Here, take a look for yourself." Conley handed him a device that didn't look much different than a latest-generation cell phone. It showed two dots moving on a digital map. "He's about a mile to the north. It shouldn't take us long to catch up. Think you can navigate with that leaky nose of yours?"

Morgan nodded and poked gingerly at it, checking for damage. At least it didn't feel broken. "Yeah, I got this. You're going to want to take the next left." Morgan unbuttoned his Hawaiian shirt, took it off, and put on a fresh black T-shirt he had brought along.

"Think he'll lead us to our man?" asked Conley.

"He'd better," said Morgan. "Because I'm getting tired of this shit."

CHAPTER 31

Morgan and Conley caught up with Hodges's town car in a few minutes, and Conley maintained a distance of a few blocks between them. They avoided visual contact—there was no need for it while they had the tracker. They drove for nearly an hour, as the city gave way to an industrial suburb. As the cars grew sparser, Conley had to keep a greater distance to avoid being seen, until they were almost a mile behind their quarry. Finally, the little dot on the map came to a stop.

They were driving alongside a row of warehouses, run-down and separated from the street by a rusty old chain-link fence topped with equally rusty barbed wire. He could see Hodges's car peeking out of a gaping section of one labeled Warehouse 6, which was about two hundred feet away. As Conley drove past without slowing down, Morgan saw Hodges get out of the driver's seat and stride furiously into the warehouse, where two guards were posted at the door. Conley turned into a narrow side street and parked the car.

"Got the camera?" asked Conley. Morgan pulled out

a digital SLR with a massive telephoto lens. They got out of the car and slinked toward Warehouse 6, which was now half a mile away. They were halfway there when Conley held up a hand, in their old signal that meant "stop." "Hold on," he said. "I think someone else is coming."

They bolted behind a Dumpster as another car, a sleek silver Audi sedan, rolled in through the gate in the fence and into the open warehouse door.

Morgan scanned the surroundings. He couldn't go in through the same gate as the car, or he would be seen, and the fence was too high to climb over. The warehouses closest to them, he had noticed, were liberally covered in graffiti. His eyes ran along the fence, looking for something he knew must be there. He found it, a short way back toward where they had parked—a gap in the fence, concealed, not large, but large enough for him to squeeze through.

"Conley, I'm going in."

"Are you crazy?"

"I need to see who it is. I need to hear what they're saying. Do you have your comm?" Conley nodded. "Good. Try to get a clear view of the inside from out here. I'll keep you posted when I can."

Before Conley could protest, Morgan ran for the gap in the fence, pulling a thread in his shirt as he wriggled through it. He dashed for the warehouse, taking cover behind car-sized boxes wrapped in tarp that were arranged in the yard, until he approached number six.

Now what? He was too likely to be seen if he approached from the front, but coming in from the back would put a huge empty warehouse between him and his targets. That's when he looked up at the graffiti again.

It hung down like a hem over the edge. The roof here was not at the very top of the warehouse but was over a squatter area that jutted from its side. The kids who tagged it had to have gotten up there somehow. If they could, so could he. He ran along the side of the warehouse through the little alley between it and the one next to it. He got his answer when he rounded the back corner and found a service ladder that led to the roof.

He climbed it, slowly, steadily, as quietly as possible, until it took him to the top. Over the edge, he saw—beyond the small nest of discarded joint tips and cigarette butts—just what he hoped for: windows, waist-high from the top surface of the lower tier.

His real problem, of course, was the roof itself. It looked strong enough to hold him, but even a light step might reverberate loudly in the expansive hollow of the warehouse. This was the time to be careful and methodical. He made his way across the roof, one . . . step . . . at . . . a . . . time.

What should have been a thirty-second walk at a leisurely pace took him nearly three minutes of cautious, deliberate movement. He could just barely hear the voices of two men barking at each other below. Standing right above them, he peeked into the window, concealing himself as much as possible. He could see them both, but it took him a few seconds to make out the other man's face through the glare from the clear blue sky. *Son of a bitch.*

"Cougar," he said, only loud enough for Conley to

hear him over the comm, "it's Nickerson. It's Senator Edgar Nickerson."

"Shit," said Conley, through his earpiece. "We got him, Cobra. That's all we needed. Now get the hell out of there."

"I need to hear what they're saying."

"Cobra, don't be stupid. We have our lead. Sticking around is suicide."

Morgan chose to ignore Conley. Chances like this didn't come around every day. He edged closer to the window. The roof underneath him creaked, and he froze. But the two men seemed to take no notice, so he leaned in and listened.

"The son of a bitch knows, Ed. He's got proof."

"He didn't ask for anything?"

"No. He basically came out and said that the point was just to rattle us."

"I'm glad to see that's not working at all."

"You think I'm scared? I'm not scared of that . . . that piece of crap. He'll be begging for me to let him die by the time I'm done with him."

"I'm sure. Do you know who that piece of crap is, Les? He's a former CIA spook. A good one, too. You think your hired monkeys can take him? You think they can outsmart a man like him? You think *you* can, Les?"

"I took care of the journalist, didn't I?"

"You sent your goons to 'disappear' some uppity little basset hound who got a whiff of a Pulitzer, and you think you can handle this?"

"And what would you do, huh?"

"Forget it, Les. I'll take care of it. Just have your men stay out of my way."

The roof under Morgan creaked again. Nickerson looked up. "What was that?"

"It's probably nothing."

It wasn't nothing. The surface under Morgan's feet was wobbling. The corroded structure of that corner of the roof was buckling under his weight.

"It's just some animal or something, Ed."

He had to get out of there. He got up, slowly, but even the shifting of his weight was too much, and the whole roof deck emitted a long, low groan.

"There's someone up there!"

It took about five seconds from when Nickerson said those words to the moment shots began flying at Morgan. With no thought of stealth, he made for the ladder. Bullets punctured the roof, which shook unsteadily underneath him. Each step telegraphed his location to the shooters, and the bullets were never very wide off their mark. He ran to the edge.

The ladder. There was no time to turn around. He bent down and, holding the top rung, swung over into empty space. But he was too heavy, the structure too old. The screws that held the ladder in place were ripped out, and Morgan, clutching the ladder tightly, fell backward into empty space.

The ladder twisted with a metallic whine, bending under his weight and hurtling him toward the ground. He braced for impact; but instead, it jerked his arm hard, holding him some three feet off the ground. It held, bent like a decrepit old man, but it held. Morgan breathed a sigh of relief and dropped to the ground.

With shots still resounding inside the warehouse, Morgan ran, taking the back route to Conley and the car. They would reconvene and find a way to get to Nickerson. They would—

A pipe swung out of nowhere in front of his eyes, and then pain, blinding pain, and he was on the ground. His addled brain tried to make sense of things. *Someone hidden around the corner of the next warehouse, waiting for him.* He was struggling to hold on, to stay awake, but oblivion washed over him in waves. Just before he was completely submerged, he saw the sinister, arresting beauty of T's face looking at him and smiling, perversely, like a rogue elf at Christmas.

CHAPTER 32

Morgan and T collapsed together on the bed, side by side, taut young bodies glistening with sweat.

"That's going to leave a mark," Morgan said, still gasping for air.

"I think it may have left a few," she said as she looked him over.

His own eyes followed the curves of her nakedness and how the morning light, filtering in through sheer curtains, played on her porcelain skin. Outside, birds chirped, and intermittently he heard the dull ring of cowbells, and an occasional moo—the sounds of an alpine village.

"I hope," said T, stretching catlike on the bed, "that we have not bothered Frau Kappel. There isn't another inn for miles and miles."

He smiled at her and stroked her soft hair. She leaned in and gave him a lingering kiss. "I love you," she said in a whisper.

Morgan, at a loss, didn't respond. He knew, of course, how to lie, and had this been an assignment, he would have reciprocated convincingly. But his relationship with Natasha had long since ceased to be an assignment, and the last thing he would do would be to deceive her. The truth was, he could not honestly tell her the same. She looked down, disappointed at his hesitation.

"Checkers?" he suggested hopefully. It was clumsy, but it was an out for both of them. She nodded weakly. He arranged the pieces on the board, which was already laid out on a table from an earlier game. She looked out the window silently, then sat across from him.

They had played more than a hundred games of checkers since that first night. Every game had been riveting, a true match of wills, and all their matches, every single one of them, had ended in a stalemate. But her game that day was slow and distracted, and she made two mistakes toward the beginning that put even the stalemate into jeopardy. She seemed agitated, nervous.

"Hey, listen, T, I . . ." he began. "I'm sorry, all right?"

She scowled at him. "It's not that, you idiot."

"Then what is it? "

"The mission. Going back there. It frightens me." She grimaced, scrunching her delicate face, and then with a roar of rage flung the checkerboard at a far wall. The board made a visible dent in the finish.

"You could just stay, you know," he said softly.

"No. I can't."

"There's no reason for you to go back." he insisted. "Stay here. Let us take care of this for you. We'll bring your brother to you."

"No. You know that if I don't go back, they will kill him."

He didn't have an answer for her. He knew it was probably true. He'd gladly trade her brother's life for hers, any day. But her feelings for her brother, he knew, went beyond just familial piety. She loved him, loved him dearly. "He kept us alive," she had once told him. "When my father died, and as my mother slowly killed herself with drink. He was my father and mother then. I owed him the shoes on my feet and the clothes on my back. I owed him my daily bread. I would have languished, cold and starving, without him. But he provided for me, and he taught me to live. If I had many lifetimes to give, it would still not repay—" Her voice cracked, and she turned away from him, covering her face. That was the only occasion he had ever seen her cry.

"Are you sure there isn't anything I can do to convince you to stay?" he asked her, one last time.

"No. Just hold me," she said. Outside, a cowbell rang.

He held her tight and made love to her one more time.

CHAPTER 33

Morgan regained consciousness with a start and found himself in a room with concrete walls, a concrete floor and ceiling, and exposed pipes that emerged from concrete to end in concrete. It was all concrete except for a rusted metal door that looked shut tightly from the outside.

Still groggy, he tried to move his arms and noticed that he was handcuffed to one of the pipes, which was thicker than his thigh and stretched from floor to ceiling. He was seated on a metal chair, his feet tied to its legs. The only other thing in the room was a table against a side wall. He saw all this by the dead yellow light of a dim, incandescent bulb that hung from a wire. The room was dark and damp. Why did these places always have to be dark and damp?

He racked his brain, trying to remember being brought there, how long he'd been out, or any clue as to where he might be, but it was no use. He wondered about Conley. Had he tried to attack T after Morgan was captured? If so, was Conley sitting in an identical room, a few yards over? Or maybe he was dead and stuffed in the trunk of a car. But there was nothing Morgan could do to help him now, and he had to assume that Conley had no way of helping him, either.

He ran his fingers along the handcuffs. They were high-security, hard to pick even if he had something to pick them with. Nor would he have time to, he realized when he heard footsteps echoing faintly from outside the door, getting louder. They stopped just outside, he heard the sliding of a dead bolt, and the door creaked open. It was T. Beautiful, deadly Natasha, wearing formfitting black pants, a black top, and heavy boots that contrasted starkly with her fair skin and hair.

"I see you are awake. I was getting concerned that you would be out for the whole day." She was calm and breezy, a cat playing with her prey.

"I'm not dead yet," he said, shaking off the haze. "Which means you must still want something from me."

"How very American of you," she said. "All business. No time for old friends." She was still stunning, and even now, her presence woke something intoxicating in him. He had the feeling she knew it, too. Even now, she moved seductively, looking at him with those deep, alluring eyes. "Well, then, here is the business, Cobra. You have some photographs. Photographs in which I believe I am featured."

"Yeah, but you don't have to worry, sweetheart. They got you on your good side."

T smirked. "Ah, yes, I had forgotten. Cobra laughs in the face of death. But you won't be laughing very long, I don't think."

"Oh, is it the threat portion of our evening already?"

"I assure you," she said, her eyes narrowing, "it will be very short."

"Then let's get to it, shall we? Tell me you're going to torture me until I tell you what you want to know. Tell me I can stop it at any time, whenever I want, that all I have to do is talk, and you'll let me go."

"I will not tell you that I will let you go. I believe that would be an insult to your intelligence. You know very well that I will not let you leave this room alive. But answer my questions, and I promise you that your death will be quick."

"Go ahead and make it slow if you want to. My schedule's wide open."

She remained unflappable. "Humor," she said. "The last refuge of the weak. You won't be cracking jokes after I've worked you over for a few hours."

"I'll be cracking jokes until long after you're dead," he said.

"Oh, good," she said. "I like it when they are cocky. It's that much sweeter when they break. Do you want to know how it's going to go, Morgan? Why don't I tell you, you know, out of professional courtesy? We are going to start off light. I start you off with no permanent damage. No toys, no tools. If you talk then, you will still be a reasonably good-looking corpse. But if you don't answer all my questions, then I start getting creative.

"I like to improvise—did you know that? I'm not one of those who likes to carry around a little toolbox with dainty little instruments like a surgeon. Why would you want to, when you know the damage you can do with everyday implements—a hammer, a pair of pliers, a vise. Who needs all this precision equipment when all you really need is access to your neighborhood hardware store?"

"I tend to prefer Home Depot myself," he said. "They have the best selection of torture gadgets anywhere in the lower forty-eight. Listen, if you're going to go on much longer, do you mind if I step out to use the bathroom?"

She didn't hold back her laughter. Morgan knew that she was in control, and so did she.

"Why don't we get started, then?" she said.

"Please, go ahead," he said, nonchalantly. "Here, I was starting to think you had decided to bore me into talking—"

The back of her hand hit him across the face before he saw it coming, stinging his cheek. The impact made his head and his injured nose ring with pain.

"Where is the memory card?" she demanded. He stared ahead. She hit him harder.

"Who else knows?" Another smack jangled his senses, followed by another and another.

He touched his tongue to where his teeth had cut into his stinging cheek and tasted blood. He looked into her eyes and gave her a mocking, red-toothed smile to mask his anger. He wasn't going to give her any satisfaction. "You hit like a girl."

"You really think you can annoy your way out of this situation?"

He shrugged. "Worked once in Nicaragua."

T laughed uproariously. "You amuse me, Cobra, even now. You really haven't changed. Still the same posturing fool you were before. Tell me, do you still believe that all you did was justified by a noble cause? Do you still believe you are an honorable man?"

"I don't believe it, T," he said, with a serious tone in his voice. "I know it."

"Ah, so certain, so pure," she said sarcastically. "A killer with a pristine soul."

"I know I'm not like you," he said. "I'm not a mercenary. I'm not a traitor." This last word had a sharp edge to it. It was meant to cut deep.

She laughed again, this time bitterly. "You are exactly like me in every way except that you will not admit it. Instead, you play house with your wife and daughter. You pretend to be a normal person in your suburban home with your white picket fence and your dog and two-point-five automobiles. But you know what you are inside. You're a killer. A willing puppet of the CIA, an agency you knew was corrupt and decadent and weak. An executioner who dresses your murderous instinct in the ideals of nationalism. But beneath it all, Cobra, you're a killer and nothing more."

"Believe what you like," he said. "I know what I know."

"Do you want to know something else?" she continued. "I was like you once. A believer. Do you think I defected to America because I found it convenient, or because the CIA offered me more money or a more comfortable life? You know different. I didn't care for those things. It hurt me deeply to leave my homeland. But I had grown to abhor the history of my country, and the crimes that persisted even after the Soviet Union fell. All the while I grew to believe in American ideals. In freedom. I truly wanted to be an American. I was willing to risk my life for it, and to continue to risk my life in the service of the country I chose.

"And then," she continued, her voice rising to a fever pitch, "I found out you murdered my brother. What hypocrites—this government, the Agency, and you, with your own double standard. You, Cobra, who's supposedly so full of honor, so loyal! But I finally found out the truth. There is no honor, no higher calling or true cause. Only petty men lusting for power and money. The truth, the truth that you know deep down inside, Cobra, is that the lying scumbags are right. Power is the only currency of the world. It is the only thing that matters in the end. I know you know this, because I learned it from you."

"That's a pretty neat story . . . very deep stuff," he said acerbically. "Except it's all bullshit."

"Liar!" she cried, suddenly livid. "Is it bullshit that my brother is dead? Is it bullshit that you killed him, murdered him in Prague when you were supposed to help him escape—when his survival was the only condition, the only thing I asked for in return for my defection? No! The bullshit, the lie, is what was fed to me after that, told to me by the people I had trusted, by the very government that I had sworn my allegiance to at great personal peril. You told me Andrei was killed by Russian Intelligence in Prague, isn't that right? Isn't that the official story? Isn't that what was told to me to cover up the fact that *you* killed him?"

He sighed, looking down. "You weren't supposed to know."

"So do you admit it, then? From your own lips? You admit you killed Andrei?"

"Yes, Natasha," he said, looking her in the eye and keeping a steady voice. "I killed your brother. I don't deny it. But I did not betray you; *he* did. He was giving you up to his superiors. It was going to be a big feather in his cap—an agent so loyal, he turned in his own sister."

"More lies!"

"It's true, T. We wanted your brother on our side as much as we wanted you. Why would we want to kill him? He had already betrayed you. If I hadn't stopped him, you would never have made it to Paris."

"No," she said, but her confidence was wavering. "Andrei would not have done that. He couldn't have!"

"Couldn't he, Natasha? Wasn't that the kind of man he was? Fiercely loyal to Mother Russia, no matter what?"

"No," she said weakly, but it didn't sound like she believed it anymore. She was hunched over, the palms of her hands on the table supporting her weight. All the catlike elegance was gone, all pretense of seduction. She seemed all of a sudden weak and defenseless.

"We're not enemies, T," he said, in the most comforting voice that he could muster. "There's no reason for us to be fighting."

She looked at him, and, for a second, he thought she was moving to untie him, that he had gained an ally, made his enemy a friend. Then, like flipping a switch, her face contorted into an expression of bitter amusement, all the vulnerability that had been there a second before, gone. She cackled like a hyena. "Well done, Cobra. No wonder you survived so long in the business. Not only are you quick on your feet, but you can spin a good story in a tight spot. You even got me— *me*—there, for a second."

"Natasha. Natasha. T, listen to me. I'm not lying to you," he insisted. "We should be on the same side."

"Of course you are lying. We are all liars." She took a dirty, oily cloth and stuffed it into his mouth. "You chose your side when you killed Andrei. There is nothing else to say."

She swung her hand hard across his face once more, and he bit down hard on the cloth in his mouth. "Okay, Cobra," she said. "Let us get started, then, shall we?"

CHAPTER 34

At age eighteen, Dan Morgan had a life and a plan. He was the star football player in high school, and while he didn't have the height or weight to play in the NFL, he got scholarship offers from a few good, small schools, through his drive and innate athletic ability, coupled with generally good grades. But things changed when he arrived at college. Frustrated with the seeming futility of his classes and with being a bench-warmer to the hulking beasts who populated the field in the Varsity team, he quit a few months in to join the Army.

Upon arriving at Fort Jackson for basic, Morgan got into trouble with his drill instructor in about the length of time it took him to get off the bus. Morgan was a patriot, but at that moment, it dawned on him that the armed forces might not be for him. His fierce independence left him with a very low tolerance for the strict hierarchy and order of the military.

The drill instructor, eyes squinted into slits, was walking down the line of drafted men in front of their bus, his chin held high, when Morgan spat on the ground. The DI marched at him with the fury of a charging bull.

"Is this the corner bar, maggot?" he yelled into Morgan's face.

Morgan looked forward blankly.

"I asked you a question, recruit!" he snapped.

"No, it isn't," said Morgan.

"No it isn't, *what*?"

"No it isn't, *sir*," said Morgan.

"I will teach you conduct befitting a soldier," said the DI. "Now, on your knees, and lick that up!"

Morgan looked at him incredulously. "No," he said.

The DI swung, and before Morgan could react, his fist connected with Morgan's gut. Morgan doubled over in pain and surprise.

"Lick it up!"

Morgan seethed. "No," he said through his teeth. *He picked the wrong guy to make an example of.* Morgan curled the fingers of his right hand into a fist. *Screw the hierarchy.* If that bastard touched him again, he wouldn't hold back.

"*Lick it up.*"

The DI hit him again, but this time, Morgan reacted with an uppercut to the DI's jaw. The DI reeled back. Morgan tensed, bracing for the next blow, when he heard someone shout, "Stand down!"

Morgan later learned that the voice belonged to a lieutenant, who had then walked over and told the DI, "Enough, officer. You'll have plenty of time to whip these ladies into shape." Morgan looked at him with gratitude, but the lieutenant's face remained stern, except for, Morgan noticed, an ever so slight, appreciative satisfaction playing around the corners of his mouth. *Hell of a start to my Army career*, thought Morgan. He spent most of the rest of the day running, submerged in constant hollering from the DI.

In basic training, Morgan had instruction in hand-to-hand combat and the use of weapons, and he excelled in both. Most of the time, however, was spent in repetitive, exhausting, pointless drills. He was afraid the DI was going to make his life hell for punching a man of his rank, but instead, the instructor evidently recognized that Morgan had a talent that set him above the other recruits. By the end of their third week, Morgan had advanced to platoon leader.

Though he had gotten on to the DI's good side, that distinction made enemies within the platoon. By the fourth week of training, he had already gotten into several fights and into a sustained feud with a loudmouth, idiot bastard named Gibbs. Gibbs was the kind of guy who liked to gang up on the smaller recruits, to intimidate them and smack them around. Morgan had never been able to tolerate petty bullying, and so he had called Gibbs out. They arranged for an after-hours fight in a pit behind the barracks.

He and Gibbs met in the dim twilight, with the whole platoon watching expectantly. Among them was the DI, standing with arms crossed. Morgan stood, facing his opponent, and someone called the beginning of the fight.

Gibbs was big, but he was slow and stupid. Morgan easily ducked his clumsy punches, hitting him with quick jabs in return. After a brief tussle, Morgan made him hit the dust. The others held him back before he could do more significant damage. But during that fight, Gibbs did do some damage—he tackled Morgan, who hit his right knee hard against a rock, the first in a series of blows to his knee that, years later, would continue to give him grief.

He was sent to the infirmary after the fight. After a short stint, during which they tended to his knee, he was told to report to the captain's office. *Oh, shit*, he thought. But when he went in, the captain wasn't there. Instead, there were two suits in sunglasses and fedoras waiting for him.

"Hello, Morgan," said one of them. "My name's Wilcox, and this here's Runyan." Each shook his hand in turn.

"We've been following your brief career here at Fort Jackson," said Runyan, "and I must say, we're very impressed."

"Very impressed indeed," said Wilcox. "Your test scores are laudable, and you've shown real leadership among the other men. You really caught the eye of your superior officers."

"We'd like to ask a few questions, if you don't mind," said Runyan.

"I guess I don't," Morgan said.

The questions were vague and circumspect, and when they dismissed him a half hour later, he thought nothing of it. Nobody else mentioned the encounter, and he had learned by now not to ask unnecessary questions. But the encounter gnawed at his mind. All through that week, it was never far from his consciousness. One week later, he was called in again, and the same two men were there.

"Are you considering a career in the armed forces?"

"How do you feel about U.S. involvement in the Middle East?"

"We see you've requested to be a Green Beret. What's your motivation behind that?"

"Tell us, Morgan, do you like the Army?"

"No, not really," Morgan had replied honestly to the last question. "Maybe it'll be different once I get out of basic training, but right now, I can't stand my superiors."

They left again with no further explanation. After yet another week went by, Morgan was called again to the captain's office.

"I think it's about time you knew the score, Morgan," said Wilcox. "We're with a certain clandestine government agency, and we happen to be recruiting. We're looking for exceptional young men, the best of the best. And we are very interested in you."

"Very interested," cut in Runyan. "There are just a few more tests we'd like you to undergo, if you accept."

Morgan agreed. This time, they sat him down with a psychiatrist, who grilled him with questions about his personal life, his political beliefs, his patriotism, and how far he was willing to go for his country, all of which Morgan answered as truthfully as he could. After that, he sat down with Wilcox and Runyan once more.

"We're with the CIA, Morgan," said Runyan. "If you decide to come with us, we'll give you the finest training a man can get, courtesy of Uncle Sam. You'll travel the world, gather intel, run operations, and help to make history."

"Just tell me where to sign," said Morgan, grinning.

Runyan smiled back at him. "Excellent! I had a feeling you would say yes. We'll get you out of here and into training right away."

"About that, " said Morgan. "I want an honorable discharge."

The two men agreed, and they kept their word. Morgan showed up at home a few days later, unannounced, on Thanksgiving, still in his Army uniform. He couldn't tell his family why he was home. He had already taken an oath of secrecy and signed half a dozen papers. His father had been nervous, thinking he had gone AWOL. It didn't help that he had told his parents how much he hated putting up with all the basic-training bullshit. So he told them he had torn up his knee during basic training and had received an honorable medical discharge.

Ten days later he took a train from Boston to DC, where he was met by his two recruiters, Wilcox and Runyan, who drove him to a top-secret training facility called The Farm that would be Morgan's home for the next year.

"I'm putting this blindfold on you for the obvious reason," Wilcox had said. "The location of The Farm is a national secret. Its entire purpose is to break you down, both mentally and physically, in ways you could never have imagined."

Unconvinced, Morgan flashed back to his high school football days—full jerseys, pads, and helmet in ninety-eight degrees, heat index of 106, double-session practices, until most of his teammates puked or passed out. But not Dan Morgan. His inner drive to be the best had kept him going. *How much tougher can this be?* he thought.

"The lead instructor is a man named Powers," Wilcox continued. "He's been an instructor at The Farm for fifteen years, as tough as they come. He washes out ninety percent of his trainees."

Sounded like just the kind of challenge Dan was looking for.

As the car came to a stop, Morgan was allowed to remove the blindfold. As his eyes adjusted to the sunlight, he saw that the facility was encircled by an electrified fence, razor wire, and armed guards and trained dogs to keep out any intruders that the surrounding dense woods and swamps hadn't already defeated.

Surveillance cameras lined the span of fence right up to a small brick guardhouse just inside the gate. The electronic gate opened, and the grim guard waved the vehicle though, saying, "They're expecting you."

They drove about a half mile and stopped in front of a small white office building. Morgan and Wilcox got out of the car to retrieve Morgan's duffel bag from the trunk.

"Good luck!" Wilcox said, echoed by Runyan from the open car window. "I have one piece of advice for you, Morgan," Wilcox said, walking back to the sedan. "If you don't want your life to be a living hell, whatever you do, don't piss Powers off."

With that, they drove away, leaving Morgan standing with his duffel bag on the curb. As he looked toward the office building, out came a large, barrel-chested man, walking straight toward him.

This must be Powers, Morgan thought. The man looked to be about forty-five years old, six feet three inches, 230 pounds. He sported a military crew cut and rough-looking skin, his deep tan offset by the white of a scar that cut into his right eyebrow. He was wearing a white tank top, black shorts, combat boots, and mirrored aviator sunglasses that hid his eyes. His choice of clothing was meant to intimidate new recruits, showing every ripped muscle in his legs and upper body. *Yep. This must be Powers,* Morgan's instincts told him. *This is the man who thinks he can break me. Let the games begin.*

Still silent and at attention, Morgan stood as Powers circled him, sizing him up, and then faced him, his mouth six inches from Morgan's nose, and barked, "Well! Aren't you the pretty boy! I bet you won't last one full day. Do you want to beat it out of here now, or should I kick your ass first?"

Morgan didn't flinch. "No!" he said.

Powers snapped back, "No, what?"

"No, I don't want to leave," said Morgan.

Powers shouted, "But you will! I promise you that, Pretty Boy. I will make your life so miserable, you'll beg to run home to your mommy and daddy. Do you understand me?"

"Yes," said Morgan.

"Yes, what?" screamed Powers. "Do I look like one of your pussy football buddies?"

"No," said Morgan.

"No, sir!" shouted Powers, with his eyes bulging and the veins in his neck and forehead popping out.

Powers face came within three inches of Morgan's as he screamed, "You call me 'sir' when you speak to me, you little pussy, or I will put my size thirteen boot so far up your ass, you'll be shitting leather for a year! Is that clear, Pretty Boy?"

"Sir, yes, sir!"

"Double-time it to that barracks." Powers pointed out a building about one hundred yards away. "Pick a cot, store your gear, change into shorts, T-shirt, and boots from the footlocker, and be out front in three minutes, or you will get your first taste of pain. Is that clear, Pretty Boy?"

"Yes, sir." Morgan took off for his new home. By the time he had stored his gear, changed into shorts, T-shirt, and boots and bolted from the barracks to the designated spot, exactly three minutes, one second had passed.

Powers again was in his face, berating him, yelling so hard, his spit frothed on his lips, spraying Morgan with his intensity. But the trainee stood his ground, showing no expression. Powers then chest-bumped him, screaming at him, chest to chest, "Do you want to go home, Pretty Boy? Do you want to cry? Do you want to hit me?"

"No, sir!" shouted Morgan.

No longer yelling, Powers asked with a stare of hatred, "Do you have a death wish, maggot?"

"No," Morgan said.

"No, *what*? You know, Pretty Boy, let's put an end to this nonsense right now. What you need is an ass-whoopin'," Powers said, pointing to a silver warehouse a few feet away. "Now, double-time it!"

Once inside the warehouse, Morgan saw a circular canvas ring enclosed by heavy ropes. He bounded into the ring and loosened up, stretching, forming his game plan. He guessed that Powers was a grappler, also trained in the martial arts. Could he beat Powers? He wasn't sure, but he had an ace up his sleeve.

He had purposely failed to mention in his military records several years of private training as a wrestler-grappler, and boxer. He had been trained by a former professional heavyweight boxing champion and considered himself to be a respectable amateur. It was a secret he had hoped would one day help him.

Today was that day, if, as was Morgan's hunch, Powers had sorely underestimated his abilities based on the information in his file jacket. At least if he put up a better fight than Powers expected, there might be a chance to gain the older man's respect.

As Powers entered the warehouse, Morgan was waiting in the center of the ring. Powers wasn't expecting much of a fight from the recruit, so he didn't bother to warm up. He only took off his boots and aviator sunglasses, placed them neatly in a corner of the ring, and stepped inside.

Powers looked at Morgan and said, "There are no rules, except avoid the eyes, throat, and balls, and," Powers said mockingly, "when you're ready to quit, Pretty Boy, just tap the mat. That is, if you're conscious."

Powers seemed surprised at the lack of fear or hesitation in Morgan's eyes. The boy looked like he was headed off to the beach.

Powers began to circle Morgan. Making his move, he slid to his left, looking for an opening to attack, then head-faked. Powers moved to leg-sweep him when Morgan threw a left hook that connected solidly with Powers's jaw, stunning the larger man.

Morgan followed up with a right to Powers's temple and another shot to his midsection. Powers doubled over and fell on one knee. It was obvious that Morgan was faster and stronger than he appeared, and that he had fought before.

Getting to his feet, Powers just smiled at him. Morgan landed a haymaker squarely on Powers's nose, breaking it and splattering blood over them both.

Morgan's increasing confidence caused him to let

his guard down for just a split second. Powers lunged, tackling him to the mat, landing on top of him, and, using every ounce of his weight and skills, finally managing to put Morgan in a sleeper choke hold until he tapped the mat. Both men got to their feet, Morgan standing at attention, waiting for the next onslaught of verbal abuse.

But instead, Powers extended his hand to Morgan and said, "I might have misjudged you. I think you may have what it takes to get through this training." Then he barked, "Shower up! Chow at 1800 hours!"

Morgan was almost at the warehouse door when Powers yelled out, "Hold up!"

Morgan stopped and turned around.

"I just had a thought. Your code name. It should be Cobra."

"Why is that?" Morgan asked.

"It's fast, powerful, and cunning."

Back in the barracks, he lay in the cot thinking about what had just happened. He was wondering if he would be treated like all the other recruits, no better, no worse, now that he had bashed in Powers's nose, when six sweat-and-dirt-covered trainees entered and dropped, fatigued, onto their cots. They introduced themselves by code name, one by one, as The Farm's instructors had drilled into them, revealing neither their real names nor where they were from.

Sizing them up, Morgan saw that they all appeared to be around his age and in excellent physical condition. He guessed that most of them were military recruits from one branch of the service or another.

The last guy to enter the room was a tall, wiry blond

man, his hair buzzed short, with a light but tanned complexion and large hands. He approached Morgan, stuck out his hand, and introduced himself as Cougar.

"Seeing as you're new here, I'll be glad to show you the ropes until you get acclimated," he said as Morgan nodded his appreciation. "We run double-time everywhere we go, all the time. If we don't, and an instructor sees us, we all pay the price." They left together, double-timing it to the mess hall.

They had exactly twenty minutes to eat, and then it was back to the barracks, a change of clothes for a five-mile run, and calisthenics before bed. Just before lights-out, Cougar resumed the orientation. Morgan learned that he'd be awakened between 4:00 and 5:00 A.M., with two minutes' personal time before formation. The length and intensity of training varied from day to day, and they had to be prepared for anything.

Over the course of that year at The Farm, Cougar and Cobra partnered up for exercises and drills. Morgan learned that Cougar's real name was Peter Conley, he was a former Marine, and his strengths were the polar opposite of Morgan's. Whereas Morgan was built tough, broad-shouldered, and thickly muscled with lightning-fast reactions, Conley was tall and lightweight, and his power came mainly from his keen intellect. He spoke seven languages and was an avid reader of history. Morgan often joked that with his high forehead, long chin, and gangly stance, he could more easily be mistaken for a college professor than a spy-to-be, although not many college professors knew six ways to kill a man with their bare hands.

*   *   *

Morgan had thought that basic training in the Army was taxing, yet nothing he did there had prepared him for training at The Farm. The drills were longer and harder, and they frequently bivouacked out in the cold, wet swamp. At The Farm, there was no such thing as being hungry or tired or sick; you did what you were told, and you didn't complain. The physical program was a constant wrench, mentally and emotionally, and it was designed to be that way.

The goal of the instructors, Morgan knew well, was to break everyone down, so that only the toughest remained and the rest washed out. *Not me*, Morgan told himself. *I'm not quitting.* With every physical challenge, he grew more determined, and each day he felt the high of having pushed himself beyond what he would have thought possible. Coming back drenched, aching, exhausted, and starving from a day of swamp training, Morgan was *happy*.

Their regimen wasn't limited to physical training. It also included technical training that far surpassed anything that was taught in basic. He was taught covert movement and how to spot and lose a tail. He learned to use state-of-the-art communications equipment. He was taught driving, from evasion and high-speed chases to rolling a car safely, to doing a 180 straight off a transport trailer. The recruits spent months working with professional role players, learning how to lie, how to beat a polygraph, and how to read tiny signals in body language. Morgan also received intense psychological training to withstand pain, both physical and emotional.

And, of course, he was taught how to kill, from hand-to-hand combat to poisons to explosives, and

how to survive each in turn. But where he really excelled was in weapons training. He was an exceptional
marksman, and he could take out a target at 500
yards—semiautomatic guns, the Glock, Walther PPK,
Beretta, or the M-16 assault rifle, fitted with a night-
vision scope. He was fastest to disassemble and re-
assemble any weapon and handled them all with ease,
as if each were an extension of his hand.

Clearly, though, Morgan wasn't very successful in
his determination to stay in the middle of the pack, so
as not to draw attention to himself. His natural ability
during runs and other PT activity and his competitive-
ness were evidence of his leadership qualities. He was
noticed not only by the other recruits but also by the instructors, especially Powers, who had taken a special
interest in him.

Morgan enjoyed the supportive camaraderie that
had developed among the men, almost all of them en-
couraging one another during long, brutal days of
physical training—all except one: Code Name Condor.
Morgan sensed he was trouble, with something nega-
tive to say about everyone, a loud, carping blowhard
who never shut his mouth. So far, Morgan had avoided
a confrontation.

But as the training got increasingly tough, and recruits were drummed out almost daily, tensions ran
high. The more Morgan tried to stay away from him,
the more Condor goaded him, and Morgan sensed the
inevitable, a fight that could cause his dismissal from
training.

One night during chow, Condor helped himself to
Morgan's tray. "What's your real name, punk?" Condor
jeered as Morgan glared at him.

"We're not allowed to disclose our names. But then, you already know that," Morgan said, as Condor put a heavy hand on his shoulder, yanking him around to face him.

Morgan pried off Condor's hand and said, "If you ever put your hand on me again, you'll regret it."

"Is that right, sissy?" Condor jeered.

Morgan's temper was almost to its boiling point. Condor got even louder, grabbing Morgan by the collar and poking him in the forehead as he spoke. Morgan had had enough. He was rising from his seat when he heard the whistle blow.

The room became dead silent. Powers was hustling toward them, and by the look on his face, he wasn't any too happy.

"So you two ladies want to fight?" he roared, standing directly in front of Morgan and Condor, withering them with a look that, if looks could kill, would have been fatal. "You apparently haven't had enough exercise today. Everybody up! Get outside to the pit! Now!"

The pit was a hole in the ground, located in the obstacle course, approximately twelve feet around and six feet deep. The troops had amassed in formation around it when Powers arrived with two other instructors.

Powers's question, "Who started the argument?" was answered by silence. "All right, then!" he yelled. "This is what's going to happen. Cobra and Condor are going to get into the pit and do a little dance. Whoever's left standing and able to get out of the pit on his own two legs will join the rest of you ladies for a ten-mile run. The one who loses goes home. Is that clear?"

In complete unison, the recruits answered, "Yes, sir!"

"The only rule is, there are no rules," Powers said, ordering Cobra and Condor into the pit. As Morgan jumped in, he noticed that the lace on his left boot was untied, but as he leaned over to tie it, Condor moved in and threw a kick to Morgan's head. He rolled away and regained his footing, assuming a boxer's position.

"I'm going to kick your ass and send you home!" the much taller and heavier Condor taunted.

"You've got a big mouth. Got the skills to back it up?" Morgan grinned, analyzing Condor's movements, guessing correctly that the larger, slower man would come at him straight on, hoping to back Cobra into losing his balance. When Condor charged, at the last second Morgan moved to Condor's left. As he swung around, Morgan hit him with a powerful uppercut, snapping Condor's head back, followed by a right cross to the center of his forehead.

As Condor went down, Morgan landed a roundhouse kick to the side of Condor's head, knocking him unconscious. The silence was deafening.

Concerned he had seriously injured him, Morgan started toward Condor, only to hear Powers yell, "Cobra! Out of the pit! You and the rest of the ladies owe me ten miles."

Morgan got a sick feeling in his stomach when he was summoned to Powers's office first thing the next morning.

"Enter," Powers said to Morgan's knock at the screen door. "Have a seat," he said.

Morgan had a feeling he was in deep shit and was about to say something, to try to avoid being thrown out of training, when Powers began to speak.

"Cobra, I've been watching you closely ever since I misjudged you on the day you arrived here. What I have come to realize is that you have all the qualities to be a great operative. You're confident, have great instincts, are smart and tough, both mentally and physically. You have great focus and are an exceptional marksman. You keep your cool and have the respect of all the men you work with. You may be the best I've ever seen, except for me," he laughed.

Then he explained why he had summoned Morgan, "We're partnering up the men, and I want you to have the first pick," he said.

Morgan felt a sigh of relief within, but without showing emotion and without hesitation, he said, "Cougar. That's who I want as my partner."

Powers gave a half grin and asked, "Why Cougar?"

"I've felt a connection with him since the day we first met. He's smart and loyal. He can fly both a helicopter and a plane, speaks several languages, knows when to keep his mouth shut, and even knows how to cook. My gut tells me I can trust him with my life."

"Okay. It's done. Head on back to the classroom."

"Sir. Permission to speak freely?" Morgan asked. To Powers's nod, Morgan asked, "Is Condor okay?"

Powers's tone warmed as he said, "You have the qualities of a true leader, concerned about one of your fellow trainees. Even though we both know he is a complete asshole. He's going to be fine, apart from taking a beating he's going to remember for the rest of his life."

CHAPTER 35

Together, Morgan and Conley made it through training at The Farm, two of the twelve recruits who did out of the ninety-nine who started in the program. The others couldn't hold up to the mental strain and the physical punishment and washed out.

Those who remained graduated in the fall. The ceremony was understated and without fanfare, but none was necessary. Every single one of the recruits standing there together knew that they had accomplished something few others could.

"Gentlemen," said Powers, standing at the podium in The Farm's single lecture hall, "you have just completed the finest training this country has to offer." He had notes on the lectern, but he spoke with the fluidity of a well-rehearsed speaker. "The skills we have taught you make you powerful, but they cannot grant you the virtues that must guide you in your service to your nation—responsibility, honor, patriotism. But above all, you will need unwavering loyalty. You, gentlemen, are special. The work you do will be crucial to maintaining America's stature as the greatest country in the world."

The recruits stood quietly, reverently, as Powers went on. "Tomorrow, you choose your assignments. Some of you will work in the headquarters at Langley as analysts, while others will be placed as attachés in foreign embassies and will be primarily responsible for gathering intelligence. These are both noble callings, vital to the functioning of our agency and, thus, to our country.

"But the boldest among you"—he looked intently at the graduates—"will choose to go into Black Ops. Those few will live lives that are dangerous and, odds are, short. They will do things that most are not capable of doing. But these men will have the unique opportunity to make history through their actions. I trust that when the time comes, you will choose wisely."

"But first," he said, breaking the solemnity of his tone, "I want you dressed in civvies and ready at 1700 hours sharp. We'll all be going out for an informal, relaxing evening at the Snapping Gator across town. There'll be good food, music, and I heard there might even be a woman or two." He finished with a smile, and a round of cheers rippled through the room.

The new graduates reported back at 5:00 P.M., and they joked with one another as they jostled for seats near the front of the bus so they could be the first out. But not Morgan, who was calm and stress-free for the first time in months. He took a seat toward the back of the bus, reclined, and sighed a contented sigh. It was over. He had done it. Even though he knew the hardest part was about to begin—actually being a spy—for the time being, he wanted to bask in the accomplishment.

He closed his eyes in the darkness of the bus, its glass windows painted black to prevent them from knowing the location of The Farm. As he felt the bus pulling away, he drifted off to sleep amid the sound of his fellow graduates roughhousing up front, until the bus brakes whined to a stop.

"Gentlemen, we're here!" said Powers. "Everybody, out!"

"Come on, Cobra!" said Conley, moving on excitedly up ahead of him. But Morgan took his time. The bar wasn't going anywhere, and after a year of constant strain, this time there was no pressure, no hurry.

By the time he had gotten off the bus, all the other graduates had run out ahead of him. He stepped down to the ground, and he knew something was wrong before he even heard the footsteps of a half dozen black-clad masked men, who surrounded him completely and cut him off from the bus. Behind him, one of them swung some sort of club, hitting him in the back. Another's fist hit him in the jaw, and he staggered and fell backward onto the gravel.

They closed in. Morgan struggled, throwing kicks and punches wildly, but there were too many of them to fight off. He felt a hand close over his nose and mouth, and the pungent smell of chloroform engulfed his senses. He faded fast, struggling with the single-minded desperation of a trapped animal, until he completely lost consciousness and his body fell limp, like a rag doll.

When Morgan woke up, his head ached, his throat was dry, and his arms were heavy and numb. He couldn't see anything, and it took him a moment to realize that this was because he had a rough canvas sack over his head. He tried to bring his hands up to remove the hood but found that they had been cuffed together behind his back to the chair he was sitting on. His next instinct was to work the sack off by moving his neck, but he found he couldn't budge. His head was taped tightly to a pole that rose from the ground behind him.

He heard voices, but he was too disoriented to make out what was being said. As the fog cleared, he realized that the reason he couldn't understand them was that they were not speaking English. It was a foreign language, one he recognized readily enough as Russian.

They pulled the hood off his head, and a blinding light shone into his face. There were at least two men in the room, but he couldn't see anything except vague silhouettes. He screwed his eyes shut, but it helped only slightly. He still felt the bulb's heat on his face like a furnace.

"Who the hell are you people?" he demanded. "What do you want from me?"

The response was a fist smashing into his face. He tasted blood.

"Shut your mouth, American," said one of them, through a thick accent. He was tall and thick like a gorilla. "You only talk if you are answering our questions."

"What the hell are you talking about?"

The man punched him hard in the gut, smashing him against the back of the chair. Morgan's reflex was to double over, but the harness on his head held him tightly. He retched in pain.

"Where is the secret CIA training center?"

"I don't know what the hell you're talking about. You people are luna—" A meaty fist smashed into Morgan's right cheek, and blood oozed into his mouth.

"What are the names of those who trained with you?"

"I'm telling you, I don't know what you're talking about!" The Russian sank his fist again into Morgan's gut. *Use your training*, thought Morgan, through the pain. *Take yourself out of yourself. Go somewhere else.*

The beating continued until Morgan lost track of time. For what seemed like days, he was brutally hammered, with no sleep, no food, and no water. They periodically cut his head free, covered it with a wet towel, tilted his face toward the ceiling, and poured water over his nose and mouth. It felt like drowning every time. They threatened him with electricity and held an ice pick to his face, hovering inches from his eye.

Whenever he lost consciousness, he was doused with cold water, and then the beatings would start again. He didn't know how long this went on—how much time passed—until one day, the enormous Russian smacked him out of his delirious fog to attention when he told him, "We have got another American here with us. Another damn spy. He is not so tough as you, but we are convinced that he has told us everything he knows."

He heard yells and detected some movement past the door to the room. "Please! Please, no!" It was a voice he didn't recognize, but it was American, all right. "I won't tell anyone—just don't kill me!"

He told Morgan, "If you do not talk, he will die."

Morgan felt a wrench in his gut worse than any of the Russian's blows, and it twisted every time he heard the man pleading for his life in an adjacent room.

"Tell us what you know!"

Morgan gave him a look of furious resolve that said everything. The Russian said something to a man, who then left the room. The American was still screaming.

"I have a family! Please! Please, d—"

A gunshot, and then there was silence.

"Bastards!" cried Morgan. "I'll kill you for this. I'll kill you all!"

The Russian crouched in front of him and said, in an almost friendly voice, "No, my friend. You will not kill anybody. You can no longer save your countryman, but you can still save yourself. Just answer our questions."

Morgan spat, the bloody saliva hitting the man in the face. The man struck back with a punch that landed squarely on Morgan's nose with a crunch. It bled profusely. The Russian got up, wiping himself with disgust, and addressed another one of the men in the room.

"He will not talk," he said. "It is time."

The Russian pulled a gun from inside the waistband of his pants.

This is it, he thought. There was no more hope of rescue or escape. His only satisfaction would be to know that he had not broken. He had not betrayed his country.

He felt the cold barrel of a gun on the back of his head.

"One last chance. Where is the secret training facility?"

"Go to hell." He waited for the gunshot. A strange thing, to wait for a gunshot he would never be aware of, that would scramble his brain before he had the chance to feel a thing. But he faced the thought of death head-on. He would die honorably rather than talk. He would not have the chance to serve his country as he had hoped, but at least he had this. This bullet would be his service, his sacrifice.

But it didn't come. The barrel of the gun was withdrawn. Through the thick haze of hunger and dehydration, he thought he heard laughter.

The blinding light in his face was shut off for the first time since he woke up in that chair, and bright, clear lights came on overhead. Through swollen eyes, he saw two men entering the room. They cut his neck loose and then undid the cuffs. Morgan tried to swing his fist at one of them, but he was too weak, and he collapsed to the floor from the effort.

One of them put a canteen to his mouth, and he drank through ragged, bloody lips, sweet, cold water flowing into his mouth, which was so parched, it hurt. The two men helped him to his feet. His knees buckled, but the men held him up. He heard approaching footsteps and saw the vague outline of a man appear at the door. It took a minute for his mind to make sense of what he was seeing.

It was Powers.

"Traitor! Goddamn traitor!"

With the last of the strength that was left in his limbs, he tried to hit him, still yelling, "Traitor! Traitor! You're gonna fry for this!" while the men supporting him held him back. He could barely tell that Powers was trying to talk to him, until suddenly the words got through to him.

"It's okay, Cobra," he was saying. "It's okay. You just passed your final exam."

CHAPTER 36

"I don't know what you think you're trying to prove, Cobra. What good are those photographs to you if you're dead?"

T pulled on the length of barbed wire. The loop tightened around Morgan's thigh, rusty teeth digging into his skin. He held back a cry of pain, but he couldn't help his breath coming out heavy and irregular, wheezing through the oily cloth in his mouth.

Not. A. Sound, he told himself, quieting his breath, trying to maintain a steady rhythm.

"This pain," she said, tugging once more, a little harder, the claws pulling on his flesh, "it can stop. All you have to do, Cobra, is give up. Just swallow your pride and tell me where the memory card is."

He heard the hum of something vibrating. Natasha looked at a small device on her waist. She grumbled something to herself in Russian, then looked at Morgan, narrowing her eyes menacingly, and ordered, "Sit tight." She walked out of the room, taking a last look at him before closing the door behind her.

Morgan listened for her footsteps, and when she was far enough away, he raised his head, fighting the exhaustion and forcing himself into alertness. He tried to turn all of his attention to escaping, but it was hard to keep his mind straight. T had left him there in the windowless cell for what he assumed was all night, with a boom box, just out of reach of his foot, blasting some awful noise that someone, somewhere called music. It kept him from falling asleep at all—the blaring music, playing on a loop, echoing around his exhausted mind. All night, desperately holding on to his sanity, he tried to break free from his handcuffs, first looking for anything that could be used as a lock pick and then, frustrated beyond reason, he tried brute force until his hands bled and his skin was raw.

But the pain was good. The pain brought adrenaline, made his body awaken. It gave him a fighting chance.

T had left the length of barbed wire embedded in his thigh. It stuck up like a dead tree, its roots digging into his leg. If he could only get ahold of it, he might be able to use it to pick the cuffs open. He contorted his body, trying to bring it within reach of his left hand. As he did, the tensing muscles in his thigh caused the barbs to bite deeper into him. He gritted his teeth and strained. The end of the wire grazed his fingertips. So close . . . if he could just get a grip . . .

Footsteps were approaching. Straining to hear, he made out two sets instead of one. Who the hell was T bringing here now? He forced his attention back to the wire. He might still be able to do it, pick the cuffs, tear his legs loose, and find a way to overpower her.

No, he decided. It was too late. He slackened his hands and waited as Natasha and her mystery guest drew closer. With a dull sound of metal against metal, the dead bolt was drawn open, and T walked in.

"Someone is here to see you," she said with displeasure. "Say hello to our guest. I believe you will recognize him."

The other person walked in. It was a man, carrying a thin briefcase. He was tall and handsome, with gray hair and a winning smile, a smile belonging to the most trusted politician in America.

"Cobra," said Nickerson, enunciating the word carefully, as he pulled the dirty rag from Morgan's mouth. "What a terrific name. What a marvelous animal. Quick, deadly, ruthless. I've been hearing a lot about you in the past few days. I must say, even though you've been a pain in the ass, I'm impressed. Truly, I am. You proved even harder to deal with than your old friend, Cougar."

So Nickerson and, consequently, T, really didn't know Conley was still alive. Good. Whatever happened to him, at least Cougar would be there to carry on.

"Edgar Nickerson, you asshole," said Morgan. "I didn't think you'd have the stones to show your face like this."

"You're right. I usually let the help deal with the vermin. But since you have turned out to be a particularly resilient specimen, I thought I would come here in person and make you a proposition."

Morgan scoffed. "You can't torture me into talking, and you think a bribe will do it?"

Nickerson looked at him with amused puzzlement. "You misunderstand me, Cobra," he said. "That's not the kind of proposition I'm here to make you. I would like you to come work for me."

"*What?*" he barked in unison with T, who looked as incredulous as he did. She moved toward him and stood menacingly close, her furious eyes locked on his. "Cobra is mine, Senator."

"Cobra has a choice to make," said Nickerson, turning away from her and toward Morgan.

"You think I'm going to bargain with you, Nickerson?" said Morgan.

Nickerson walked over to Morgan and crouched in front of him, so they were eye to eye. "You're not going to hold torture and attempted murder against me, are you?" he said, with gentle mocking. "After all, a man like you should know, it's just business."

"You didn't just mess with me. You messed with my family, my friends, my *dog*. And trust me, Nickerson, I'm a son of a bitch who can hold a grudge. So tell me, what in the world do you think could convince me to work for you? What do you think you can offer me that would be more valuable to me than bashing your face in?"

"Simple. You want to do the right thing, in your own stubborn way. Don't forget, I read your file, and the Agency knows everything there is to know about you. You can be a merciless killer, but you are a principled man, Mr. Cobra. You want to be a force for good in a dangerous world. I can offer you that power."

"I gave that up when I left the CIA. Turns out it wasn't all it was cracked up to be."

"You know as well as I do that the CIA has grown gutless and officious. The government is inept. They aren't willing to do what it takes to protect this country. Hell, they were spineless even back when you worked for them. Remember Libya? We could have eliminated

Gaddafi then and there. No bombing, no collateral damage, just one bullet from your rifle to the bastard's head."

Morgan looked at him with faint surprise.

"Oh, yes, I know about that," he continued. "State secrets aren't so secret when you know how to ask. Come work for me, Cobra, and you will live a life that matters again, and even more so than before. None of that congressional oversight nonsense, no weak-willed pencil pushers backing out at the last minute. With me, you can help shape the world in our image."

"By moving opium and using the drug money to fund the enemy? By supplying the weapons that put American soldiers into danger?"

"Necessary evils, I'm afraid," said Nickerson, with just a tinge of feigned remorse. "I believe it is something you are personally familiar with. It's no simple matter to make enough money to change the world, and change the world I will. We will not allow bloodthirsty, America-hating dictators to live. We will hunt terrorists and criminals down wherever they may hide. We will be a force for good in the world again."

"Bullshit," said Morgan. "You don't give a shit about the world."

"Perhaps," said Nickerson candidly, "but even so." He picked up his briefcase, set it down on the table, and opened it. Morgan watched as he pulled out three large photographs and set them on the floor in front of him, where he could see them.

"Do you know this man?" Nickerson asked, pointing at the first photograph. It was a video still of an Arab with a long, scraggly beard and crazy-looking eyes. "Jawhar Essa. Propagandist for Al-Qaeda. Hiding in Yemen and untouchable by our government. Killed two months ago by one of my agents."

Nickerson moved on to the next one, a long-range shot of a laughing Latino man wearing a Panama hat and large gold chains around his neck that hung down on his chest, visible through his open shirt. "Porfirio Aguilar. Head of the Juárez cartel—that is, until we got to him in January of this year."

He moved on to the third picture, a middle-aged, Eastern European–looking man with graying temples and mustache. "Janek Kovar. Czech arms dealer and human trafficker. Killed not two weeks ago by—you guessed it—us."

"What's your angle, Nickerson?" said Morgan. "I *know* you're not doing this shit out of the goodness of your heart."

"What does it matter?" said Nickerson silkily. "Good work is being done. Thanks to me. To us." He nodded to Natasha, who was leaning against the wall in a corner, watching him with contempt. "I can offer you that opportunity again, Cobra. To change things the only way they ever get changed. To shape the world according to your own ideals."

"Maybe, Nickerson. But you forgot one thing."

"Yes?"

"My ideal world doesn't have you in it."

Nickerson laughed, as if Morgan had told a very funny joke. "Is that your answer, then? You won't reconsider?"

Morgan spit on the floor in front of him, spattering the pictures Nickerson had laid out.

"Very well. He's all yours, Natasha. Enjoy yourself."

"I'm going to kill you, Nickerson," Morgan said,

with a strange calm that surprised even himself. "I promise you. You will die. Soon."

"I'm trembling in my shoes, *Cobra*," said Nickerson, deadpan. He turned to Natasha, who was looking at him with anger. "You're wasting your time with this nonsense. So what if he doesn't talk? If he dies, the photographs are lost forever, and that's that. Meanwhile, you have more important things to worry about. The big day is Saturday."

She looked at him incredulously, motioning toward Morgan.

"Oh, what's he going to do?" said Nickerson. "He's a corpse. He just doesn't know it yet. And let me make this clear—make sure he's goddamn certain of it soon. You have more important things to do. "

She took a lingering look at Morgan and said, without turning away, "Cobra and I are not done yet."

Nickerson scoffed. "Revenge. So tacky, so small-minded!" He pulled the door open to leave. "It just better not interfere with the plan."

Natasha followed him and closed and latched the door behind her. Morgan wondered how long she would keep him alive. This could be the last time he was alone in the room. It might be his final chance for escape.

He shifted his body, again trying to grab hold of the wire, contorting his torso, stretching his right arm around the pipe behind him. He edged closer, closer, his thigh screaming in pain until, *yes!* Two fingers wrapped around the wire, which he carefully bent so that he could hold it in his hand. Working it slowly, carefully, he unwound it from his thigh, each barb stinging as it came out. It made him bleed more, but it came loose. He held it firmly in his hands. *Now for the handcuffs.*

The wire was thin, but it was still far thicker than ideal for the task. He tried to work an end of it into the lock, but it kept slipping out.

Focus. You can do this, he said to himself.

Again, he worked it in, and it slipped out. Frustrated, he tried to jam it in carelessly. A barb caught his finger unexpectedly, ripping the skin, and he released reflexively. The length of wire, which had curled into a loose spiral, bounced and rolled just out of reach. *Shit.*

Morgan tried to snag it with his foot and came up a few inches short. He strained and shifted, trying to bring the chair closer to it, trying to give himself a few extra inches, but it was no use. It was out of his reach, and there was nothing he could do to get it back, nothing he could do to open the handcuffs, and nothing to do now but wait for T to come back and, if he was lucky, kill him right away.

And then he heard a loud hissing, like radio static. He whipped his head around, looking for the source, until he realized the shushing sound was closer than he thought. The earpiece! It had gone dead with Conley out of range, and he had forgotten all about it.

"Come in, Cob . . . " said Conley's voice, breaking up in static.

"Cougar!" he said, in a loud whisper, splitting the difference between his excitement and his fear that T might hear. Given the range of the device, Conley couldn't be farther than 500 yards away, and probably closer, considering the apparent thickness of the concrete around him.

" . . . bra c . . . in. Are yo . . . ere?"

"Cougar, Congar, come in, can you hear me?"

". . . obra? Cobra, is that you?"

"Cougar, I'm in a small room, behind a heavy iron door. I think I'm underground somewhere."

"I'm coming, Cobra."

"Be careful. T and Nickerson are around here somewhere."

"Roger that."

There was silence for some time, and then Morgan heard hurried footsteps outside the door, coming his way. The door unlocked, and in burst Natasha, murder in her eyes.

"Looks like you and Nickerson aren't quite on the same page," said Morgan calmly.

Natasha went straight for him, put one heavy boot against his chest, and grabbed him by the hair. "I'm no longer amused by this, Cobra." She slapped him across the face. "I'm going to go get a hammer and some pliers, and I'm going to start doing some serious damage." She pushed off him with her foot and stormed out, banging the metal door behind her.

Shit.

"Cougar," he said. "Cougar, come in. Where are you? Now would be a really great time for you to show up!"

He heard footsteps approaching. *Goddamn*, he thought, bracing for what was coming. He heard the dead bolt on the door being undone, and the door swung open.

But it wasn't Natasha. It was Peter Conley, gun drawn. Morgan had never been happier to see him.

"Cobra? Oh, Christ. Come on, man, let's get you out of here."

"I'm handcuffed," said Morgan, knocking the cuffs

against the metal pipe. "You're going to have to find a way to open them."

Conley pulled out a knife to cut Morgan's legs free and then examined the handcuffs.

"I don't have anything to pick these with," said Conley.

"There's some wire on the floor."

"You mean this *barbed* wire?" Conley asked, dubiously. "I don't think I can use this. It's too thick. I'm going to have to shoot them apart."

"Do you have a silencer for that thing?"

Conley shook his head.

"We're going to have to hightail it out of here, then," said Morgan. "Okay." He spread his hands so that the chain was taut against the pipe. "Ready."

Conley placed his gun point-blank against the handcuff chain and fired. The gunshot rang in Morgan's ears and reverberated in the enclosed space. Morgan held his hands apart, free, a few links of the chain dangling from each cuff. Conley helped him to his feet. He stumbled, but he didn't fall.

"Are you okay to walk on your own?" asked Conley.

"Just go!" said Morgan.

They dashed out of the room and heard T's heavy boots pounding the concrete, around the bend of the hallway, barreling toward them.

Conley shouted, "This way!" and sprinted in the opposite direction, deeper into the facility. Morgan battled to run as best he could, with a stinging left thigh on top of the burning in his knee. T sped toward them, her footsteps echoing closer behind them.

"In here!" Conley led him into a room about twice

as big as the one in which Morgan had been held, with the same heavy metal door, which Conley closed and bolted behind them.

Inside the room were the rudiments of a home. There was a mattress on the floor covered with rumpled sheets, and a worktable with a lamp on it. In one corner was a ladder that led upward, out of sight, into a narrow vertical tunnel.

"This is her safe house!" Morgan realized. T, meanwhile, had caught up to them. She kicked and banged loudly against the door, but it didn't budge.

"Come on, Cobra," said Conley, making for the ladder. "This has to lead somewhere. Let's get out of here."

Natasha shot three times at the door, making the room ring deafeningly. Although the slugs punched deep dents in it, the door held. Morgan scanned the room. On the table, under a pool of light, was spread a large blueprint.

"Let's go!" shouted Conley. Morgan heard the faint sounds of footsteps as T ran away from the door.

"Wait!" Morgan went to the table and hastily folded the blueprint into a jumbled mess. "Okay," he said, carrying it with him. "Let's go."

They climbed the ladder through a manhole that led to the ground level, Morgan with the blueprint tucked under his arm. When they emerged, Morgan saw that they were on a construction site for what might have eventually become a processing plant of some kind, but the build-out had been long abandoned. Sunlight filtered in through high, paneless windows.

His body screaming with agony, Morgan struggled

to keep up with Conley as they ran out into broad daylight. He looked back, concerned that their pursuer was still hot on their heels, but the way around was long. She wasn't going to be able to catch up. When they reached Conley's car, hidden a few hundred feet away, Morgan was confident that they were safe. For now.

CHAPTER 37

Once they had driven far enough away that they were sure T had not followed them, Morgan flipped down the visor and looked in the mirror. He looked exactly like he felt. His face was bloody and bruised, his left eye swollen half-shut, his lips cut in several places.

"We've got to get you to a doctor," said Conley.

"No hospitals," he grunted.

"You're right," said Conley. "That would be less than wise. But you need a doctor. Don't worry, I know a guy. We can get you to his clinic, and he'll take care of you, no questions asked."

Morgan looked down at his thigh. Blood was oozing out, staining the upholstery of the seat. He pulled up his shirt and examined his bruised torso.

"Anything broken?" asked Conley.

"A few cracked ribs, maybe," said Morgan, wincing as he prodded them with his hand. "Nothing I can't handle."

"Okay," said Conley. "We'll get you looked after and then find a place where you can rest."

"Are you kidding?" asked Morgan, incredulously. "With all this going on, you're thinking of resting?"

"Morgan, I've been up all night trying to pick up your signal, and *I'm* exhausted. I can only imagine what state you're in."

"I'm fine," Morgan said curtly.

"I don't know what happened in there, but let me tell you, I wouldn't be fine if I were alone in a room with T for a few hours. You were in there for almost a day. I'm sorry, Morgan, but there's no way you're fine."

Conley was right. He wasn't fine. His head was fuzzy, his flesh sore and throbbing. The light was painful to his eyes, and he could barely stay awake as Conley drove on. His body ached for rest. He was aware that, now that they knew for sure that Senator Edgar Nickerson was behind all this, the right thing to do was to regroup and rethink their strategy.

But Morgan resisted it, with the same instinct that told him to never give in, never surrender. That instinct had saved his life more times than he could count, and he had learned to trust it.

"We see a doctor, and we keep moving," he said. Conley looked at him disapprovingly but didn't press the point further.

Morgan remembered the crumpled blueprint from Natasha's hideout, which he had placed in between his seat and Conley's when they took off in the car. He picked it up, and, unfolding the wispy paper, he laid it out on the dashboard, part of it hanging down over the edge like a tablecloth. He examined the writing on it, blinking hard to keep himself awake and concentrated.

"What is it?" asked Conley.

"It's RFK Stadium," he said. "A detailed floor plan."

"That can't be good," said Conley. "You don't think she could be planning a terrorist attack? A few well-placed bombs . . . if the stadium is packed . . ."

"I don't know," said Morgan, looking closely at the blue lines on the paper. "Look, this isn't old like the rest of the notes on the blueprint—an X drawn in pencil, here in the middle of the field. And there's a number written off to the side here: 340."

"What do you suppose that is?" asked Conley. "A seat or section number?"

Morgan shook his head. "I don't know. But Nickerson said something before he left. Something about Saturday being a big day."

"Who's playing Saturday at RFK?" Conley wondered aloud. And then it hit Morgan.

"I know what the number means. Nobody's playing on Saturday. That senator, McKay, she's giving a speech there. I imagine that X is right about where her podium is going to be. Conley, that number is a range, as in for a rifle. T is planning to assassinate Senator McKay."

CHAPTER 38

Dennis Poole walked into Senator Lana McKay's office to find her sitting at her cluttered desk, with a pen in her hand, poring over a thin document, deep in concentration. She looked up at him from the paper and smiled, that sincere, guilelessly disarming smile of hers that he had always found so compelling, that had won him when he had first met her. And yet he knew there was a fighter behind that smile, one who could be as hard and unyielding as steel.

"Hi, Dennis," she said. "Tell me, how are things looking out there?"

"Crazy as usual. But it's all going to work out."

"God willing," she said wearily.

"Ritchie wants to know what you think of the speech."

"I'm looking it over one last time now," she said. "Tell him I have some notes to go over with him, but it's powerful. Between you and me, this is his best yet." She sighed and sat back in her chair. "I just hope it's good enough to get people to take notice."

"It will be," he said. "You're going to make sure of that."

"I'm glad one of us has that kind of confidence," she replied. "I just hope it's not misplaced."

"I've seen how people respond to you, Lana. They see you, and they know you're the real deal. It's going to happen."

"It is, isn't it?" she said, perking up. "We're going to stop them. No more using taxpayer money to fund thuggery. No more profiting off the blood of American soldiers."

"You made a believer out of me, Lana. You're going to do this."

"*We're* going to do it, Dennis. You've been a crucial part of everything I've done in office. This is going to be your big day as much as it is mine."

He flashed her a broad, grateful smile. "We're gonna push this law through," he said. "No compromises, no derailments. We'll expose the opponents of justice and transparency, and they will be shamed into voting for us. If politics is the only thing they believe in, then that's what we'll play. We'll expose their hypocrisy and corruption. The electorate won't stand for maintaining the status quo."

"I wish it didn't have to be this way," she said.

"You've made me believe that it doesn't, Lana. Even when I was a kid fresh out of college, I knew that most politicians didn't act against their own interests, that they voted with their biggest donors, always seeking out money and votes, almost never giving a damn about justice or the people their policies affected. But this, this is different. Lana, you made this cynic believe in our government again."

She smiled softly at him. "It truly makes me happy

to hear you say that, Dennis. All that's left now is to reach everyone else."

"That will come. Just wait and see. The American people will be on your side."

Her office phone rang.

"Sally," she called out to her assistant in the other room, "did you send this through?"

"No, Senator. Whoever it is called your line directly."

"Hmm," she said, and she picked up the receiver. "Hello, you've reached Senator McKay."

"Senator." It was a man's gruff, unfamiliar voice. "You don't know me, but please don't hang up."

"Who are you? How did you get this number?"

"I can't tell you who I am. But what I can tell you is that your life is in danger. There is a plot to assassinate you on Saturday. You need to call off your speech."

"What? Are you threatening me?"

"No!" said the voice. "But someone *is* going to kill you, Senator. You need to cancel the rally."

"That's not going to happen. If you have information, why don't you call the police?"

"They won't be able to do anything about it. Not against the people who are plotting to kill you. You need to go somewhere secret and safe and stay there."

"And who are these powerful people who want me dead?" she asked, affecting mild amusement.

"Look, I know you won't believe me. But think about whether Senator Edgar Nickerson might have the means and the motive to take you out of the picture."

"Edgar Nickerson!" she laughed, skeptically.

"This is serious, Senator!"

"Look, sir," she said, losing her patience, "if you have information about an assassination plot, please contact the authorities. If you have information that implicates Senator Nickerson in this kind of conspiracy, by all means take it to the newspapers. But don't ask me to cancel my speech on hearsay. I won't be stopped by vague threats." She slammed down the receiver hard and sat back, fuming.

"Are you okay, Lana?" asked Poole.

She waved him off, but he could tell she was shaken. "This isn't my first death threat, Dennis. Just alert the security team that there's been another one, and have them do what they do."

"Are you sure you're okay? Can I get you something?"

"I'll be fine. These . . . these thugs think that they can intimidate me. Well, I'll show them. If they want to stop me from making my speech, if they want to stop this bill from becoming law, they'll have to make good on their threats and kill me. Because anything short of that will not hold me back."

"Aren't you worried that they will?" asked Poole, who was himself more than a little apprehensive. Still, he couldn't help admiring her grit.

McKay looked out her window with steely resolve. "If they do, if all the powers in Washington are arrayed against me, then I suppose I can't stop them. But backing down is one thing I will not do."

"You really think this reform is worth your life, Lana?" he asked.

"Yes. But even if it weren't on the face of it, I wouldn't let that stop me. If I back down now, it'll be the same thing next time, and the next. And next thing I know,

I've got a lifetime of backroom deals and compromised principles. And then I'm no better than any of them."

"If that's your decision," he said, "I'll be right there with you."

"I know you will, Dennis," said the senator. "I know you will."

"Do you think she believed you?" Conley asked Morgan.

"Not enough." He looked down at the prepaid cell phone, its face still glowing from the call.

It was the afternoon of the same day that Conley had rescued him, and they were sitting in Conley's car in a supermarket parking lot. Morgan had been stitched up and had bandages wrapped around his thigh and torso. The bruising on his face, if anything, looked worse. But although he hadn't rested, he had taken a shower and eaten, and he felt refreshed and alert.

"What do we do now?" asked Conley.

"I don't see that we have a choice," said Morgan. "We can't let Nickerson win. We have to stop him."

"We can't do this alone, Morgan."

"And who are we going to call, Conley? If we call the Feds with a story about a CIA conspiracy but no credible evidence to back it up, they're just going to think we're another couple of crazies."

"Then we have no one else to turn to. We have to contact the Agency," Conley reasoned.

"Are you crazy? They tried to kill me and my family, and you want to trust them with this?"

"This is about saving the senator, Morgan. We have

to do something. Not everyone in there can be compromised. Even with the mole, they can still protect her. They have resources that we don't."

"I don't know, Conley," he said, looking away.

"I'm not willing to gamble with the senator's life. I hate this just as much as you do, and I trust them about as far as I can throw them. But it's our best shot at stopping Nickerson."

"Fine," said Morgan, gritting his teeth. He didn't like it at all, but Conley was right.

"Here, give me the phone. We'll call Boyle directly."

"No," said Morgan. "We shouldn't let anyone know you're alive. I'll do it."

"Are you sure?" said Conley.

"You mean, am I going to lose my temper and tell him to go to hell?"

"I mean, you've been beaten and deprived of sleep. I don't mean to have this conversation all over again, but are you sure you're up for anything right now?"

Morgan glowered at him. "Yeah, I can handle myself. Just tell me how to get his direct line."

Conley dialed for him instead and handed the phone back to Morgan. It rang twice, and then he heard the voice on the line.

"Boyle."

"You son of a bitch. This is Cobra. I have some information for you. Now listen closely, and if for a second I think you're stalling to keep me on the line, I'll hang up."

"Cobra, you need to turn yourself over to us right now," Boyle demanded. "Tell me where you are, and I'll send someone to get you."

"Like you sent that sick bastard to get me and my family?" said Morgan acerbically.

"Wagner veered off mission. He was supposed to bring you in, that's all."

"Bullshit. But that's not why I called you, Boyle. I have information. I want to tell you who really killed Eric Plante and Zalmay Siddiqi. It was Natasha Vasiliyevna. Now she's plotting to assassinate Senator Lana McKay at her rally on Saturday." He decided against mentioning Nickerson. Morgan knew how it would sound, and there was no need to make it less believable.

"That's impossible," said Boyle incredulously. "She's not even in the country."

"You're being played. She's here, and she's been after me ever since I was in Afghanistan."

"If that's all true, Cobra, then it's all the more reason for you to turn yourself in and let us take care of the investigation."

"Damn it, Boyle, there's no time for an investigation! You need to find her now, before she kills the senator!"

"Just come in, and we'll discuss this calmly. You can present everything you have, and we can determine whether it's credible here at headquarters."

"No. I told you what I know. What you do with this information now is your problem."

"I can't act on your word alone," he said.

"Bullshit."

"Why don't you just turn yourself in . . ."

"*Why don't you go to hell?*" Morgan threw the phone hard onto the dashboard, and it bounced back, landing on Conley, who turned it off and popped out the battery.

"No luck, then?" he said glumly.

"Looks like we're on our own." Morgan glanced at him. "What now?"

"Like I said before," said Conley, "we check into a hotel so we can both get some sleep. Tomorrow morning we begin planning. It looks like we're running this solo."

"Maybe not entirely," said Morgan. "I know someone who might be able to help."

CIA Director Boyle laid down the receiver, thought, and then picked it up again.

"Get me Kline."

"Yes, sir?" came Kline's voice, after a few seconds.

"It's Cobra. He just called me."

"Did you record the call? Did you trace it?" asked Kline.

"No, it happened too quickly, and I wasn't fast enough. But what he told me was concerning. He raved about some sort of conspiracy against him and talked about a rally that Senator McKay is holding on Saturday. I'm afraid he's planning something and that it's happening there."

"Sir, what do we do?" asked Kline. "Deploy another operative?"

"No. Alert Homeland Security. I want every officer in that stadium to have a photograph of Cobra. Give them a story about him being some kind of anti-government extremist. And tell them he should be considered armed and dangerous. If he is spotted, orders are to shoot on sight."

CHAPTER 39

The rain poured mercilessly as Morgan sloshed through the streets of Prague on a dark spring evening, a briefcase in his hand. It was an ancient city and looked older still after enduring decades of Soviet rule. That night, however, there was electricity in the air, and the city buzzed with an atmosphere of vibrant youth and new possibilities.

Revolution, however, was not Dan Morgan's business in Prague that night. After one last quick look backward to check that he wasn't being followed, he turned in to the Three Hunchbacks Hotel, in the Zizkov district. Soviet rule had not been kind to the once-beautiful façade, which was now stained and dilapidated. The inside, dusty and smelling of mildew, had not fared much better. Morgan walked up three flights of stairs, then down a dark, wood-paneled hallway to the third door on the right. He knocked, tapping out a prearranged code. He heard footsteps, and the heavy door swung open.

"Andrei," Morgan said to the man at the door.

"What news do you bring, Cobra?" Andrei said,

dripping with anxiety. "Tell me we have not been found out. Tell me my sister is alive and well." He was impeccably dressed, as usual, in an elegant brown suit and slicked back sandy hair. But the bags under his eyes were more pronounced, and his cheeks were sallow and more sunken than usual. He held a small weapon loosely in his hand, a Makarov semiautomatic.

"Everything's okay. Natasha's fine, and everything's still according to plan," Morgan replied.

"Good, good," Andrei said, relieved. "Please, come in."

Morgan walked into the room. A stiff bed lay on warped floorboards. Everything that belonged to Andrei was arranged in an open suitcase on the dresser. He seemed to be ready to go at a moment's notice.

"I have some documents for you," said Morgan, motioning to his briefcase. "A passport and entry papers that will get you through the border. We take the morning train to Vienna."

"Do you know how long I have been here, Cobra? Trapped, in this apartment? Two days!" he exclaimed, keeping his voice low. His eyes were wide, wild. "Do you know what my people are capable of? Do you know what they would do to me if they caught me?"

"I'm sure you know better than I do," said Morgan.

"The penalty for defection is death. And not quick death, as you Americans do it. Americans, even coldhearted ones like you, are merciful. In Russia, we like our executions slow and painful."

Morgan sighed. "I came as soon as I could." He tossed Andrei's suitcase onto the bed and placed the briefcase on the dresser.

"And left me nearly mad in the meantime!" he exclaimed. "But tell me, Cobra, where is my sister?"

"Natasha's safe," said Morgan. "She's with Cougar."

"We will not be going together, then?"

"Soon, Andrei. Once you're both in Paris. Then you'll come together to the United States."

"I must see her now, Cobra," Andrei said, and he walked to the window. "I must see her before I go. Is she here? Is she in Prague? I must know."

Morgan opened the briefcase and shuffled through the papers inside. "You'll see her in good time," he said. He pulled out a manila envelope and tossed it onto the bed. "There's your ticket out of here."

Andrei walked over and bent down to pick up the envelope. As his back was turned, in one fluid move, Morgan slipped a length of wire from his coat pocket and looped it around Andrei's neck, pulling it taut. Andrei, startled, reached up, but he couldn't get his fingers under the wire. He tried to wriggle himself loose, then heaved back, trying to knock Morgan against the wall behind them. Morgan held firm, the garrote biting into his hand. Andrei thrashed, kicked, and elbowed him, his strength slowly withering, until finally, after two minutes, he went limp. Morgan held the garrote tight until he was sure the man was dead, then laid him on the bed, facing away from the door. Morgan packed up his briefcase and gave the room a quick sweep to make sure he had left nothing behind that could identify him, then left.

He made his way out of the hotel and walked down a few streets before hailing a cab to the Old Town Square, where Conley sat at a café, wearing an elegant

European overcoat and sipping an espresso as if he'd been living in the city his whole life.

"It's done," Morgan said. "Clean and quiet. Nobody saw me leave. How's T?"

"In the safe house, eager to get out of here. We're driving out right away, headed for the Austrian border. Hopefully we'll make it before they find Andrei."

"Don't count on it," said Morgan. "The Russians will be expecting him to report back on her whereabouts. They'll know he's dead before the day is done. But don't worry. I'll make sure they're busy until your trail is nice and cold."

Conley laughed. "I'm sure you will. Give those bastards hell." He took a few bills from his wallet and put them on the table. "Good luck, my friend. I'll see you on the other side."

"God willing," said Morgan, shaking his hand. "Oh, and, Peter," he added, as he got up. "T never finds out about this. Deal?"

"She'll never hear it from me," said Conley.

CHAPTER 40

Saturday was a bright, beautiful day, and although the senator's speech wouldn't start until seven that evening, which was more than three hours away, the people who had trickled in since noon were already waiting in line at the gate, wearing shirts or hats or carrying signs with McKay's name on them. All in all, a casual observer might have mistaken it for a ball game. Natasha, who was most certainly not a casual observer, watched with unmitigated contempt, this audience in the circus world of political rallies. Well, there would be a spectacle tonight. She would make sure of that.

"Vera!" came a voice from behind her. She turned to see Dennis Poole, in a white button-down with the collar open and sleeves pushed up to his elbows.

"There you are!" said Natasha, her voice suddenly laden with enthusiasm, all traces of her accent gone from her voice.

"Hello, Vera," he said. After a faltering greeting, he seemed to draw some courage and kissed her as passionately as he knew how. It was still pathetically clumsy and awkward, Natasha noted. "I'm glad you

came, although I'm afraid you'll be doing a lot of sitting around until it's time for the speech."

"Oh, I don't mind," she said. "It's all so exciting!"
She, Natasha, would normally have regarded Poole
with nothing but disdain. But she was not herself now.
She was Vera, a superficially adventurous publicist
from Brooklyn with big soft eyes and a tender smile.
She appeared to be the kind of woman who might con-
ceivably, even if improbably, fall in love with a bore
like Dennis Poole, as well as a woman who might feel
genuinely sorry for manipulating him.

"You're dressed up," he remarked. She was wearing
a crisp gray pantsuit over a dark red shirt.

"Well, I don't go to one of these events every day,
you know!"

He led her toward the service entrance to the stadium, his hand in the small of her back. "She's with
me," he said to the guard at the door, flashing the badge
he was wearing on a lanyard around his neck.

Inside, the tunnel-like halls of the stadium were
pulsing with their own energy. But unlike the festive
mood outside, the atmosphere inside was tense, and
everyone was working hectically, preparing for the big
event.

"I'm really not supposed to bring you back here," he
said, with far more pride than remorse.

"Oh, what harm could there be?" she said.

He eyed her, raising an eyebrow in mock suspicion.
"You're not a spy, are you?"

"*Nyet, comrade*," she said with a sly smile, in an
American accent, and he laughed.

"Do you want to see the war room?"

He led her down the long, curved hallway, past a

steady stream of event staff, and through a door into the home team locker room, which had been repurposed for the rally, furnished with a long table that was stacked with boxes and papers. In the far end of the room, a minifridge hummed, with a jar and a glass sitting on top of it on a circular platter.

"It's not exactly what the space was designed for," said Poole, "but the location couldn't be more convenient in terms of proximity to the stage. Just hold on a sec. I need to take a look at something while I'm here."

Natasha slowly made her way around the table, trailing her left hand on the outer surfaces of boxes and the papers that lay strewn about. She reached Poole, who was rummaging through a box, and snaked her hand around his neck, pulling him in for a kiss. He offered only token resistance before leaning in.

They were interrupted by the ringing of his phone. He looked at the display and grimaced apologetically. "I'm sorry, but I need to take this."

"I'll hold the thought," she said, giving him one more lingering kiss.

He took the call and wandered toward a corner of the room, while Natasha continued to make her way around the table, affecting flawless nonchalance, running her hands over the documents, her fingers slipping lightning-quick into a box and taking out an ID badge with a lanyard hanging from it, which she dropped into her purse.

Poole glanced at her as he talked, and she gave him a sweet grin as she continued to walk the length of the table. On reaching the end, she sauntered off at an angle as her fingers crept into her purse and found a small rectangular plastic case. She looked at Poole, smiling, but he was looking away. She clicked the case, and a small, clear strip stuck out like a tongue. It was adhesive, and with the exact refractory index of glass. Handling it took extreme care. Just one slip of her finger, and—

She was startled by Poole's voice, coming from a mere few feet behind her. "Come," he said. "I have a surprise for you."

He ushered her out of the locker room, locking the door behind him, and then walked with her out to the field. Half of the verdant sports turf was covered with folding chairs sectioned off with rope, and an open stage had been erected in the middle of it. On the sidelines was a well-dressed woman surveying the scene, flanked by a couple of men in suits.

"Dennis!" exclaimed Natasha. "Is that . . . ?"

"The one and only. She arrived a bit early, so I thought I might bring you around to meet her." He called out to Senator McKay. "Lana! Lana, good to see you made it. How do you like the setup?"

"You've done a hell of a job here, Dennis."

He beamed. "I'm glad you like it." He pulled lightly on Natasha's hand. "Lana, I'd like you to meet Vera Blackburn."

The Senator extended her hand. "It's a pleasure, Vera. I've heard a lot about you," she said, smiling warmly.

"It would be a great understatement if I said the same about you," said Natasha, ebulliently. "I am a great admirer of your work, Senator."

McKay smiled graciously. "Thank you, Vera. I've tried to do my best to serve the people of this country. But I owe many of my accomplishments to Dennis."

"Oh, please," said Poole bashfully.

"He'll deny it, but it's true. You have a fine man here, Vera. This one's a keeper."

"Don't worry, Senator. I'll treat him right."

Natasha looked at her watch. She had to extricate herself if the plan was to stay on schedule. She pretended to dig through her purse for something and made her phone ring.

"Oh!" she said. "I'm sorry, Senator, would you excuse me please? I need to take this." She walked a few feet away, took the phone from her purse, stopped the ringing, and put it to her ear. "Hello?" she said. "Oh, you're kidding. No, in DC. Yes. Yes. Listen, is there anyone else you can call? Howard? Ugh. Okay, fine." She huffed and put the phone back into her purse.

"I am so sorry, but I need to go," she said to Poole and the senator. "Work emergency, and apparently there's no one who can deal with it except me. Please excuse me, Senator. It was such a pleasure to meet you, and I so wish I could stay."

"It was nice to meet you too, Vera. Pity you have to go."

She stepped aside, and Dennis walked with her.

"I am so sorry, Dennis," Natasha reiterated.

"It's the peril of being indispensable," he said with a good-natured shrug.

"You are sweet."

"Can you find your way out okay?" he asked, and he planted a kiss on her lips.

"I'll manage, I'm sure."

She walked into the bowels of the stadium, and whatever softness had been there before left her eyes.

She was Natasha again, coldly alert, and the lightness in her step was replaced with steely determination.

This whole show was all Nickerson's idea. If she had had her way, she could have already killed McKay a hundred times over. And now Cobra knew about it, and if she knew him, he would be here, trying to stop her. But Nickerson wanted to make a splash, a god-damn spectacle. She wished she could dispose of him and be done with it, wipe that grin off his face for good.

Patience, she told herself. Even *he* would outlive his usefulness, sooner or later. She wished it could be sooner rather than later, but Nickerson played a long game. And so she would, too. She could wait.

Meanwhile, she had to get everything ready for the night's show.

Morgan sat in the back of an unmarked white van in the RFK Stadium parking lot, dressed in a stiff black suit and tie. He looked into a small pocket mirror, checking his hair, now all black, and his matching fake mustache, which looked like the one he'd had when he had just started work as an operative.

"Damn it," he said. "Where's Cougar?"

"In the parking lot," said Grant Lowry, who was hunched over a keyboard in front of four computer screens, as he motioned distractedly toward one of the monitors. The van had been fitted with cutting-edge surveillance equipment and an impressive array of computers, all according to Lowry's exacting specifications. "He'll be here in a minute or two."

Morgan had approached Lowry as the man had arrived home, walking from his car to his front door, on the day after he had failed to convince Boyle to help them. Lowry had fumbled ineffectively for the pepper spray until Morgan assured him that he wasn't there to hurt him. Morgan briefly explained the situation and asked for help.

"No way," he had told Morgan, outside the door to his apartment building. He was jiggling his keys nervously. "No chance in hell."

"I can't do this without you."

"You're going to have to."

"She's going to assassinate a senator, Lowry. And there is no one to stop her but us."

"Look, Cobra, I'll bring this to Kline for you. I don't even have to tell him I saw you. We'll look into it and take the necessary precautions."

"I've already talked to Boyle, Lowry. He wasn't exactly receptive."

"So now you want me to go against the Director? Cobra, that wouldn't just be career suicide. That would be real, honest-to-God suicide."

"Then you're just going to let the senator die?"

"I don't even *like* her," said Lowry.

"What about Nickerson? What about Natasha? You're going to let them win?"

"You're the action hero, Cobra. Look at me." He motioned down at his dumpy figure. "What do you think the odds are that I would survive an encounter with an operative?"

Morgan threw up his hands. "I told him! I told him you wouldn't do it."

"Told who?"

"Cougar," said Morgan. "I told him you'd side with the pencil pushers."

"Did you say Cougar? Are you by any chance implying that Cougar's *alive*?" said Lowry, astonished.

"Yeah," said Morgan. "And he said you'd help us, that you'd do the right thing. I said you didn't have the spine."

"Do you really expect that reverse-psychology trick to work?" asked Lowry.

"No," said Morgan. "That's what I'm telling you. I said you wouldn't help us."

"Because it's not working, Cobra."

"I didn't think it was," he said. "That's what I told Cougar. But he insisted that you would come through. I guess I was right, after all."

Lowry turned around to leave, faltered, and then glanced back at Morgan with a look of annoyed frustration. "Okay, fine," he said. "You win. I'll listen to what you have to say."

"I appreciate it, Lowry."

"I'm not agreeing to anything yet!"

"I know," said Morgan.

Three days later, they were in the back of the van in the RFK parking lot.

"He had better be treating my car right," said Morgan, as he put his foot up on Lowry's chair and strapped a holster to his ankle. Then he picked up the gun, the small and easily concealable Walther PPK, his gun of choice from his days in Black Ops. He inspected it one last time, clicked the safety catch, and slid it into the holster. He looked at Lowry impatiently. If there had been more room, he would have been pacing.

"When did you say Conley was getting here?" Morgan asked.

"Three . . . two . . . one . . ." said Lowry, and, right on cue, there was a knock on the back door of the van. Lowry opened it to let Conley in, dressed in a suit to match Morgan's.

"That GTO steers like a dream," he said, smiling broadly.

"Don't get too comfortable," grumbled Morgan. "You're not the one who's driving it out of here."

"If things don't go right, neither of us is," said Conley.

"Shit," muttered Lowry to himself. "Tell me, why am I helping you guys again?"

"Because you're an honorable man working for a corrupt organization," said Conley. "And you want to set things right."

"Yeah, that must be it," Lowry said wryly. "Now, look here. We'll go over this one more time before you jokers go in. Natasha will be a needle in a haystack, but we're not flying blind here." He pointed to one of the screens. Morgan and Conley bent down to look at it.

"That number on the blueprint, 340. The section numbers don't go that high, so our best guess is that this is a range. That's the distance she will be shooting from. Here"—he gestured to a screen in front of him, which showed a seating diagram of the stadium with a circle superimposed on it—"is the perimeter drawn by that range, measured from the stage as marked on Natasha's blueprint, plus or minus ten feet. It just happens to intersect with the newly built luxury boxes, and Natasha's blueprint is recent enough to include them."

He indicated the seating diagram on the computer, a row of squares, and pointed to the edge of the upper level. "And this one here, L13, was requested by none other than Senator Nickerson. From there, Natasha would have a clear view of the stage, as well as total privacy."

"You go in using these." He handed each of them a ticket printed on fancy card stock. "Those will get you into the box seats. And these"—he gave each of them a laminated security badge—"will get you in without attracting much attention and let you move around the off-limits areas."

"Have you had any luck tapping into their security network?" asked Morgan.

"It's about to come online. As soon as it does . . . There." He brought up a map of the stadium on the screen, and a few dozen red dots appeared, moving jerkily like a squadron of fleas. "Each of those is a member of the event security team. There's a small delay, but I can pinpoint each man's location within a few feet."

"You're the man, Lowry!" said Conley.

"I am, aren't I?" He turned back to his computer and flicked through windows faster than Morgan could keep up.

"Uh-oh," said Lowry.

"That's not a good sound. What is it?" asked Morgan, alarmed. Lowry leaned back to let them see the screen. On it was a photograph of Morgan. He looked slightly younger in it, but it was no more than five years old. "What the hell is this?"

"I guess someone knows you're coming," said Lowry.

"This is on the network. Says here it's supposed to be distributed to all security personnel. They're going to be on the lookout for you, Cobra."

"Shit."

"Maybe you should sit this one out," said Conley.

"There's no way in hell I'm hanging back," said Morgan. "But we go in separately. That way, if I get caught, you still have a fighting chance."

"If you're sure . . ." said Conley.

"Yeah, I'm sure. Let's do this."

"All right, fellas," said Lowry. "It's showtime. Earpieces *in!*" Morgan popped the little device snugly into his ear.

"Just like old times, eh, Dan?" said Conley, looking at him.

Morgan looked at Conley and grinned. "Ready?"

"Let's go."

Natasha was outside the stadium again, walking toward the same service entrance she had used when she walked in with Poole earlier that day. This time, she was wearing a business-casual outfit that concealed a skintight black catsuit underneath. A strap over her shoulder supported a heavy black bag, and around her neck hung the event staff ID she had swiped, now with a picture of her. She flashed it to the security guard at the gate, who waved her in stiffly but did not ask to check her bag or frisk her.

Once inside, she took a left and walked briskly down the long corridor that earlier had been so busy with scrambling staff but now was empty. A right turn up ahead led to the locker room and the senator, but

Natasha's destination was straight ahead and up. She pressed on, approaching the turn, when she heard echoing footsteps. She looked back, unsure of where they were coming from, and ran bodily into a man who had just rounded the corner. She raised her eyes and saw that she was face-to-face with Dennis Poole.

"Vera?" he exclaimed, befuddled. "What—"

Before he could say any more, she wrapped her hands around his head and snapped his neck. He stopped talking midsentence and collapsed like a hunk of meat on the floor of a butcher shop. His lifeless eyes stared up at her, frozen in an expression of utter astonishment.

She looked around and found a narrow broom closet a few yards ahead. She drew an automatic lock pick from her pack and in seconds opened the closet door. It was cramped, but it would do. She dragged Poole's limp carcass across the dirty concrete floor. Dragging corpses was always heavy and cumbersome, and for all her training, her frame was still not cut out for it. With a great deal of effort, she managed to heave the corpse inside and shut the door, locking it again. It was a hasty hiding place, but the closet should keep its secret long enough. As she turned away, a small part of her felt a twinge of remorse. Perhaps it was whatever aspect of Vera that still existed in her. But in any case, it was short-lived. Her attention was soon drawn to the applause that had erupted from the stadium. The event was about to begin, and she needed to get into position.

CHAPTER 41

In a few minutes, the rally would start, and all the VIPs had apparently already been seated, judging from the absence of a line at the gate for the luxury boxes. Morgan knelt between two cars and waited for Conley to go in ahead of him. Two alert security guards were working the entrance, however, and Morgan decided there was no way he could make it past them with a gun. He unstrapped his ankle holster and tossed it under one of the nearby cars. Someone would be surprised to find it later that night, but by then it wouldn't matter anymore.

He saw Conley disappear into the stadium. He counted to one hundred and then emerged from between the cars, walking toward the gate. He could only hope the guards wouldn't recognize him, with his current disguise, from the old photograph. If they did, this mission was over for him, and it was all up to Conley.

Morgan walked confidently to the nearest guard and presented his ticket. The man scanned it, saying courteously, "Good evening, sir." He motioned for Morgan to open his arms and spread his legs, then ran the metal detector baton along the outline of Morgan's frame. "Enjoy yourself, sir," the guard said, waving him in. Morgan walked past the guard into the stadium, then breathed a sigh of relief.

"Sir! Hold on!"

Shit, he thought. Had they recognized him? Could he take on both guards at once? His mind raced to devise a strategy, and his eyes hunted his surroundings for possible ad hoc weapons. He turned around to face the guard.

"Yes?"

"Don't want to forget this." He had Morgan's ticket in his hand. "They won't let you in without it."

Morgan thanked him and walked away, into the stadium. He went up a flight of stairs, and Conley was there waiting for him.

"No trouble?" Conley asked.

"All good," he answered. They walked together up more stairs. There was another pair of security guards, dressed in sharp black suits. Morgan and Conley offered their tickets.

"That would be about halfway down and on your right," said one of the guards, after examining the tickets.

The doors to the luxury boxes were on their right along an elegant wood-paneled hallway. The number of each box was emblazoned on the door. Together, they reached the one they had come for, number thirteen. Morgan caught Conley's eye and held up three fingers. He counted down, and on his mark, he turned the knob, pushing the door open and rushing in, expecting violent resistance from T.

But, as they stood in the luxury box, with its lounge

chairs and bar and wall-mounted high-definition TV, they didn't see Natasha but rather just a man, handsome, silver-haired, looking at them indignantly.

"Nickerson!" Morgan gasped. He expected the senator to yell for help, but instead he composed himself and then looked at Morgan and Conley with controlled nonchalance.

"I can't believe how shoddy the security in this place is," Nickerson said.

Morgan twitched, ready to go for his jugular.

"I wouldn't do that," said Nickerson. "All I have to do is call out, and there will be a dozen security guards in here."

"So why haven't you already?" asked Conley.

"Ah, you must be Cougar," he said, with mild amusement. "Alive and kicking, I see. I'll have to let Natasha know that she failed even worse than she thinks."

He cleared his throat. "The reason I haven't called the guards is that I have no interest in seeing you captured by them. I must admit, I thought you would have skipped the country by now. But the truth is, I don't want to attract any attention to myself, which having two men arrested or killed in my box would certainly accomplish. So let me tell you what's going to happen. You'll have thirty seconds to leave this stadium before I let security know you're here. You've gotten this far, but I doubt you will be able to evade them if they know you're inside and what you're wearing."

"Or maybe I'd rather snap your neck before I go," said Morgan.

"No doubt you'd like to. But we all know why you're

here today, and it's not for me. *She* is not here, obviously, and your time is running out. Try anything, and I'll yell. Even if you do manage to kill me, you will risk capture. Get captured, and there's no one left to stop her. So, what will it be?"

Morgan's fury was close to flash point, but Conley put his hand on Morgan's shoulder, which calmed him enough to control himself.

"One day, sooner or later," said Morgan, "you're going to pay for everything you've done."

"I'm sure," said Nickerson dismissively. "Now, off you go."

Enraged, Morgan stormed out of the VIP box, with Conley behind him. They walked down the hallway they had come in through and past the two entrance guards, who merely regarded them blankly.

"I can't believe we just left like that," said Morgan.

"But he's right, Cobra," said Conley. "It's a stalemate situation."

"And meanwhile, we're back at square one," said Morgan.

"There are more than twenty thousand people in this stadium," said Conley, "we have no idea where to even begin looking for T, and the speech is about to start. So the real pertinent question is, What now?"

Morgan visualized the stadium in his head, analyzing it for secluded vantage points. If he were in T's position, where would he be? The answer was obvious.

"Lowry, Lowry, come in."

"This is Lowry," came his voice in Morgan's ear.

"Lowry, the roof! Where does the perimeter intersect with the edge of the roof?"

Morgan heard clicking on Lowry's end. After a few seconds, Lowry told him, "That would be . . . at the stadium lights right above you."

It made sense. The light arrays would be a perfect cover from any eyes scanning the roofline, making anyone looking directly into them effectively blind. He mentally kicked himself for not thinking of it sooner. "Then that's where she'll be," said Morgan. "Lowry, how do we get there?"

"Let me see . . ." Morgan heard typing on the other side. Then, "There's a door down the hallway to your left that will take you to the maintenance area. Gain access to that, and I'll direct you from there."

They walked down the hallway. Finding the door, Morgan tested the knob to check if it was locked, when a voice from behind him bellowed, "Hey, what are you doing?"

It was one of the upstairs guards, in his black suit. Morgan noticed the bulge of a gun under his jacket.

"I'm sorry, sir, we were just looking for the bathroom."

"Well, that's not it," he said brusquely. And then he stopped, as if he were listening to something in his earpiece. As he looked at Morgan and Conley, his eyes went wide, and his hand went for his gun. But he was too slow. Morgan elbowed him in the face and followed with a left hook to his temple. The man fell down, out cold.

He took the guard's gun, a Colt semiautomatic, and checked it for ammo—a full clip. Morgan tucked it into his pants behind his back. Then he took the earpiece from the man's ear and crushed it beneath his foot.

"Can you get that door open?" he said to Conley. Morgan kept lookout while Conley worked the lock with his tools. He opened it in under a minute and helped Morgan drag the unconscious man inside.

"Lowry, we're in. Where now?"

"Up, baby, up." He directed them through the twisting tunnels, past exposed pipes and raw concrete, until they opened a white door and saw, in the distance, the brightly illuminated dome of the Capitol and the Washington Monument towering behind it. They were on the flat top of the main section of the stadium, and on that rested the roof itself, white and undulating.

"On your left, you'll find a ladder to the top," said Lowry.

Morgan climbed first. When he reached the top, he looked around. There were four arrays of stadium lights, two on each side. "Lowry, which one is it?"

"How am I supposed to know? They're all about the same distance from the podium."

She could be at any one. Morgan looked in both directions. There wasn't time to think about this. "I'll go left," he said, and he ran toward the nearest array, while Conley took the cue and ran right.

He scanned the scaffolding on the light arrays, each of which had four levels of narrow catwalks for maintenance. No sign of her on the nearest one. He sprinted toward the far lights. Below, in the stadium, the people were cheering. Senator McKay had just been announced.

Morgan approached the next group of stadium lights and saw a figure crouching on the second-tier catwalk, looking through the scope of a rifle whose muzzle extended out, in between the lights. T. He slowed his pace, stepped lightly, and didn't say a word, careful so as not to alert her to his presence. Morgan climbed quietly onto the platform, the din below concealing whatever noise he made, his gun on her the entire time, and, once on his feet, he yelled over the applause, "Natasha! Step away from the rifle!"

CHAPTER 42

Immersed in the noise of the cheering crowd below them, Natasha looked at Morgan and the gun in his hand without emotion. She took her hands slowly and deliberately off the rifle. She looked at him without speaking. Slowly, her lips curled into a smirk.

"Away from the rifle. Now!"

She got to her feet and raised her hands, palms out. "So, you've found me. I suppose you think that means you won, don't you?"

"I seem to be the one with the gun," he said.

"Maybe. But I know something you don't."

"Oh, yeah? What's that?"

"Fail-safe. Redundancy. Shooting her, this whole business with the rifle, this is Plan B. The backup. You can kill me now, and she still dies. In fact, kill me now, and you have no possibility at all of preventing her death." She continued to smile, and Morgan recognized that she was triumphant.

He kept the gun on her. "Is there any chance you're going to tell me how to save her?"

"Perhaps, Cobra. As I see it, we are in a position to make an exchange here."

"Yeah? What do you want?"

"Drop the gun and let me go. I'll shout it to you as I run away."

"You think I'm falling for that?" he asked, unmoved. "You'd say anything to get out of this."

"A fair point. But do you think you have a choice in the matter?"

"Yeah," he said. "I shoot you here and now."

"You are going to gamble with the senator's life?" she asked. "Perhaps I am lying. You know that I am perfectly capable of it. That if it were not true, I would make it up. But the cost of calling my bluff is too great."

He stood there, the gun pointed at her chest, sweat dripping down his forehead from the heat of the stadium lights. The cheering of the crowd began to die down, and he heard McKay's voice reverberate throughout the stadium, "Thank you! Thank you so much!"

"Tick-tock, Cobra. In a minute or two, the senator will be a corpse unless I tell you how to save her. Make your choice. What does Cobra care about more? His duty or a personal score?"

His hand twitched on his weapon.

"Move, slowly. Leave the bag, and keep your hands where I can see them," he said.

She stood from her crouch. Morgan was standing between her and the ladder down to the stadium roof, and she had to get past him. She took her time walking toward him, never breaking eye contact.

"Thank you," the senator said again. Then she began, solemnly, "We are living in a time of deep moral crisis in our government. A time when corruption has become so entrenched that we are no longer surprised by each new scandal."

As Natasha squeezed past Morgan, brushing up against his body, she puckered her lips and blew him a kiss. He jabbed the barrel of the gun against her side.

"Okay, okay," she said. "Such impatience."

She descended the ladder, lingering just a fraction too long on each step.

"Our leaders have betrayed our trust, forsaking their oath of office for power and petty personal gain." McKay's voice was clear and passionate.

Natasha looked up at him, her eyes at the level of his feet.

"Well?" he demanded.

"The gun, Cobra. Toss it."

Grimacing, he released the clip, which fell with a clang at his feet, then tossed the gun onto the stadium roof near where she stood.

"And for the sake of Beltway cronyism, this treachery"—McKay's voice rang out over the speakers—"and it *is* treachery, folks, a betrayal of the trust of the American people—goes unchallenged and unreported."

"That was my end of the bargain," said Morgan. "Now let's hear yours."

"On second thought," said Natasha, with a superior smile, "I think I'll let you figure it out on your own. Let's just say I left a little present for her. Now we find out whether you can still think on your feet, Cobra."

She turned around and ran from him, toward the outer edge of the roof. He tensed, ready to go after her, but stopped midstride. Had she lied? If not, what was Plan A?

"Seeing all of you here tonight, I know that I am not the only one who thinks this cannot go on," said McKay.

"Cougar, Cougar, come in," said Morgan.

"I'm here, Cobra. What's happening?"

"Cougar, she's making a run for it. I need you to go after her. Keep as close to her as you can!"

"Got it," said Conley.

"Lowry, did you catch that?" said Morgan.

"I got the gist. Do you believe her?"

"I don't think I have a choice," he said.

"What do you figure it is, a second shooter?" asked Lowry.

"No," said Morgan. "That's not her style. She likes to take care of things herself. She wouldn't trust someone else with this."

"Could be a bomb in the podium," said Lowry. "Did she have a detonator on her?"

Morgan looked down to where Natasha had left her pack.

"But what do we do about it?" asked McKay.

The pack was mostly empty. The rifle, he figured, would have taken up most of the space, and apart from that there were some tools and some folded-up straps of some kind, like narrow seat belts. But as he rummaged, his hand found a small cylindrical object, bright orange with a white cap.

"No. But there is something here. A pill container. The label says it's . . . " He strained to read the tiny print, "Hydrosol . . . Hydroxocobalamin."

"Hydroxo . . . cobalamin . . ." he heard Lowry murmuring and typing. "Apparently that's another name for vitamin B12a. But I don't know why that would be . . ."

It dawned on him almost immediately. "I know," said Morgan. "It's an antidote for cyanide. "

"Why would she . . . Oh, God."

"She's going to poison the senator," said Morgan.

"How was she going to do that?"

"Not from a distance, she couldn't. Whatever it is, it's already in place." He thought for a moment, looking at the senator through the scope. Then he said, "The water!"

"What?" asked Lowry.

"She said it's going to be a spectacle. There's no way she can deliver the poison from here. That means the cyanide is already there. The only way she could be sure the senator would take it when she was onstage would be to put it in the senator's water. The water that's sitting on the podium right now."

"Are you sure, Cobra" asked Lowry. "This whole thing could be nothing but misdirection."

"It fits her MO."

"So what are you going to do?"

"The only thing I can do from here," said Morgan. "I shoot at her and take care that I miss."

He knelt at T's rifle and looked through the scope.

"Cobra, are you crazy?"

"It's the only way to save her now. The only way to interrupt this speech right now."

"There are times when we despair," continued McKay, "and it seems like there is nothing we, as citizens, can do to change anything."

There was no wind. It was a straight, clear shot. The heat off the lights was a furnace, and sweat ran down his brow and dripped from his nose. He tore off the fake mustache, not needing it anymore. He took off the suit jacket and laid it on the platform in front of the rifle.

"Even if Natasha wasn't lying," exhorted Lowry, "and even if you manage to pull this off, you'll cause a panic. They'll think you're shooting at her, and all twenty thousand people in this stadium are going to rush for the exits. People might die."

"I need to do it. I can't let Nickerson win." He looked through the scope. A shot straight through the podium would do it. It would hit the stage, McKay would be unscathed, and her security detail would usher her off to safety.

"Cobra, think about this!"

"But I, for one, believe that in a democracy, it is in the citizens' power to change things," said McKay. "So consider this a call to action!"

The crowd erupted in wild cheering and applause.

And then it happened in a split second. She took the glass and began to raise it to her mouth. A shot through the podium would no longer be enough. He had to act immediately. There was no time to take careful aim, yet if he was off by a hairbreadth, he would be doing T's job for her.

He squeezed the trigger.

The glass shattered in Senator McKay's hand. Ten thousand screams rang out, a thousand cameras flashed, and her security detail sprang into action.

He didn't have time to observe the aftermath. It wouldn't be long until they worked out a rough trajectory from the bullet hole in the stage. They were probably scanning the roofline now for him. He'd done what he had come to do. Now he had to get the hell out of there. Morgan left the rifle where it was, climbed down onto the roof, and ran back in the direction from which he had come.

"Now you've done it," said Lowry.

"How's Cougar?" Morgan asked.

"Still on Natasha's tail. He's almost out to the parking lot. Cobra, you have to get the hell out of there. Guards are swarming up to the roof. At least five are going to be there in under two minutes."

"Can I get down the way I came up?"

"Not unless you're planning on shooting your way out of there."

"Then find me a way to get the hell off this roof!"

"I'm trying!"

He was almost to the edge of the roof, with nowhere to go. "Lowry, which way did Natasha leave?"

"Same way you got there. Why?"

She couldn't have counted on leaving the same way. If she had shot the senator, she would be in exactly the same predicament he was in now. She wouldn't have trusted her escape to chance. There had to be another way out of there. He looked along the edge of the roof, and then he saw it.

"Lowry, I think I've found the way down."

The rope was sitting in black coils, anchored tightly to a sturdy railing. He ran toward it and found it already threaded through the rappel device, with a locking carabiner attached to it. But there was no harness—that was in Natasha's pack, two hundred feet away.

There was no time to go back for it now. He'd have to make do with what he had. Morgan attached the carabiner to his belt and pulled hard. He could only hope that it would hold. He removed his button-down shirt, leaving him in his undershirt, and wrapped it crudely around his right hand. Then he looked down. At the bottom of the first drop was the main body of the stadium, on which the roof sat, and over that edge was a long, sheer drop with nothing but thin, vertical slats for support. Below, people were swarming out of the stadium. He climbed over the railing and stood with his back to empty space.

I hate this part, he thought.

He pushed off, and his feet flailed in the air. As he swung himself back in toward the side of the roof, he was thrown off balance, and he hit his shoulder hard. He released more rope but too fast. His feet hit the ground on the lower level, and the impact made him fall onto his right knee with a scream of pain.

"Cobra," came Lowry's voice. "They're coming! Get out of there!"

He got up and tossed the rope over the side, down to the ground below. There would be no do-over this time. He stood with his back to the edge.

Only one way to go, he thought, and he dropped backward into the air. He had better control this time, and he stabilized himself on the slats with his feet. He zipped down quickly, and soon his feet hit the soft ground no harder than if he had jumped off a curb.

"Conley, what's going on?"

"Natasha's got wheels," said Conley through his earpiece. "I'm going after her. Where are you?"

"I'm right by the main gate. Where are you?"

He didn't need a response when he heard the rumble of his GTO approaching, maneuvering through the crowd. The car stopped right in front of him. Conley got out.

"You drive."

Morgan ran around the car to the driver's door. As he got in, he looked up and saw three security guards looking down at him from the roof. *Hell with them*, he thought, and he sat down, feeling the powerful rumble of the engine through the wheel. Conley was already in the passenger seat.

"Get ready to see some real driving," he said, and they peeled off, roaring down toward Independence Avenue, toward T, leaving a dozen guards scrambling behind them.

CHAPTER 43

Morgan stepped on the gas, and the GTO roared down the avenue. Tires squealed as he swerved around cars, which he passed so fast, it looked as though they were hardly moving at all, honking at him as he cut them off. Far ahead, Natasha was threading an agile little Japanese sports car through traffic, driving west toward the National Mall. Her car was newer, lighter, and easier to maneuver through tight spots, but it couldn't match the raw power of the GTO.

"Don't let her get out of our line of sight!" shouted Conley over the roar of the engine.

"What the hell do you think I'm doing?" Morgan exclaimed.

And then, through the rearview mirror, he saw flashing red and blue lights and heard the siren of the police car.

That didn't take long, Morgan muttered to himself, stepping harder on the gas. But the police car came with one great benefit: the other cars, hearing the siren, were now parting, opening a way for Morgan and Conley to pass. But still, Natasha was getting farther and farther away.

"Lowry, do you copy?" Morgan said.

"Copy, Cobra," came Lowry's voice, barely audible in his earpiece.

"Is there any way you can track her?" said Morgan.

There was a pause, and then Lowry said, "I can, but it's going to take a few minutes."

"We don't have a few minutes!" said Morgan.

"I'm going to have to tap into a military satellite," said Lowry. "This isn't exactly a walk in the park." There was a pause, and then he said, "Listen, Cobra. Once I'm in, I'm going to need to get a bead on her visually. I need to find her by tracing your signal. That means you need to stay on her tail until I can access the feed."

"Can you say that to me in plain English?"

"If you lose her, I won't be able to find her again."

"Copy that."

"Cobra!" yelled Conley. They were approaching an intersection, and the lights had just turned red. The cars in their lane came to a stop, blocking their way. With no time to stop, he veered into the opposite lane, narrowly missing a car that had turned into it. The cars at the intersection stopped as they saw him careering toward them, leaving a sliver of an opening for the GTO. Morgan scraped another vehicle as he negotiated the narrow gap between cars. The pursuing police car came to a screeching halt behind them, not daring to make the same dangerous maneuver. But the victory was short-lived. The tail they lost was soon replaced by two others.

They steadily gained on Natasha as they drove past Lincoln Park and merged onto Massachusetts Avenue, until Morgan was close enough to drive in her wake. The call had definitely gone out on the police frequency, because cop cars were now attempting to cut them off. There would only be more of them the closer they got to the National Mall.

"Lowry, do you have the trace on her yet?" barked Morgan.

"Almost! Keep her in your sight!"

They zoomed down Constitution Avenue, passing the illuminated Capitol on their left. Two more cop cars turned on their flashing lights, straight ahead and hurtling toward them. Natasha took a sharp left, tires squealing. Narrowly missing the oncoming police cars, Morgan turned in pursuit of her, so that the Capitol remained on their left. Up ahead, there were another two squad cars closing in fast.

"Only one way out!" said Morgan. And, sure enough, Natasha veered right, climbing onto the sidewalk at the access ramp and onto the lawn of the National Mall, barely avoiding the scrambling pedestrians.

"Oh, shit!" exclaimed Conley as Morgan turned hard, the GTO pitching violently when they hit the ramp. They followed Natasha's car, which was whipping up dust in its wake. The police cars scrambled to pursue them by the road alongside the lawn. Morgan and Conley were trailing Natasha closely now, and their car handled better on the grass than hers.

Even though they had caught up with Natasha, they were faced with another problem. The police cars were converging around them, attempting to cut them off from any escape routes.

"Lowry, now would be a really good time for you to get a lock on her car!" Morgan snapped.

"Tracing now! Just keep with her for a few more seconds!"

They were fast running out of lawn, and the police cars were attempting to block their way forward.

"Cobra!" shouted Conley. "Forget Natasha! We need to get out of here!"

"Not until Lowry gets the trace!"

"We're not going to be able to escape the cops unless we split off from her!" Conley insisted. "Now!"

He was right. The Mall was a wide-open space, but the cops were closing in. There was a far better chance of escape if they gave up the chase.

"Lowry! We can't hold on much longer!"

Through the rearview mirror, Morgan saw that two police cars had climbed onto the lawn after them, far behind but gaining. If they didn't separate, this was going to be over pretty quickly.

"Lowry?"

"Got it!" exclaimed Lowry triumphantly. "Now you two get the hell out of there!"

Morgan pulled the hand brake, making a 180 that pinned him against the door and sent dust up all around them. The car stopped mere feet from the curb, and he instantly hit the gas hard, back in the direction they had come from. Natasha raced on, just making it between two police cars that were attempting to block her way. Now turned to face the two police cars that had been coming up behind them, Morgan feigned a turn to the left, then made a sharp right. One of the police cars, trying clumsily to respond to Morgan's maneuver, spun out and hit the other. Morgan could still see them, motionless, in his rearview mirror as he drove back onto the street and turned right at the National Gallery. He sped down Constitution Avenue, turning at the Canadian embassy. As they drove farther from the Mall, the sirens faded behind them, and Morgan pulled the car into a darkened alley.

Conley, sitting beside him, breathed a sigh of relief. "Jesus, Cobra. I'd almost forgotten how *crazy* you are behind the wheel."

Morgan smirked. "A little fast for you, Grandpa?"

Conley grinned back at him. "How about you get on an F-22 with me someday, and we'll see who the *grandpa* is."

Morgan chuckled. "All right, Lowry," he said. "Tell us where to go."

CHAPTER 44

Natasha parked her car at the sharp elbow of a residential road that bordered the arboretum. Beyond a couple of old concrete barriers to the east was a dark, abandoned lane. She got out of the car, surveyed the street once more for any trailing police cars, hopped over the barrier, and ran down the road, into the darkness and away from civilization. She spotted the chopper about three hundred feet away, and even with it on the ground she could see its beams, brilliant in the twilight. She could hear the rotor from where she was, too, powered up and ready for takeoff. She looked back, half expecting to see Morgan's headlights behind her. But no; everything was dark.

As she approached the chopper, she saw a man standing in front of it, facing her. In the half light, she could just make out his facial features. It was a beefy man with greasy black hair and bulging eyes. Roland Vinson.

"What is going on here?" she demanded, shouting over the roar of the motor and blades of the helicopter.

"Change of plans, sweetheart," he shouted back.

She reached for her weapon, but he was faster. He aimed the sleek black silencer at her chest and fired twice. She collapsed, her legs splayed at awkward angles. She gasped, and then her breathing settled into a labored wheeze. Her lungs, she realized, were filling with blood. She tried to get up, but it was as though there were a heavy rock on her chest. Her mind was already far away. It felt as though to move a finger would take all her strength. Vinson walked toward her until his feet, huge in ugly crocodile shoes, were planted next to her head. He aimed right between her eyes.

"It's too bad I gotta mess up such a pretty face."

She kept her eyes firmly on him, defiantly. If he was killing her, she would make her death her own and stare down the barrel of the gun that did it. She fought through the haze. She wanted to be fully conscious for it.

But it didn't come. There were gunshots, and before she knew it, Vinson looked up and retreated toward the chopper, shooting back at an unknown target. She lay there languishing as the firefight raged around her. She was enveloped in a whirlwind as the chopper took off. Her blond hair whipped across her face. The miasma of death was setting in now, and everything seemed distant. The shooting continued as the rotors slowly faded into the distance. Then there was silence.

Her eyes flicked upward, and through the haze she saw Cobra standing over her in the twilight. The world was far away now, as if she was underwater and sinking deeper. *Not yet*, she thought. *One more thing*. It took all her willpower to move her trembling hand into the secret pocket in her pants and to drag out with her weak fingers the small object. She closed her palm around it. Then she forced her laboring lungs to say one last word, in a weak wheeze.

"Andr . . ."

The name of her brother died on her lips, and the world went dark.

Morgan knelt over T's lifeless body as Conley approached and asked, "Is there any chance you saw who was on that helicopter?"

Morgan shook his head distractedly. He was looking at her face, contorted with pain. Her beautiful sky-blue eyes still retained their wild intensity, even in death. He shut them gently and looked at her in the quickly fading light. As much as he could never forgive her for what she had done, their enmity seemed not to matter as much now that she was dead. Instead, he felt a strange camaraderie with her, as if she hadn't been hunting him, but rather, as if it was still that first night at the ball; as if she hadn't been told a lie and had lived her life without bitterness and had had no score to settle with him; as if they had remained friends to the end, and resentment had not turned her into a cynical, amoral, rogue agent. In silence he honored her as the friend she once was and the great warrior that she had been to the end. He took her hand in his one last time and was surprised to find that there was something nested in it.

He gently pried apart her fingers and found a small, featureless black metallic chip. He held it up to Conley. "You know what this is?" Conley shook his head. Whatever it was, it might be important. Morgan slipped it into his pocket.

"Lowry," Morgan said. "Lowry, come in." He got no response.

"I guess we're out of range," said Conley. "Come on. Let's get back."

They walked briskly back up the dark road and got into the GTO.

"What now?" asked Conley.

"We regroup," said Morgan, starting the engine and rolling out. "T may be dead, but Nickerson isn't. There's still a mole in the CIA. They're still arming Afghan insurgents."

"Cobra," Conley cut in softly.

Morgan continued. ". . . and for all we know, they're going to try to kill Senator McKay again, and I'm betting they're going to go for the quick and dirty kill this time."

"Cobra," Conley repeated, "Morgan. Maybe it's time for us to cut our losses and leave. Take Jenny and Alex and get out of the country. Find a nice, quiet place to retire."

"And what? Let them get away with it?"

"They already have, Morgan. The Agency wants to kill us. Nobody else is going to believe our word. There's just two of us against all of them."

"Then we keep fighting, Conley. We keep coming at them until we win."

"Or until we die, Morgan? Is that it?"

Morgan didn't answer because their discussion was cut short. Three squad cars turned onto the street they were on, tires squealing and lights flashing.

"Shit!" Morgan downshifted to second gear, and with a twist of the wheel the car turned a complete 180, rubber burning on asphalt. They tore off in the opposite direction, away from the approaching squad cars. Almost immediately, four more turned onto the street ahead of them. Morgan tromped the gas pedal.

"Cobra, what are you doing?" Conley exclaimed.

"We're going to get past them!"

The cars ahead massed rapidly, blocking the road ahead. Morgan accelerated.

"Cobra!"

"We'll plow through if we have to. We can make it!"

"No, Cobra, we can't!"

"*We can make it through!*"

"Cobra! We can't! Let it go!"

Gritting his teeth, Morgan pulled the hand brake and stopped the car with a controlled spin. The cars that had been chasing them closed in a circle around them. At least a dozen policemen scrambled out and took cover behind their cars, guns aimed at Morgan and Conley.

"Get out of the vehicle with your hands up!"

They were completely surrounded. There was nothing to do but surrender.

CHAPTER 45

For nearly an hour Morgan and Conley sat hand-cuffed in a stationary squad car, guarded by two shotgun-wielding cops, while other officers talked among themselves and made phone calls. There seemed to be some confusion about what to do with them. With nothing really to be done, the two sat tight and waited.

Eventually, a conclusion was reached, and about half of the police cars dispersed, while the rest of the force remained to guard them. Finally, a small caravan of black town cars pulled up alongside them, and from the lead car emerged the weasel, Harold Kline, looking smug.

"These boys are ours, Sergeant," he said, presenting a piece of paper to the officer in charge. "That little document means they're under our purview. Your discretion in this matter is both appreciated and absolutely mandatory."

The police sergeant looked at him with an expression that said, "*What a jack-off!*" But he talked to some of his fellow officers, pointing at the two captives.

Morgan and Conley were yanked out of the car and re-cuffed behind their backs with the CIA's high-security restraints.

"You fellas going to behave?" said Kline.

"Where are you taking us?" demanded Morgan.

"You'll find out," said Kline. Then he addressed the agents. "Load them up. I want them in separate cars, in full shackles. Keep your guns out of their reach, and watch their hands! The last thing you want to do is underestimate them."

They led Morgan to one of the cars, and once inside they cuffed his ankles. There was an agent on either side of him, and he was instructed not to move. The cuffs dug into his back uncomfortably.

As the car began moving, he wondered where he would end up. They wouldn't bring formal charges against him, not with everything he knew from his past missions. There was a lot of dirty laundry that nobody wanted aired.

Plus, there was plenty the CIA could do if they wanted to make him disappear, and the fact that he lived mostly off the grid would only make that easier for them. Would they ship him off to a secret prison in the Middle East? Or would he be the victim of an un-fortunate "accident"? And, most of all, what would happen to Jenny and Alex now? But as they drove, it became abundantly clear where they were going.

The car came to a stop sometime later at CIA Head-quarters. They yanked him out the door. Conley was brought out of his car just a few feet away from him, being escorted, like him, by two men.

The procession walked into the building, and even

though it was a Saturday night, the place was still fully manned, with suits walking in and out. Whatever time it was, it was always noon somewhere in the world.

Morgan saw a small group of people standing and facing them and realized that among them was Jeffrey Boyle, looking stiff and official, flanked by several security officers.

"Gentlemen, kindly detain him," Boyle said calmly. Morgan braced himself for rough treatment. But to his surprise, they surrounded Kline, two of them with weapons drawn.

"What the hell is going on here, Jeffrey?" Kline demanded.

One of the officers handcuffed him and patted him down.

"You are being charged with conspiracy to commit murder, for the attempted assassination of Senator Lana McKay," said Boyle.

"What? Is this some kind of joke?" asked Kline, perplexed and indignant. "I had nothing to do with that! On what evidence are you arresting me?"

"It's all here, page after page, the record of your electronic communications with the operative implicated in an assassination attempt," said Boyle. "All of which point to your direct involvement in the planning and execution of the attempt on Senator McKay's life."

Kline's eyes widened, and the color drained from his face. "I don't know what those documents are. It's a frame job! A dirty frame job! Jeffrey, you have to believe me!"

"Spare us," said Boyle dispassionately. "You'll have an opportunity to defend yourself in court. Now, take this traitor away."

They escorted Kline, still protesting his innocence, out of the building. Boyle's attention turned to Morgan.

"Seems like I owe you an apology. You were right all along: there was a mole in the CIA, working right under our noses. I was a fool not to see it. But it became increasingly clear to me that something didn't add up, so I had Kline investigated. And you were right."

Morgan regarded him with undisguised animosity.

"In light of these developments, I consider your hostile actions entirely justified." He looked at Conley. "The same goes for you, Cougar. You can't imagine how happy I was to discover you were alive."

Then, addressing their guards, Boyle said, "Please release them from their handcuffs." He turned back to Morgan and Conley. "Your names will be cleared. If you wish, Cougar, you will be reinstated as an operative, pending an investigation of the events of the past two weeks. We will also choose to overlook the involvement of a certain Mr. Lowry, who is already inside being debriefed. Fair?"

Morgan walked up close to him and spoke in a menacing whisper. "You sent an assassin after me and my family. That's not something I'm going to forgive and forget."

"I sincerely hope you will put yourself in my shoes one day and change your mind about that. But I am truly sorry, Cobra. I hesitated to believe that there was a mole, because I did not want to believe that such a grave breach had happened on my watch. It was my mistake, and I openly admit that."

Morgan swung his fist and let him know what he thought of Boyle's apology, and his point hit the director right in the jaw. Morgan was tackled to the floor and restrained by four agents.

"Let him go," said Boyle, touching his jaw tenderly. "That was a freebie, Cobra, because I happen to be in an apologetic mood. I recommend that you don't try it again."

Morgan glowered at him. As Boyle's eyes then focused somewhere behind him, Morgan turned around to see that a lean and muscular woman, dressed professionally and with a no-nonsense, close-cropped haircut, had just walked in from outside.

"Ah, Julia, just in time," said Boyle. "Cobra, this is Julia Carr. She was Kline's second-in-command at the NCS. Julia, it seems you just got a battlefield promotion. You'll be taking over Kline's duties provisionally as Deputy Director, effective immediately."

"Is that why I was called in? What happened to Harold?"

"You will be filled in on everything shortly. Now please ensure that these two gentlemen are debriefed."

Julia Carr nodded.

"Gentlemen," she said, and the three of them walked together into the bowels of the CIA.

CHAPTER 46

Morgan was up most of the night going over in excruciating detail everything that had happened since Eric Plante visited him at his home. Earlier that evening, they had let him contact Jenny and Alex, who had been staying at an out-of-the-way motel in Pennsylvania. There was no harm in disclosing their location at this point and no reason to prolong their anxiety and discomfort. Two agents were sent to pick them up. Morgan would have liked to go himself, but they wouldn't let him leave. He also told them where to collect Natasha's body.

At about 3:00 A.M., they gave him some fresh clothes, a cot, and an electronic ankle monitor, the kind used for people under house arrest. He resented being treated like a prisoner, but it was no use arguing with them. Then they told him to get a few hours' sleep. He couldn't, so he lay on his cot, still in his undershirt and pants, thinking about the chip he had taken from Natasha. They had taken it on his arrest, but promised to give it to Lowry for analysis.

"I've seen this before," said Lowry the next morning, turning the chip over in his hand. He had also been kept overnight but had managed to find a shower and a change of clothes. They were now in his office, which was about as big as a broom closet and was plastered with comic strips clipped from the newspaper. "Data storage, but far from your garden variety USB flash drive."

"So what can we expect to see here?" Morgan asked.

"On a chip like this? The more advanced ones can store upward of one terabyte of data."

"Which means?" asked Morgan.

"Which means she could have put everything on there. Documents, recordings, video. You can fit more than a hundred DVDs' worth of video in a terabyte. I assume this was her insurance, something to keep the people she works for from disposing of her. So there might be some seriously damning evidence in here. This might be everything we need. To put the final nail in Kline's coffin *and* get Nickerson."

Then this was it. This little thing could put an end to this whole situation for good.

"It's got some impressive hardware-based encryption," Lowry continued. "Very difficult to crack."

"Can you do it?"

A sly smile played on Lowry's face. "We'll have to brute-force it. Luckily, we have just the tool for the job."

"How long will it take to decrypt it?"

"On your average home PC? About thirty years."

"Thirty *years*?"

"Yeah," said Lowry. "But don't worry. In our machine, it shouldn't take more than a couple of days. I just have to log it in, and we'll get it started."

"Log it in?" asked Morgan. "You mean, tell them about it?"

"There's no way I can keep this a secret, Cobra. I'm here, but I'm on thin ice. They're watching my ass so closely, they'll know if I get a wedgie before I do."

"Lowry—"

"What are you afraid of, anyway? It's over already, Cobra. Relax. Everything will be fine."

Jeffrey Boyle was sitting at his desk when his personal assistant announced that Julia Carr was there to see him.

"Send her in."

Carr walked into the office, her confident façade cracking around the edges.

"I've been working on getting up to speed on this Cobra/Cougar situation," she said. "It's a lot to take in. We're looking at a government contractor gone rogue—it's the only term I can use to describe it—coupled with a mole in the CIA and—get this—a senator mastermind. Edgar Nickerson."

Boyle looked at her, deep in thought. "Do they have the evidence to back up all of this?"

"Oh, there's no doubt Acevedo International is into some serious illegal activity," she said. "We're talking treason, and they have the surveillance photos to prove it. Lawyers might get the higher-ups off, but if we allow this to get out, the company's finished when it comes to government contracts."

Boyle nodded. "And what about the link with Nickerson?"

"They've got nothing conclusive to show for it, although they seem thoroughly convinced."

"I see. Well, keep me posted, Julia. This situation even now calls for special attention. Remember, I want you to oversee this personally. Nobody else gets the full picture, and none of this information leaves this department. And I want to be informed of any new developments. You understand?"

"There is one thing, sir," she said. "Cobra apparently took a memory chip of some sort from Natasha Vasiliyevna's corpse."

Boyle looked at her with rapt attention. "What was on it?"

"We don't know," said Carr. "Apparently, it's got some serious encryption. But we have Lowry looking at it, and he says cracking it will be a real intelligence coup."

He frowned. "I see. How long until he is done decrypting it?"

"He says not for a few days, sir."

"Good," he said. But she didn't move. "Anything else?"

"Well, sir, I thought I might tell you that Cobra's wife and daughter are about to arrive at headquarters. Within the next"—she checked her watch—"fifteen minutes."

"Thank you for letting me know, Julia. Is that all?"

"Yes, sir."

"Then, if you'll excuse me, I need to report to the Director."

She took her leave and shut the door behind her. Boyle picked up the phone. "Jordan? Clear my schedule. I'm going to be absent from the office for the rest of the day."

"But sir, you have a conference call with the Director of National Intelligence at three."

"Tell him I'm up to my neck. Reschedule it for tomorrow," he said. "You know the drill." He put the phone back into its cradle. Then he got up, picked up his briefcase, and walked out the door.

"I'll take over from here," said Boyle to the two agents accompanying the Morgans. Then he turned his attention to the wife, whom he knew only from her pictures in Cobra's file. Jenny Morgan. She was younger in the photos, but her beauty had aged well. What the pictures hadn't shown was the innocent gullibility betrayed by her eyes, even while her body language showed tension and mistrust.

"Mrs. Morgan," he said, extending his hand to her. "My name is Jeffrey Boyle, and I'm director of the National Clandestine Service."

"Nice to meet you," said Mrs. Morgan, not entirely convincingly.

"And this must be Alexandra," he said, looking at the girl. She had her mother's looks, but there was definitely something of Cobra in her. Young as she was, she sported a distinct fortitude and shrewdness.

"Please accept my sincere apology, Mrs. Morgan, and Miss," he added, nodding to Alex, "for our involvement in this affair. We were deceived by one of our own, and that led to some bad decisions. I am very sorry." Jenny looked at him without friendliness in her eyes. "I'm afraid I need to follow that up with a request," he said. "I'd like you to answer a few questions about the events of the past two weeks."

"I'd like to see my husband first," replied Jenny.

"That will be arranged. But he isn't here right now. We put him up at a hotel a few miles away. Needless to say, your husband can use some rest."

"Then we'll go right to him," said Jenny.

"I'm sorry, but I thought this was explained to you. We will have to interview you right away. We have to ask you to remain here at headquarters for a few hours."

"A few *hours*? I'm not going to wait that long to see my husband, Mr. Boyle."

"It's important for us to determine everything that happened as soon and in as much detail as possible. I promise you that we'll get you to your husband as soon as we're finished."

"Mr. Boyle—" began Jenny.

"Mom," interrupted Alex, touching her arm, "it's fine. Let's just do this and be done with it."

Jenny sighed. "I suppose that would be all right, if you feel up to it," she said uneasily. "Let's go, then."

"I'm afraid you can't be together for this," he said. "We need to interview you separately. It will give us a more accurate picture of what happened."

"Frankly, Mr. Boyle, I don't care what picture you get. My daughter is a minor, and I'm not leaving her side," she said, instinctively moving between him and Alex.

"What if we were to take her directly to see your husband?" said Boyle. "I will personally see to it that your daughter gets there safely. You have the word of the director of the NCS."

"With all due respect," said Jenny, "I don't think your word is worth very much to me right now."

"Mom," Alex interjected, "it's okay. I'll go with him."

"But, Alex—"

"I appreciate it, Mom, but I'll be fine." Jenny looked at her daughter, her forehead lined with concern. "Really. Let's just get it over with, okay?"

"You are a brave young woman," said Boyle. "Don't worry. I'll make sure that she gets to your husband right away. I will go personally, as a small token of apology. We do appreciate your cooperation, Mrs. Morgan. Now please, Miss Morgan, if you would come with me, I'll take you to your father, myself. Hopefully it will help me make amends to him."

As Jenny made her way through security, Boyle escorted Alex out of the building, into the chilly, bright sunshine outside.

"Is it just you?" she asked. "No . . . guards or anyone?"

He chuckled. "Of course not. You're not my prisoner, are you?"

They walked in silence for a few seconds, and then Boyle spoke again, asking tentatively, "How are you feeling, Miss Morgan? Eager to see your father, I'm sure."

"Yeah," she said sullenly, looking away. Boyle glared at her, unseen. In another situation, he might be tempted to teach her a lesson in manners.

"He's certainly eager to see you."

"I know he is," she said.

"It must be difficult for you," he said. "This whole situation. How your father's work put you into danger."

"*You* put me into danger," she said.

The cheek! "And I can only apologize for that. This is the car here," said Boyle, stopping at a navy blue Mercedes. He unlocked it with the remote on his key chain and held open the passenger door for her. "But still," he continued, as he got into the driver's seat and buckled in. "I can't imagine it's easy for you, finding out about his secret life like this."

"My father loves me," she said stiffly.

"Oh, I'm counting on it," he said, and he turned the ignition key.

She shifted uncomfortably in the passenger's seat as the car rolled out.

After he finally received the required clearance to walk around freely, Morgan joined Lowry in his office, where the analyst was huddled in a chair, his face inches from the screen.

"Sit down, Cobra," he said, without looking away from the monitor. "I haven't started the brute-force decryption yet, but so far, this isn't presenting any challenges beyond what I expected. I suspect the protections on this thing go a little beyond encryption, but it's nothing we can't get around."

"It's all Greek to me," said Morgan. "But I'll trust that everything you're saying makes sense."

"God, I need an energy drink," said Lowry. "Something for you, Cobra?"

"Nah," he said distractedly, "I'm good."

"Okay, then, I'll be right back. You, behave. Oh, also, the bigwigs said they might need you soon, and they know you're out here. So if the phone rings, pick it up. It might be for you."

Morgan waited to sit at the computer until Lowry's footsteps faded away. He had been hoping for some time alone with this thing ever since he was brought to headquarters. Lowry had left the code-cracking program open and ready to begin. But Morgan had a hunch. It didn't take long for him to find a field labeled ENTER PASSWORD. His hands hovered over the keyboard.

If she had wanted the drive to be accessible to no one but herself, the password would be a random string of letters, numbers, and symbols, and guesswork would be a waste of time. But Morgan knew that this drive wasn't only for her. It was insurance, something that she would want others to be able to access if she died. She had taken it out to give it to him as her last living act. Natasha had wanted him to have it. He tried to put himself in her situation. If he were giving this to someone as the last thing he did on this earth, he would damn well want to make sure they had the password. And the easiest way to do that would be . . .

To tell them. Of course. It was obvious; how could he have missed it? He typed in *andrei*, but he knew it was too short without even trying. But that, of course, wasn't his full name. He carefully typed: *andrei-vasiliyevich*. He hit the Enter key. He fully expected an error message, but instead, a window opened with a long list of folders, each with a separate date on it. He was in.

He examined the files, running the cursor over each

one as he scanned it. The earliest ones dated back ten years, but the bulk of them were more recent. He clicked on the last file, from only a few days previous, labeled with the date, time, and *CIA*.

He heard Natasha's voice from the speakers. "I can do it. I can bring him down!"

"No. You failed, and now I'm sending Wagner to finish what you couldn't."

He stopped the recording. The voice was not Kline's. It belonged to NCS Director Jeffrey Boyle.

Morgan sat there in shock. It was Boyle. Morgan had been played all along, from the moment Boyle had let him in on Cougar's mission in Afghanistan. Boyle had leaked information to Nickerson and Natasha, and he must have bugged Plante, as he probably did his entire senior staff.

When he found out Plante was on to him, Boyle and his stooge, Nickerson, assigned T to take care of people who might implicate him—Plante, Cougar, Zalmay, and Morgan. It all fell neatly into place. Boyle had sent Wagner after Morgan, and when all his schemes had at last failed, he had set up Kline to take the fall. *The bastard*. But now Morgan had the evidence. Now he knew, and he'd make sure that Boyle would pay for what he did.

The phone rang, and Morgan looked at it as if it were a hissing snake. He picked up.

"I'm trying to reach Cobra."

"That's me," he said.

"Mr. Cobra, please hold. It's your daughter on the line."

He waited a few seconds and then heard Alex's quavering voice say, "Dad, it's me."

"Alex? Is something wrong? Is your mother there?"

"No, Dad, he's got a gun." She sounded like she was crying.

"Who has a gun? Alex, what's going on?"

"I don't know what he's talking about, but he says you have to bring the chip, and that you have to come alone and not tell anyone or he'll kill me. The ankle monitor—he says the code is 254766. He says to come to the barn at the Old Mill Road outside Arlington. Please, Daddy, please—!"

And someone hung up before she could say any more.

He heard Lowry's footsteps, heading back into the room. Morgan stood up as he appeared at the door.

"I really needed this," Lowry said, holding up a can of energy drink. Then he spotted the screen. "Hey, Cobra, what did you do there?"

But Morgan had already made his way behind him and deftly locked him in a sleeper hold. Lowry, whose natural response was not to struggle, was easily subdued and fell unconscious quickly.

Morgan set him down in the chair and then disconnected the chip from the computer and pocketed it. *I give it to Boyle, and then what?* he thought. *He lets me and my family go? Not likely.*

But what choice did he have?

He was about to walk out when he saw Lowry's smart phone on the desk. He had a crazy thought, and a desperate plan began to form in his mind.

He had to do it. He had to go face off against Boyle. But he wasn't going in empty-handed.

CHAPTER 47

Morgan spotted the grain silo first, towering above the trees, dirty white with rust peeking through the old paint. The air was quiet here, the noises of the city far behind. He stopped at the side of the road. Through the trees, he could catch glimpses of a run-down barn, and he wondered if there was a slaughter-house here, and at what distance it was possible to hear the screaming of dying cattle. He decided to approach on foot and rolled to a stop.

Before he got out of the car, he reached into the glove compartment and pulled out his backup gun. Then he picked up Lowry's phone from the passenger's seat and looked at its glowing screen. God, he hoped his plan worked. He reached for the ankle monitor. *Here goes nothing*, he thought, as he reconnected the loop. It began blinking red, while emitting a high-pitched, droning buzz. Someone, somewhere now knew that he was far out of his designated perimeter.

Morgan got out of the car and zigzagged his way to the barn door, taking cover behind Boyle's Mercedes, and then running to stand flat against the barn itself.

He peered through the cracks in the decaying planks that made up the wall. Light filtering in through the crumbling roof revealed Boyle standing in the hayloft, holding a weapon in his hand, his eyes fixed nervously on the door. Alex was there, too, sitting beside him on a bale of hay and sobbing quietly. If it were anyone else, he would go in guns blazing. But not this time, not while Boyle had Alex.

He pulled the heavy barn door, and it creaked loudly. The drifting dust motes glowed in shafts of sunlight that poured inside. He walked in, hands raised. Boyle moved fast, grabbing Alex by her hair and holding his gun under her chin.

"Cobra!" said Boyle, looking down at him from the hayloft. "How nice of you to show."

"Dad!" screamed Alex.

"Stay calm, sweetie," said Morgan. "I'm going to take care of this. It's going to be okay."

"You got a gun, Cobra?"

He reached for his weapon, tucked in the rear of his pants at the base of his back, and, holding it by the muzzle, dropped it at his feet.

"Kick it away."

Morgan did. It scraped noisily against the dirty barn floor.

"And the chip?" said Boyle.

He took the small black square from his pocket and held it up for Boyle to see.

"I've got a little something else, too," said Morgan, and he took Lowry's phone out of his shirt pocket. "Marvelous things, these phones. Did you know I can get an Internet connection all the way out here? Did you know, in fact, that I can send an e-mail to the editors of every major newspaper with the click of this one tiny little green button?"

Boyle glared at him, understanding plainly what Morgan was really telling him. Morgan went on.

"There were an awful lot of incriminating files on that chip. It would be a shame if a handful of them happened to be attached when this e-mail message goes out."

"You're bluffing!" said Boyle. "There were layers of encryption on that chip. There's no way you could have broken it already."

"No, there's no way. Unless, of course, I happened to know the password."

Boyle glowered, his eyes slits, and then burst into derisive laughter. "Nice try, Cobra. But you're a rat backed into a corner. There's nothing you wouldn't say to escape. Do you really expect me to fall for that?"

"'You failed, and now I'm sending Wagner to finish what you couldn't do, Natasha.' Sound familiar, Boyle?"

Boyle's gloating expression took an apprehensive turn, and he looked at Morgan in angry, stunned silence. Then he screamed, "Drop the phone. Drop it now! Or the little bitch gets it!"

"You touch a hair on her head—"

"And what?" Boyle pulled harder on Alex's hair, and she whimpered. The two men looked at each other in silence, furious. Then Boyle said, "You think I care about my reputation as much as you care about your daughter, Cobra?" Morgan just looked at him, concentrating to keep his anger in check. In another situation, he might try to go for his gun and shoot. But if he did, he knew Alex would be the first to die.

"See, Cobra, that's your problem. Your attachment

to your family. It stops you from going all-out. Keeps you from taking the risks that made you a great operative. Keeps you from making the hard decisions."

"Like you did, Boyle? Betraying your country? Was that a hard decision?"

"You don't know the first thing about patriotism, Cobra," he fumed. "You risked your life, yes, but you hid behind your code name. You still do. And you never had to make the decision to kill a person, or twenty. You just followed orders. You were never ultimately responsible for the security of this country. You have never made a decision to kill fifty people today to save a hundred tomorrow. You don't know what it means to make that kind of decision!" In his anger, he pulled Alex's hair. She sobbed.

"Look, Boyle, I don't care," said Morgan. "You did what you did for your own reasons, and I don't give a shit what they are. I just want my daughter back. So I'm forcing a draw. You toss away your gun, and we make the exchange. My daughter for the phone."

"Are there any more copies?"

"This is the only one," said Morgan.

"Suppose I believe you. How do I know that no one at the Agency has seen this?"

"Do you really think that they would let me come out here alone?" said Morgan. "This place would be swarming with Feds if I had told them."

"How do I know it isn't?" said Boyle.

"If it is," said Morgan, "then you've already lost."

Boyle watched him, as if mulling it over, and then said, "Okay. Come up. Slowly."

"Lose the gun first," said Morgan.

Boyle tossed it behind him, and it hit the wooden

loft with a thud. Morgan walked to the ladder that was propped up against the loft and climbed, slowly, his eyes steadily on Boyle and his daughter, who was no longer sobbing but still shaking.

Finally, he stood on the loft, about fifteen feet away from Alex, facing Boyle. The wooden floor seemed shaky, the wood itself rotted through. Morgan took a step toward him.

"Easy now," said Boyle. Morgan looked at the phone in his hand and then at Boyle. He had gotten close to Boyle and, more important, to Alex, But this was about as far as his plan went. Now he had to improvise.

"So what are we going to do once we make the exchange, Boyle?" It was an awkward question, but then again, they were far past social niceties.

"I should ask you the same, Cobra. How can I believe that you'll just back off?"

"Give me my daughter, Boyle, and I disappear. I take the blame, just like you planned. The operative gone rogue. You go back to selling out your country, to being some senator's bitch, and you never hear from me again."

Boyle cringed in anger at his words. "And suppose I don't believe you?"

"What do you think I'm going to do, Boyle? You control the intelligence. I give you the chip, and it's the last bit of evidence that connects you with any of this. I disappear as a fugitive. Who's going to believe anything I say?"

As Boyle paused, thinking, Morgan gave Alex a look that he hoped would be comforting. *It will be all right,* he wanted to say. *I'll die before I let anything happen to you.*

"So do we have an understanding?" Morgan said instead. "Give me my daughter, and we all walk out of here unscathed. After that, I disappear."

Boyle nodded. Morgan approached him, one tiny step at a time. He extended his hand holding the cell phone and the chip. Alex was just beyond his arm's reach.

Morgan tossed him the phone, then the chip, and Boyle shoved Alex forward into her father's arms. Morgan's stare never left Boyle, whose eyes went wide as he examined the phone and realized Morgan's deception. He looked fiercely at Morgan for a split second, and then his hatred erupted in a determined lunge to recover his gun.

Morgan pushed his daughter to the side into a bale of hay. He rushed at Boyle, hitting him in his midsection. They toppled over together and hit the loft floor hard. It splintered under their weight, and they fell through the stale air.

Morgan hit the ground hard and then felt piercing, disorienting pain. His bad knee had made contact first and absorbed much of the impact. After lying for a few moments dazed and in pain, he tried to get up but stumbled, falling facedown in the dirt.

He raised his head and saw Boyle on his feet, panting, incensed. He limped to the nearest wall, where several rusty farm implements were hanging, and grabbed a large, rusty machete. Morgan tried to get up again, but again the pain was too much, and his knee buckled.

Boyle shuffled back, his fist wrapped tightly around

the handle of the machete. With a great roar of triumph, he raised the machete over his head, ready to strike.

Alex's voice pierced the air. "Stop!"

She yelled it through her tears but still sounded commanding and self-assured. Boyle froze and turned around slowly. She had come down from the hayloft and picked up Morgan's gun, which was now in her trembling hand. Boyle took a step toward her.

"Stay back!" she screamed, no longer tearing up. She was angry. Enraged. And it seemed to give her power. "Stay back, or I'll shoot!"

"Do you know," said Boyle, panting, "how to use one of those?"

"I'm pretty sure it's just point and shoot," she said with resolute bitterness.

"There's a little more to it than that," Boyle told her. "Put it down, little girl, or you might hurt yourself."

She sneered at him. "I'm not a little girl." And she squeezed the trigger.

One shot—*BAM!*—hit Boyle squarely in the chest, and a red bloom grew on his shirt around the wound. He stammered, as if to say something, and then he fell as if the ground had shifted beneath his feet.

"Dad!" Alex exclaimed, and she ran over to him. He had crawled to the wall of the barn and was leaning against it, next to the hanging tools, trying to get up on his own. She extended her hand and helped him to his feet.

"You know something, kid?" He was half hugging, half leaning on her for support and glowing with pride. "You're my hero." She beamed and hugged him.

Morgan almost didn't see him. Boyle, blood-drenched,

had staggered to his feet, machete in hand. He was breathing in wheezing gasps, and his eyes were wide like a cornered animal's. With an inhuman scream, he raised the machete and charged. Alex screamed.

Morgan, with no time to think, grabbed the first thing his hands found on the wall—a pitchfork. He swung it to parry Boyle's attack, but the man didn't stop. His own momentum impaled him on the rusty tines of the pitchfork. They broke through his flesh and pierced him upward, from his gut into his chest. The machete dropped to the ground. He let out a weak grunt, gurgled, and tipped over onto his side, twitching, the pitchfork still sticking out of his torso.

Crying again, Alex fell into Morgan's arms.

"It's okay," he said, holding her tightly. "It's okay. Everything's okay now."

"Daddy," she said, sobbing, "can we go home now?"

"Yes, honey," he said, as he heard distant police sirens approaching. "We can go home."

CHAPTER 48

Edgar Nickerson looked out the plane's window at the fields far below. They were over—what?—Alabama? Tennessee? In any case, it was flyover country. He looked for Vinson to ask him, but Vinson was up in the cockpit with the pilot.

For the past hour or so, Nickerson had been replaying the same scene in his head, again and again—Cobra, bloody and tied to a chair, right in front of him. Except now, in the vision in his head, there was no offer. This time, Nickerson didn't leave, didn't entrust Natasha with the task of killing him. Instead, Nickerson himself killed the agent, each time a different way—a bullet to the head, a knife to the gut, a length of pipe, a two-by-four.

He tried to suppress those thoughts and relax. Fine, Boyle was out, and the CIA had some dirt on him. So what? They wouldn't go public with it, not the CIA, and in this business, it was the votes that counted. And fine, that goddamn McKay would get her law passed. After the assassination attempt, she had a Swiss bank's worth of political capital. Yes, that would hamper his influence in Congress and probably necessitate that he sever all his dealings with Acevedo. And even if, in the worst-case scenario, this shit did go public, he'd be gone long before they could grab him, and he'd live out his days in a tropical paradise with more money than he could count. And as worst-case scenarios went, how bad was that, really?

His reverie was interrupted by a sinking feeling in his gut. The plane was losing altitude, fast enough for him to notice. He was about to shout for Vinson when the man emerged from the cockpit, calmly strapping himself into a parachute.

"What's going on?" demanded Nickerson, gripped with fear. "Is the plane going to crash?"

"Yeah, 'fraid it is," said Vinson, without looking up from adjusting the ties on the parachute.

"What did the pilot say?"

"Pilot's dead," said Vinson. "And the autopilot is a couple of seconds away from getting fried."

"What? Then what are you waiting for? Give me a parachute!"

Nickerson got up from his seat, but before he could take a step, Vinson drew his gun.

"You want to stay in your seat." He motioned with the firearm, and Nickerson sat back down.

"What the hell are you doing?"

"Don't take it personally, now, boss. It's just business."

"Who's paying you? How much? I'll double it!"

"Sorry, Ed, but you can't pay me enough. You're out. History. And I'm not hitching my wagon to a dead horse." Vinson pulled down the lever to the cabin door, braced himself, and with a heave, opened it.

A buzzing alarm rang, and the emergency lights tinted everything red as air rushed out, sending loose sheets of paper and cups flying; then the roaring wind began, a hurricane inside the tiny jet's cabin. Vinson, holding fast on to a hand strap, gave him a little wave, and then he was gone, out into the blue expanse.

The plane bucked wildly. Nickerson held on, white-knuckled, to his armrest, tying to remember the emergency positions on the card he never read. Then the plane pitched into a nosedive straight down, lifting him from his seat so that he was held down only by the seat belt, so hard that he wondered whether the force might be enough to break every bone in his body. Squinting his watering eyes, he glanced out the window just in time to see the ground, so close, he could make out individual branches on the trees, reaching up at him like a giant hand swatting him out of the sky. Nickerson closed his eyes and hoped that it would be quick.

CHAPTER 49

Morgan and his daughter were brought back to CIA headquarters in handcuffs while a team stayed back to analyze the scene. They had to practically pull Alex away from him when they separated them for one-on-one questioning. Morgan went over the story in detail and produced Natasha's chip along with the password to access it. Then they locked him up in a holding cell, only to return a short while later to get him for further interrogation. Finally, they locked him up and left him in holding overnight.

The next day, they let Conley talk to him under heavy supervision.

"Jenny and Alex are together, and they're okay," said Conley. "From what they told me, which, granted, was not a whole damn lot, they'll let you out once they determine that the recordings on Natasha's chip are legit. What I do know is that there's a hell of a lot on it. More than we could have hoped—a heck of a lot more than the memory card we started with. I think we're going to nail Acevedo good. Hang in there, Morgan. You'll be out soon."

It was another day before they called him out of confinement again, and this time he sat down at a table with Julia Carr, who looked both weary and hardened by the recent events.

"Cobra, we need to know that we can count on your help in this time of crisis," she said. "There's a lot of turmoil in the agency at the moment, and we are hoping to be able to deal with it . . . in-house."

"I see," said Morgan. "So you're here to negotiate my silence—is that it?"

"We were hoping we could appeal to your loyalty and patriotism in the matter," she said. Then, with a thin smile, she added, "Or, failing that, your self-interest."

He didn't smile back. "There are two things I'm going to need from you," he said. "First, my file is purged. I walk out of here accused of no crime, and the CIA never bothers me or my family again. Is that clear?"

She nodded. "That can be arranged. And the other?"

"I need to know that Nickerson and Acevedo are going down. Keep secret what you have to keep secret, but they do not get away with what they did. Deal?"

"We have no interest in protecting Acevedo," said Carr. "They will suffer a very thorough, very *public* investigation. We will do everything in our power to air out the extent of their crimes. You have my personal guarantee about that," she said. On that point, Morgan remained doubtful. But there was one more important matter.

"And Nickerson?" he asked.

"They didn't tell you?" she said, with a smile.

"Tell me what?"

"It seems," she replied, "that someone has already

taken care of that for us. His private jet crashed this morning, and he was confirmed dead just hours ago. Senator Nickerson will no longer be a problem."

They made him sign about two dozen nondisclosure agreements and then let him go. He walked out to find Conley waiting for him.

"I brought your car," he said, holding up the keys to the GTO.

As they drove away together, Morgan behind the wheel, Conley told him everything that he had gleaned from the CIA. "Apparently Nickerson was using the drug money to create a whole web of influence. It wasn't just assassinations but also a wide campaign of bribery, blackmail, and intimidation. Boyle was feeding him information and also gave him access to some of the CIA's operatives. Like Natasha."

"What about Acevedo?" asked Morgan, looking forward as he drove.

"A marriage of convenience. Nickerson could offer protection, and they had money, lots of money. Enough to fund Nickerson's wild power trips. Looking over this stuff, I'm just glad we stopped him before it got any worse."

"And what are you going to do now?" asked Morgan.

Conley sighed. "I'm going to do what I've always done."

"Back to work for the CIA? After all that's happened?"

"It's the life for me," said Conley. "I've known it for a long time. I think you understand what I'm talking about. I think you feel it, too."

"I quit, remember?"

"I know, Morgan. But part of you never did, the part of you that loved this job. It never really went away, did it? A part that loves danger and excitement and being a part of something great. It's like Cobra still exists in there, inside you, and all this time was just waiting to come out. I know it's not *all* you are. You're also Dan Morgan, family man, who would do anything for his wife and daughter. Hey, maybe you can be just Dan Morgan for the rest of your life. But I'm not so sure that you can. Maybe you need this. Maybe you need to let Cobra out now and then."

They arrived at the hotel, where Conley had left his Sebring.

Morgan embraced his old friend. "Take care of yourself, Cougar."

Jenny and Alex were waiting for him in the lobby. As soon as he walked in through the revolving doors, they ran to him, Alex exclaiming, "Dad!" The three of them hugged, and Morgan couldn't help the tears that streamed down his cheeks.

They returned to Massachusetts that very night to find Neika lying on the mat at their front door. Her fur was matted with dirt and blood, but she leapt up as soon as she saw them, prancing around them, if a little stiffly, in a state of pure joy. Morgan laughed as she jumped on them to lick their faces, leaving dirty brown paw prints everywhere. Jenny and Alex, dirt all over the front of their clothes, laughed along.

EPILOGUE

It was Sunday. The Boston Common was alive with couples, families, and solitary people taking in the sun. The landscape was speckled with vibrant tulips and cherry blossoms, and the trees were as green as they ever get. Morgan took his time, enjoying the warm breeze. It was a beautiful day.

He walked onto the footbridge and spotted Senator Lana McKay with a hand on the railing, looking absentmindedly at the swan boats out in the water. He caught her eye as he approached her and smiled.

"Senator? Dan Morgan." He extended a friendly hand.

"It's such a pleasure to meet you," she said. "Thanks for driving into Boston, Mr. Morgan."

"I'm surprised you found me," he said.

"Information about you is indeed hard to come by, even if you have a seat in the United States Senate."

"But you have your ways?"

"Don't we all?"

She looked out at the water and sighed. "I owe you a debt of gratitude, Mr. Morgan. What you did . . . well, I hesitate to use the word *heroism* in almost any context, but it certainly seems to apply here."

"Honestly, Senator, I didn't really see it as a choice." he said. "I did what I had to do, and that's about it."

"The longer I live," she said, squinting at the water, "the more clear it is to me that the virtue of doing what is right is a rare thing in this world." She paused. "The bill failed, you know. The corporate oversight bill. 47–51. Even without Nickerson, the favors and the campaign donations spoke louder. I suppose the irony here is that, if only Nickerson had left me alone, I would have failed all the same."

"You'll get another chance," said Morgan.

"I certainly hope so," she said, in a disheartened tone. She sighed deeply and spoke again, looking away. "Do you ever wonder whether all your efforts are for nothing, Mr. Morgan? Do you ever lie awake at night asking yourself if what you do is ultimately right?"

"To tell you the truth, Senator, I don't. I know that maybe I should. It's a messy world, and right and wrong aren't always clear. But long ago, I learned to trust my gut and to never stop fighting."

"And how has that worked out for you?" she asked, with sincere curiosity.

"Better than the alternative."

She sighed. "I hope you're right, Mr. Morgan. This political game in Washington makes me question myself sometimes."

"That's the reason I never got into it in the first place."

She thanked him again and wished him luck. He

made his way along the path toward his car. As he walked into the entrance to the underground parking garage, he spotted a man on his tail, maybe forty to forty-five, in a dark suit and tie, wearing sunglasses.

Morgan walked quickly downstairs and waited around the corner at the landing for the man. He heard the dull knocking of the man's shoes on the steps. When he turned the corner, Morgan wrapped his right arm around the man's neck, pinning him in a choke hold.

"What the hell do you want?"

"Hello, Mr. Morgan," said the man, unfazed. "My name is Smith. I've been sent to make you a proposition."

Morgan frisked him with his free hand and then released him. "Whatever it is, I'm not interested."

"I hope you will at least listen, Mr. Morgan."

Morgan walked toward his car, and the man who called himself Smith walked alongside him.

"I work for a certain organization. Officially, we have no name. Officially, we don't exist. But we are there, behind the scenes, deeper than the CIA. We are pulling the strings and making this world a safer, better place. Mr. Morgan, we are in the business of writing history."

Morgan couldn't help giving the man a quick glance that betrayed his intrigue.

"We would like you to join us, Morgan. We have much use for a man like you. There's no need to answer now." The man handed him a business card that contained nothing but a phone number printed on cream stock. "Just call us when you have made your decision." He turned around and took two steps, then stopped, and said, "Ah, I nearly forgot. We have contacted your friend, as well. A man who goes by the name of Cougar. We made him the same proposition."

"And?"

"He accepted. We hope to hear from you soon, Mr. Morgan." He walked away down the long garage, his footsteps echoing in the vast parking facility. Morgan contemplated tossing the card. Instead, he tucked it into his shirt pocket and got into the GTO. He turned his head to catch a last glimpse of Smith, but the man had already vanished. Morgan smiled to himself as he started the car and headed home.

ACKNOWLEDGMENTS

Writing this novel was a three-year journey with many exhausting days and sleepless nights, yet it was also one of the most exhilarating experiences of my life. I want to thank my wife, Lynn, who put up with my mood swings and who believed in and encouraged me through the process. I love you and appreciate all your help.

I was extremely fortunate to team up with my talented co-writer Caio Camargo, who spent the better part of a year listening to me tell stories from my past and then helped me create this book. It was a joy working together, and I look forward to our next collaboration.

I am very lucky to have been surrounded by such loyal friends during the writing of this book. One of my oldest and dearest friends, Nancy Schneider, carefully reviewed the many versions of the manuscript as it evolved. Hermann Schaeffer, Nick Julian, Rodney Jones, George Mitrano, Ruth Shuman, and Randi Swartz all provided feedback from a reader's perspective.

I also want to thank Michaela Hamilton and the rest of the team at Kensington Publishing Corp. for taking a chance on an unknown writer and giving me the opportunity to tell my story.

Finally, I want to thank my readers . . . I hope you enjoyed the adventures of Dan Morgan.

Don't miss the next exciting thriller featuring Black
Ops specialist Dan Morgan

Silent Assassin
by Leo J. Maloney

Coming from Pinnacle in 2013!

Turn the page to read a preview excerpt . . .

"I'm here to see Roman Lubarsky."

The voice was self-assured—brash, even—and if the accent had not given away that it belonged to an American, then surely the characteristic lack of subtlety would have been plenty to identify the nationality of the speaker.

"I'm afraid Mr. Lubarsky isn't seeing anyone at the moment, sir," said the girl at reception, offering him a practiced look of slight commiseration from across the counter.

"Oh, I think he's going to want to see me," the man said, and then he grinned. He was approaching middle age but still handsome in that rough American way, with a full head of dark hair with gray streaks, and a trim beard and mustache. He was not tall but had broad shoulders emphasized by his gray pin-striped suit. He had a briefcase in his right hand, which she had noticed when he walked into the lobby. She had also noticed that he was unusually fit and vigorous. The kind of man who could cause a lot of trouble if he wanted to. And she couldn't quite tell, but he might have had a well-concealed gun holster tucked under his suit jacket. It was the kind of thing she was paid to notice.

She did not smile back at his comment. She could tell she wouldn't get rid of him easily, but he wasn't the first person who had insisted on coming in off the street to see the boss. She knew how to deal with them.

"Mr. Lubarsky does not receive anyone without an appointment," she told him. She leaned in closer, as if to say something confidential, just between him and her, and said, "Trust me, sir, it will do no good to insist." As she spoke, she reached down discreetly with her right hand and pushed the tiny button hidden on the underside of the counter.

"I have a standing appointment with your boss," said the man.

"It's not in my book," she said, offering him a *What can I do?* shrug.

"Oh, I think he's going to want to see me, anyway."

This was getting tiresome. "I insist, sir, that even if you are the Pope himself, Mr. Lubarsky will not—" She was interrupted as Marko and Lyudmil emerged from the door next to the reception desk and flanked the American.

"This guy giving you trouble, Rositsa?"

"Some men just can't take no for an answer," she said, teasing the man by looking straight into his eyes as she spoke.

The man did not stop smiling. "Some just know when not to fold."

"Come on, asshole," said Lyudmil, grabbing the man's left arm. "The lady has had enough of you."

The American, totally unfazed, did not move. Instead, he reached into his breast pocket. The two men seemed alarmed by the gesture and moved to restrain him, but they relaxed when they saw him pulling out a business card. The American offered it to them, holding it between two outstretched fingers. One guard took it, examined it, and then handed it to the other. They exchanged nods.

"Please follow us this way, sir," said Marko.

The three disappeared through the door the two security men had emerged from. Rositsa looked down at the counter and saw that they had left the card. She picked it up and looked at it curiously. On it was no name—in fact, no words at all. All there was on it was a drawing of a snake, a cobra, coiled and ready to strike.

Dan Morgan, Code Name Cobra, was taken into a back room off the lobby of the Sárkány, where the bare concrete walls and fluorescent lighting stood in stark contrast to the elegant wood paneling and soft incandescent lighting in the reception area. He had been led there by the two hulking grunts in black suits who had come, originally, to kick him out and maybe leave him in the back alley with a couple of cracked ribs and internal bleeding.

One of the two, tall and broad-shouldered with a jutting chin, scowled down at him while the other, a squat and wide man who might have been mistaken for an ape if he weren't wearing such a dapper suit, tried to take his Walther. "No guns in the hotel," he said, though of course he meant no guns that weren't in their possession.

"My weapon stays with me," said Morgan.

"Are we going to have to take it away from you?" said the tall one.

"You can try."

The two looked at each other and then at him as if they wanted to take turns breaking his neck.

"Any funny business," said the short, squat one, "and you leave this hotel in little tiny pieces—is that clear?"

"Crystal."

They X-rayed his briefcase, scanned him for bugs, and then escorted him back to the lobby. Then they ushered him to an elevator that they opened with a key. The interior was red-carpeted and wood-paneled to match the lobby, and it had only two floor buttons, un-marked. The short one turned another key and pressed the top button.

The elevator was not large, and Morgan was wedged uncomfortably between the two guards. The cabin began its ascent, the movement imperceptible but for a gentle tug at Morgan's gut and at the leather satchel he held in his right hand.

The elevator stopped as discreetly as it had started, after what seemed like too short a time to cover the necessary distance. The doors slid open, right into the penthouse foyer.

The first thing to hit him was the smell. It was a heady mixture of stale vomit, rotting food, alcohol, and sweat mingled with a few other bodily odors. Obscene squeals and moans from a pornographic movie drifted in, and it seemed like an appropriate soundtrack. The foyer itself was decorated in the most expensive poor taste achievable. He briefly wondered how much worse it would seem to Jenny's professional eye—only a fleeting thought before his mind began to formulate his reaction in case things took a turn for the worse.

It was automatic, part of his training. Possibilities played in his head in short clips of sudden violence. The bigger one would go down with a swing of the suitcase in Morgan's hand—a well-placed blow would be enough knock him out. He'd likely have to draw his gun to take down the other goon, but he could not count on doing it fast enough and might have to improvise. Morgan had a keen sense of his environment, and this one provided more than enough for him to work with: here a bronze bust of Elvis that could easily crack open a man's skull, there a gold-framed mirror whose shards could slice open a carotid in a split second.

A guttural voice spoke from the next room, in Russian. The short one responded in kind, and Morgan made out, in his speech, the word "Cobra." The man in the other room responded.

"Go on," said the short one thickly. "He is waiting."

Morgan stepped through a columned arch, and the scene that had been only suggested by the acrid and intensifying smell appeared before him, inspiring in him alternately nausea and rage. The Sárkány was elegant and expensive, and the penthouse, on a good day, was by far the best suite in the hotel. But whatever class the place might have had was subsumed into the filth of the man he had come to see.

"Lubarsky."

"Please, please, call me Roman," said Lubarsky jovially. "Have a drink. Make yourself at home."

Husks of top-shelf Champagne and vodka bottles lay strewn about, along with two upturned velvet-upholstered chairs. Slumped on the bed, half-covered by a stained white sheet, was a woman who wouldn't have looked out of place on a high-fashion runway. She lay slack on the bed, her white-blond hair hanging off its side, her eyes eerily blank. Another woman, black with high cheekbones and wearing mussed-up lingerie, was huddled over an end table from which she had pushed off a wrought iron lamp. She was frantically cutting with a razor at a small mound of cocaine. Victims of human trafficking, most likely. Morgan knew what women went through to become playthings for the rich and unscrupulous. What he saw disgusted him, and made him want to kill Lubarsky even more.

"Lubarsky," said Morgan.

The man himself was naked, rolls of flesh pendent between his open legs, his body hair so thick, he might as well have been wearing a sweater. Greasy black locks clung to the sweat on his forehead, and his eyes were open wide, red and manic, with pupils so dilated that they almost reached the outer edges of the iris.

"How long have you been on this bender?" Morgan asked.

"I take it that's my money in that suitcase?" He snorted.

"Answer the question, Lubarsky."

The Georgian looked at him with murder in his eyes. "Are you telling me what to do in my own hotel?"

"You and I have things to do today, and I want to know that you're able to keep up your end."

Lubarsky looked at him as if he were about to lunge for his throat, then burst out laughing, a hacking, throaty laugh. "Why all business, Cobra? Sit down. Have some cocaine. Have a whore. I just got these two fresh from a new shipment." He looked at the woman who had been huddled over the table snorting coke. "You! Come here."

She did her best to slink over, stumbling as she did.

"What is your name, sugar?" asked Lubarsky.

"My name is anything you want, baby." She spoke in a lewd tone, rendered especially cartoonish by her heavy accent. Her eyes, red and heavy-lidded, were void of all emotion.

Lubarsky snickered and said, "You see? I have them well trained."

"I'll pass," said Morgan.

"Are you sure?"

Morgan scowled at him.

"Fine, fine. You are a modest man. I cannot say I understand, but I respect it." He waved absently at the woman, and she stumbled away. "Have a drink, then. I have a single malt from the highlands—"

"I don't drink."

Lubarsky laughed his hideous laugh again, and it made Morgan want to break his nose. "That's the trouble with you ex-intelligence types. Always with the discipline. You make obscene amounts of money, but you never do anything obscene with it!"

"I hear Novokoff can really put away the vodka."

"Yes, true," he said, laughing. "But that is like the milk of his mother to Novokoff. He has the resistance of an ox. It doesn't count as debauchery if he does not become drunk."

"Speaking of the devil—"

"Yes, yes, I have not forgotten the business, Cobra. Your end first."

Morgan set down the briefcase on the table in front of Lubarsky. "It's all in there," he said.

Lubarsky opened it and looked through the stacks of bills inside, a smile widening on his face.

"You are a man of your word, Cobra."

Morgan wasn't interested in compliments. "Novokoff?"

"It is set up for today, like we discussed."

"Where?"

Lubarsky snorted. "He will not say until we are on the road. He is a paranoid bastard."

"I'm guessing he learned it the hard way," said Morgan. "Twenty years in the KGB will do that to a man."

"And your side of the bargain?"

"Don't worry, I've got it. All loaded up in a freezer truck and ready to take it wherever he is," said Morgan.

"I tell you, Cobra, you are in the wrong business. This high-tech junk—biological weapons and nerve gas and smart bombs—they are crap business. All the special transportation, the lack of supply. And it's all middlemen, middlemen, middlemen. Never a direct sale. The percentage is shit. The good business is in selling Kalashnikovs and grenades to African warlords. Get paid in diamonds, and no middlemen to pay."

"But you're still gracing us with your presence today, Roman?" said Morgan.

Lubarsky laughed. "I am making an introduction. Whole other animal. Little exposure, cash up front. Plus," he added, "for Novokoff, I do this."

"How sweet of you."

"It is good for business. Not to mention, I'm scared shitless of the bastard." He seemed serious all of a sudden. "You do not mess this up, you hear me, Cobra?"

"*You're* telling *me*? Screw you, Lubarsky. Are you even planning on putting on some clothes?"

Lubarsky laughed. "You know, I like you, Cobra. I believe this is—how do you say?—the start of a wonderful friendship."

Morgan looked at him disdainfully and hoped that he might have the opportunity to kill the man before this was over.

D r. Eugenia Barrett opened the metal crate slowly and deliberately, and a thin mist poured out from inside, slowly dispersing to reveal four rows of cylinders.

"This is the real thing. A tiny whiff of this stuff will kill a grown man in forty seconds," she said. "Same if you get any on your skin. Violent convulsions, projectile vomiting. The good news is, you probably won't be conscious for most of it."

"Yeah, I got the CliffsNotes stateside," said Morgan. He looked down at the sixteen canisters, the mist from the refrigeration still playing around them. Morgan shivered, but not from the cold.

"I'd say in this case you could use the refresher." She unbuttoned her lab coat to climb down from the back of the truck. Morgan followed her, being careful as he touched his right foot to the ground, and was slightly relieved not to feel any pain in his knee.

They were in an otherwise empty loading dock on the edge of Budapest, and Lubarsky was waiting in a car outside with the two hulks from the hotel. Barrett was a slight woman with close-cropped hair, no older than thirty, a fast-talking prodigy without an ear for social graces. Her directness had made Morgan like her right away.

"The one upside," she continued, "is that the half-life for this baby is only about a minute in the atmosphere. If there's any kind of leak, hold your breath, and get the hell out of there." She reached into a bag and brought out a syringe in a hermetic plastic sheath. "You'll still absorb it through your skin, but you just might make it if you inject yourself with this."

Morgan eyed the size of the needle warily. "This is what, an antidote?"

"Atropine. It'll counteract the effects of the gas. Plunge that son of a bitch right into your heart, and it could save your life."

"My *heart*?" He took it into his hands and stared at the three-inch-long needle. "Remind me, Genie," he said, "why we're not giving this bastard a goddamn decoy?"

"If he's half as competent as he's supposed to be, he'll make damn sure he gets what he's paying for. And if he finds out we've filled these canisters with weapons-grade air, the whole operation is blown."

"That fail-safe had better work."

"Don't worry. We tested the hell out of those incinerators. They're on timer *and* remote control, and there's enough thermite in each canister to melt an Eskimo's ass."

"Just take care that it doesn't melt mine."

Barrett laughed. "Don't worry, Cobes. If everything goes according to plan, you'll be gone and he'll be captured before long before that timer goes off."

"And if it doesn't?"

"How about we choose to keep a positive attitude about this?" she said. "It goes well, we take a couple of nasty arms dealers out of commission, and maybe get their suppliers to boot."

"We can do that by *killing* them," said Morgan.

"Hey, I'm not the one you need to talk to here. I don't make orders; I take them, say thank you, and ask for another. And if the brass wants Novokoff captured alive, then that's what they're gonna get."

"And why the hell *do* they want him alive?"

"You're asking the wrong girl here," said Barrett.

He heard a long beep of a horn coming from Lubarsky's car outside.

"Your date is getting impatient," she said.

"Tough. Where's Ferenc?"

"Just inside. Ferenc!" she yelled out to him. "Come on out here—we're ready for you."

The tall, blond Hungarian with a youthful, rectangular face appeared, sauntering toward them and the truck, his footsteps echoing in the hollows of the loading dock.

"Hello, Cobra," he said. "Are you ready to bag a weapons dealer?"

"I'm glad you're so chipper about this," said Morgan. "Is the team ready?"

"They're in position at a safe house a few blocks away," said Ferenc. "They'll be tracking us to our destination."

Morgan climbed into the passenger side of the truck while Ferenc got into the driver's seat. Ferenc turned the key, and, after whining, the engine rumbled awake. Morgan opened his window.

"You're all set, Cobes," said Barrett, who then walked to the garage door control. "Try not to get killed."

"Thanks for the advice. I'll keep that in mind."

"All right, then, here we go." She pulled the switch, and the garage door started rolling up. She winced as the cold air rushed in, carrying with it flurries of snow.

"I'm trying to avoid bodily injury, thank you very much."

Ferenc pulled the truck outside, where Lubarsky was waiting, huddled and leaning against his black town car.

"We're here," said Morgan through the truck's window.

"About time," said the Georgian. "I am freezing my nuts off out here." He typed into his burner phone.

"I thought you Russian assholes were supposed to be used to the cold," said Morgan. "Or at least not to whine like a little girl about it."

Lubarsky's phone beeped, and he looked at the screen.

"Okay, I know where we are meeting. It is a long drive. I take it you want to ride with the merchandise?"

"You take it right," said Morgan.

"Okay," said Lubarsky. "Follow me."

Lubarsky set off, and Ferenc followed.

"So how do we do this?" asked Ferenc.

"You hang back," said Morgan. "Near the truck—remember, you're just the driver. Keep a close eye on the situation and your weapon ready."

They drove in silence behind Lubarsky for a few minutes, until Ferenc spoke.

"So this Novokoff—he's ex-KGB, right? Cold War dinosaur type? Still active in intelligence?"

"Yeah."

"And you knew him from back in the day?"

"I knew *of* him," said Morgan. "Killed at least three Agency men, one of them a good friend of mine. Likes murder and tortures in cold blood. Made a fortune cashing in on weapon stockpiles after the fall of the Soviet Union."

"Sounds like a nasty piece of work," said Ferenc.

"You don't know the half of it."

Lubarsky pulled into an abandoned factory complex and was waved in through a truck-size door by a man in combat armor holding a semiautomatic. Ferenc followed Lubarsky's lead.

"Oh, boy," said Morgan.

Morgan counted three more men similarly armed, and at each of their belts he could make out the bulbous shapes of three grenades. Ferenc parked the truck behind Lubarsky's car, and the men converged on them, forming a perimeter.

Morgan stepped out. He saw Novokoff standing in the middle of the abandoned factory floor next to a single, featureless, surgical-aluminum table, wearing a black turtleneck sweater with suspenders, a pistol at his hip. Morgan had known him from pictures, but there was something unnerving about his personal presence, even at a distance. He was aloof, his carefully coiffed gray hair and beard giving him the aspect of a well-groomed wolf. His eyes had the quiet calm of a fearless killer. There was also one new feature—a scar, bright red and not fully healed, streaked across his face.

"Bringing a gun to an introduction is no way to make friends," said Novokoff.

"You're one to talk," said Morgan. "Why the army? Expecting an invasion?"

"I am not a trusting man, Cobra. Let's just say I had some relevant prior experience. And after all, we were *de facto* enemies for the better part of a decade, were we not? Oh, you did not expect me to come to this meeting without finding out everything that I could about you, did you, *Mr. Morgan*? You don't mind that I use your real name, do you? All this code name business is so passé."

Morgan did not react. "There aren't many who know that name and survive."

"Ah, but therein lies the beauty of commerce, Mr. Morgan. It brings even enemies together in the bonds of trade. It creates a connection of trust and mutual need."

"I think even you understand the irony of those words coming out of your mouth."

"Ah, that is true only if you believe that the game at the KGB was really about the Revolution, Mr. Morgan. Ah, it was for some, those hopeless young fanatics who readily gave their lives for this . . . *cause*. It is alien to me and most of the men of my time. We understood that it was not about Socialism. It was not about Mother Russia. It was always, really, only about power."

"So this should be right up your alley," said Morgan.

"Very much so. And apparently yours, too," Novokoff said, shifting gears, "or you could not offer me such a rare item."

"Exactly. So how about we get to it?"

"Very well. I have money for you, Mr. Morgan, and I trust you have product for me."

"In the truck," said Morgan.

Novokoff motioned to his men. Two of them opened the back of the truck, took down the crate, and with some effort placed it down next to the table.

"Be careful with that. I do not want to die here," said Lubarsky.

Another of Novokoff's men brought out a seamless Plexiglas cage that held five large lab rats and set it down on the table. He placed next to it a short mesh hose with complicated attachments at the ends. One of the men who had taken the metal crate from the truck opened it and removed a canister, spreading billows of smoke from the dry ice. He held it carefully, walking slowly to the table and setting it down as gently as he could.

He took the hose and connected one end into the air nozzle on the rat cage, and the other to the canister. There was a faint hiss as colorless, odorless gas seeped into the cage. The rats were at first paralyzed, then began to seize madly, foaming at the mouths, scratching at one another involuntarily until their white fur was stained red. Slowly, the seizing tapered to stillness but for an odd twitching leg.

"It appears you are a man of your word, Mr. Morgan," said Novokoff. He motioned toward the hose, and the nearest man moved to disconnect it. He undid the lock on the nozzle and pulled, but it seemed stuck. He pulled harder. It gave, but the man lost his balance, knocking back against the canister. Morgan's heart skipped a beat as the canister teetered uncertainly. He prepared to bolt, certain that it would fall. He exhaled, relieved, as it fell back upright. Then he looked at Novokoff.

His face was changed entirely, contorted with anger.

He growled something in Russian to the man. The man started talking apologetically, holding his hands at chest level. He noticed the other guards looking on uncomfortably. And then, faster than anyone could react, Novokoff drew his pistol and cold-cocked the man on his temple. The guard sprawled onto the ground, and Novokoff was immediately on him, swinging his pistol again, this time against the man's face.

Two other guards rushed to him as he hit the man in wild fury. They managed to wrench him off the man and hold him back. Novokoff growled, struggling for a few seconds; but as suddenly as it had come on, his fury seemed to die down. His face changed back to an eerie calm, and he looked at Morgan as if nothing had happened.

"Your product is good, Cobra," he said. "And your asking price is fair."

The man on the floor groaned, and it seemed to flip a switch in Novokoff. He wheeled around, and the two guards ran to hold him back again.

What happened next seemed to move in slow motion. Novokoff struggled and pushed one of the men back. He staggered against the table. The canister tipped again, and for a split second it seemed like it might teeter back to its standing position. But it moved an inch too far, and it dropped to the ground. The struggle ceased, and everyone froze as the canister rolled a few feet and came to a halt. Then, there was a bright flash, and a wave of hot air blew into Morgan's face. The fail-safe had gone off.

Novokoff turned to him with snake's eyes, and Morgan knew that he understood exactly what had happened. Novokoff drew his gun and shot, but Morgan had already anticipated this and dodged the first salvo of bullets. Novokoff's men, however, took the cue and fired bursts at Morgan and Lubarsky's goons. These two drew their own guns and shot back.

"Stop that!" yelled Lubarsky.

Novokoff shouted in Russian, and it was obvious why: the crate with the canisters was dangerously close to the line of fire. One of Lubarsky's men was hit. Morgan saw another of Novokoff's men fall, near him, and saw that the bullet had come from Ferenc, who had joined the fray. Novokoff retreated behind a pillar, and Morgan kicked over a table and hid behind it. He listened for the gunfire, waiting for a lull. He pictured the position of one of the shooters. His eyes met Ferenc's—the other man was crouching behind the truck. He made the sign for covering fire. Ferenc nodded.

Ferenc emerged, shooting. A split second later, Morgan stood, and with another split second to aim, fired. He hit the man squarely in the forehead. He crouched and looked at Ferenc but saw him sprawled on the floor, inert, blood pooling underneath him.

Shit.

He heard moans. Lubarsky was several yards away, shot in the gut.

"Damn you . . . Cobra . . ." he said, with labored breathing.

"You are alone, Mr. Morgan!" Novokoff yelled out to him. "Come out now, you double-crossing son of a bitch, and I promise you a quick death!"

The bastard. Morgan was half-tempted to make his an ending befitting Butch Cassidy, but instead he took a deep breath. There was a burst of gunfire in his direction, hitting the table deafeningly. But the table held the bullets. He was safe until they realized he was out of ammunition.

He looked around. A few feet away from him was the crate, and next to him was the body of one of Novokoff's men, the first to fall. His gun, however, was several feet out of reach, in the path of enemy bullets.

What wasn't out of reach were the man's grenades.

He took them. There were only two; he would have to make them count. He couldn't rely on killing both his enemies with grenades—they were too mobile, the space too open. But there was one possibility.

He took one grenade in each hand and held them to his chest. One chance, and he would probably die. But if he did, he would go out fighting. With his mouth, he pulled the pin on one grenade and sent it sailing in the direction of Novokoff. He removed the pin from the other and, in the cover of the first explosion, tossed it into the crate with the canisters. And then he ran.

The burst came along with a heat wave from the thermite, which was what he had hoped for. Almost immediately he heard Lubarsky gag and cough, and he turned to see him start convulsing. He had released the gas.

And then the tingling hit him. At his extremities, at first. He had to run, had to get out of there. He stumbled out the door the truck had come in.

He panted, his nose running. He stumbled and fell into the soft snow. Consciousness was fading; he knew he didn't have long. He reached into his pocket and brought out the syringe Dr. Barrett had given him. He fumbled to open it. His hands were already losing their grip. With all his effort, he ripped the package and removed the needle's cover with his mouth. He looked at it: it was one big mother of a needle. This had a slightly sobering effect. He tried to concentrate on the target on his chest. His hands were about to give out. He had one chance to do this, or he was dead.

He plunged the needle into his chest. His heart raced, and he began to black out just as he heard the sound of approaching vehicles.